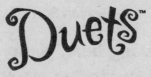

Duets™

**Two brand-new stories in every volume...
twice a month!**

Duets Vol. #77

Talented Darlene Gardner returns with another
funny story about two rival reporters who *live* to
scoop each other...especially when it comes to love.
Darlene spins "a delightful tale with an engaging
set-up and lovable characters," says *Romantic Times*.
Joining her is Temptation author Dawn Atkins, who
also delivers a wonderful story about two rival
cohosts of a quirky TV relationship show.

Duets Vol. #78

Bestselling author Jacqueline Diamond
takes you to Skunk's Crossing, Texas, for a
wacky tale about a nanny who takes on not only
two kids, but a ranch full of sexy cowboys...
with unexpected results! Meet another unusual
nanny in Nancy Warren's debut Duets novel,
also available this month. Nancy's stories are
"playful and great fun...highly recommended,"
according to The Best Reviews Book Review.

Be sure t̶   s today!

Heaven Scent

"You belong here, Nancy."

A man could wait only so long. Words weren't Max's strong point, not with this beautiful, sweet lady standing right in front of him.

In one short step he gathered her into his arms. No more of that tentative exploratory stuff they'd tried before. This time he meant business.

He didn't know where to start, or how to stop, so he did everything at once. Hugged her tight. Kissed her madly. Lifted her top and slipped it off, removing her bra in the process.

"You don't fool around, do you?" Nancy whispered, sounding awestruck.

"I think of myself as a man of action," he said, and proceeded to demonstrate by devouring her perfect breasts.

"I guess this is the way people do things on a ranch," she said breathlessly, and made short work of his belt. Not an easy chore, but Nancy seemed determined.

He couldn't wait to see what else she was determined to do.

For more, turn to page 9

Shotgun Nanny

"That's what you're wearing for a day at the park?" Mark demanded.

Annie glanced down. Her paisley-printed Capri pants were zipped, her purple crop top was clean. Her purple sandals with the big plastic daisies were on the correct feet. "What's wrong with it?"

"There's so much skin showing." He dropped his voice. "And I can see you're not wearing a—um—" His gaze fastened on her chest.

"A bra, Mark. It's called a bra. I hardly ever wear them. *Too* restricting."

"It's a good thing I got that dog to protect you," he grumbled, forcing his gaze straight ahead.

"From who? You? You're the one who can't keep his eyes to himself."

Mark tossed the picnic basket in the back of his SUV with a thump and she knew the flush on his face wasn't from exertion.

Annie lifted her sun hat and slipped on dark glasses, then held out her hand for the keys. "Any more orders?" she asked, and stuck out her chest as far as a 32B with attitude would go.

For more, turn to page 197

HARLEQUIN DUETS

ISBN 0-373-44144-4

Copyright in the collection:
Copyright © 2001 by Harlequin Books S.A.

The publisher acknowledges the copyright holders
of the individual works as follows:

HEAVEN SCENT
Copyright © 2002 by Jackie Hyman

SHOTGUN NANNY
Copyright © 2002 by Nancy Warren

Visit us at www.eHarlequin.com

Printed In U.S.A.

Heaven Scent

Jacqueline Diamond

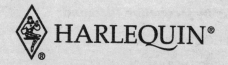

HARLEQUIN®

TORONTO • NEW YORK • LONDON
AMSTERDAM • PARIS • SYDNEY • HAMBURG
STOCKHOLM • ATHENS • TOKYO • MILAN • MADRID
PRAGUE • WARSAW • BUDAPEST • AUCKLAND

Dear Reader,

Nancy Verano, the child psychologist who gets itchy around children and can't figure out what she wants from life, first turned up in my previous Duets novel, *Excuse Me? Whose Baby?* as the hero's fiancée.

If you read the book, you know that Nancy graciously stepped aside so the hero, who was her old friend, could marry the woman he really loved. When last seen, she was contentedly showing Fellini movies to babies to test the effect on their language acquisition.

My editor, Jennifer Tam, and I couldn't let Nancy disappear from view without finding her own true love, however. We're just softies that way.

It was clear to me that Nancy needed a kind of shock treatment to make her see life in a new way. The notion of throwing her onto a ranch in Texas as a nanny brought out my mischievous side, so I did.

Hope you enjoy the results! If you like the book, please let me know at P.O. Box 1315, Brea, CA 92822.

Warmly,

Jacqueline Diamond

Books by Jacqueline Diamond

HARLEQUIN DUETS
37—DESIGNER GENES*
44—EXCUSE ME? WHOSE BABY?
55—MORE THAN THE DOCTOR ORDERED**
65—THE DOC'S DOUBLE DELIVERY

*The Bachelor Dads of Nowhere Junction
**The Mail-Order Men of Nowhere Junction

To my husband, Kurt, who once
chased a skunk with a hose and lived to tell the tale.

1

"I THINK IT'S A GREAT idea," said Nancy Verano.

"You do?" Her younger sister Hayley stared at her hopefully.

"I'll do-si-do right down to the general store and buy me a cowboy hat," Nancy said in her best mock Texas accent. "I'll put on the cutest little apron you gosh-darn ever did see. I jes' can't wait to put my arms around those two little tykes. You did say they were out of diapers, didn't you?"

"Nancy, they're six and nine, and I'm counting on you!" wailed Hayley, pacing around Nancy's small over-the-garage apartment. She'd arrived early for her sister's thirty-fifth birthday party in order to have this discussion. "Somebody has to fulfill my housekeeping contract, and you've got the summer off!"

As an assistant psychology professor at De Lune University in Clair De Lune, California, Nancy had only to finish grading exams for her spring semester classes and she would, indeed, be free. In addition, she'd recently fulfilled a yearlong grant to show Fellini movies to infants and measure the impact on their language development.

Nancy had submitted a grant proposal for another linguistics study. If that didn't come through, she would apply for a summer counseling job at the local Marriage and Family Center.

After all, she had college loans to pay off. More than that, Nancy had been the first in her family to go to college and had always felt she had to work extra hard at her career to prove that her success wasn't a fluke. The very last job she would ever consider was to work as a housekeeper and nanny on a Texas ranch.

"It's out of the question." She crouched in front of her low mirror, which had been hung by a previous, shorter tenant, and brushed out her shoulder-length blond hair. "Tell the rancher you changed your mind."

Tears glittered on Hayley's lashes. "I can't. Mr. Richter's a card-carrying Neanderthal. After I signed the contract, he told me that if I didn't keep my promise to work for at least three months, he'd hunt me down and make me sorry."

"I thought you hadn't actually met him," Nancy said.

"He told me that on the phone."

"Did he growl when he said it? Could you hear him spinning the barrel of his six-gun?"

"Practically!" Hayley flung out her arms dramatically. In the June sunlight slanting through a window, she looked younger than her twenty-nine years and, as always, breathtakingly beautiful.

Although she and Nancy both had light coloring, Hayley benefitted from having bright blue eyes rather than gray and a softer set of features, along with a theatrical nature. Even a casual observer could see that Hayley was photogenic.

It was a valuable trait for an actress, although, until recently, the would-be star had landed only occasional small roles. Now Hayley had unexpectedly been hired for a situation comedy that began shooting next week.

It was her big break. Too bad she'd already agreed to a different sort of contract.

"You're due to leave—when?" Nancy asked.

"Next Saturday."

"I'll give you a lift to the airport."

"You know I can't go, but you're free. Please! We can't let him down," Hayley wailed. "He interviewed I don't know how many people over the Internet before he chose me. I'm the only one he trusts."

"I can't understand why you applied for the job in the first place," Nancy said. "Why not go for coal-mining in Siberia? Or sign on as a mercenary in some third-world country? That's no more ridiculous for a mall-rat like you than relocating to a ranch."

Hayley shrugged. "I figured that if I was over-the-hill as an actress, I needed to make a clean break. To reinvent myself."

"As a nanny?"

"When I saw the ad on the Internet, it reminded me of when I did *The Sound of Music* in dinner theater," her sister said. "I pictured the kids dancing around wearing the curtains while I taught them to sing 'Do-Re-Mi.'"

"You have a weird take on reality," said Nancy. "I, on the other hand, know exactly what's true and what isn't, which is why I have no intention of replacing you."

"You'd make a better nanny than me," Hayley pressed. "You practically raised the six of us."

"Not voluntarily."

"Motives don't count."

Nancy's mother had loved babies. Unfortunately, she'd lost interest once they passed the toddler stage, and had turned them over to her eldest daughter. Her mother had tried to delegate the cooking, too, until the whole family landed in the hospital with food poisoning.

Growing up, Nancy might have avoided being chained to the stove, but she couldn't avoid a succession of younger siblings. Grudgingly, she'd come to cherish the little pests. She'd also, however, developed an aversion to matters domestic.

"I'm sure Mr. Big, Tall and Tough will be thrilled when you send a substitute who can't cook, screams when the vacuum cleaner turns on and gets itchy around children," she said.

"He wouldn't have to know you were a substitute. My middle name is Nanette, so my nickname could be Nancy," Hayley argued.

"And the smell of burning food that first morning wouldn't give him a clue?"

"Max Richter has to own a microwave." Hayley folded her hands in a semipraying position. "Besides, you could meet a lot of well-built guys on the Rolling R."

"Like who?"

"There's Max himself—"

"The handsome Neanderthal hunk?"

"Also a foreman and a couple of hired hands," said her sister. "Think of the rugged physiques."

"Think of the tobacco chewing, chili chomping and gas-passing around the campfire. I can hardly wait." Nancy tucked her blouse into her slacks and eyed her shoe rack. She decided on flats for her birthday celebration.

"They don't cook around a campfire," Hayley said. "There's a ranch house and they're only about five miles from town."

"What town?"

"I forget the name. It involves some kind of animal," her sister said. "I think it starts with an *S*."

"Snakes? This town has so many snakes it's named after them?" Nancy groaned.

"Not snakes, skunks!" said Hayley, her memory miraculously restored. "It's called Skunk Crossing."

"That's no better."

"I'm sure they're all deodorized," she said. "Almost sure."

Nancy wished her sister would take no for an answer and deal with her own problems. Unfortunately, Big Sister had always been a soft touch for her siblings. They counted on her, and she usually came through for them.

Not this time. Skunk Crossing? Honestly!

It was a relief when someone knocked at the door. Her other siblings had arrived. Since their parents had retired and moved to Florida, it would be just the seven of them celebrating Nancy's birthday.

They were going to an amusement park for the rest of the day and half the night. With luck, there would be no more talk about nanny jobs in Texas.

A thousand miles away...

GRIFFIN HAD STUCK sausage crumbles up his nose.

"That looks disgusting," said Melissa, his nine-year-old sister.

Her six-year-old brother tried to answer and accidentally blew the sausage out of his nose. "It isn't 'gusting," said Griffin. "Is it, Daddy?"

Max Richter dragged his attention away from the kitchen window. From here, he could see how badly the horse corral needed repairs after last week's storm. Also, the sight of the machine shed reminded him that the tractor was overdue for maintenance. "What I think is that you should both settle down."

"I don't like brunch," said his daughter. "Grampa and Gramma let us eat anything we wanted whenever we were hungry. I never ate eggs *or* sausages."

"Sausages make my nose itch." Griffin snorted, and wiped the result on his sleeve.

"Mind your manners," Max said.

"They don't have manners because they never got taught any," said JoAnne Ortega, the ranch foreman's wife and temporary housekeeper and nanny. She clattered a few pots in the sink. "I guess they're looking to you to set the pace."

"I am setting the pace, darn it!" Max barely averted the use of stronger language. He didn't want to antagonize JoAnne, who was an old friend as well as an employee.

"Lately, you've had the temper of a yellow dog that backed into a cactus," she said. "Don't worry. I do understand, but that doesn't mean I have to like it."

Max supposed he had been kind of grumpy for a while. Three years, give or take a month.

That's how long it had been since his wife ran off with their marriage counselor. Faced with working long hours at the ranch, he'd entrusted his two young children to their maternal grandparents in Houston.

The elderly Ardells had let the children run wild. Six months ago, as the couple's health declined, Max had reclaimed his children only to discover that he had no idea how to deal with them.

He'd tried military discipline, and encountered tears and tantrums that drove away the first nanny. Next, he'd suffered through a period of benign neglect, demolishing two more nannies in the process.

When he advertised the job for a fourth time in the nearby town of Skunk Crossing, there hadn't been a single response. No one from neighboring towns responded to his ads, either, because of fears about a growing wild skunk population in the area. In desperation, he'd turned to an Internet site.

There he had found a number of unsuitable applicants and one winner: Ms. Hayley Nanette Verano. She had the experience and can-do attitude he was looking for. With any luck, she'd stay permanently, becoming part of the infrastructure like the foreman and the cattle barn.

"The domestic goddess is leaving now." JoAnne hung her apron on a peg.

"You haven't finished the dishes," said Melissa.

"It's Sunday. I only came over after church because you all looked so pathetic," the housekeeper answered. "Besides, if I don't show up at home, Luis is likely to forget what I look like."

"Melissa, you shouldn't criticize your elders," added Max. As he spoke, he could hear his own father, long-deceased, barking similar words at him. "It wouldn't hurt you to do a little more work around here yourself, young lady."

"I'm not your slave!" cried his daughter, whose

red-gold hair and flashing green eyes reminded him painfully of her mother. She stomped out the side door and pelted away.

"I'll wash the dishes." Griffin hopped up. "Okay, Dad?" He snatched two plates and promptly dropped one of them. The plastic dish rolled several feet before clattering to a halt, spewing food onto the tile floor. "Oops."

"I'm going." JoAnne ignored Max's pleading look.

"Any suggestions about what I should do for the rest of the day?" Although he loved his two children, he had trouble devising ways to entertain them.

"Pray for a strong wind," said JoAnne. "Whichever kind it is that brings Mary Poppins."

She swept out the side door. A moment later, he heard her four-wheel drive roar off.

Max was cleaning the soiled floor, a job made more difficult by Griffin's clumsy attempts to help, when the phone rang. *Please let it be Ms. Verano to say she's arriving early.*

"Yes?" he said into the receiver.

"Max! Man, it's been a long time!"

It was his brother, Bill, enthusiastic as always. "How's it going?" Max asked.

"Great! Well, not bad. Could be better." Although he'd been born on a ranch, Bill's heart was in the advertising business he owned in Dallas. He instinctively put a positive spin on everything, which meant that, since he'd backpedaled from "great" to "could be better," something terrible must have happened.

"What's wrong?" Max frowned at Griffin, who was pulling a chair to the sink. His son ignored him.

"It's Beth and me," Bill said. "We're having a few problems. You know, she's much better at explaining this kind of thing than I am. Maybe I should let her handle this."

In the background, a woman shrilled, "You're not laying this one on me!" Max winced. Although he liked his sister-in-law, her strident voice made his teeth ache. In a pinch, he imagined she could substitute it for the drill in her dental practice.

Nearby, Griffin turned on the water full blast, splattering it across the counter. Stretching the phone cord as far as it would go, Max couldn't quite reach the faucet to turn it off.

Bill was talking again. "You know how you're always inviting us to the ranch?"

"Sure. I'd love to have you." Although Max had bought out his brother's share of the spread, he considered it their family home.

"I'd like Kirstin to have that wonderful old-fashioned ranch experience." Kirstin was Bill and Beth's twelve-year-old daughter. "For a whole summer, not just a few days."

"You're coming for the summer?" This was terrific news. Having more grown-ups on the premises was exactly what his kids needed. Not to mention that it was what Max needed.

"Not me and Beth," Bill said. "Some time alone would do us good."

Griffin stuck a frying pan under the water. It caught the spray at an angle, spewing out greasy water that soaked the little boy's shirt and intensified the mess on the floor.

"Turn that thing off!" Max said. "Not you, Bill. It's my son." Griffin stopped the tap and burst into tears.

"Kids can get into so much mischief," his brother said. "Kirstin will be a big help. She's old enough to learn to baby-sit."

"Da-a-a-ad!" came a second female voice in the background. The high-pitched tone sounded stingingly like her mother's. "I hate little kids!"

Better and better.

"You always told me the ranch was where we Richters belong, deep down inside," his brother said. "How do you expect Kirstin to love the place if she never spends any time there?"

Max knew he was being manipulated. He didn't care. His niece was growing up with two parents who worked long hours and substituted expensive gifts for parental attention. "I'll take her."

"Also, I'm sure she'll..." His brother stopped. "You will?"

"She's my niece." That said it all, as far as Max was concerned.

"Great! I'll drop her off on Wednesday. I'm going to a conference in El Paso and it's not far out of my way."

Although Max would have preferred a few more days to prepare the kids, what difference did it make? "Fine. I'll see you then."

When he hung up, Griffin was sniffling. At a suggestion of visiting the kittens in the barn, however, the boy brightened.

Although Max hated to leave the kitchen in this

condition, he had to set priorities. First, distract Griffin, and second, locate Melissa.

Later, they could eat supper at the Black-and-White Café in Skunk Crossing. In the morning, JoAnne would return before breakfast in time to clean.

As for Kirstin, the only thing Max remembered about his niece was that she changed clothes three times a day. A real city girl, but it didn't matter.

She belonged here. Besides, according to Ms. Verano, she'd once supervised seven children in an Austrian family. Adding Kirstin to his brood shouldn't pose any problem.

ON MONDAY EVENING, Hayley made the hour drive from Hollywood to drop off a thick envelope. "Here's your plane ticket, which Mr. Richter paid for, so we'd better use it," she said, "and some information I downloaded from the Internet about ranch life."

"This would interest me…why?" With difficulty, Nancy tore her attention from the exam papers spread on her kitchen table for grading.

In answer to one of the questions, "Why did Freud and Jung disagree?" a student had written, "Maybe they, like, went to rival high schools."

"You might want to buy some new clothes before Saturday," Hayley went on. "Boots, jeans, that kind of thing."

"No," said Nancy. "Now if you'll excuse me, I've got work to do." Seizing the top paper, she began marking it. When she looked up again, her sister was gone. The envelope remained.

On Tuesday, Nancy's grant application was rejected. "Superficial," the letter called her linguistics idea. "You appear to lack passion for the project."

That was true, she admitted. Not since she came up with the Fellini proposal had she gotten excited about doing research. So, Nancy drove to the Marriage and Family Center and filled out a job application.

On Wednesday, the director called to say the organization was changing its name to The Home Healing and Housebreaking Institute. Instead of providing child and marriage counseling, it would now serve families having problems with their pets. The man politely informed Nancy that her skills didn't suit the center's new direction.

On Thursday, she got out the Yellow Pages and looked up other counseling centers. After struggling to compose a letter that achieved the right balance between professional confidence and begging, she fell asleep with a headache.

At midnight, Nancy was awakened by a dog howling at the moon. She was sleepily dialing The Home Healing and Housebreaking Center for advice when she realized it was not a dog but English Professor Hugh Bemling, serenading her.

Nancy pulled on her robe, a gag gift from Hayley that had a bikini-clad woman's figure superimposed on the front. After zipping it, she shuffled onto the landing.

Below stood the bearded professor, intermittently lit by the flashcube from a camera belonging to her neighbor, Mrs. Zimpelman. From a small tape recorder slung around Hugh's neck issued the tinny sounds of a guitar.

The professor, a slim fellow with flyaway hair, was bellowing a love poem set to the tune of "Greensleeves." "O Maiden Fair, O Ph.D., you've won the heart of poor lovelorn me."

For a moment, Nancy allowed herself to fantasize that he'd accidentally arrived at the wrong address. This was not impossible, as Hugh was noted for his absentmindedness.

However, it wasn't likely. He'd been following Nancy around campus all year, except when he myopically followed other people by mistake.

At last Hugh ceased howling and retrieved his wire-rimmed spectacles from his shirt pocket. Clearing his throat, he eyed Nancy adoringly. "Lovely Dr. Verano, allow me to press my suit."

Nancy descended the stairs. First things first, she decided. "Mrs. Zimpelman, go home."

"But this is interesting," said her gossipy neighbor, who was on her cell phone describing Nancy's bathrobe to a friend.

The front door scraped open on the dark-shingled house adjacent to the garage apartment. Out peered retired dean Marie Pipp, Nancy's landlady. Her hair was covered by a turban.

"Beat it, Esther!" she called. "Or I'll hex you!"

Mrs. Zimpelman, who had never been entirely convinced that Dean Pipp was not a witch, dashed across the street to her own home. With a wink at Nancy, the dean went inside.

"Hugh," Nancy said. "Please don't do this again."

"Someone has to love me," he said, "and I've decided it ought to be you."

"Love isn't that simple," she said. "As a specialist in the Romantic poets, you ought to know that."

He tried to find a comfortable position in which to stand, which necessitated much twitching and changing of arm positions. "I decided I've been going about my courtship all wrong."

"You're wasting your time," Nancy said.

"I haven't pursued you ardently enough. Now that it's summer and I have some time off, I'm going to give it a go," Hugh said. "We should be able to wrap this thing up by August."

She was too tired to continue the discussion. "Go away. I don't want to be pursued."

"I'll be back," Hugh said jauntily, and departed whistling. Remarkably, he did it on key.

Nancy took two aspirins and went back to bed.

On Friday at the beauty salon, she read three women's magazines while waiting for a haircut. They were replete with ugly belly-button-baring fashions, star gossip and pop psychology articles about men.

People got paid for writing this foolishness? she mused, after finishing an article called "Hunky Subway Token Sellers: How to Live With Them, How to Live Without Them." Goodness, she could write something like this with one hand tied behind her back.

Or perhaps it wasn't foolishness. The president of De Lune University loved to see faculty members publish in large-circulation periodicals.

If Nancy came up with a pop psychology subject, she could create her own summer job by making observations and composing an article. In addition to possibly earning some money, she might further her slow but, she hoped, inevitable rise toward tenure.

A title sprang into her head. "The Modern-Day Cowboy: Observations of a Psychologist Incognito on a Texas Ranch." It was as if some power greater than herself had whispered in her ear.

How could she resist? Nancy wondered, and knew she wasn't going to.

2

ON SATURDAY MORNING, Max awoke from a nightmare. He lay in bed, his heart pounding as fragments of a dream fleeted through his conscious mind.

Hordes of skunks were attacking the ranch. They edged backwards toward him, tails raised, paws beating a tattoo. The forces of chaos were closing in, waving a battle flag of black-and-white.

Gradually, the images faded, leaving Max with a keyed-up sense of tension. Well, that was a fun dream, he thought grumpily.

It wasn't the first time he'd had this sort of nightmare, although until recently they'd involved giant ants. It wasn't the first time he'd faced financial losses, either.

After his parents died when he was sixteen—more than half his lifetime ago—Max had nearly lost the ranch to bad weather, ailing cattle, rising costs and falling meat prices. Things had begun looking up a few years ago, though, when he'd netted some serious money from oil leases.

Over the objections of his then-wife, who'd wanted to spend the money on travel and home improvements, he'd invested it in several non-oil related businesses in Skunk Crossing. They'd prospered until the past year, when the skyrocketing skunk population had chased away ranch-loving visitors. Now Max and his friends faced losing their investments.

He sat up, stretching stiff muscles. He'd spent much of the week repairing fences from the recent storm and, since Wednesday, trying to pacify his niece.

Kirstin objected bitterly to sleeping on the couch in the family room. "I'm part of the family," she said. "Who is this Ms. Verano, anyway? She can't expect to have a whole entire room to herself!"

"Sorry," he'd said, "a private room is part of her contract." Although it wasn't, he knew for dead certain that the city lady would depart in a huff if she didn't get one.

His niece, who lacked the option of departing, showed her unhappiness by continually praising the city life she missed. "At least Dallas smells like civilization," she'd said yesterday when Melissa defended the ranch. "Instead of like skunks!"

"You're the one who stinks!" his daughter had snapped.

Furious, Kirstin had locked herself in the bathroom for an hour. It was, she said later, the only place where she could be alone.

Max stared at the *Gladiator* calendar on his wall. It was Saturday, he registered with a leap of glee. The day of salvation.

At breakfast, he said, "Who wants to ride to San Angelo with me to meet the nanny?"

"You mean that *creature* who's taking *my* bedroom?" Kirstin tossed back her long hair, which was streaked with shades of brown and blond. "Not me!"

Until now, Melissa had held a similar attitude. Seeing Max scowl at her cousin, however, she changed course. "I'll come, Daddy. I'm sure Ms. Verano is very nice."

"Me, too!" said Griffin.

"You're both trying to make me look bad!" Kirstin's lower lip quivered.

"It's not hard," Melissa said.

"Can't you girls be friends? That's what cousins are supposed to do, isn't it?" Max appealed to Jo-Anne, who was tidying the pantry.

She smacked down a can in annoyance. She was probably irritated at her husband, Luis, who'd been acting strange lately. "If you ask me, some of us females are a little too nice. I hope Ms. Verano gives you-all what-for."

"When are we leaving, Dad?" Griffin asked.

Max checked his watch. "Right now. All aboard!"

While Kirstin sat with her arms folded, the two younger children scrambled to their feet. None of them offered to help clear the table and for once he didn't bother to nag.

That was going to be Ms. Verano's task from now on.

NANCY HADN'T KNOWN propeller planes still existed, aside from those tiny Cessnas that buzzed over the campus towing advertising banners. Yet here she was, winging from Dallas-Fort Worth into the hinterland on a cute little turbo number with a couple of dozen commuters who acted as if it were normal to fly this way.

Those whirring blades, like something out of the 1950s, gave her the impression of journeying into the past. Instinctively, she hugged her laptop computer as if it were a last vestige of the real world.

What had she let herself in for?

Blithe self-confidence had carried Nancy through organizing a rapid departure from Clair De Lune. Dean Pipp had agreed to sublet the apartment to a summer-school student and return it in August. Mail would be held until a post office box was obtained in Skunk Crossing, since it might look strange for the nanny to receive letters addressed to Dr. Verano.

Much as she hated being underhanded, Nancy had decided it was best to let the rancher believe she was Hayley. Remaining incognito was essential for her to make meaningful observations.

As the plane descended toward San Angelo Regional Airport, Nancy's spirits quailed. All she knew about ranches was that they had cattle stampedes. And all she knew about nannies was that, in *The Sound of Music,* the children had put something nasty on their nanny's chair. Or was it in her bed?

The plane landed smoothly, and, after the flight attendant opened the door, the passengers strolled across the tarmac. Hot, muggy air wilted the curl from Nancy's hair.

Among a cluster of waiting people, she spotted a man and two children who fit the description of the Richters. They hadn't noticed her yet, so Nancy had a chance to study them unobserved.

With that bright red-gold hair, the little girl was a knockout. The small boy, wearing chaps and a yoked shirt, had a cute round face, although no doubt he hid frogs and lizards in his pockets.

The man was not what she had expected. As Nancy caught her breath, her target audience shifted from a traditional ladies' magazine to *Cosmopolitan.*

Only the tanned skin, jeans and yoked shirt

matched her expectation of what a rancher looked like. Otherwise, he had nothing in common with the crew-cut, musclebound, tight-faced lout she'd anticipated.

He was a lean six foot three, she estimated, with thick brown hair that softened the commanding effect of his high-boned face. Even from a distance, she could feel the melting effect of those intelligent, chocolate eyes. As for his full mouth, it looked as if it wanted to smile, but rarely did.

The man's gaze flicked over her and stopped. An instant connection sizzled through Nancy, all the way down to her toenails.

Time to step forward and make a good impression. "Mr. Richter?" she asked, moving toward him. "I'm Ms. Verano. And these must be the children. Well, of course, they're children. What else would they be? Did you all have a nice flight? I mean, I certainly did."

There, she'd handled that with aplomb, Nancy thought. She smiled, held out her hand and awaited his response.

In the photo she'd sent, Hayley Nanette Verano had appeared sweet and naive. Although at twenty-nine she was only seven years younger than Max, he'd felt old enough to be her father. As a result, he hadn't considered the possibility of male-female vibrations.

Now, as he shook hands with her, vibes jolted him so hard it was a wonder his teeth didn't rattle. Honey-blond hair, beautifully defined lips, a knowing tilt to her chin and, oh, those long legs. He was getting hard all over.

Max gritted his teeth. Ms. Verano had a confident,

breezy air that reassured and disturbed him at the same time. Heck, he wasn't even sure he'd reacted this strongly to Lilia the first time they met, although it was hard to remember.

From the region of his brain into which the dream of massed skunks had disappeared, there emerged a new and much more pleasant series of images. Ms. Verano draped invitingly across Max's bed. Ms. Verano slipping off that perky gray jacket and pearl-buttoned blouse. Ms. Verano sliding her charcoal skirt down her hips...

No, he thought firmly as he introduced himself and the children. He was reacting to a physical presence, not the woman. He didn't even know her and, seeing as she was his employee, he didn't intend to. Not in the biblical sense.

"What's that?" Griffin pointed to a briefcase the nanny carried.

"My laptop computer," she said.

"What do you need it for?" asked Melissa.

"All nannies carry them in L.A.," she said.

"Why?" Max, leading the way toward the baggage claim, didn't recall any of his previous housekeepers bringing such equipment. Still, they'd come from Skunk Crossing, where the general store owner still rang up purchases on a manual cash register.

"To organize my notes," she said. "About, oh, cleaning products. And recipes, of course."

"That sounds very efficient." Max, having earned a degree in agriculture despite the rigors of running a ranch, was a strong believer in modern technology.

Mary Poppins, twenty-first-century style, had arrived.

ON THE WAY to the ranch, Nancy made mental notes. For her article, she would need to describe not only the cowboy but also his native habitat.

Goodness, there were miles and miles of it, filled with wild grasses and cattle and fences and thickets of low-growing trees that Max explained were mesquites. As Hayley had promised, there was a dearth of shopping malls.

"Do you ride the range?" she asked.

"This is the Double Bar L," he said as his extended pickup truck rumbled along the highway. "If I rode it, I'd be arrested for trespassing, since it isn't my ranch."

"They'd have you arrested? Is there a range war?" she asked, making furious mental jottings.

"I was joking. Actually, the owners are my friends." He gave her a crooked smile that set Nancy's heart pounding. "We haven't had a proper range war around here in, oh, at least three or four years."

He was exaggerating again. She hadn't expected to find a sense of humor in a Neanderthal, Nancy thought.

She returned to her research topic. "Do you ride a horse or use some kind of motorized vehicle?"

She was hoping for the horse. It was lovely to picture this handsome semigiant loping through the sagebrush atop a fierce, snorting animal. His knees would grip the saddle, his hips would sway invitingly, and...

Why did Freud and Jung quarrel? Because Freud thought everything about human psychology was sexual and Jung disagreed. Until this moment, Nancy had sided with Jung. After meeting Max, she might have to rethink her position.

"Trucks and ATVs tend to spook the cattle," Max said. "They also have a hard time with ravines."

"Do you ride, Ms. Verano?" asked Melissa from the back seat.

Nancy was about to respond with a truthful no, when Max said, "Of course she does. Hayley grew up on a farm, didn't you?"

So her sister had lied about her background, no doubt basing her fabrications on the time she'd played the lead in *Oklahoma! May her forked tongue twist her lines, and may her on-screen love interest have bad breath.*

As far as Nancy knew, the closest Hayley had ever come to a farm was visiting a petting zoo. As for Nancy's own riding skills, she'd honed them on the carousel at Disneyland.

Instead of giving a direct answer, she said, "I use my middle name, Mr. Richter. That's Nanette—Nancy for short."

"People around here call me Max," he said.

Nancy liked plain names. His wife apparently hadn't shared that point of view, however, since she'd bestowed Griffin upon her son.

What had the former Mrs. Richter been like? Nancy wondered. She supposed the woman must have died, probably of boredom.

The truck swerved to avoid a small black-and-white creature in the road. "A skunk!" she said. "How cute."

"It wouldn't have smelled cute if we'd hit it," Max said.

"We've got lots of skunks," Griffin added.

"In your room?" Nancy asked.

Melissa giggled. "No, they're wild."

"Usually they're nocturnal," Max added, "although recently we've been seeing more of them in the daytime. It's nothing to worry about."

"Who's worried?" On principle, Nancy had decided not to show fear no matter what kind of creature she encountered. If she did, the children might feel challenged to put one in her bed.

They turned off the highway at a sign that read The Rolling R, and stopped at a wide gate. To her surprise, it opened automatically, like a garage door. Nancy supposed she should have expected that. After all, she'd grown up on a farm. She'd probably raised goats, milked the cows and plowed the back forty every morning before school, too.

Through the car window drifted the acrid scents of cow dung and hay. If it were possible to bottle the odor, Nancy would give some to her sister for Christmas.

"That's the equipment shop and the machine shed right there." Max pointed to their right. As his arm invaded her airspace, an appealing aroma of soap and leather tickled Nancy's senses.

Warm sensations stirred beneath her tailored skirt and short-sleeved cotton sweater. She felt an urge to wiggle closer to Max.

Melissa spoke from the back seat. "That's the horse corral over there, and we've got two barns. One for horses and one for cattle."

"The kittens are in the horse barn," Griffin added.

"There's bunnies, too," said his sister. "We collect the eggs every morning."

"You raise Easter bunnies?" Nancy asked.

Max's masculine chuckle rumbled through her like a 4.3 earthquake. "The bunnies share the chicken coop,'' he said. ''I'm afraid all we produce are ordinary hens' eggs.''

''JoAnne cooks them and I hate them,'' Melissa announced.

Nancy's spirits soared. ''You have a cook?''

''The foreman's wife has been helping out. Of course, she won't have to, now that you're here,'' Max said. ''We understand you're a terrific chef.''

Nancy groaned inwardly. Hayley had worked as a short-order cook among her many temporary jobs, so she hadn't lied about that skill. Except, of course, that it wasn't Hayley who'd hied her rear end to Texas.

Max halted the truck in front of a sprawling one-story house. Two young men ambled toward them from the corral.

''Howdy, ma'am,'' one of them called to Nancy, and swept off his baseball cap.

''Likewise,'' said the second, following suit.

The pair were a matched set, gangly and sunburned, with reddish hair and freckles. The only distinction was the gap between their front teeth: one had a straight space, while the other was crooked.

''Meet Rudy and Randy Malone.'' Max collected his cowboy hat, which had been sitting between him and Nancy, and wedged it on his head. ''My hired hands.''

''They're twins,'' said Melissa.

''They live in the bunkhouse,'' added Griffin. ''I want to sleep there. Can I, Dad?''

''When you're older.'' His father opened the driver's door.

As Nancy reached for her handle, the passenger door was flung wide by the man with the straight gap. ''Call me Randolph 'stead of Randy,'' he said. ''You sure are purty, ma'am, if you don't mind my saying so.''

He was staring at her legs, either from lust or because he was too embarrassed to look at her face. ''I don't mind, but it would help if you took a step backward so I could get out, Randolph,'' Nancy said.

''Oh, yes'm,'' he muttered and ducked away.

''Don't mind him. He fell off'n a horse and hit his head when he was ten.'' Rudy reached into the bed of the truck. ''I'll take your bags inside, ma'am.''

''I'll carry this here briefcase.'' Before she could protest, Randolph seized the laptop and scurried off.

Nancy was amazed that two cowboys living in the middle of nowhere could have so much in common under the skin with an English professor from California. At least she hoped they didn't write bad poetry.

They would make fine subjects for her article. Max had mentioned a foreman, also, and the foreman's nephew who sometimes helped out. Four or five men ought to be enough cowboys to satisfy an editor, Nancy hoped.

''Just ignore them.'' Coming around, Max took her elbow to steady her as she eased out of the truck. His fingertips heated her skin, making her sharply aware of the size and strength of his hands. ''They're like overgrown puppies.''

''So I noticed.'' It was ridiculous, the effect this man had merely by touching her, Nancy thought. Up close, she noticed how his shirt stuck to his chest in the heat, and that one of his shirttails had come untucked. She fought the urge to tuck it in for him.

She'd never had such feelings around Jim, a long-time friend to whom she'd briefly and foolishly been engaged the previous year. It must be the cowboy mystique, Nancy decided, tilting up her chin and discovering she was much closer to the man's mouth than she'd calculated.

"Thanks for the help. You can let go of my arm now," she said.

To her disappointment, Max obeyed. If not for the presence of a small audience, kissing the man would have been interesting. For research purposes, of course.

"Let's go see the bunnies!" Griffin caught her hand.

"I ought to change into pants first," Nancy said.

"It's not far," Melissa said. "Besides, you look really nice in a skirt."

"Thanks."

Max didn't second the compliment. Had he even noticed her as a woman? Nancy wondered.

"I hope you brought jeans," he said. "You'll need them to survive around here."

"I did. What's my schedule, by the way?" she asked.

They'd eaten lunch in San Angelo, and a few hours remained before dinner. Nancy hoped one of the mesquite thickets they'd passed hid a take-out pizza restaurant, although it seemed unlikely.

"I've got a few chores to tend to," Max said. "I'll see you at dinnertime. Matter of fact, I'm looking forward to it. You might want to defrost some meat from the freezer."

"Meat?" she said weakly. Terms like *roasting, stewing, broiling* and *barbecuing* were part of Nancy's vocabulary. So were *space travel* and *break dancing,* and she didn't do those, either.

"We've got a freezerful," Max said. "Take your pick." Out of Nancy's mouth popped the words, "I'm a vegetarian." She was shocked to hear herself utter such a blatant lie, when she ate restaurant-fried chicken and canned stew all the time.

If she really did become a vegetarian, starting now, it wouldn't be a lie. Plus, how hard could it be to toss a salad or stick a zucchini in the microwave?

"You didn't mention that in the interview," Max said.

Nancy gazed at him innocently. "I thought everybody was a vegetarian."

"On a cattle ranch?" he asked. "So what kind of cooking do you do?"

"Not eggs!" begged Melissa.

"We'll figure out something," Nancy promised.

"I'm sure you will," Max said.

She could see doubts fleeting across his expressive eyes. Ah, so he was having second thoughts about her. By August, when she announced she was leaving, he'd be glad to get rid of her.

For some reason, as she watched Max's lithe figure stride away, Nancy didn't find that prospect as pleasant as she had expected.

3

A VEGETARIAN? Deep down, Max had known there must be a flaw in his seemingly ideal nanny, a reason why she hadn't found a housekeeping job in Los Angeles. Apparently even West Coast health nuts liked to eat steak and chicken for dinner.

Still, Max conceded as he headed for the machine shed, anything Nancy cooked would probably taste good. So, he imagined, would she.

Whoa. You, mister, are not going to find out.

Nancy worked for him. Besides, after his disastrous marriage to a hothouse flower, Max knew better than to fall for a city lady with a floating mane of blond hair, big gray eyes and long, stocking-smooth legs.

Abruptly, he realized he'd been so intrigued by his new nanny that he'd forgotten to tell her about Kirstin. His niece was old enough to introduce herself, he decided, and continued on his way.

"Max!" His foreman, Luis Ortega, halted his SUV on the driveway. Strapped to the roof were a half-dozen weathered two-by-fours. "Any suggestions where I can put these so JoAnne won't see 'em?"

"Where'd you get the wood?" Max asked.

"From that barn they tore down over at the Flying Jockstrap," said Luis, using his nickname for a nearby ranch, the Flying J. Its pretentious "nouveau ranch'' owner sailed colorful windsocks from his flag-pole right below Old Glory. Luis claimed the things resembled men's underwear.

"I'm afraid to ask what you're building." Max didn't object to his men undertaking personal tasks when ranch business was light, since they put in long hours when necessary. He was a bit concerned about the direction his foreman's interests had taken in the past year, though, because they had been upsetting JoAnne.

"It's something I've got to do." Luis's heavily tanned, creased face took on a stubborn set. Built like a bulldog, the man had a stubborn temperament to match.

"Who's arguing?" said Max. "I was curious."

"It's a bigger and better trebuchet," said Luis.

"That's what I figured."

Building trebuchets, a type of medieval-style cat-apult once used for hurling objects at castle walls, had become a craze. Here in Texas, a catapult society had built a trebuchet with a hundred-foot throwing arm capable of tossing a 1957 Buick, although no one had ever explained to Max why people wanted to do that.

Some folks attributed the trebuchet's popularity to an episode of the TV program *Northern Exposure,* in which a character had built one. Luis had learned about them from a British TV series called *Junkyard Wars* that he captured via satellite dish.

"I always had an itch to hurl things, but I figured it was because I was irritated at my kids," he'd told Max months earlier. "After they grew up and left home, I realized they had nothing to do with it. I just like throwing things."

In the pasture behind his house, he'd built a medium-size trebuchet. On a sunny afternoon, Luis could be found lobbing bowling balls across the meadow, competing for distance with Rudy and Randy. It drove JoAnne crazy.

Now, for whatever reason, he planned to build a bigger one. "You can stack the wood behind the corral chutes," Max said. "It'll look like we plan to reinforce the corral, which isn't a bad idea."

"No swiping my lumber," said Luis. "Not unless it's an emergency." He put the SUV into Reverse.

"Wait!" Max said. "What are you planning to throw with that thing?"

"My boat!" called Luis. He backed down the drive and turned onto a branch road that ran to the chutes.

Luis had bought the motorboat, named *Free At Last,* at JoAnne's insistence after their kids left for college. They'd spent many weekends hauling it to a lake several hours away and sailing the thing, which turned out to be in constant need of repairs.

After giving up boating in disgust, Luis had tried fruitlessly to sell the *Free At Last.* Since his wife wouldn't let him give it away, he stored it under a tarp behind the equipment shop and snarled every time he passed it.

JoAnne was already angry about the abandoned boat, the thud-thud of bowling balls and the amount of time her husband spent on his pointless hobby. When she learned about the bigger trebuchet, she was going to be furious.

Max guessed that Hayley—make that Nancy—would approve if he built a catapult, as long as he used it to launch frozen cuts of meat across the field.

Or maybe not. He didn't know much about vegetarians, although apparently he was going to learn, since he'd hired one to cook.

As he got out his tools and set to work on the tractor, he reminded himself that he was not going to think about how pretty she looked or that appealing, slightly dazed way she had of smiling at him. If he didn't concentrate, he might...squirt oil all over himself.

Max stared down at the goop on his shirt and pants and muttered a few curses in Spanish that Luis had taught him. It was what he deserved for daydreaming, though.

The ranch, and everyone on it, depended on him. He had no business wasting his time on fantasies.

Grimly, he pulled off his shirt and went to rinse himself.

NANCY LINGERED among the bunnies and kittens, enjoying the way Melissa's and Griffin's faces shone with enthusiasm. She might even enjoy her summer job, if she could dodge the booby traps set by Hayley's fabrications.

There were wads of loose kitty fur on her jacket by the time she and the children came through a side door into the sunny kitchen. The flowered wallpaper, sprigged curtains and ornamental tile were, Nancy assumed, a legacy of the late Mrs. Richter.

Her mind buzzed with notes about Max and the ranch that she wanted to write down. "Do you two take naps?"

Griffin snorted. "We're too old!"

"I like to curl up in the afternoon and read," Melissa admitted.

Reading! Perfect, Nancy thought. "That's outstanding. Do you read, Griffin?"

"Sure," he said.

"He looks at the pictures," Melissa said.

"I can so read! A little."

"I'll help you with it," Nancy said. "Later. Meanwhile, we're going to have an hour of quiet time. You can both play in your rooms and I'll take a nap."

They laughed. "You're too old to take a nap," Griffin said.

"That's what you think," Nancy said. "Where's my room, by the way?"

The children led her through an elegant living room into a hallway. Nancy glimpsed other rooms at the back of the house. One, Melissa said, was a den where Kirstin was sleeping. Kirstin must be one of the cats, Nancy thought. Off the hallway, the children pointed out their rooms. Across from them lay a bathroom and the master bedroom.

Max's room. Nancy restrained an urge to peek inside. Even so, as she passed, she caught a whiff of leather and a trace of indefinable male essence.

Questions filled her mind. What kind of woman his wife had been. Whether he had a girlfriend. If anyone ever helped him tuck in his shirt, or, better yet, ripped it off his lean torso and threw him across the bed.

She wasn't likely to get answers. In any case, it wouldn't be her.

"Your room's at the end." Melissa pointed down the hallway. "It used to be a porch."

"You can see the bunkhouse if you stand on your bed," Griffin said. "Want me to show you?"

"No, thanks."

"What are you really going to do?" Melissa asked.

Nancy decided not to insist she would be napping, although she might. "Unpack. I hope Rory and Ronny put my bags away like they promised."

"Not Rory and Ronny! Rudy and Randy," corrected Griffin.

"Roly and Poly?" Nancy asked in mock confusion.

Griffin giggled. "You're doing it on purpose."

"I like you," said Melissa.

Nancy surprised herself by bending down and hugging them both. Since they were all covered in loose fur, little tufts of it wafted into the air.

Someone was going to have to vacuum this hallway one of these days, Nancy thought. It might even be her.

"See you in an hour," she said.

"See you!" They disappeared into their rooms.

Thank goodness things were going smoothly, she thought, as she opened the door to the end bedroom. Shaped like a long rectangle, it was furnished in cheerful country fabrics, with a daybed against the far wall. The only indication that this had once been a porch were the floor-to-ceiling shutters on the wall opposite the door.

The most curious aspect was a girl with long, expensively streaked hair. She sat at the small desk, logged on to the Internet with Nancy's laptop.

"Find anything interesting?" Nancy asked.

"Maybe." The girl finished sending a message before turning toward her.

About junior high age, she was pretty despite too much makeup. Her expensive if minuscule top bore a designer's name emblazoned across the front.

"I've been e-mailing my friends in Dallas," the girl said. "This place is positively primitive. The only computer belongs to Uncle Max and it's password-protected."

Although Nancy sympathized with the girl's sense of isolation, that was no excuse for invading another person's privacy and making free with her possessions. Also, there were a lot of documents on that computer that were nobody's business. "I'm afraid your uncle forgot to introduce us."

"I'm Kirstin," the girl said. "You must be the nanny. Well, I don't need a nanny, and besides, this ought to be my room."

The picture came into focus. "You're sleeping in the den," Nancy said. "Just visiting?"

"For, like, the whole summer." Kirstin pouted.

"Not willingly, I take it." Reaching past her, Nancy logged off the Internet. "From now on, you'll only be able to use this under my supervision. It has my personal files on it." And, as soon as she borrowed the appropriate software from Max, it would have a passcode, too.

"Whatever." Kirstin folded her arms. "My parents are busy working, so they dumped me here instead of paying for summer camp."

"I see." Nancy had learned that her siblings respected her most when she treated them like adults. She decided to start immediately with Kirstin. "I hope your uncle explained to you about doing chores.''

"Chores?'' The girl's nostrils flared. "You mean like collecting eggs and feeding the animals?''

"I take it the younger children do those things.'' Kirstin hadn't mentioned milking the cows. Nancy hoped that meant it was done by machine, because Hayley had no doubt won blue ribbons in milking at some make-believe state fair. "Do you cook?''

"That's your job.''

"You didn't answer my question.''

"I can make brownies,'' Kirstin said.

"Good. That's your chore for today,'' Nancy said. "Go make brownies.''

The girl studied her dubiously. "You're not going to watch to make sure I don't mess up?''

"Do you need me to?''

"No. I know how to light the oven with a match. This ranch is so out-of-date the kitchen doesn't even have pilot lights.'' Kirstin got to her feet. "I saw some mix in the cupboard. Don't complain if they're underdone. I like them gooey.''

"Sounds perfect.'' Nancy had made brownies once in the microwave. They'd come out tough in some places and rock-hard in others.

She made a mental note to get Kirstin to show her how to light the oven. But she could probably figure it out, now that she knew it required matches.

"Don't expect me to do your work for you every day,'' grumbled the girl as she departed, leaving a residue of adolescent angst.

Well, there was an unexpected challenge, Nancy thought. An angry preteen. Unless Kirstin was deeply troubled, though, she'd get tired of acting bad-tempered before long.

Nancy stood in the middle of the room, rooted by indecision. She ought to make notes on the computer. She ought to unpack her suitcases, which were sitting on the floor. She ought to do a lot of things, none of which interested her at the moment.

If only she knew why she was so restless, she mused as she removed her suit and brushed off the cat fur. The suit went into the back of the closet, awaiting a trip to the dry cleaners, if such a thing existed in Skunk Crossing. Nancy pulled on a pair of jeans and a short-sleeved pink blouse.

A faint stuffiness in the air indicated the room hadn't been used in a while. She folded back the shutters and discovered a sliding-glass door behind them. Easing it open, she felt a soft breeze play through the screen.

Below her stretched the private road, with smaller paths branching off. To her left sprawled a jumble of outbuildings and corrals where a few horses lazed in the afternoon heat. Farther downhill, Max emerged from a large garage-type structure.

He walked with a swinging stride to a pump and began to work it. Perspiration glistened on his bare back and shoulders, and strands of brown hair clung to his well-shaped head.

When the water gushed, he stopped pumping and splashed himself, rinsing oil from his arms. They were powerful arms, corded with muscles.

Using a bucket, he poured more water over himself. His jeans had slid down on his hips, revealing a flat, bare stomach and wet skin that gleamed in the sunshine.

Max Richter was more than a cowboy. He was pure, unabashed masculinity.

Nancy wanted to dash down the slope and run her hands over his rib cage. To catch a glint of laughter in his deep eyes and seduce him with a kiss. To press herself against his wet body and unwork the fastener on those tantalizingly tight jeans.

She'd never wanted a man this way before. Didn't have much experience with sex, to tell the truth. There'd been a boyfriend in college who'd faded from memory, and another, equally unmemorable, in graduate school. Plus one brief and platonic engagement. Nancy had, in short, reached the age of thirty-five and earned a Ph.D. in psychology without ever, she realized now, becoming sexually awakened.

This wild pounding in her veins made her understand why men wrote bad poetry and women took ridiculous chances with their futures. Nancy gripped the edge of the shutters. She had never dreamed she was so susceptible.

From now on, she would carefully control her feelings. No more daydreaming about Max Richter's half-naked body and no more speculating about how he would feel in her arms.

Otherwise she was going to land way, way over her head.

Sitting at the head of the table, Max studied the food before him. Around him, everyone grew quiet.

Amazingly quiet. He hadn't known Griffin to sit still for more than thirty seconds without offering to help someone. And for once, neither his daughter nor his niece was glaring at him.

The architect of this miracle sat across from him, a few strands escaping the twist into which she'd tucked her hair. Nancy, like everyone else, awaited his judgment.

Having been reproved by Lilia numerous times for his lack of suaveness, Max knew he should compliment his new housekeeper on her cooking. The problem was, he couldn't think of what to say because he couldn't identify the food in front of him.

On one platter, a gooey mass of melted cheese covered a greenish mound. In a bowl, odd-looking bits and pieces of nuts and vegetables sagged inside a red ooze of not-quite-firm Jell-O.

Another bowl offered chunks of lettuce half-buried beneath gobs of white dressing. The centerpiece was a towering plate of rough brown chunks that might have been brownies, except that, if so, what were they doing on the dinner table?

"Everything looks great." Max hoped that was enough, although no one responded. "It's time to bow our heads," he added, to break the silence. He hadn't said grace in years.

All heads dipped. "Now I lay me down to sleep." Max stopped. Uttering the first prayer that popped into his mind hadn't been such a good idea.

"Amen," said Nancy. She nodded at the children, who chimed in, "Amen."

"Try one of the brownies," said Kirstin. "I made them."

Under such circumstances, Max's father would have delivered a lecture about the importance of nutrition. The only part Max remembered, however, was "Eat beans. They keep you regular." After his gaffe with the prayer, he decided to play it safe and omit the lecture.

Instead, he tasted a brownie. "It's good." Seeing his niece's frown, he realized that he hadn't spoken strongly enough. "Terrific. The best I've had in ages."

"It's just a mix." Kirstin's smile belied her disparaging words.

Griffin and Melissa started talking at the same time. "I helped Nancy... I showed her where to find... She let me pour the salad dressing... The Jell-O was my idea..."

Max bathed them all in a smile as he contemplated whether there was anything here he could eat, and realized he had no choice. A man needed sustenance to do his work. Besides, if he declined to eat, he would offend everyone and ruin the rare good mood.

He passed the platters around, taking a modest serving from each. The children dug in with gusto exceeded only by Nancy's own enthusiasm. The woman appeared to enjoy this odd collation.

Max indicated the cheese-covered mound. "What is—I mean, does this dish have a name?"

"It's frozen broccoli," said Nancy. "There were hardly any fresh vegetables."

Here at last was a point to be seized on. "You're right," Max said. "What this ranch lacks is a vegetable garden."

"That's a terrific idea." Nancy beamed at him.

"There's a plot out back where my mother used to

garden," Max said. "Once you get the soil turned, we can pick up seeds and seedlings for you in town."

Nancy paled. "For me?"

"You don't think I'd let such a valuable resource go to waste, do you?" Max asked. "All those prizes for your tomatoes! I'm looking forward to tasting what you cook with them."

"Oh, yes, my tomatoes." Nancy waved her hand dismissively. "Really, they weren't all that...I mean, they were big, but..."

"I haven't eaten homemade spaghetti sauce since my mother died." Max could still taste the notes of sweet tomato, fresh basil, garlic and onions. "What else do you grow?"

"Lemons," Nancy said. "Of course, that requires a tree, doesn't it? Radishes. I just adore radishes, don't you? And there's nothing like zucchini. My neighbor, Mrs. Zimpelman, put in a bunch of plants and she was giving zucchini away up and down the street. People used to turn out their lights when they saw her coming."

"The soil might need a little improvement," Max said. "I'll have Rudy and Randy bring a pile of composted steer manure to get you started."

"Let me dig, please!" said Griffin.

"I guess I could try," said his sister.

Kirstin made a face. "I'm not rooting around in any steer manure. You can make your kids do it, Uncle Max, but you won't turn me into some hick farmer."

Melissa's green eyes narrowed. "Are you calling our grandmother a hick? She was your grandmother, too!"

Dismay flashed across Kirstin's face, that her cousin had gotten the better of her. She wasn't going to back off, though, Max could see.

Nancy spoke. "Kirstin can help plan the, er, layout so the plants don't, uh, shade each other."

Max was impressed, both by Nancy's skill with the children and by her knowledge of gardening. Given her background, though, it was no more than he'd expected.

"I can't wait," he said. "Pass me another of those brownies, would you?"

The only thing he didn't understand was why his new housekeeper had ever left farm life when she appeared so suited for it. He would have to watch her carefully for clues.

4

NANCY COULDN'T BELIEVE she'd pulled it off. Max was eating the food. Not with great relish, but he hadn't rejected it. Nor had he threatened to put her on the next plane to L.A.

The harsh pucker lines between his eyebrows had softened this evening, Nancy noticed, and his cocoa-colored eyes appeared lit from within. In defiance of all common sense, he'd accepted her as a nanny. She was safe. Well, almost.

The problem was that she'd spotted a can of Vienna sausages in the pantry while searching for the box of Jell-O. She loved Vienna sausages.

Maybe she could sneak in here late at night— No, of course not. If she got caught, the jig would be up. Plus, if her boss discovered she wasn't a vegetarian, she might have to chicken-fry a steak, whatever that meant.

So far, he seemed respectful of her accomplishments. More than that: proud of them. Oddly, she wanted him to be proud of her, even if she was a complete phony.

"I'm glad you like the food," she said.

"It's…fascinating." Max regarded his plate with an unreadable expression. "Keep up the good work."

"Promise we won't have eggs for breakfast tomorrow," said Melissa.

"I like eggs," said Kirstin.

"Nothing says 'breakfast' like waffles from the freezer," Nancy announced. "I don't suppose you have any?"

Max got to his feet and opened the freezer compartment. He was so tall that he had to bend, even though it was on top of the refrigerator section. "No. There might be some in the freezer in the utility room, but I think that's all meat."

"Cereal is fine, too," said Nancy.

"Isn't that too much sugar?" Max regarded her dubiously.

"Sugar gives you energy," she said. "Exactly what you need to go out and rope calves."

"I'm surprised to hear you say that," he said, "after you took first place in the state Young Dieticians' contest."

Somebody just shoot Hayley. Please!

Nancy recalled a bit of medical news she'd read in the newspaper. "Sugar isn't as bad as saturated fat, which you find in meat and whole dairy products." And commercially baked goods, which she wasn't going to mention because she couldn't bear to give them up.

"I'll take your word for it," said Max.

After dinner, while the family watched a game show on TV, Nancy retreated to her room and fired off an emergency e-mail to her landlady. If anybody in Clair De Lune knew about gardening, it was Dean Marie Pipp.

The dean must have been on-line, because while

Nancy was trying to figure out how to flame Hayley without running afoul of any e-mail regulations against profanity, she received a reply.

"You'll love gardening!" wrote her landlady. "Here's a list of Web sites where you can place orders and get information."

Nancy sent back a thank-you, accessed the Web sites and downloaded as much gardening information as she could find. Then her attention returned to her sister.

She was too angry even for an e-mail, Nancy decided, and picked up her cell phone. A musical voice answered, "Hayley here."

"First place in the Young Dieticians' contest?" Nancy demanded. "4-H medals for your tomatoes? You don't know a radish from a turnip!"

"That's not true," Hayley said. "Remember when I was in the musical *The Fantasticks?* We planted a vegetable garden. There's a whole song about it."

"That wasn't your character, and the vegetables were made of posterboard," Nancy said. "I'm going to be knee-deep in cow manure, thanks to you."

"So otherwise, how's it going?" Hayley asked.

"The kids are cute. As for the rancher, it's too soon to tell." The undercurrent of toughness, the glimpses of vulnerability and the beautifully developed hard body were none of Hayley's business.

"Started work on your article yet?" Her sister had loved the idea when Nancy mentioned it. No doubt it had eased Hayley's feelings of guilt, if she had any.

"Not yet," she said. "How are rehearsals?"

"We start next week," Hayley said. "It's still Saturday, remember? You left this morning."

"Seems like I've been gone for years."

"Thanks for calling. You've certainly eased my mind," said her sister. "I know this is costing you a bundle in phone charges, so next time, let's e-mail, okay? Bye!"

As Nancy hung up, she recognized that, once again, she'd been manipulated. That was less significant, however, than the fact that, as the conversation had reminded her, she was more concerned about the vegetable garden than about her article.

She didn't dare let herself get sidetracked. Coming from a nonacademic family, Nancy felt vulnerable to any implication that she lacked mental incisiveness. She had to do an outstanding job on this article, even if it was intended for an audience more interested in belly buttons than psychology.

USUALLY, Max enjoyed watching TV in the family room. Tonight, however, while Griffin perched on his lap and Melissa curled beside him on the couch, Kirstin kept glaring at them.

"What's the matter?" he asked during a commercial.

"Other than the fact that you're sitting on my bed? Nothing," she snapped.

She'd sunk into a beanbag chair near the patio door, her long hair falling over her face. Mad at the world.

Max couldn't figure out why. Sure, she was being inconvenienced, but spending time on the ranch was a privilege, not a prison sentence.

"Define 'nothing,'" he said.

"This ranch is crummy! There's nobody interesting

for miles around. Is that good enough for you?'' snarled his niece.

"We think it's a great place," Melissa said.

"That's because you never lived in Dallas."

"Griffin and I lived in Houston," she said. "We're not hicks, so stop being such a snob."

"I'm not a snob!" Kirstin said. "I just hate this place. I've got a right to hate it, okay?"

Nancy sailed into the room. For Max, the atmosphere immediately brightened.

The woman looked amazing in jeans and a pink shirt. Such a simple outfit, no different from what JoAnne might wear or any of the women he saw in town, yet for some reason it made Max acutely aware of the fact that he was a man. A man with red blood in his veins and a lot of healthy body parts he wasn't using.

"What's going on?" Nancy asked.

"Kirstin hates the ranch," Max said.

"Surely not," Nancy began. "She just isn't used to it yet."

"I wish she'd go home," said Melissa.

"I wish I could," replied her cousin. "My parents are too cheap to pay for summer camp, that's what."

"You got kicked out of summer camp last year. I heard Uncle Bill tell Dad," said Melissa. "They sent you here because they're fighting all the time and you get in the way."

"Stop right there!" Max had worried that his brother spoke too freely when he dropped by on Wednesday. Until now, however, neither of his children had mentioned anything and Kirstin had stoutly maintained she was here in lieu of camp.

"You're lying!" Kirstin wailed.

"Then why did your father say..."

"That's enough!" Max roared.

Melissa flew to her feet, bristling with outrage. "I'm telling the truth. I want to go back to Gramma and Grandpa's. They never yell at me. I hate this place, too!"

"Not as much as I do!" shouted Kirstin.

Both girls stomped out of the room. A moment later, Max heard two doors slam. Kirstin, he guessed, must be in the bathroom.

"Ouch, my ears! I haven't heard a door slammed like that since *I* was a teenager." Nancy folded herself into the beanbag chair. Even in such an awkward position, she managed to cross her long jean-clad legs seductively.

Max forced his attention onto his son. "Griffin, it's time for bed."

"I was enjoying the game show," the boy said. He hadn't taken his eyes from the screen during the entire uproar.

"It's over." Nancy indicated the closing credits.

"Okay." Griffin gave his father a hug. After a moment's internal debate, he went and hugged Nancy, too. "Good night."

"'Night," said Max.

"Sweet dreams," said Nancy.

The boy's small figure disappeared into the depths of the house. "Are boys always easier than girls?" Max asked.

"Only until they start driving cars into trees," Nancy said. "Or riding horses into gulches, whatever teenagers do around here."

"Both." Max was surprised at how easy he felt with this woman who'd only arrived today. The house had been lonely at night since Lilia left. That was one of the reasons he so often worked late.

Nancy fluffed back a sweep of blond hair, which she'd brushed out of its earlier twist. Max preferred it loose this way.

"It would help me deal with Kirstin if I knew more about her family situation," Nancy said.

Max leaned forward, elbows resting on his knees. "My brother and his wife are having problems, as you must have gathered. Bill figured that without Kirstin around, they'd have more time to talk."

"Are they seeing a counselor?" Nancy asked.

A sudden rage nearly blinded him. "They're not wasting their time on that exploitive garbage," Max said tightly. "Either they love each other enough to stick it out or they don't."

Nancy held up her hands, palms out. "Don't shoot, mister. I was only asking."

"Things here are different from in L.A.," Max said, a little embarrassed by his outburst. "We keep our personal business to ourselves."

"Okay." Nancy cleared her throat. "If it isn't too personal, however, I'm eager to learn more about how you do things here on the ranch."

"Like herding steers?" Max wondered if she was volunteering to help. "You've got your hands full already."

"I didn't mean the technical details!" Nancy said. "I mean, I want to understand the masculine perspective."

"The masculine perspective?"

"How real he-men on a ranch look at things. The macho point of view, so to speak."

Max raised one eyebrow. "According to the macho point of view, the best masculine perspective is on top. Not that I'm trying to be forward."

He feared for a moment he'd offended Nancy with his attempt at humor. She didn't look offended, though, merely curious. "Do you know a lot of macho men? Are most ranch hands like that?"

"Heck, no," Max said. "The guys out here respect women. They'd better, if they want to work for me."

"I can see you've got high standards for your employees. How'm I doing so far?"

"I like the way you take charge of the children," Max said. "You're not at all what I expected, though."

"You didn't expect your nanny to take charge of the children?" Nancy asked.

"I didn't put that very well." Being a man of action rather than words, Max prayed silently each time he opened his mouth that whatever was in his brain would somehow communicate itself accurately. That worked about half the time. "I thought you'd be younger and more unsure of yourself."

"I see," Nancy said. "Which version of me do you prefer?"

"The competent one," Max said. "For me to go out and battle the elements with a clear mind, I need to have confidence in the woman who's guarding the home front."

"That's an interesting use of warlike metaphors," Nancy said.

"Metaphors?" To the best of Max's knowledge, he hadn't twisted his brain around a metaphor since high school. "I mean it. In some ways, it's a war zone around here. This isn't the big city where the food arrives prepackaged in the supermarket."

"I'd like to ride the range with you sometime. Would that be all right?" Nancy asked.

The woman sure did jump from one topic to another, yet she seemed sincere in everything she said. Still, he couldn't picture her dragging a calf out of the muck. "If it's riding you want, we've got some decent trails."

"I don't want to ride for its own sake. I'm curious about what it's like to be a cowboy," she said.

"I'm not a cowboy," Max said. "I'm a rancher."

"What's the difference?" She clasped her hands together and leaned forward, riveted, although he couldn't imagine why.

"A cowboy's a loner. He's got no desire to be in management," he said. "Even if he can scrape up the money to buy a ranch, he doesn't want the hassles."

"Are Rudy and Randolph cowboys?" she asked.

Surely this beautiful woman couldn't be interested in those two juveniles, Max thought with a flare of jealousy. He almost wished he hadn't denied being a cowboy, since she apparently found the type romantic. "Naw. They're too green and gawky."

"Not seasoned enough. I get it." She stretched, a motion that put eye-catching curves into her pink shirt. "Well, I'd better turn in. That plane ride wore me out. Besides, I'll bet Kirstin would like her bedroom back."

"I forgot about that." Max stood when she did. "If she were staying on, I'd build another bedroom."

"You've got a dining room," Nancy said. "How often do you use it?"

"Not much," he conceded. "I suppose we could put a foldout cot in there, although it wouldn't be as big as the couch." Now that Nancy mentioned it, he could see what a good idea it was.

"She won't mind a smaller bed. And I'll bet she'd love it if you fix a rack for hanging her clothes," Nancy said. "We could empty the sideboard for storage, and if we remove a leaf from the table and push it aside, that'll give her a little leg room."

"I'll get right on it," Max said. "My ex-wife left a fancy bedspread I can hang in the doorway for privacy."

Half an hour later, the dining room was transformed. Max called his neice, and once he explained what he and Nancy had done, her frown disappeared. A reinvigorated Kirstin transferred her possessions in a rush. "Nobody comes in without my permission!" she announced.

"Absolutely," Max agreed.

Griffin studied the space enviously. "Right next to the kitchen! You can eat any time you like."

"There's room on the table for your Beanie Babies," Melissa said, having emerged from the bathroom when she heard all the moving. "Maybe mine can come and visit them."

"Maybe," Kirstin said. "But you have to ask first. No barging in here."

With peace restored, Max shooed everyone to bed and went to his office, whistling under his breath, to take care of paperwork. Soon he'd be able to leave the household entirely in Nancy's capable hands.

That was a good thing, since his blood insisted on heating every time she came close. With luck, he'd be able to stay so far away, he'd forget she was around.

NANCY STRUGGLED to write what Max had said about cowboys. She had trouble remembering the details as she worked on her article because her brain was filled with images of his intense, thoughtful expressions.

Nancy half-wished that, when they stood up after talking in the den, she hadn't distracted him by suggesting they turn the dining room into a bedroom. Maybe he'd have held out a hand to assist her to her feet. She might have stumbled against him and found her cheek pressed to his chest as she inhaled his tangy scent.

Or they might have continued their fascinating conversation about the masculine perspective. It called for being on top, he'd said.

Not all the time, though, surely. Nancy didn't have much experience in these matters—because of her drive to succeed, she'd spent little time dating—but she supposed that, with a man like Max, a woman would want to roll around and try different positions.

She couldn't have dreamed up a more appealing cowboy, even if he did claim to be more of a rancher. If the magazine readers weren't careful, they'd fall in love with him.

It was surprising that a man like him should be single for long. Nancy frowned as something Max had said earlier nagged at her.

He'd called Lilia his ex-wife, not his late wife. Come to think of it, there were no photographs of her among the framed shots hanging in the family room. Just the kids, Max and some older people.

A living ex-wife had a claim on Max and the kids.

Not that she was any of Nancy's business, but it was odd that nothing had been mentioned about her.

What was she like? What had gone wrong between them?

It was hard to imagine a woman giving up on Max, although Nancy supposed it might be hard to live with a man who had such old-fashioned ideas. He saw himself fighting the forces of nature while the woman stayed home with the kids. Hardly anybody thought that way these days.

Yet tonight, she'd enjoyed their conversation. She'd cherished Max's subtle reactions to her, and a couple of times she'd nearly lost track of the topic as she focused more on the rhythm of his voice than on the words.

With a groan, Nancy stopped typing and stared at her laptop screen. Max fiercely resisted being relegated to the category of test subject. In order to write about him, she had to regain her objectivity.

She lifted a nightgown from the closet and began to change. Through the partly open window drifted the scent of hay and, from far off, the acrid scent of *eau de skunk*.

Sporadic noises intruded: cattle lowing, a dog barking, the whinney of horses. There was also an odd thudding, repeated at uneven intervals. Tomorrow, she'd ask Max about that.

When Nancy peered out the side window, she could see a structure that must be the bunkhouse and, beyond it, another house. She presumed that belonged to the foreman and his wife.

So many people to meet. So many impressions to absorb. It was hard to separate herself as a person from her self-imposed assignment as an observer.

Maybe that was because, to some extent, she wasn't suited to be a psychologist. A familiar dart of insecurity pierced her usual self-confidence.

She had all the credentials, of course. She'd earned a Ph.D. and landed both a fine teaching position and a research grant.

Lately, though, she'd been barren of new ideas for projects. Maybe, deep inside, she wasn't cut out to reach such a high level of success. Sometimes she felt as if she were faking it and that sooner or later her colleagues would find out.

For years, Nancy had crammed her days with schoolwork, struggling to get through college and become a woman of accomplishment. If she didn't succeed, she'd felt that she would simply disappear. That she'd be nobody.

Well, she certainly wasn't nobody on this ranch. Max and the kids liked her and, she could tell, needed someone like her. Unfortunately, their good opinions were based on a lie.

She ought to do Max a favor and tell him the truth. She could still serve out the summer…watching resentment and disapproval in his eyes at every step.

No. She wasn't going to give up on her article so easily. Or make herself and Max miserable, either. Where was the harm in pretending for a little while longer?

Nancy spared one last frustrated glance at the blinking cursor on her laptop before turning it off. Maybe tomorrow she'd get her objectivity back.

5

    "I'M BEING HAUNTED by the ghost of a skunk I ran over last month," said Idabelle Babcock. The large, forthright woman owned the Skunk Crossing Bed-and-Breakfast as well as the Black-and-White Café and the town's gas station, Max had explained.

    The sixtyish woman was among a number of congregation members who'd gathered outside church before the service. To Nancy, they formed a charming picture in their Sunday finery against the Spanish-style structure, with its picturesque bell tower and red-tile roof.

    "Mama, please don't say that! Everybody'll think you're a nutcase," said Idabelle's daughter, JoAnne Ortega, the wife of Max's foreman. An attractive woman in her late forties, JoAnne had the same dark hair as her mother.

    When they arrived, Max had introduced Nancy to the pair and to his foreman, Luis. The conversation had soon turned to skunks, prompting Idabelle's startling announcement about the ghost.

    "I hit that durn polecat right in front of your ranch, Lorrin," she told a sunburned man, who joined the group with his red-haired wife. "Since then, I've seen his pointy little nose poking out of the bushes and his tail following me down the street 'most every night."

The sunburned man glanced nervously toward a half-dozen people standing apart. In contrast to most of the congregation, they wore crisply new Western clothing that ranged from jeans and yoked shirts to Stetsons, boots and, in one ridiculous-looking case, chaps.

"Try not to let my customers hear, all right?" he said. "I'm sorry, Idabelle, but you know how tough it's been trying to get people to stay on the Double Bar L once they hear about the skunks. My guests believe every polecat in Texas must have rabies."

Next to Nancy, Max murmured, "Lorrin Witherspoon and his wife, Lenore, run a working dude ranch."

"Mama, I never heard of a skunk having a ghost," JoAnne said. "There's plenty of the little stinkers wandering around. It's no wonder you keep seeing them."

"Maybe so." Her mother didn't sound convinced.

The church bell clanged. The children, who'd been playing with the Witherspoons' three youngsters, came running. Max escorted Nancy into the building, his hand lightly touching her waist.

Her cheek came to his shoulder. It was a straight, broad shoulder, perfect for resting her head against should she feel sleepy. Indeed, she had to fight a tendency to take a little nap right now.

At every step, people greeted them and welcomed the new nanny. Nancy couldn't help responding to their open friendliness, although she knew she ought to maintain a professional distance. Some of them might turn out to be material for her article.

As she sat down, a man sitting across the aisle two

rows down caught her eye because of his showy cowboy hat. When he turned toward her, she saw that he
had the kind of smooth, pretty features common
among Hayley's actor friends.

Giving her a grin that bordered on a smirk, he
winked. The man had gall, flirting with a stranger in
church!

"He sure thinks well of himself," Nancy muttered.

"That's Dale Dwyer," Max said. "He made a fortune with an Internet company, cashed out before it
went bust and bought the Flying J ranch. He's doing
his darndest to turn it into the Playboy Mansion."

"Where does he find the 'bunnies'?" Nancy asked.

"He flies them in, along with his friends, from back
east," Max said.

Dale Dwyer definitely wasn't a cowboy, Nancy
thought with relief. Otherwise she might have felt obligated to interview him.

Griffin settled on Max's left and Melissa slipped
into the pew on Nancy's right. That left Kirstin, who
flipped back her long hair and went to join the Witherspoons' daughter.

"I'm glad the two of them are hitting it off," Max
said. "They're a good match. Lynn's only a year
younger."

"I thought Lynn was *my* friend." Melissa scuffed
the pew ahead of her.

"She's probably flattered to be pals with an older
girl who's new in town," Nancy said. "That doesn't
mean she likes you any less."

"She'd better not," the girl said.

"Stop kicking the pew," said her father.

The minister, who had been talking with some congregants, lifted his guitar from a cloth-covered side table and approached the altar. "Let's sing our opening hymn, folks."

"Audey used to be a country singer till he got the call for preaching," Max whispered. "We have a lot of music in our ministry."

"His real name's Audacious," added Melissa. "The Reverend Audacious Powdermilk. Isn't that cool?"

"It sure is," Nancy said.

The pastor, a man in his fifties with more wrinkles than a bloodhound, was indeed cool, she decided as he swung into a tune that had the entire congregation singing. The exception was Dale Dwyer, who kept turning and mouthing words at Nancy. She made no attempt to understand him.

A prayer followed the opening hymn. Then Max, JoAnne and Lorrin and Lenore Witherspoon formed a quartet next to the minister.

They launched into a religious song with an irresistible melody. Nancy's foot insisted on tapping, even though such a thing would have been unthinkable in her parents' church.

Griffin stood on his pew so he could see better. Since other children were doing the same and no one seemed to mind, Nancy didn't object.

"I like it when Daddy sings," Melissa said.

"Me, too," Nancy said. Max's baritone, rippling through the other voices, raised prickles along her spine. It was utterly and completely male.

With a shiver, she wondered if he was singing directly to her. Words of love, although not romantic love.

"Nancy." Griffin tugged at her left hand. "What's that?"

Her gaze followed his pointing finger to the cloth-covered table behind and slightly to one side of the altar. The cloth rippled as if in a slight breeze.

"There must be a draft," she whispered.

"Look down," he said.

Nancy shifted closer to aisle so she could see better. That was when she spotted the small black-and-white nose poking from beneath the table.

"I think it's a dog," she said.

An undercurrent ran through the congregation. Whispers, gasps, and then someone said aloud, "Good Lord! It's a skunk!"

Pastor Powdermilk raised his hands. The singing stopped, along with most of the noise. "Folks, let's not alarm our small striped friend."

"He's not my friend!" a man shouted.

"That must be the skunk I was telling you about," Idabelle informed her daughter loudly enough to be heard from one end of church to the other. "The one that's haunting me."

"It's not a ghost, Mama," JoAnne said. "It's as solid as cow poop."

One of the tourist women jumped to her feet. "You people must be crazy. Why are you sitting here? Don't you know all skunks are rabid?"

"It's not attacking anybody," the minister pointed out. Indeed, as far as Nancy could see, the skunk, which was peering around as if seeking an escape route, was as frightened as anyone.

"No sane person would come anywhere near this

town. Skunks in church!'' The woman stalked down the aisle, followed by the rest of the tourists.

Reluctantly, the Witherspoons left the altar. ''I brought them in my van, so I've got to take them back to the ranch,'' Lorrin explained. ''We have to do something about this here skunk problem before it bankrupts us all.''

''I'm calling a meeting this afternoon, two o'clock at my ranch,'' Max said. ''All interested parties are welcome.''

His jaw tightened, and Nancy realized that Dale Dwyer's cowboy hat was bobbing in agreement. Max could hardly rescind the open invitation, however.

A rustling noise reflected growing nervousness among the rest of the congregation. When the skunk took a tentative step forward, people leaped to their feet and ran for the door, with Dale Dwyer leading the pack.

''I refuse to yield to mass hysteria.'' Nancy stood still, holding the children's hands. ''That's how people get trampled.''

Kirstin, who had rejoined them after the Witherspoons left, folded her arms uneasily but held her ground. That showed courage, Nancy thought.

Max strode toward them. ''What if the skunk nukes us?'' Melissa asked him.

Her father reached the end of their row. ''It's facing us. A skunk that's about to spray turns its back and beats a rhythm with its paws.'' He surveyed the church, which by now was almost empty. ''I'm glad you didn't panic. Let's walk out quietly, shall we?''

''What about the skunk?'' Nancy asked.

JoAnne came by, on her husband's arm. ''Pastor

Audey's got it under his spell. Music soothes the savage beast, they say."

Sure enough, the minister was plucking his guitar and crooning "Love Me Tender" to the skunk. Gathering its dignity about it, the small creature listened for a moment before meandering toward a side door.

"I guess the Lord has seen fit to end this service early today," Pastor Powdermilk told them. "You folks don't have to stick around. Good luck with your meeting. Whatever you decide, I hope it will be done with respect for God's creatures."

"We'll figure out something," Max said.

"That's the most exciting church service I ever attended," Nancy remarked as they strolled outside.

"You didn't even seem scared," he said.

"I wasn't." She took a deep breath of the clean air. "Although I don't suppose I'd like it if I got sprayed."

"It's not true about them all having rabies, by the way," Max said. "They're like any other animal. If they're exposed, they can get the disease. Otherwise, they mind their own business."

"Did they have a lot of skunks where you grew up?" asked Melissa.

"Sure," Nancy said, thinking of Hayley. "Some of them are even members of my family."

JoAnne spotted her mother lingering in the parking lot. "Admit it. It was no ghost," she said.

"All right," said Idabelle. "I've figured this thing out now."

Everyone waited.

"I'm being stalked by the mate of that skunk I ran over," she said. "It even followed me to church."

"I didn't notice it singling you out," said her daughter.

"I guess it got confused in the commotion."

"Mama!"

Luis shook his head. "Let's go lob a few bowling balls. It'll take our minds off the situation."

"What scares me," said his wife, "is that I'm beginning to think you have a point."

Nancy decided not to ask for an explanation for Luis's offer yet. She needed all her energy to figure out what to fix for a vegetarian lunch.

IN PREPARATION for the afternoon meeting, Max set out a plate of leftover cream cheese and cucumber sandwiches in the living room. For lunch, the children had preferred the hot dogs he'd fixed.

Nancy had worn a peculiar expression as she munched her veggie sandwich and watched the rest of them eat wieners. He could have sworn it was envy, not disapproval.

"Let me tidy up in here." She appeared in the doorway, wearing the same gauzy rose-print skirt and blouse from church. The material clung to her rounded bosom and nipped waist.

While he was bringing in extra chairs, Max forgot everything except how delectable Nancy looked. "I'd appreciate it," he managed to say, although he couldn't remember what she'd just offered to do.

She plumped the imprint of Griffin's small body from the couch cushions and, with a rag, wiped fingerprints off the coffee table. Outside, a thumping noise shattered the Sunday peace.

"What's that?" Nancy asked.

"I'll show you." Max escorted her down a small passage that led between his office and a utility room. It ended at the back door. Through a glass pane, he pointed to a field. "See that?"

She squeezed beside him to look. This close, he noticed how the sunlight picked out strands of honey and wheat in her hair and that she smelled like the coffee she'd brewed for lunch.

"What's that contraption?" She indicated a wheeled wooden chassis supporting a waist-high crossbeam and throwing arm.

"It's a trebuchet. A kind of catapult." While he explained, they watched a couple of bowling balls whiz into the distance. At this angle, the orbs seemed to disappear into the sky. "Luis's passion for throwing things irritates the heck out of JoAnne."

"It must be part of the primitive male psyche," Nancy said. "It probably comes from thousands of years of hurling rocks and spears at their prey."

"You sure don't talk like a nanny," Max said.

Wide gray eyes blinked at him. "I don't?"

"Especially one who dropped out of college after her freshman year." He'd reread her résumé last night, looking for clues to why he found her presence so unsettling.

"I guess I speak that way because I read a lot." Nancy whirled at the buzz of the doorbell. "They're here!"

Max could have sworn he detected relief in her voice. He made a note to probe further when he got the chance.

Lorrin and Lenore Witherspoon had brought their daughter and two younger sons. When they entered, the children scampered through the house to find their playmates.

Dale Dwyer followed them, doffing his hat to Nancy and then, uncouthly, putting it back on indoors. Maybe he was trying to disguise his receding temples and thinning pale blond hair, Max thought.

Idabelle, who had a great deal to lose from the skunk invasion, arrived shortly afterwards. JoAnne walked over as soon as she spotted her mother's car. The continuing thuds from the back pasture accounted for Luis's absence.

Max waited a few minutes in case anyone else showed up. "I expected a better turnout," he said.

"A number of people asked if I was coming." Idabelle settled her large frame on the couch. "They said they'd support whatever I want to do."

"That's because you own most of the businesses that cater to visitors," her daughter said.

"Me and my partner here." She nodded toward Max, who straddled a reversed straight chair.

"I'm only a twenty-five-percent partner," he reminded her.

"That's the twenty-five percent I needed to renovate," she said. "The café and the B and B looked sorrier than a plucked chicken. If it weren't for you, I'd be losing business even without the skunks."

"It was a good investment," Max said. "Regardless of what happens in the short-term."

In truth, he might have earned a better return in the stock market. Or he could have pleased Lilia and squandered the oil lease money on shopping trips to San Antonio.

The bottom line wasn't financial, though. It was loyalty to his community and to old friends.

Lenore reached for one of the sandwiches. "We've all got an economic stake in this skunk problem. Almost all." She eyed Dale questioningly.

"I don't like the smelly things cluttering up my property. Still, getting rid of them shouldn't be hard once we agree." Stretching out his legs, he tipped back his chair. "I vote we hire an exterminator to gas or poison them, whatever works best. I'll fly someone in, if that's what it takes. Guess this is going to be a short meeting, huh?"

He bestowed a cocky grin on Nancy. Perched a few feet away on a chair by the china hutch, she ignored him.

"You scare them critters and this whole county'll stink to high heaven," grumbled Lorrin.

"I'm sure they can be harvested without setting them off like stink bombs. It just takes a man who knows what he's doing." Dale scooted his chair a few inches closer to Nancy's and tried another smile in her direction. Again, no reaction.

Much as he disliked the oily newcomer, Max had to admit that Dwyer could be accounted handsome. He was certainly rich.

It spoke well for Nancy that she didn't give the oaf the time of day. Perhaps she was inured because there were so many handsome men in L.A. Max wondered how he measured up and then dismissed the thought, because, much as he liked Nancy, he couldn't bring himself to worry about such things.

"I don't like skunks any more than the next person," JoAnne said. "And I sure don't want Mama to lose her customers. I think we ought to remember, though, that these animals have a right to be on this earth, same as we do.''

''Hardly!'' Dale snorted. ''I paid top dollar for that ranch.''

Lorrin tapped his fingers on his knee. ''I hate to go against you, JoAnne. The trouble is, we've got pitiful few bookings for the rest of the summer, and there'll be nothing at all by next year if we don't solve this thing.''

Max brought up other options he'd been weighing. Unfortunately, he could see the weaknesses even before the others pointed them out.

Although neutering skunks might be humane, they couldn't capture enough to make a serious dent in their reproductive rate. The other possibility, spreading public information about the harmlessness of skunks, was impractical, since the Witherspoons' customers hailed from across the country.

''May I say something?'' asked Nancy.

''Please do, pretty lady.'' Dale sure didn't give up easily.

''I want to make sure I understand the situation,'' she said. ''It isn't really the skunks that are the problem, right? It's the fact that they scare the tourists.''

''That's true.'' Idabelle eyed a cucumber sandwich warily and passed on it.

''Why do tourists come to this area?'' Nancy asked. ''Other than the ones staying at the dude ranch.''

''City folks sometimes drive through Texas searching for a down-home experience,'' JoAnne said.

"This little town with its funny name appeals to them."

"Honeymooners with a sense of humor like to lodge at the B and B," Idabelle added. "They send postcards to all their friends with the official Skunk Crossing postmark."

"Also, we stage an Old West Festival in August," Max explained. "The town puts on a small rodeo and hires a petting zoo. It draws a lot of families from the area."

"This year, we haven't even started booking acts," Idabelle said. "I'm chairman of the carnival committee, but, to tell you the truth, I doubt anyone's going to attend."

"If you can't lick 'em, join 'em." Nancy crossed her legs demurely. They were slim, shapely legs, and Dale was paying far too much attention to them, Max thought.

"I'm not sure I follow you," Lorrin said.

"The town's called Skunk Crossing," Nancy said. "Any town could have an Old West Festival. Only this one could celebrate a Skunk Days festival."

"I don't see anything to celebrate about skunks." Dale's nostrils flared.

The man was too stupid to recognize a brilliant idea. Everyone else got it, and Max saw excitement growing in their faces as Nancy explained, "Don't get rid of the skunks or pretend they're not there. Make a fuss about them!"

"We could paint Main Street black and white," Idabelle said. "I'll draw up a special theme menu at the café."

"Over in Groundhog Station, they had skunk racing one year. We could hire the same operators," added her daughter. "And how about a pet show with prizes for black-and-white animals? Big ones, little ones, smelly ones."

"Wonderful! Skunk Days is a natural for offbeat publicity," Nancy said. "What do you think, Max?"

"My brother owns an advertising agency and he owes me a favor," he said. "I vote aye."

Lorrin and Lenore added their approval. As a hum of discussion swept the room, it became clear that everyone but Dale loved the idea.

"Even though you're new to the area, you should be on the Skunk Days committee, Nancy," JoAnne said.

Quickly, she shook her head. "I have duties here."

"We can work something out," Max said. "Only if you want to, though."

"I'll help you set up a Web site," she said. "Other than that, well, I can't get involved."

He saw no reason why not, unless Nancy was afraid of incurring publicity for herself. Had she come here to hide from her past?

Unlikely, Max decided. When he'd checked out her references, there'd been no mention of problems. Still, she *was* a lot sharper than her résumé had suggested.

Soon afterwards, the meeting broke up. Dale left first, disgruntled. While the Witherspoons collected their children, JoAnne hugged her mother.

"Thanks for not bringing up the stalking business," she told Idabelle.

"I know how foolish it sounds," her mother said. "I'm not making it up, though. I saw that skunk watching me as I left the house, and it'll be waiting when I get back.''

JoAnne released an exasperated sigh, the kind she usually reserved for her husband. ''Oh, Mama!''

''I'm glad we're not killing a bunch of them,'' added Idabelle, ''seeing how vengeful they are.''

''The Night of the Vengeful Skunks,'' Nancy said. ''Wouldn't that make a good title for a movie?''

''You could give it three sniffs instead of three stars,'' Max said. ''Say, we should add a skunk film festival to our agenda. Are there any movies featuring skunks?''

''*Bambi*,'' Nancy said promptly.

''How about that cartoon character, Pepe Le Pew?'' said Idabelle. ''I'll get right on it.''

Max escorted the visitors to their vehicles. His children ran alongside, making plans to picnic with their friends the next weekend.

A few minutes later, he found Nancy clearing the living room. She picked up the sandwiches with a touch of pink enlivening her cheeks. ''I guess these weren't such a hit.''

''You more than made up for it.'' He touched her arm. ''That was a terrific idea for the festival.''

''Thanks.'' She was still regarding the sandwich plate ruefully. ''I'm sorry about this vegetarian business. I'm kind of new at it, to tell the truth. It just seemed...healthier.''

That, at least, explained her awkwardness in the kitchen. ''If you're not committed to it, I'd appreciate your calling a time-out for a few months.''

''Does that mean I get to eat the can of Vienna sausages in the pantry?'' she asked.

Max laughed. "You certainly may." In light of her confession, his suspicions about her hiding out struck him as paranoid. Apparently, her recent decision to become a vegetarian had been the root of her problems.

On the other hand, there was something about Nancy that still didn't fit with what he'd expected. A man had to find out everything possible about the woman to whom he entrusted his children.

Max remembered something Nancy had said earlier, and it gave him an idea. Tomorrow, he was going to catch her by surprise.

Her reaction would tell him a lot.

6

JoAnne showed up while Nancy was starting break-fast. When she entered the kitchen, she immediately homed in on the withered bacon in the frying pan.

"I know there must be a way to cook them in the microwave, but I figured I'd do it the old-fashioned way." Nancy adjusted the grease-splattered apron over her shorts and T-shirt. "They turned black all of a sudden."

The older woman set the burned bacon aside. "Our dog will enjoy those. Let me show you how it's done."

"Thanks. I'm kind of butterfingers around here." As she watched JoAnne lay out fresh rashers, Nancy got out the eggs the children had collected. "I was thinking of scrambling these. I know Melissa doesn't like them, though."

"Give her a box of cereal," JoAnne advised.

"I was thinking of it." Although a few days ago she'd have handed over the cereal without a second thought, Nancy had begun to worry about following her instincts. Her lack of culinary aptitude was becoming a bit too apparent.

The foreman's wife turned the frying bacon with a fork. "You have to remove them from the pan when they're not quite done. The fat gets so hot, they keep on cooking.''

"That's sneaky of them.'' Nancy cracked eggs into a bowl and picked out a few errant pieces of shell.

"We ran out of pancake batter. You can pick some up in town this afternoon,'' JoAnne said. "You need groceries and Max mentioned starting a garden, so I thought you and I might drive in and do some shopping.''

"I'd love to.'' Nancy beamed at the other woman. Her assistance would be invaluable.

JoAnne, who announced that she'd already eaten, fixed herself a cup of coffee and called in the troops. They dug into the bacon with gusto.

Melissa even consumed her eggs without complaining. By comparison to overcooked broccoli and cucumber sandwiches, ordinary food must taste good.

Max smiled as he watched Nancy take several bacon strips. Sparks zinged down her spine. The fact that he was amused at her expense didn't make him any less appealing.

While they were eating, JoAnne said, "This afternoon when we go into town, we can take the kittens. They're old enough to give away.''

"They're our kittens!'' Melissa cried. "I won't give them up!''

"We don't need seven cats on the Rolling R,'' Max told her. "I should have had Colonel Pickering neutered long ago.''

His daughter stared at him, stricken. "Daddy!''

"They're very fond of those kittens,'' Nancy said.

"I wuv them,'' said Griffin, reverting to baby talk.

Max considered. "I'll let you pick out one kitten to keep."

"One apiece?" Kirstin pressed. "I can take mine back to Dallas. My parents won't mind."

"Please, Dad?" said Melissa.

"All right," he agreed. "Pick them out this morning."

"That leaves three to find homes for," JoAnne said. "I'll help you make a sign after breakfast. You can station yourselves outside Mama's café while Nancy and I shop."

"Nancy, you pick my kitten for me," said Griffin.

"How sweet." She tousled his brown hair. It was soft, like his father's. Or like she imagined his father's to be, since she hadn't actually touched it.

"JoAnne will look after you till noon." Max set aside his napkin. "Nancy and I are going to check on a couple of horses that keep wandering near the creekbed."

"We are?" She could see in his face, and JoAnne's, that they'd arranged this outing beforehand.

"You said you wanted to ride the range with me." On his feet, Max towered over everyone. "Here's your golden opportunity. Unless you've changed your mind?"

"No way." Nancy stood up. "I'll go throw on some jeans."

"Don't forget the sunscreen," JoAnne said. "You don't want to burn that fair complexion."

"Right you are." Realizing she'd left a request unfufilled, Nancy added, "Griffin, you like the kitten with the brown splotches on his nose. Keep that one."

"How do you know which one he likes?" Max asked.

"I saw him playing with it Saturday."

"Dibs on the black-and-tan one." Melissa scraped back her chair.

"I haven't made up my mind," Kirstin said. "It might take a while."

"You've got three hours." JoAnne set down her cup. "And you all have to help clear before you start."

Grumbling good-naturedly, the children pitched in. They were so keyed-up about their kittens, they scarcely noticed when Nancy slipped out.

She wondered if there was an Internet site that taught horseback riding. And knew that, even if it existed, it wasn't going to help.

MAX COULD TELL from the way Nancy regarded her horse that she hadn't done much riding. She appeared to be measuring the distance from the ground to the stirrup as if to figure out whether her foot would reach that high.

"You don't have to go if you're frightened," he said. She'd been a good sport when he surprised her by mentioning the ride, but he didn't want to push her too far.

"I'm out of practice. That doesn't mean I'm scared." She reached behind her neck and looped the rubber band one more time around her hair. At least she'd groomed herself sensibly. "Animals don't frighten me. Does this one tend to bolt?"

He'd picked the oldest, gentlest mare in the stable.

"Nutmeg's the horse the children ride." He walked to the horse's mouth and held the bridle. "Ready?"

"You bet!" She inserted her shoe and swung into place, landing with a small jolt. Although Nutmeg quivered, the horse settled down immediately.

Max had to hand it to Nancy. She had guts, he thought as he mounted his burnished gelding, Copper. Also, she had a natural seat. She perched straight in the saddle, balancing herself against Nutmeg's shifting.

At a click of the tongue and a nudge with his knees, Copper started forward. Nutmeg followed suit.

"So you've always wanted to ride the range," Max said. "You must have been eager to get a job on a ranch." Eager enough to lie about her background?

"Taking care of houses and kids tends to be confining," Nancy said. "Doing it on a ranch, though, that's different. I like being out of doors."

They passed between the machine shed and the corrals. Rudy and Randolph, who were repairing a cattle chute, waved as they went by, their gazes lingering on Nancy.

Those boys ought to find themselves girlfriends, Max mused. At twenty-five, they remained bashful and socially awkward. He'd make sure they attended the next community square dance.

Leaving the outbuildings, they rode alongside a pasture dotted with cattle and spring calves. Animals raised their heads to watch them pass.

Although the pungent odor of cow droppings wafted through the air, Nancy's face was alive with curiosity as she took in the panorama. "This place is splendid and timeless. It makes me feel connected to the past.''

Normally, Max didn't indulge in romantic notions. Today, however, he registered the sweep of clear sky, the wind rustling through the trees and the calves playing bucking games in the meadow.

''I love it here,'' he said. ''After my parents died, when I was sixteen, most folks believed Bill and I should be adopted by relatives. The problem was, there weren't any close by, and I didn't want to leave.''

''You took over the ranch when you were sixteen?'' Nancy swayed easily as Nutmeg skirted a low-growing clump of cactus.

''Luis had been my dad's foreman,'' he said. ''He offered to stay, and Idabelle knew a lawyer who got me declared an emancipated minor. Ranchers around here chipped in to help, and we muddled through.''

''You've done a good job,'' Nancy said. ''Everything's so organized. The fences are fixed, the barns are painted.''

The horses picked their way downhill along the path. ''Structures fall apart fast if they aren't maintained.''

''It's more than that.'' Nancy turned her cool gaze on him. ''People show us on the outside what they're like on the inside. Whether they're disorganized, or egotistical, or in control.''

''You can read my mind from the paint on the barn?'' Max asked.

''Not your mind,'' she said. ''Your approach to ranching.''

''What else do you know about me?''

"Not much." Her tone became brisker. "Not as much as I'd like to. Tell me what a rancher does all day. What you think about."

"I pray for rain, but not too much of it," he said. "You want me to walk you through a day in the life? All right."

He described the events he took for granted. She clearly relished every detail, from feeding the horses in the morning and oiling the saddle and tack, to digging postholes and maintaining the roads.

She expressed surprise that he handled his own routine veterinary work, maintained his own equipment and mended his fences. "You're so self-sufficient."

"It goes with the territory," Max said. "Surely your dad was that way on your farm. Down in Imperial County, wasn't it?"

"A farm isn't a ranch," Nancy said. "We, you know, grew things."

Like tall tales? Still, he didn't want to call her a liar. Apparently she'd exaggerated her background because she hankered to live in a place like this.

A man could hardly blame her for that. Max would have gladly told a few whoppers himself to get a job on a ranch if he hadn't inherited one.

NANCY WISHED she could take notes on what Max was saying. Still, she didn't expect to have trouble remembering, because it was so absorbing.

During her Fellini project, she'd found it easy to concentrate because she really wanted to know how babies acquired language. The ranch intrigued her in the same way.

Max's account drew her right into his life. She

could smell the leather, taste the beans he heated over a campfire when he stayed out late, hear the sizzle of a brand when he marked his calves in the spring.

It bothered her a little that she wasn't staying objective. On the other hand, this was hardly some experiment with rats in a maze.

She was observing a real situation for a popular audience, Nancy reminded herself. Surely her emotions were part of the story. As the narrator, she could strike the correct tone of cheeky aloofness later.

They found a small band of horses grazing on the edge of a creek, near a permanently installed trailer where Max explained that he slept when caught in bad weather. "This fellow's the problem." He indicated a stallion standing with head up and ears pricked. "His name's Felonious and he's got a knack for kicking down fences."

"What are you going to do with him?"

"Put him in jail." To his mount, he said, "Let's go, boy."

Copper swung around the strays, herding them toward a gap in a nearby fence. Max guided the gelding with light tugs on the reins, a slight lean of the body and the grip of his muscled thighs.

His low clucking noises tickled Nancy's ear like a lover's whisper. At a slight motion in his hips, heat shafted through her. She felt as if she were the one held tightly between Max's legs.

She was glad for the distraction when Nutmeg started forward, following Copper. Once they reached the downed fence, Max chased the loose horses inside, pulled some tools from his saddlebags and dropped to the ground.

"I'll help." Nancy swung one leg over Nutmeg.

"I've got you." He hurried over in time to grip her waist. For a moment, she seemed to be flying as his large hands eased her to the ground.

Her leg grazed his as she alit. He tensed, perhaps steadying himself against the impact. Every muscle in his body must have gone rigid, she thought, and wondered what else had hardened.

Shame on you!

She stepped away reluctantly. "I'm not much with a hammer, but I can hold the boards in place."

"That'll help." Max showed her how to position each crosspiece as he nailed them in with speed and precision. A thin sheen of sweat stood out on his skin as he worked, and she noticed he had rolled up his sleeves.

Someone ought to write a poem about those powerful forearms, Nancy thought. The only words that came were, "Oh, rancher strong, oh, horseman brave, you've made this fluttering heart your slave."

It must be the lingering Hugh Bemling influence. She would have to exorcise it immediately.

Max rapped in the last nail and stood back to examine his work. Nancy remained in a crouch. Her body, which had aged fifty years while she was riding, was in no hurry to follow his example.

"How will you keep the horses from escaping again?" she asked.

"It shouldn't be a problem. Felonious can't jump this high, and he can't kick down a fence unless it's weakened. I'm guessing this section sagged after the last thunderstorm that…"

Abruptly, he went deadly still. He was staring at the ground a few feet past her.

Nancy started to turn.

"Don't move." His low voice carried urgency.

"What is it?"

"Rattlesnake." He edged toward his horse. It gave a low whinney and performed a nervous dance. "Calm down, boy. Let me get into my saddlebag."

Nancy wondered if it was better to stand here not knowing what the snake was doing or to peek and find out for sure. Then she heard an unmistakable, dry rattling noise that froze her in place.

"Don't even twitch," Max said in a low, hypnotic voice. As the horse nickered uneasily, he slid his hand into the side pouch and took out a gun.

As a rule, Nancy wasn't keen on firearms. That, however, had been in town. Out here, there were no police to call.

Max eased to one side, taking aim. The snake rattled again.

The shot rang out, stunningly loud. Then another, and another. Her ears pounding, Nancy braced for the sharp sting of fangs in her ankle.

Max walked past her and fired again. She quaked so hard she nearly lost her balance.

"That did it," he said. "It's about as dead as any snake would want to be. You can turn around now."

Nancy managed to change position enough to see the scattered remains of a diamondback. Harmless now, but she still feared it.

Standing over the vanquished menace, Max formed the classic image of a cowboy—Stetson tilted, tanned face examining the battle remains, gun smoking in his hand. He was so sexy that, if she hadn't been scared out of her wits, Nancy might have done something foolish. Like kiss him.

She knew she ought to say something. It took a moment to remember what that was. "Thank you."

"You've got strong nerves." He returned the gun to the saddlebag. "I expected you to shriek and take off running."

"I'm not the hysterical kind," Nancy said. "I prefer to stand here and have my heart attack quietly."

"You're trembling." Concern darkening his eyes, he gathered her into his arms. "Lean on me."

"Okay." She drooped against him, grateful for his solid support. Luxuriating in his heat. Wondering if that kiss wouldn't be a good idea, after all.

Max caught her upper arms and held her back for inspection. "You're not going to faint, are you?"

"Nannies don't faint. We spank bottoms. This one's already been spanked to bits, I'd say." She indicated the remains of the snake.

"I'm glad we stumbled across him," he said.

"You're happy I nearly got snakebit?"

"Not that part," he conceded. "I meant, I'm glad he isn't still wandering around. Rattlers can kill calves, chickens, bunny rabbits and children."

"Then I'm glad I played a useful role as bait," Nancy said.

"Think you can ride?"

"It beats walking."

She let Max help her onto Nutmeg, subduing the impulse to cling to him. He smelled wonderful, like exertion and saddle and horse. Until today, none of those odors had been on her Top Ten list, but from now on, they went to the head of the queue.

Only when they were safely on the path heading toward the ranchhouse did she realize what a perfect incident this was to include in her article.

IT WAS THE first time Max had ever almost for sure saved somebody's life, or at least prevented a lot of pain and suffering. He'd pulled a hired hand out of quicksand once, but the fellow could have swum to safety if he hadn't been roaring drunk.

Max had gone ice-cold when he saw the snake menacing Nancy. It had been as if, in that instant, everything he'd worked for was threatened.

He was glad it hadn't affected his aim. No matter how well a man thought he knew himself, he didn't know everything until the chips were down.

By the time they reached the corrals, Nancy's color had returned, and she showed no sign of shock. Max knew he probably looked and acted pretty much as always, too. Inside him, though, something had changed during their ride.

He just wished he knew what the heck it was.

A HUNK OF black-colored cabbage and two white licorice strips decorated the plate. Idabelle waved them proudly under her visitors' noses.

"Mama, that's disgusting," JoAnne said.

The café owner clunked the platter onto the counter. "If you ask me, it's durn clever. My cook's calling it White-Striped Skunk Cabbage. We're going to fix up a whole special menu by August."

"I'm not eating that," Melissa said.

"Gross-out." Griffin made a barfing noise.

"You two are so juvenile," Kirstin declared. "I think it's…cool."

"Why aren't you eating any, then?" demanded her cousin.

"Because I'm not hungry."

At midafternoon, the Black-and-White Café was nearly empty. Among the handful of coffee drinkers, no one paid any attention to the mewing noises emerging from the basket over Nancy's arm.

"We ought to set up the children out front," she said. "I'm stiff from my ride and I'd like to finish shopping before rigor mortis sets in."

"I forgot about that," JoAnne said apologetically. "You must be in quite a state."

"Pish and tosh," said her mother. "She's a farm girl. Isn't that what you told me?"

"Something like that." JoAnne ushered them all out onto the sidewalk and set up the sign that read Free Kittens in large letters. Lower down, Melissa had scrawled, "You better be nice to them."

The children settled on borrowed chairs. "I can watch them from inside," Idabelle assured the adults.

"That's so kind of you." As she spoke, Nancy saw something from the corner of her eye. She turned in time to glimpse a black-and-white nose retreat into a crawl space across the street. "What was that?"

"My stalker," said Idabelle.

"You mean, your stinker!" Griffin grinned.

"I think it was a rabbit," Kirstin said.

Melissa groaned. "Who ever heard of a rabbit stalking anybody?"

"It's gone now," JoAnne said. "Mama, whatever it was, it's more scared of you than you are of it."

"How would you know?"

"You should set a trap for it." No sooner had Nancy made the suggestion than a problem occurred to her. "Of course, I don't know how you'd get a skunk out of a trap without setting it off."

"It's not a bad idea," Idabelle said. "I'll think on it." She went inside.

"Let's get the gardening supplies first," JoAnne said.

"Fine with me." Nancy was glad to have someone else take charge. She was so light-headed from this morning's near-death experience that she could only concentrate on one moment at a time.

They'd gone half a block when an SUV rumbled past, towing a motorboat. Nancy wondered if she were hallucinating. "If that thing fits in a creek, I'll eat your mother's skunk cabbage."

"There's a lake a few hours' drive from here," JoAnne said. "After the kids grew up, Luis and I bought a boat ourselves. It cost a bundle to run the durn thing but it was the only time I got my husband to myself, out there alone on the water."

"It sounds lovely," Nancy said.

"Not to him it didn't." JoAnne scowled. "He tried to sell the boat and when that didn't work he wanted to give it away, but I won't let him. Now all he does in his spare time is stand out in the pasture lobbing bowling balls and laughing like a loon."

"You think he'll ever go boating with you again?"

"He'd better do something if he wants to keep me.

I'm not going to sit around in my old age listening to thump-thump-thump all day.''

At the general store, they selected fertilizer, seeds, wire supports and tomato plants. "Max has everything else," JoAnne said, and instructed the storekeeper to put the goods on the ranch's account.

In the grocery store, JoAnne pushed the cart. She had an amazing ability to keep track of a weekful of meals and what was needed for each, Nancy discovered as the items piled up. JoAnne even gave verbal cooking tips as they shopped.

When she mentioned barbecuing, the idea delighted Nancy. It didn't sound hard to fix meat that way.

Of course, one of these days, she might decide to become a vegetarian for real. Only after securing enough decent recipes, though, and most likely not while living on a cattle ranch.

In the produce section, Nancy picked out a couple of potatoes before she saw JoAnne's disbelieving stare. "What's wrong with them?"

"Nothing, if you're cooking for one or two." The other woman hefted a ten-pound bag of spuds into their cart. "You're not used to making meals for a family."

Nancy couldn't pretend otherwise. "I guess I tweaked my résumé a little."

"You did more than tweak it," JoAnne said. "You're not the person you claim to be."

"You mean that stuff about the farm?"

"That and more." The older woman stared her in the face. "You're not twenty-nine, either."

"Do you think Max noticed?" Nancy asked.

JoAnne burst out laughing. "You're cheeky, I'll give you that. You don't even bother to deny it!"

Nancy sighed. "How can I? My sister Hayley sent in that résumé, which wasn't entirely true for her, either. She did mean to take the job, except that something better came up. I had the summer off and she talked me into taking it for her."

"Only for the summer?"

"I'm afraid so," she said. "So, what do you think? Is Max suspicious?"

"He'd have to be an idiot not to notice there's something funny going on." Getting back to work, JoAnne picked out a couple of heads of cauliflower. "But he's a guy, so he'll look right at the bottom line, which is that you're a good nanny and he needs one."

Nancy added a bag of apples to the cart. "Should I tell him the truth?"

"That depends." JoAnne mulled the subject. "What do you usually do for a living?"

"I'm a psychologist," she said.

"Ouch." The older woman grimaced.

"Why 'ouch'?"

"Max's ex-wife, Lilia, ran off with their marriage counselor," she said. "He hates psychologists. I dislike keeping secrets from the man, but if I were you, I'd save that one. He'd go ballistic."

Nancy could see Max standing over the dead snake this morning, gun in hand. She didn't think he'd shoot her. He might kick her out, though.

"Do you think I'm morally obligated to leave?" she asked.

"Nope." JoAnne added a pineapple to their purchases. "The kids need you and you're getting the job done. Besides, I've seen the way Max looks at you. You could be good for him."

"But he hates shrinks."

"People change their minds, given enough time." JoAnne examined a couple of avocadoes. "Who knows?"

Several other shoppers entered the produce section, putting an end to the conversation. Nancy had plenty to think about, anyway.

Even knowing the truth, or most of it, JoAnne believed in her abilities as a nanny. It seemed odd, because to Nancy her ambition was an intrinsic part of herself.

Since childhood, she'd been propelled by a need for accomplishment. As she matured, it had turned into a drive to demonstrate that, despite her blue-collar background, she belonged in the academic world.

Now she was surprised to find how much she enjoyed taking on mundane chores like cooking and child care. But it was only temporary.

Nancy could never settle for anything less than national recognition in her field, no matter how much she liked living on a ranch.

7

AFTER NANCY and JoAnne returned from town, Max found the twins and asked if they'd be willing to help with the garden. "I'm sure Ms. Verano would like to get things under way tomorrow."

"We don't mind at all," Rudy said. "Do we, bro?"

Randolph stopped chewing, took a straw out of his mouth and said, "'Specially not for such a purty lady."

"We should start first thing." Rudy spit on his hands and slicked back his hair, accidentally depositing a few wisps of hay in the process. "It being hot like this, we ought to get them seedlings into the ground quick."

Randolph hitched his jeans higher on his skinny hips. "I hope she don't mind the smell of cow manure."

The conversation Max had had with Nancy a few days earlier flashed into his brain. So she thought cowboys were romantic? A few hours with this pair ought to change her mind.

"She grew up on a farm," he said. "She's used to it."

"Now 'member," Rudy told his brother. "I saw her first, so I get the first chance to ask her out."

"You didn't!" Randolph glared. "I may be the younger by five minutes, but that don't make you king of the mountain."

Max held up his hands in a Stop! gesture. "Whoa, boys. Nobody's asking anybody out."

"Why not?" they both asked.

Max realized he couldn't very well answer, "Because I'm the one who really saw her first." Instead, he said, "Because she's an employee and I don't want her to feel uncomfortable. Give her time to settle in."

"How much time?" Rudy asked.

How about forever? Although he didn't believe Nancy would be interested in either of these fellows, the idea of them hitting on her bothered Max. "You fellows ought to remember she's a good four years older than you."

"That ain't so old," Randolph said.

"Who cares anyway?" added his twin.

"You wait and see if she acts interested," Max said. "Get to know her gradually. If I hear a complaint from her about being pestered, you boys are in trouble."

Rudy and his brother exchanged glances. "I got dibs," Rudy said.

"Maybe so, maybe not."

As he walked away, Max wondered if his own interest in Nancy was equally obvious. And equally foolish.

EXCEPT FOR helping her landlady weed her herbs on occasion, Nancy lacked experience with gardens. Yet, as she watched the twins rake the rich soil flat, she was eager to get started. She got a warm, nurturing feeling whenever she thought about tucking little plants into the ground and standing back to wait for an avalanche of tomatoes.

How convenient it was to have a garden outside the back door, she thought. With luck, she might even figure out how to serve some of these vegetables.

"How's that, miss?" asked Randolph Malone, wiping his sweaty forehead with his sleeve. Beneath the baseball cap, his hair looked wet.

"Beautiful," Nancy said.

"That ain't the only thing that's beautiful." Rudy gave her a big, gap-toothed smile. "Not that I'd want you to feel like I was pestering you or nothing."

"Thanks for the compliment." For the past hour, they'd worked so hard that Nancy hadn't wanted to trouble them with questions. However, she did need material for her article, and these boys seemed eager to help in any way they could.

A short distance away, she spotted Griffin and Melissa crawling around in a fenced enclosure with their bunnies. They seemed content for the moment. Kirstin, when last seen, had been reading a Jane Austen novel.

"So what do you fellows do, most days?" she asked. "What kind of chores?"

"Let's not talk about that. It's boring," Randolph said. "I'd rather show you my rock collection. You oughta come up to the bunkhouse sometime."

"Is that like inviting me to see your etchings?" Nancy asked.

"I don't have no etchings, miss," he said.

Rudy frowned at his brother, then turned to Nancy. "We feed the barn animals," he said. "Then we do whatever's needed. Plant hay, move the cattle between pastures, fix stuff.''

"How about entertainment?'' she asked. "I don't suppose you put on rodeos, do you?''

"No, miss,'' he said. "We woulda liked to join a rodeo when we was younger but our mama said she'd whack us a good one if we tried.''

"She said if we tried to ride a bronco, we'd land on our heads, and we don't have any brains to spare as it is,'' Randolph explained.

Nancy laughed. "I'm sure she was kidding.''

"Oh, no, miss,'' Rudy said. "If we done wrong, she smacked us with a frying pan, even when we was growed up.''

A curtain stirred in the back of the house. That must be Max's office, Nancy thought.

Sure enough, there he was, peering out with a disapproving furrow between his brows. Surely he didn't object to the twins taking a well-deserved break.

Rudy noticed his boss. "Oops. We better go on our way now, miss.''

"I wasn't done telling her about my rock collection,'' said his brother.

Rudy poked him with an elbow and gave a sharp nod toward the office window. "Oh,'' said Randolph. "Well, we'll see you later, miss.''

As they walked away, Nancy heard Rudy say, "You call that pathetic bunch of pebbles a rock collection?''

"You don't collect nothing but nose hairs,'' retorted his twin. "I think for Christmas I'm gonna break down and buy you tweezers.''

At the window, Max watched the pair leave. As

soon as they were out of sight, he ducked back, apparently satisfied.

One thing she'd learned about cowboys today, Nancy reflected—they certainly had a jealous side.

THE IDEA of a Skunk Days festival spread like wildfire, bringing three or four calls a day from enthusiastic ranchers. It reached the point where the cattle hardly looked up when Max's cell phone rang.

JoAnne booked the skunk racing organization. Instead of a petting zoo, she found a skunk club to sponsor an adopt-a-baby-skunk booth.

Idabelle, going bonkers over her new menu, plucked some strange recipes from the Internet. She swore she was going to make Possum Sausage and something called Roadkill Squirrel Squares. Max hoped she was kidding.

As for Nancy, she designed a delightful Web page with animated skunks and funny sound effects. The woman had amazing talents. She was also turning into a halfway decent cook, if you didn't mind barbecue every night.

At bedtime on a Saturday, three weeks after Nancy's arrival, Max sat in the den with his children. While reading to Griffin, he listened with part of his mind to Melissa's chatter about the Witherspoon kids and the three kittens they'd adopted that day in town.

Finally he hugged them good-night. Although both children clamored for more attention, Max had too much work, so he sent them to bed and went into his office.

With the festival a definite go, it was time to consult his personal publicity expert. Max rapid-dialed his brother and put him on the speakerphone.

"Richter here," Bill answered, as if he were at the office.

"Richter on this end, too."

"Hey, bro. Glad to hear from you." Although he and his wife phoned Kirstin occasionally, Bill rarely talked to Max beyond a casual greeting. "What's up?"

Max told him about the plans for the Skunk Days Festival.

"I love it. Including the 'Pepe Le Pew' film festival. Make sure you notify any cartoon-related Internet sites," Bill said. "You'll want to print up Skunk Days T-shirts and souvenirs, of course. Try a couple of different designs, with varying degrees of coarse humor. Here's the name of a novelty company that can take care of it."

Max made notes. "Think you can generate any publicity?"

"Sure. E-mail me the info when it's firmed up, and I'll put out a press release," his brother said. "So, honestly, how's my kid doing?"

That was hard to answer. "She seems to fit in," Max said cautiously. "She misses you and her friends back home."

"Man, I wish we could bring her back right now." Bill's voice took on a ragged edge. "I figured some private time with Beth would bring us together. It isn't working."

Some marriages couldn't be saved, as Max had learned with Lilia. His brother and sister-in-law, however, seemed well matched in many ways. "What's the problem?"

"She's angry at me all the time," Bill said. "Hey, owning an ad agency isn't any easier than running a dental clinic. She's not the only person under pressure."

"Maybe you need a vacation." Max knew better than to suggest they come to the ranch. Neither his brother nor his sister-in-law enjoyed the rustic life. "Take a second honeymoon in New Orleans or Santa Fe."

"One of her dentists just quit and she can't spare the time," Bill said. "You know, I always thought we'd have more children. I'd really like a son. Doesn't look like there's any chance of that."

With a rush of love, Max pictured the two children he'd just sent to bed. At least Lilia, despite her infidelity, had given him the two most precious people in his life.

"Have you talked to her about it?" he asked. "Maybe she wants more kids, too."

"Are you kidding? If I brought up something like that, she'd bite my head off," Bill said. "These days, we never connect. It's as if we're speaking two different languages. I hate to say it, but we might be better off separating."

"I'm sorry." It was the only thing Max could say.

When he hung up, he heard a rustling in the hallway outside his office. He went out, but saw no one.

It occurred to him, belatedly, that he should have taken Bill off the speakerphone when they started discussing personal matters. His brother's comments hadn't been intended for Kirstin's ears.

He was about to go check on her when the phone rang again. It was Lorrin Witherspoon.

"Lenore and I got a great idea!" he said. "We're going to beef up our fall and winter business with skunk themed activities and we want to promote them during the festival. What do you think of the Autumn Skunk-Watching Tour and A Black-And-White Christmas on the Range?"

Max finger-combed his hair as he dragged his thoughts back from his niece. "Run that by me one more time, please, Lorrin?"

NANCY COULDN'T FIND her cell phone. She'd left it on her bed before dinner to remind her to call her parents in Florida and wish them a happy anniversary.

She poked her head into Griffin's room to see if he'd taken it to play with. He slept curled beside his kitten, Patchy Nose.

The little critters were supposed to stay in the barn. However, since she saw that the boy had placed a bowl of water in the corner and, nearby, a box of sand, she decided to leave the pair in peace until morning.

There was no sign of her phone in Melissa's room, either. The little girl lay half-buried among stuffed animals, her red-gold hair spilling around her.

She had such lovely coloring, Nancy thought. Her mother must be gorgeous.

JoAnne had explained that Lilia came from Houston, where she and Max had met. He'd been attending a ranchers' convention at a hotel where Lilia had worked as assistant to the manager. She'd been quite a beauty. Unfortunately, she'd also been spoiled and self-centered.

When she left him, she'd made no attempt to seek custody of her children. She'd seen them occasionally while they lived with her parents, but since her new husband didn't like kids, Lilia had essentially shut them out of her life.

It amazed Nancy that a woman could abandon her children, as well as a husband like Max. Some people didn't appreciate life's greatest gifts.

As a teenager, Nancy had undergone surgery for a benign but painful condition. The doctor had warned that it would leave her infertile.

At the time, she hadn't minded. Burdened with six younger siblings and eager to embark on a professional career, she'd welcomed the prospect of staying child-free.

Later, when she got engaged, friends had encouraged her to look into treatments. A doctor at the college's infertility clinic had been happy to look at Nancy's records. Unfortunately, it turned out that the treatment for her condition would be expensive, painful and lengthy, with only a slight chance of success. At thirty-five, she'd resigned herself to childlessness. Now, watching the covers rise and fall as the little girl slept, Nancy realized for the first time just how much she'd lost.

Lilia had held these babies in her arms, yet had chosen to give them up. What motivated a woman like that? Nancy wondered again.

And where the heck was her cell phone?

She decided to reinvestigate her suspicions about

the house's resident preteen. Tightening the sash on her bathrobe, Nancy set out through the house.

From the living room, she could see light shining under Max's office door and hear him talking to someone about the festival. Light also spilled around the flowered bedspread that covered the opening to the dining room.

As she neared it, she heard Kirstin's tear-filled voice saying, "I want to come home, Mom. I can take care of myself. Nobody needs to watch me."

Nancy didn't like to eavesdrop, even though she was paying for the charges on her purloined phone. Still, Kirstin's well-being was her responsibility, and she could hardly help the girl if she didn't know what was going on.

After a pause, Kirstin said, "Please, please, please. Don't you love me anymore?"

She must have received a sharp response, because she responded, "Well, fine! Excuse me for asking!" Then came the smack of a small, borrowed object hitting the wall.

Nancy knocked on the doorframe. There was no response.

"Excuse me. I can't find my cell phone," she called through the bedspread. "It's a family heirloom and I'd hate to lose it. My ancestors brought it over on the *Mayflower*. Have you seen it?"

A quavery voice replied, "They didn't have cell phones on the *Mayflower*."

"You mean my grandmother lied?" Nancy said.

The only response was a loud snuffling.

"I'm coming in." Not hearing any shrieks of protest, Nancy brushed aside the heavy cloth.

At the far end of the room, in the circle of light from a table lamp, Kirstin lay huddled on her cot, face buried in her arms. Her shoulders heaved.

The cell phone lay on a table to one side, where it must have landed after hitting the wall. A quick inspection showed it to be undamaged.

Nancy dropped it in her robe pocket. "In case you're wondering, I accidentally overheard part of that conversation. I hope we haven't made you feel unwelcome here."

Kirstin sat up. With her puffy, tear-streaked face and tangled hair, she looked like a little kid.

"I don't want to be here," she sobbed. "This isn't my home and you can't make me stay. I'll hitchhike back to Dallas."

Nancy sat down near her. "Your Uncle Max and I don't want to put you in any danger. If you feel that strongly, we'll drive you home."

She had no idea whether that was feasible, and knew Kirstin's family wouldn't like it. Both her training and her instincts, however, told her Kirstin needed to know that she and Max weren't enemies. If she felt trapped, the girl really might do something foolish.

"You're just the nanny! You can't make promises like that," Kirstin flared. "Go away!"

"I know you miss your parents," Nancy said. "It must feel like a rejection, being sent away for so long."

"You don't know anything!" Tears ran down the girl's cheeks.

"They love you, even if they don't always show it," she said. "Parents get caught up in their own problems, just like you get involved in schoolwork or with your friends. That doesn't mean your family stops caring about you."

"I'm not going to have a family," Kirstin said. "They're getting a divorce."

This was the first Nancy had heard of it. "Who told you that?"

"I heard Dad talking to Uncle Max on the speakerphone," the girl said.

"They're divorcing?"

"He said they might get a separation."

This was a rotten way for their daughter to find out, Nancy thought. "One of the problems with eavesdropping is that you don't hear the whole story," she said. "For one thing, a separation isn't a divorce. Besides, even if the worst happens, lots of kids with divorced parents do just fine."

"So I get to stay here and go to some hick regional high school for the rest of my life?" Kirstin muttered angrily.

"Who says you'd have to stay here?"

"I'm here now, aren't I?"

"If they do divorce, they'll be leaving each other, not you," Nancy said.

Footsteps creaked outside the dining room and the impromptu curtain moved aside. "Who's talking about divorce?" Max asked.

Nancy glanced at him, concerned that he might object to her discussing such a delicate subject with his niece. It was impossible to read anything in the strong, controlled lines of his face.

"My dad," Kirstin said.

Max came inside, standing in the shadows outside

the lamp's bright sphere. "Nobody's getting a divorce."

His niece folded her arms. "I heard him."

"Your dad was speculating." Max gave her a wan smile. "I won't let them break up. If they try it, I'll crack their heads together."

"Like that would really work!" Kirstin snapped. "You couldn't even keep your own wife from running away." She stopped at the flare of emotion on her uncle's face. "I'm sorry, Uncle Max."

Silently, he turned and walked out. Seeing Kirstin's stricken expression, Nancy said, "He'll get over it. Your uncle and your parents love you a lot."

"I could make him pancakes for breakfast tomorrow," she said in a small voice.

"He'd like that." Nancy reached for the girl and was pleased when she submitted to a hug. "Things aren't as bad as they seem, honest."

"I hope not," Kirstin said. "I'm sorry for what I said about you just being the nanny. And I'm sorry about your phone. Did I break it?"

"Nope," Nancy said. "You didn't break anything, trust me."

She tucked Kirstin in and brought over a couple of stuffed animals for company. The girl squeezed her hand before she left. To Nancy, that meant a lot.

Now she wanted to find Max and see if she could ease some of that pain from his eyes.

8

STANDING IN THE KITCHEN, staring at a cup of decaf he didn't really want, Max felt ashamed of reacting so strongly to a childish taunt. Yet Kirstin's remark had stung, because the memory of Lilia's defection still rankled.

Why? He certainly didn't love her anymore. Maybe it was guilt, for failing her in ways he was only beginning to understand. If he'd talked to her more, tried to make the ranch more comfortable, spent some of that oil lease money the way she'd asked...

No matter what, it wouldn't have worked. It had been a mismatch from the beginning. He took a sip, then set the mug aside.

Nancy came in. "Kirstin wants to make pancakes for your breakfast tomorrow to apologize."

His chest tightened. "Should I go in there and let her know she's forgiven?"

"She's settled down for the night," Nancy said. "You can heap praise all over her pancakes tomorrow."

"Thanks for talking to her."

"I didn't mean to interfere in family business," she said. "By the way, can she hear us in here?" The dining room connected to the kitchen through a heavy door.

"My parents had that door soundproofed after a dinner party where nobody could talk over the racket from our dishwasher. And you weren't interfering, you were doing your job."

He stopped, noticing that, on her bathrobe, a voluptuous female figure in a bikini overlay Nancy's body. Max knew it was a gag. It reminded him, however, of the real woman beneath the fabric.

"What?" She looked down. "Oh, my goodness. My sister Ha…Helen gave it to me for my birthday."

"Hayley and Helen?" he said. "Your parents must have liked the letter *H*."

"They were crazy about it," Nancy said.

And I'm crazy about you. That was how Max felt, suddenly, like a teenager getting his first crush. Young and bashful.

His hands reached and caught her shoulders, registering the delicacy of her bones through that ridiculous robe. Nancy leaned toward him, face uptilted.

The kitchen filled with their quiet breathing and Max's tumultuous heartbeat. In her gray eyes, he saw hints of violet glimmering as her lips parted.

Two people alone at night. His bedroom so close. One kiss and they might both be lost.

Fiercely, Max reminded himself that Nancy worked for him. That it was his responsibility to keep his distance while they were on his property.

"I can't do this." With a ragged sense of disappointment, he released her and stepped back. "It isn't right."

"Right and wrong are relative." Nancy's eyes had a glazed look. "Within reasonable parameters."

"Excuse me?"

"I'm babbling." A tendril of blond hair wisped across her temple. Max brushed it back, and felt again that rush of longing. Again, it hit the brick wall of propriety.

"This isn't the way I normally behave," he said.

"Max, we didn't do anything."

"We almost did."

"You're cute when you're befuddled."

"Glad to hear it." He'd made a fool of himself, approaching her and then withdrawing, yet it didn't matter. Somehow, with Nancy, he felt comfortable making mistakes.

This wouldn't be the last encounter between them, Max knew. He itched to take her in his arms on neutral ground, with no bed looming temptingly in the background. That gave him an idea.

"Next Thursday's the Fourth of July," he said. "There's a square dance and potluck in town. If we all go, you could save me a dance."

"You'll have to refresh my memory," Nancy said. "I'm rusty with my do-si-do."

"Sure." Max wished a torrent of light banter would spill out of him to hold her here in the kitchen a while longer. If only he had his brother's glibness.

He didn't, though, and, with a fleeting "Good night, then," the object of his affections sauntered out.

On the back of her robe wiggled the rear side of a bikini-clad woman. Max groaned.

The six days until next Thursday seemed like a very long time to wait before he could hold her again.

DURING THE NEXT WEEK, Kirstin calmed down. Her outburst about her parents must have temporarily relieved her tension.

Melissa, by contrast, complained bitterly about her father's extended absences. From moving the herd to a fresh pasture to mowing the hay, there always seemed to be a reason for him to work late and, twice, sleep at the trailer.

Nancy suspected it was partly her fault. Although he continued to act friendly when they were thrown together, Max clearly wanted to avoid her.

Why had he beaten a retreat because of the other night? Granted, if they had kissed, it might have progressed to some mild fondling. Followed by heavy fondling and bodies pressing together...

Good heavens, she was fantasizing again. On Thursday, as she retrieved a large Jell-O salad from the refrigerator for the potluck, Nancy gave herself a mental shake.

She'd been a basket case all week. Barely able to keep her mind focused on the children, she'd neglected to weed the vegetable garden and had hardly worked on her article.

Amazingly, the tomatoes, beans and zucchini continued to grow. Vegetables had energies of their own, just like children.

The notes for the article, however, sat in the computer, refusing to expand or arrange themselves. She still needed to ask more questions of Rudy and Randolph, for one thing. For another, she hadn't yet sorted out her own feelings about her subject matter.

''Where's Dad?'' Melissa popped into the kitchen, proudly outfitted in a red-and-white checked blouse over a blue denim skirt. "I want him to see how I look."

"He should be back any minute." Max had gone out earlier to move some wood with Luis. Nancy wasn't sure why they'd chosen a holiday to do it. Or why they'd waited until after JoAnne left to decorate the community center.

"Everybody ready?" Entering, Max went to the sink to wash sawdust off his hands. "Melissa, you're a darn pretty sight."

"Thanks, Dad." Merrily, she whirled to show off her outfit. "Grampa and Gramma sent it to me."

"We'll go visit them, come fall," Max said. "Would you like that?"

"Sure." She studied him worriedly. "You aren't going to leave us there, are you?"

"No." He dried his hands on a towel. "I thought you missed living in Houston."

"Not anymore."

He hugged her. "Glad to hear it."

The cell phone rang in his pocket. Max released his daughter to answer, then made an annoyed face and clicked off. "That's the second time someone's called today and hung up."

"You think they're having trouble getting through?" Nancy asked.

"I can hear breathing. Probably some smart-aleck kid." He returned his attention to his daughter. "Well, sweetheart, ready for a good time?"

"I sure am!" She reached up for another hug.

Melissa bubbled with happiness all the way to town. Although crammed into the middle of the back seat, even Kirstin was smiling. Her parents had called that morning and promised to visit for Skunk Days and take her home afterwards.

Griffin kept leaning forward in his seat and tickling his father's neck with a new toy action figure his grandparents had sent. After the third time, Max threatened to make him dance with a girl, and the little boy subsided.

Although she went into town twice weekly for shopping and church, Nancy was surprised to see how many vehicles crowded the parking lot and street outside the one-story community center. She hadn't realized that this many people lived in and around Skunk Crossing.

A large American flag flapped in the twilight, and many vehicles sported red-and-white bunting. "People go all out for Independence Day around here," she said.

Max squeezed the truck into a space. "We take our patriotism seriously in ranch country."

As they got out, she heard the lively scrape of square-dance music and inhaled the scent of hamburgers on the grill. "That smells great."

The children raced ahead, eager to see their friends and get first pick of the desserts. For once, Nancy decided not to chide them about nutrition, even if she had won first prize in whatever-it-was.

Inside the main room of the community center, dinner offerings jammed a long table. From a large rear patio rang the cheery notes of the band and the chant of the square-dance caller, weaving his commands into a singsong.

"Hi, Nancy. We'll put that right here with the other

salads,'' said Idabelle, appearing from the crowd and taking the gelatin mold.

''Thank you.'' A visual check showed that the children were with their friends. It had become second nature for Nancy to keep an eye on her charges.

Max and the café owner exchanged information about the latest Skunk Days plans. ''Any luck catching your striped stalker?'' he asked.

To Nancy, Idabelle explained, ''I decided to put out some cat food and see if I could get a good look at the critter.'' She led the way to the long table, where she wedged the new dish between a three-bean salad and a bowl of coleslaw.

''Did it work?'' Nancy asked.

''A family of possums found it first.'' Idabelle shifted dishes to make room for more new arrivals. ''A mother and her three babies. I have to stop putting out the food long enough to break their habit before I try again.''

''Good luck.'' A light touch on her arm made Nancy's knees tremble. She knew what it meant. Max was ready for their dance.

''Are you hungry?'' he asked politely. ''We could eat now.''

''Not unless you are.'' Although it was after seven o'clock, Nancy had shared a late snack with the kids.

''Then let's go.''

Outside, darkness was rolling in. In the brightness of the patio, people laughed and swung their partners beneath hanging lanterns. A mild breeze softened the day's lingering heat.

While they waited for the dance to end, Max greeted friends and introduced Nancy to ranchers from around the county. Their names blurred. Each welcoming face stood out, though.

Standing beside Max, she measured his sturdy length at the points where she swayed against him. Her knee. Her hip. Her shoulder. His scent of wood chips and leather and masculinity blotted out the smokiness of the barbecue.

The music stopped amid applause. Some dancers left the floor, and new sets began forming.

Max's hand on the small of Nancy's back propelled her to the center of the patio. They joined Luis and JoAnne, the Witherspoons and a couple introduced as the town's mayor and his wife.

When a catchy number started, everyone whirled into motion. Although she'd tried square dancing in college, Nancy couldn't follow the caller's rapid patter. Instead, she did her best to imitate the other dancers.

Whirling and pacing, catching hands with Max and then being launched away from him created a flirtatious pattern. When they separated, she could hardly wait to greet him again. Each time she rejoined him, she gladly slipped into the protective shelter of his embrace.

"I told you. You're good for him," JoAnne said as they passed each other.

Nancy didn't know if it was true, but Max was definitely good for her. Tonight, she allowed herself to forget that she was anything other than a woman in a small Texas town, enjoying her growing attraction to a very sexy man.

Despite a slight shortness of breath, she was sorry

when the music stopped. Regretfully, she applauded the musicians.

"We'll check on the children," Lenore Witherspoon said as she and her husband left the dance floor. "Don't you worry about them."

"Thanks." Nancy blushed, realizing the woman was giving her a hint to go off with her man. All the same, she appreciated the assistance.

"Let's take a little walk." Max spoke close to her ear.

Nancy nodded.

In one direction lay a fenced swimming pool. He steered her along a different path, through a grove of low-growing trees.

"What are these?" she asked.

"Pecans," he said.

"Oh, that's right. They do grow on trees," Nancy dithered. "I mean, they're nuts, and most nuts grow on trees, except, of course, peanuts."

Max spun her toward him and stopped the flow of words with his mouth. Nancy gripped his shoulders to anchor herself before she drifted, flew, soared with the buoyant power of his kiss.

Lightly, she touched his hair and cheeks as she'd longed to do for weeks now. She ran her palms down his chest, and replaced them with her breasts, the nubs erect and almost painfully sensitized.

"Wow." Max lifted his head. "I'm on fire, honey. You sure know how to arouse a man."

She, who was so good with words, had none to explain what she felt. That for the first time in her life, she, too, was on fire.

It scared her.

This man. This place. This scratchy fiddle music wailing behind her. They weren't Nancy's man, her place or her melody.

She was pretending. Not just to Max, but to herself. Pretending that she belonged here, when she knew she didn't and never could. Pretending she could give as much as she was taking.

Nancy ducked his attempt to kiss her again. "I got a little carried away."

His arms tightened around her. "Let's get even more carried away."

"It's time to go inside," she said.

"You can't mean that. Not yet."

Nancy tried to answer and discovered she was breathless. From the dance, still? Hardly.

"We're not thinking straight," she said. "We'd better go eat."

Max dropped his arms. Moonlight glinted on his dark eyes. "Go on, then. I need a minute to think." He spoke in a neutral tone. She wondered if anger lay underneath.

She was not going to apologize. This was not the kind of thing a person could explain or ask forgiveness for, not when every fiery cell of her body urged her to grab him and get, oh, so very reckless. Besides, he was the one who'd called a halt to their near-embrace last week.

"I'll save you some food." It was a silly remark, given that the table practically sagged beneath its load. She hoped to win a smile.

Seeing none, she turned and fled.

Good job, Nancy. How very mature and professional of you. Still, she'd done the right thing, she thought, by calling their actions to a halt. Not that Max was likely to believe it.

HE SUPPOSED he'd deserved her sudden withdrawal, the way he'd moved in on her. She'd responded, though. What could have spooked her that way?

Maybe Max had misread her. Whatever made him think he knew anything about women? He certainly had a less than stellar track record.

He searched his memory, trying to discover what had put her off. He'd mentioned wanting to get carried away. Was that it?

Heck, he desired her, and she desired him, too. That didn't mean he had expectations of the bedroom variety.

From a short distance, Max heard two people laughing quietly. A man and woman, getting together. Relationships seemed to come so easily to other people.

He would give Nancy a few minutes to eat and then he'd ask for another dance, he decided. That was all. Just a dance.

To Max's irritation, his phone rang. Although it might be the same jokester, he didn't dare ignore it. Luis's nephew Manuel, who worked part-time at the ranch, was keeping an eye on the place tonight with instructions to call if any problems cropped up.

He flipped it open. "Richter here."

Heavy breathing, like before.

"Who is this?" he snapped.

"Max?" The voice was soft, almost childlike. It resonated through him like a brass gong.

"Why are you calling me, Lilia?" Instinctively, he

headed toward the unoccupied pool to get away from the couple in the woods. He didn't want anyone overhearing this conversation.

"Oh, Max." She heaved a long, self-pitying sigh. At least, he assumed from experience that it was self-pitying. "Things are such a mess."

"What things?"

"I...left my husband. Marrying him was a mistake," she said.

"It took you three years to figure that out?" He heard his own bitterness, and it irked him. After so long, he ought to be indifferent.

"I've been trying all day to work up my nerve to talk to you." She released a shuddering breath. "Oh, Max, I'm so unhappy." Choked sobs issued over the phone.

Unlike during their marriage, Max had enough objectivity to recognize that she was trying to manipulate him, although he couldn't guess toward what end. Also, her speech sounded a bit slurred. "Have you been drinking?"

"Only a couple of beers. Everybody drinks beer on the Fourth of July."

"That reminds me, you're interrupting my holiday. Whatever you called to say, please get to the point."

She sniffled. "I want us to try again."

Although Max recoiled at the suggestion, a tiny part of him ached for what had been lost. It was like an old wound, long healed, that still twinges on a rainy day. That was Lilia, one big thunderstorm in his life. "No," he said.

"I want to see the children."

He would have liked to say no to that, too. By law,

however, they shared custody. "Fine. I'm going to arrange a visit with your parents in September. We'll meet you then."

"Sooner," she said.

Max didn't want to be having this conversation, but he knew better than to antagonize his ex-wife. She had claws, as he'd learned during the agonizing process of their divorce. "If you insist. When?"

"I—I don't know." Helplessness vibrated over the phone. Lilia was issuing a siren call for a big, strong male to come and rescue her.

She'd better find some other hero. "Call me when you figure it out," Max said, and clicked off.

Then he went in search of Nancy.

NANCY HAD ENTERED the community center before she realized she'd lost her appetite. Even the smells of roasting chicken and sizzling hamburgers failed to stir her.

She paused long enough to see that the children were eating with the Witherspoons, before retreating outside. It had a been a huge mistake coming to Texas, she thought. Never, never, never would she let Hayley talk her into anything like this again.

"Excuse me, miss." Rudy Malone swept off his baseball cap. "May I trouble you for this dance?"

His freckled face reflected such hope that Nancy couldn't refuse. Besides, this was a good chance to question him again for her article.

"Sure," she said.

The band had segued to pop music. On the patio, couples slow-danced to a country tune, holding each other with degrees of ardor that ranged from the snuggling of young sweethearts to the amused courtesy of long-married couples.

Rudy tried to draw her against him. Nancy stiffened, keeping space between them.

"So, uh, how's the cooking going?" he asked, having heard, no doubt, of her struggles.

"Just fine." Nancy decided to plunge in. "Tell me, have you always been a cowboy?"

"Who, me?" Rudy said. "Uh, yeah, I guess so."

"What do you like best about it?"

"Dancing with purty ladies on the Fourth of July," he said gallantly.

She chuckled. "That was right nice of you."

"You're startin' to sound like a Texan already." He made another attempt to pull her close.

Nancy held her ground. She was already near enough to choke on his excess aftershave lotion. "Do you prefer riding a horse or driving a truck?"

"What? Uh, riding a horse," he said.

"Why?"

"You don't have to stay on the road. You've got more freedom," he said. "You're closer to the land and everything."

"You mean, there's a sense of wildness about riding?" she said.

He nodded. "And I like the feel of a horse between my legs." His jaw dropped in dismay. "Excuse me, miss."

"That's all right." Nancy squeezed his arm to reassure him. "We'll forget you said that."

His eyes shone feverishly. "I'm not sure I want to forget it."

A male hand clapped on his shoulder. For a delirious moment, Nancy hoped it belonged to Max.

"Mind if I break in, partner?" Dale Dwyer, even paler than usual in the uneven lighting, tried to insinuate himself between her and the ranch hand.

Disappointment colored Rudy's face, but he knew his manners. "I guess I don't." With a polite nod to Nancy, he withdrew.

"Enjoying the local yokels?" The rancher, she noticed, wore a gaudy red-white-and-blue shirt over designer jeans. He stood out from the crowd like a tulip in a patch of daisies.

Nancy bristled at his condescending remark. "I live here now. That makes me one of the yokels, too."

"You're from L.A., I hear. I like California girls."

"How interesting." Unlike Randolph, Dale had a sneaky way of getting close that made it difficult to keep him at arm's length. Nancy kept having to back away.

At last, the song ended. Dale caught her wrist. "I see plenty of folks going for walks. Why don't we?"

"Sorry, the lady's taken." Max appeared beside Nancy. Not a happy Max, judging by his glower, but a very welcome one.

Dale released his grip. "I didn't know I was poaching, Richter."

"Well, you know now." After Dale strutted away, Max said to Nancy, "We need to talk."

In the commotion as other dancers changed places on the patio, she hoped not many had noticed the interchange. It was a small town, though. "Let's go someplace private, okay?"

He led her around the side of the building to a

sidewalk that ran alongside the parking lot. ''I thought you were going to eat,'' he growled.

''I got waylaid.''

He didn't meet her gaze. From the way a muscle jumped in his jaw, Nancy could tell she'd infuriated him.

She wished she could fast-reverse the last ten minutes. Back to the pecan grove. Back to their kiss.

Instead, she waited quietly, wondering why he was so angry and what he was going to do about it.

9

MAX HAD EXPECTED better of Nancy. One minute she'd been giggling and flirting with Rudy, and the next she'd been hanging all over Dale. Or, at least, letting him hang all over her.

It made Max look like a fool in front of his friends and neighbors. They'd seen him walk out with Nancy, and here she was a few minutes later, flaunting herself with other men.

He knew he might be overreacting because of his disgust with Lilia. He didn't buy that Nancy had been waylaid, however. She'd proved to him that she knew how to say no if she didn't want something.

"I see you found yourself a couple of admirers," he said. "I'd prefer you picked one for the evening so it doesn't look like I'm trusting my children to a flirt."

"Come on, Max, you can't take this seriously," Nancy said. "Are you jealous?"

Yes, darn it, he was jealous. Nearly overwhelmed by his longing to possess her, and intensely frustrated.

He hadn't intended to get involved with a woman at this point in his life. Romance was too much of a roller coaster, as tonight had just confirmed.

"This has gone too far," he said.

"I'm not planning to marry either of them, if that's

what you mean,'' Nancy said. "Dale is a dweeb, to tell you the truth. Rudy's a sweet fellow, but he should go easy on the cologne.''

She looked so cute and unfazed that Max wanted to forgive and forget. At the same time, this evening had reminded him of how vulnerable he could be when he fell for a woman.

And of how much it hurt when that woman turned on him.

"You need to show more discretion," he said. "So do I. As your employer, I shouldn't have stepped over the line.''

"If I did anything wrong, I apologize," Nancy said. "Can we forget about all this and go back to being friends now?''

"I'm afraid not.'' Max stared unseeing across the rows of cars, hating what he had to do, certain he had no choice. "You work for me and I should never have kissed you or touched you in any way. I won't make that mistake again and I'd appreciate your keeping your distance as well.''

Disappointment shadowed her eyes. "I suppose you're right.''

"There's one more thing,'' he said.

"Yes?''

"If you have another bathrobe, I'd appreciate your wearing it from now on.''

"Oh. Right,'' she said.

Randolph Malone came around the corner of the community center. "Boss? You'd better get in here. Luis let it slip that he's building a bigger trebuchet and JoAnne's chewing his head off.''

"So that's what the lumber was for,'' Nancy said.

"She's probably after my head, too." Almost relieved at the diversion, Max escorted her in.

"You want to act like a two-year-old and spend all your spare time throwing things? You can do that to your heart's content. I'm moving in with Mama."

The people in the large room had given center stage to the outraged JoAnne. She didn't appear to notice her audience, not even her mother, who was making distressed hand signals that Nancy interpreted as meaning, "Don't say anything you'll regret."

"Don't move out. The ranch is your home." Judging by Luis's deer-in-the-headlights expression, he was suitably chastized. Not beaten, though. "I won't build the new trebuchet right away."

"Use those boards to fix the corral." JoAnne turned her attention to the new arrivals. "Max! Tell him!"

"It's his wood," Max said. "For the record, I don't want you to move out, either."

Nancy decided not to second the motion. She was, as Max had noted, merely his employee.

She knew he'd done her a favor by stopping any involvement before it really began. Why, then, did she feel so bad?

"Are you giving up the lumber or not?" JoAnne demanded of her husband.

"Are you giving up the boat?" he shot back.

"What does that have to do with anything?"

"Seems to me we're both stubborn," he said. "I don't see why I should be the one to knuckle under."

If only he realized that his wife simply wanted to

be closer to him, Nancy thought. This was obviously not the time to bring it up.

"Mama, get my old room ready," JoAnne said.

"You don't need to, Idabelle," said Luis. "I'll move into the bunkhouse. My wife can get rid of me, if that's what she's so keen to do."

"Fine," JoAnne said.

The mayor raised his hands to catch everyone's attention. "Folks, it's time for the fireworks."

"We just saw the fireworks," said Lenore.

Gradually the room emptied as the townspeople followed the mayor outside. Nancy joined the exodus, holding on to a yawning Griffin.

Outside, she sat in a folding chair cradling the boy, while Max stood with one arm around Melissa and the other around his niece. To a casual observer, they must look like a family.

In six weeks, they would celebrate Skunk Days. Soon afterward, Nancy would have to leave for the start of the fall semester. By next summer, the Richter children would scarcely remember her.

Would Max? she wondered. And if he did, how would he think of her?

Overhead, fireworks boomed and blossomed. Applause rose from the audience.

"I wuv you, Nancy," murmured a sleepy Griffin, and wound his arms around her neck.

If tears pricked her eyes, she was the only one who noticed.

WHEN THE DESIGNS for the T-shirts arrived for his approval, Max drove into town to get Idabelle's opinion. He found her at the gas station, making sure the attendant kept the paper towel dispenser full for customers.

"Details count," she told him as she checked the squeegee for signs of wear.

"It's not as if you have competition," the youth pointed out.

"Honey, if you antagonize the customers, the next thing you know, competition will come to town." Pushing a lock of gray-streaked black hair off her temple, the large-set woman accompanied him next door to the café.

Max followed, impressed as always by Idabelle's boundless energy. The woman supervised the bed-and-breakfast, the café and the gas station, yet when her grandchildren were young, she'd always found time to baby-sit them.

It was she and her late husband, along with Luis and JoAnne, who'd helped Max survive as an orphaned sixteen-year-old trying to do a man's job. One time when Bill was having trouble in school, Idabelle had driven out to the ranch and given the boy a stern lecture, followed by hugs. On Christmas, it was to her house that they'd gone to celebrate.

When Max had received the oil lease money, he hadn't hesitated to invest it in badly needed upgrades to her businesses. He'd never regretted it, even if it had delivered yet another blow to his crumbling marriage.

Inside the Black and White Café, a handful of people were eating a late lunch. The colorful sundresses—one pink, one purple—of a pair of ranchers' wives softened the starkness of the Art Deco tile.

Idabelle poured two cups of coffee and spread the

sketches on a table. One showed a cartoon skunk sitting with paws raised as if begging, above the slogan Skunk Days Festival, and, on the line below, Skunk Crossing, Texas.

The second said I Survived Skunk Days—Ain't That Scentsational? Two skunks, tails turned toward the viewer, peered back over their shoulders as if taking aim. "These are adorable," she said.

"The novelty manufacturer in El Paso says he can have the T-shirts ready in plenty of time," Max told her. "In fact, he's so amused that he plans to attend with his family."

"We've got ourselves a winner," Idabelle said. "I don't mind telling you, I was barely hanging in there financially. We owe that Nancy of yours for the idea."

"She's pretty sharp," he agreed.

"If you don't mind my asking," she said, "what's going on between you two?"

"Nothing," Max said a little too quickly.

His old friend studied him. "That's not the way it looked on the Fourth of July."

"We decided to cool it," he said. "It's better that way, believe me."

"I know how bad Lilia hurt you." Idabelle nibbled at a Danish pastry. "You wait too long, though, and somebody else is going to grab that girl." Slyly, she added, "Maybe Dale Dwyer."

"She wouldn't be interested in a weasel like him!" Max flared.

"I guess not." Idabelle drummed her fingers on the table. "How're the concert rehearsals going?"

"Fine." He was grateful for her switch of subjects.

"Your daughter's got a gift for writing parody."
Members of the church choir were preparing skunk-
themed song takeoffs for the festival.

After discussing a few other items of business, he
took the sketches and drove back to the ranch. So
Idabelle was trying to pair him off with Nancy, he
mused. Although Max respected the older woman's
judgment, it wasn't that simple.

He'd struggled to keep his housekeeper at arm's
length since the Fourth of July. It meant retreating to
his office every evening after the kids were in bed to
avoid being alone with her. It meant halting himself
from sharing the details of his days with her, too.

Still, he knew how quickly the early stages of love
degenerated into pitched battles. It was better this
way.

He'd set his course and he planned to stick to it.
No matter what Idabelle might think.

IN EARLY August, a series of thunderstorms hit the
ranch. Day after day, downpours undermined fences
and turned pastureland to mud. Once a twister appeared in the distance, but it never made landfall.

Confined to the house and barn, the children grew
restless and grouchy. Melissa complained frequently
as her father, running damage control, stayed out until
dark every evening and often slept over at the trailer.

Her carping got on her cousin's nerves. Following
one long, tearful conversation with her parents that
failed to bring an early reprieve from exile, Kirstin
yelled at the younger girl. At least she got to see her
father once in a while, Kirstin snapped.

"Oh, quit feeling sorry for yourself!" Melissa

yelled back. A moment later came the much-too-familiar sound of doors slamming.

Max's absences wore on Nancy's nerves, too. He looked so tired when he came stumbling in at night that she wanted to run a hot bath and give him a massage. Instead, the best she could do was heat some food and listen while the children chattered to him.

She missed Max in all sorts of ways. She missed his deep chuckle when they talked, and his gaze lingering on her when she walked into a room, and the strength of his arms.

He gave no sign of relenting about their relationship. Although, from the corner of her eye, Nancy sometimes saw him watching her, he averted his gaze the instant she turned around. When he had to address her, he spoke briefly and with bland courtesy.

The bright spot in her days was the good-natured Griffin. Appointing himself beastmaster, he spent hours feeding and playing with the rapidly growing kittens. His other favorite activity was "helping" Nancy maintain the Skunk Days Web site. At least, that's what he claimed to be doing as he sounded out letters while she updated the items.

"R-a-c," he read, sitting beside Nancy as she typed on her laptop.

"What does that sound like?" she prompted.

"Rac," he said. "Is it raccoon?"

"It sure is." She ruffled his hair. "This story's about Idabelle."

After the possums stopped searching for the absent cat food, the café owner had tried putting some out again. This time, she'd attracted a pair of large raccoons, and had to take another break before trolling once more for the mysterious skunk she still claimed was stalking her.

Nancy had been reluctant at first to put Idabelle's saga in the "Aroma Around Town" column. Jo-Anne's mother had earnestly requested it, however, and soon e-mails had poured in from curious readers. Already her bed-and-breakfast was fully booked for weeks before, during and after the three-day festival.

Griffin leaned forward, searching the screen for more words to decipher. By the time he started first grade next month, he'd learn to read easily, Nancy thought with satisfaction.

It amazed her that helping one child acquire language was at least as satisfying as working with a whole roomful of babies. Every day, his vocabulary—verbal and written—grew and his mind developed in its own unique way.

Nancy hadn't experienced her siblings this way because she'd still been growing up herself. Now she was ready for the adventure, and grateful that at least she had this summer to enjoy it.

"I'm going to go see if JoAnne's dog had her puppies yet," Griffin announced when he lost interest in the Web site. "Look, it stopped raining."

Nancy peered out the window. The sunlight might be weak, but at least there *was* sunlight for a change.

"Be sure to put your boots on and go out through the back." The area around the utility room had been unofficially designated Swamp Central. Since Nancy had covered the floor with an old tarp, she didn't mind the mess.

"Sure thing." Griffin darted out.

As it was too early in the afternoon to start dinner,

Nancy decided to query magazines about her article. One advantage to being ignored by Max was that it had given her time to put her notes in order and get down to work.

In writing the first draft, she'd worried that the tone was too light and affectionate to be taken seriously. On the other hand, since her targets were women's magazines, perhaps that wasn't a bad thing.

Nancy tried to capture the same cheery tone in writing her query letter, of which she addressed copies to half a dozen magazines. Pleased with the result, she copied her work to a disk and slipped into Max's unoccupied office.

Using his computer, she printed the letters. In her opinion, regular letters looked more professional than e-mail, and she could receive responses at the post office box she'd rented in town.

"Nancy?"

She gave a little jump. She hadn't heard Melissa come in. "What's up?"

"I want to bake a cake," the nine-year-old said. "Dad's got to come home tonight, since it stopped raining."

Nancy turned the letters facedown, in case Melissa took a peek, and removed her disk from the computer. "Sure. Let me put these away and I'll help you."

Max had been gone for two days, phoning in at bedtime from his trailer. First a couple of dozen cows and calves had escaped through a downed fence, then the horses had gone AWOL again. There always seemed to be some problem keeping him away.

"Can we make a lemon cake?" Melissa asked. "That's his favorite."

"There's a box of mix in the pantry." While shopping, Nancy could now run a mental list of what they needed almost as well as JoAnne. "Let's do it."

Her spirits brightened as they headed for the kitchen. The prospect of seeing Max again delighted her almost as much as Melissa.

IN LAST NIGHT'S DREAM, a pitchfork-wielding Max had staved off a circle of huge, rabid skunks. Close behind him, Nancy had huddled with her laptop, busily describing the battle to legions of mesmerized Web site fans.

He wasn't sure at what point the skunks had been replaced by the devilish figure of Lilia. She'd waved her arms and screamed something he couldn't understand.

Hours later, his heart still pounded at the memory. Although his cell phone had remained hauntingly quiet since the Fourth of July, Max knew he would hear from his ex-wife sooner or later.

He dragged his thoughts away from last night's scenario. Darn, he must be really worn out if he was mulling over dreams in the middle of working.

"I think that does it...." After breaking off to sneeze, Luis slogged to where Max stood surveying the range with binoculars. They'd recovered the last of the stray horses earlier and, with the aid of the twins, had patched the fence.

"You've got a cold. Get on home," Max said.

"Aren't you coming?"

"I want to ride the fences one more time to make sure we didn't overlook anything. We don't need to have to chase that bunch again."

Luis squinted at the thin sunshine. "This break won't last. There's another storm rolling in."

"I can hole up in the trailer," Max said. "One more night won't hurt me. You get on back. I'll bet JoAnne misses you."

"Not that you'd notice. She'll feed me because she cooks for the twins. That's about it." The couple had remained at arm's length all month, neither willing to budge an inch.

"You're two of a kind," Max said. "Stubborn as mules."

"If I give in, next thing you know I'll be spending every weekend patching that darn boat," Luis said. "A man's got to stand up for himself."

"I guess so." Max had stood up for himself where Nancy was concerned, and, as a result, spent a painfully lonely four weeks craving her nearness. It was easier when he kept physical distance between them, so he did it as often as possible.

He shooed his foreman home, and whistled for his horse.

MELISSA AND KIRSTIN iced the cake together with none of their usual bickering. When Nancy heard the back door open and the sound of masculine footsteps, she decided this day was turning out to be a real winner.

On reaching the rear hall, however, she saw that it was Luis, not Max. "Sorry to bother you," he said. "Do you have any cold medicine?"

"I'll look." Nancy checked the nearest bathroom. She was returning with some pills when she heard Melissa ask, "Where's Dad?"

"Staying over in the trailer one more night."

The girl stared at Luis as if he'd announced the end of the world. "He's got to come home. I baked a cake."

"He'll drag his sorry tail in here tomorrow, I'm sure. Save him a slice. I'm sure he'll enjoy it." The foreman grabbed a tissue from a nearby holder and sneezed into it.

Melissa ran off, her eyes glistening. Nancy's heart ached for her.

"He's overdoing it," she said. "Not that I know anything about ranching."

"The man's got inner demons," Luis said. "As for me, I've got an outer demon."

"JoAnne hasn't eased up, huh?" Neither Nancy nor Idabelle had been able to persuade her to give the man a break.

"Nope," he said. "The truth is, I don't care so much about the new trebuchet. I only want to build it to fling the boat so I can get rid of it."

If Nancy had been the couple's marriage counselor, she'd have urged them to explore the root of their problems. To deal with issues of control and personal space and so on.

But these weren't her clients, they were her friends. And what they needed was practical advice, not soul-searching.

"May I make a suggestion?" she asked.

"Go right ahead." Mud-encrusted and bedraggled, Luis had lost some of his usual bravado. Rainstorms and a cranky wife clearly had a draining effect on a man.

"Idabelle was saying the other day that she needs

more wood to build booths for Skunk Days,'' she said. ''She's also looking for a raffle prize.''

''Something like a boat?'' Luis asked.

''She didn't specify.''

He considered the implication in silence. Luis was not one to react hastily.

After a while, he said, ''It would be a fair trade-off. JoAnne gives up the boat, I give up the lumber.''

''And you make her mother happy.''

''Much obliged, Nancy,'' he said, and went out.

Nancy's thoughts returned to Melissa. A trip to the girl's room showed she wasn't there. Not in the bathroom or the den, either.

In the kitchen, Kirstin said, ''She went outside.''

''Outside?'' It was close to dinnertime, with twilight closing in. Through the window, Nancy saw dark clouds gathering.

She hurried out. No sign of Melissa in the yard. At a sudden movement, her hopes leaped, and then she spotted Griffin trotting toward her. ''No puppies yet,'' he said.

''Have you seen your sister?''

''Yeah. She was running that way.'' He pointed past the barn toward open ranchland. ''She didn't have her boots on, either.''

Nancy swung toward the door and saw the twelve-year-old watching anxiously. ''Kirstin, you take care of Griffin, okay? I'm going to go look for Melissa.''

''Okay.'' The girl gestured her cousin inside. ''Let's go turn on some cartoons.''

There was no sign of Melissa anywhere around the ranch buildings. Doubly worried when she felt the first drops of rain on her face, Nancy went inside and phoned Luis.

"She'll probably come back once the rain gets heavy," he said. "In case she doesn't, I'll get the boys and start searching. You'd better call Max."

The children were her responsibility, Nancy thought. She should have paid closer attention to Melissa when she knew the girl was so upset.

Her nerves tight as violin strings, she dialed Max's number.

10

IF ANYONE had asked Max before he became a father, whether he'd have worried about a nine-year-old girl wandering around the ranch after dark, he'd have shrugged it off.

Heck, he and his brother had camped out by themselves many a night while growing up, including once in the rain. There were few dangerous wild animals, and, this being the middle of summer, it was plenty warm.

If this theoretical girl wasn't stupid enough to drown herself in the creek, interfere with an enraged bull or step on a rattlesnake, she'd come home sooner or later none the worse for wear, he'd have said.

He'd have been an idiot.

When Max heard that his daughter was missing, his adrenaline slammed into overdrive. His little Melissa was wandering around in the dark, in the rain? Who the heck had let such a thing happen?

"You have no business working as a nanny if you can't do a simple thing like keep an eye on the kids," he snarled into the phone.

After a moment's shocked silence, Nancy said, "Luis and the twins are searching. I have a suspicion she might be heading for the trailer."

"The trailer?" He couldn't imagine why his

daughter would want to come to this place. After several days of men slumbering unshowered on its hard beds, it looked and smelled like a kennel. "She's only been here once. I doubt she has any clear idea where it is."

"I'm going to talk to Griffin and Kirstin," she said. "Sometimes kids know each other a lot better than we do."

He was ashamed of having yelled at her. It wasn't as if he kept his kids under constant surveillance when they were under his supervision, after all.

Max was too keyed-up to focus on nonessentials right now, however, and that included apologies. "I'll start looking from this end."

"Stay in touch," Nancy said.

"Right." He rang off.

He went outside. A weary Copper was eating hay in the shed. It was risky to take the overworked animal out in the dark. Even a savvy horse could turn an ankle in this mud.

Besides, on horseback a man was likely to miss a small girl. He might not hear her over the horse's heavy breathing, either.

Instead, he set out on foot. Playing his large flashlight beam around, Max called Melissa's name as he walked. No answer.

He'd expected none. She didn't know the ranch well enough to make it here even in good weather and bright light.

If only he'd kept the children on the ranch all these years instead of entrusting them to his in-laws! The girl would know every trail and pasture by now, the way Max had at her age.

He was wasting his time on useless recriminations. Grimly, he set out toward the house, calling her name and stopping from time to time to listen for a response that didn't come.

NANCY SAT BOTH children at the kitchen table to pick their brains. It didn't take more than a minute before Kirstin admitted that her cousin had vowed openly to go to the trailer.

"She asked me to come with her, but I didn't want to," she said. "I'm sorry. I should have tried to stop her."

There was no point in laying a guilt trip on a twelve-year-old. Besides, Nancy's immediate concern was to learn in which direction the younger girl had headed.

"Kirstin, when you and Melissa went on a picnic two weeks ago, how far did you go?" she asked.

"No farther than the water tanks, like we promised."

The tanks, which sat on a hill behind the barns, commanded a view. "Could you see Max's trailer from there?"

"Sort of, through some bushes. Melissa pointed it out."

"Are you sure it was the trailer?"

"It was painted yellow," Kirstin said. "Does that help?"

"The trailer is silver," Nancy said. "Can you draw me a picture of where on the ranch this yellow thing is?"

The girl jumped up. "I'll do it right now." On a

sheet of computer paper, she sketched a bird's-eye view of the ranch's central section.

Mentally, Nancy compared it to a chart JoAnne had shown her and realized that Melissa had pointed toward a storage shed. "Good job!" she said. "Now we know where she's really going."

Kirstin looked relieved that she'd been able to help. Griffin clapped his hands. "I want to draw a map, too!"

"Okay, you do that while I call your father."

The boy grabbed some crayons and paper and began scribbling eagerly. Kirstin fetched several cans of chili from the pantry. "I'll start dinner," she said.

"That's a wonderful idea. Melissa will be starved when she gets home." Nancy picked up the phone. "After I call Max, I'll go outside. Who knows, maybe she's trying to find her way back."

With luck, they'd find her soon. The sooner the better.

AFTER NANCY CALLED, Max saddled Copper and headed for the shed. In the last half hour, he'd shouted himself hoarse. He'd also had time to recognize why his daughter had gone out in the rain.

She was looking for her father.

He'd been so busy hiding from his emotions that he hadn't considered the impact his absences might have on his family. Realizing that he himself was at fault made Max feel even worse for snapping at Nancy.

Mostly, though, he wanted to find his daughter.

For once, the weather cooperated. The shower

stopped, a possible sign that the storm had passed them by.

The shed, when he reached it, proved empty. Max backtracked toward the ranch buildings, shouting for Melissa. Finally, miraculously, he heard a high-pitched response. "Daddy! Daddy! I'm over here!"

She huddled beneath a mesquite tree, staring around with wide eyes. "Baby, are you all right?" Max hit the ground and raced to her.

"I feel stupid," Melissa said. "I was going to bring you this." She held out a napkin filled with something crumbly. Max caught the smell of lemon.

"You baked my favorite cake?" His throat clamped shut with emotion.

"I want you to come home." She snuggled against him.

He swallowed hard. "I'm going to do that right now," he said. "And stay there."

THE NEXT DAY, the sun shone merrily. TV reports called for clear weather, although it would be a while before the mud dried out.

Luis removed his boat from its covering and set it in the marshy yard. "We're having an after-the-rain party," he announced. "Everybody come sail with me in Noah's Ark."

The children piled in, bringing their kittens as a substitute for Noah's animals. They were extra happy because Lenore Witherspoon had called that morning to invite them to a sleepover party for Lynn's twelfth birthday.

Standing on the porch, Nancy was pleased to see

Max join the others. He had to fold his long legs to avoid kicking Luis.

"Seaward ho, me hearties!" The foreman waved a pair of oars. "Who'll row the first shift?"

"Me!" said Griffin.

"What in the heck are y'all doing?" Rudy ambled from the barn, scratching his head through his baseball cap.

"Letting off steam," Max said.

"Well, y'all look like fools."

"I like your serious, nose-to-the-grindstone attitude," Nancy said. "In fact, Rudy, I've got a little present for you and Randolph."

"Yes'm?" he asked hopefully.

"Hold on." She returned minutes later, bearing a bucket, sponge, soap and a pile of clean sheets. "You two are appointed to clean out the trailer. I hear from Max it's a sty."

"But…"

"Make sure you leave that cabin shipshape, you landlubber!" roared Luis.

"Don't forget to restock the larder," Max called.

Muttering to himself, Rudy departed in search of his brother. "I'm glad we got out of that thankless task," Max said.

"I'm glad nobody asked *me* to do it," Kirstin said. "After all, I cooked dinner."

"And did a terrific job." Her uncle's praise brought a smile. "As for that lemon cake, I'd have come home earlier if I'd known about it."

He gave his daughter a squeeze, stopping only to help Griffin pretend to row. This morning, with his amber eyes dancing in the sunlight, the rancher seemed to have shed ten years. Nancy would have hugged him if she'd dared.

Last night, there'd been hugs all around. Once Melissa got over being upset, she was thrilled to take credit for bringing Daddy home, and they'd all enjoyed the cake.

Today, even Luis was in better spirits. He'd discussed Nancy's proposal with his wife, although so far she hadn't agreed to anything.

"Where's JoAnne?" Nancy asked.

"She drove into town," said the foreman. "To see what her mother thinks about raffling off this here fine seagoing vessel, I presume."

"Fine? I thought you hated it," Max said.

"It's only a fine seagoing vessel when it's sitting on dry land. Or semidry land, in this case." Luis waved his oar and let out a shout. "Pull hard for open sea, me boys! There's a pirate ship on the horizon!"

The "pirate ship" turned out to be JoAnne's green station wagon. It jounced along the newly potholed roadway and halted in front of them.

"Just what I wanted," she said as she emerged. "A work crew."

Both men got stricken looks much like the one Rudy had worn moments before. Luis made an attempt to scramble to his feet, but succeeded only in frightening a kitten, which hid beneath a seat.

Producing a couple of paint buckets and brushes, JoAnne marched toward them. "We're going to paint black-and-white stripes on this old clunker and rename it *The Stinker* before Mama raffles it."

"We're getting rid of it?" Luis carefully disentangled the kitten.

"Mama's delighted. She's been telling everyone the raffle prize would be 'something big,' and they were beginning to complain that she hadn't produced anything," said his wife. "She's eager to get her hands on that lumber for booths, too."

It was hard for Nancy to believe that only a week remained before the festival. Two weeks after that she would have to leave, a subject she seriously didn't want to think about. It was much more fun to reflect on how happy Luis and Joanne looked, grinning at each other like newlyweds.

"I'll paint!" said Griffin.

"I'll go fix sandwiches," Nancy said. "So you don't have to interrupt your work to come inside." She paused on the porch. "Cucumber and cream cheese okay with everyone?"

Silence fell over the boat. It was broken only by the mewling of a kitten.

"That was a joke," she said. "How about bacon sandwiches with lettuce and tomato from the garden?"

Cheers went up. As Max chuckled, his gaze met Nancy's and she saw a glint of unaccustomed tenderness.

She hurried inside, hoping it meant that the general thaw applied to her, too.

COMING UP with last-minute birthday presents for Lynn posed less of a challenge than Nancy had feared. Kirstin decided to give a new doll that her parents had sent. Melissa contributed a young-adult novel by Cheryl Zach, since she had two copies, and Griffin drew a big picture of a skunk.

Late that afternoon, they all climbed into the pickup and drove over to the Double Bar L. Halfway there, a skunk meandered onto the highway and stood regarding the oncoming truck with mild curiosity. Max veered sharply around it.

"The problem with skunks is they aren't afraid of much," he said.

"That's because they're *pee-yew!*" said Griffin, and the two girls laughed.

As they rattled onto the dude ranch, Nancy noticed half a dozen guest cabins clustered near the main house. In the corral, a couple with a toddler were riding ponies under Lorrin's supervision.

Lenore and her three kids ran out to greet them. "Come join us for dinner," she said.

"We snacked all afternoon," Max said. "I'm not hungry. Nancy?"

"Me, either. Thanks, though."

How could she be hungry with butterflies performing an Irish jig in her stomach? She and Max were going to be alone for the first time in weeks.

Nancy wasn't sure what she wanted to happen and was in no hurry to get there, either. She had an uncharacteristic feeling of simply wanting to exist in the here and now, as long as the here and now included Max.

He called farewells to the children, who waved and vanished around a corner with their friends. "Gee, I was expecting some clinging," he said. "They made such a big deal about me being gone."

"That's different," Nancy said. "You left them stuck at home. This time, they're the ones out having fun."

After promising to collect the kids in the morning, they rode home with a view of a glorious sunset. "If you don't mind, I'd like to stop by the trailer and see what still needs to be done," Max said. "There's a shortcut from the highway."

"You mean we have to work?" Nancy asked, disappointed.

"Just a little inventory," he said. "I suspect the twins' idea of restocking the larder is a box of crackers and some spray cheese."

"Okay, let's stop." Nancy was in no hurry to return to the house, anyway. Before they left, Max had announced that he planned to spend the evening catching up on paperwork.

At the trailer, Nancy hopped out. Although she'd seen it from the outside before, she was curious to inspect the interior.

It was definitely a no-frills operation, she saw when she climbed inside behind Max. The roof was so low he had to stoop. A tiny kitchenette occupied the center, with a double bed on one end and two foldout couches on the other. Cramped quarters indeed.

"We've got electrical hookups from the highway," Max explained, checking the cabinets. "Gee, I was wrong. It isn't crackers and spray cheese, it's Froot Loops and snack cakes."

"Health food," Nancy teased. She was glad he'd never seen her larder in Clair De Lune. It wasn't much better.

"Next time you're in town, stock up on canned goods, would you? We need to refill this."

"Sure." When he swung to face her, Nancy had a hard time catching her breath. It was due less to any lack of oxygen than to the way the small space compressed and intensified Max's presence.

Those high cheekbones. That shaggy hair. She wanted to touch them again, but didn't dare.

It was a moment before he spoke. "I guess this is as good a time as any to apologize."

"For what?"

"The unkind things I said last night." He cleared his throat. "Blaming you for Melissa's disappearance. She's not a toddler. You can't be expected to keep her under lock and key."

"I knew you didn't mean it," Nancy said. "We were all upset."

"You don't have to be so nice about it," he said.

"Why shouldn't I?"

"Because I'd feel less guilty if you subjected me to a little verbal abuse," he admitted. "You know. 'Max, you're an arrogant jerk.' 'Max, you're a lousy father.' That kind of thing."

"You're neither of those," she said. "You're a wonderful man. When you relax, you're funny and charming, and everyone on the ranch relies on your strength."

"You think I'm funny and charming?" He quirked an eyebrow, inviting further flattery.

"Yes, I do." Nancy couldn't believe she'd once considered him a Neanderthal. That was before she'd met him, she reminded herself.

"I'm enjoying this conversation," Max said. "Tell me more."

A dozen compliments sprang to mind, all of them true. Yet she had no right to go on flirting while she was committing fraud. It wasn't fair to go on deceiving this man. He deserved the truth.

"I'm the one who doesn't deserve your good opinion," Nancy said.

"If it's about last night..."

"It isn't." Although she wanted Max to like her so much that her entire body trembled, she couldn't proceed under false pretenses. It was time to take her medicine.

And hope that, by some miracle, he would forgive her.

11

MAX KNEW HE OUGHT TO concentrate on what Nancy was saying. Obviously, her shortcomings, real or imagined, preyed on her mind.

The truth was, he didn't care. Over the past two months, he'd come to know this woman thoroughly.

Whatever she believed she was hiding, he was wild about her. Totally gone. Right now, he wanted her almost beyond enduring.

"I'm getting a neck cramp standing here with my head tilted." His shoulders ached, too, from not being able to straighten. "Why don't we sit down?" There was nowhere to sit except on one of the beds.

"We could go outside."

"It's getting dark," he replied, although it was barely dusk.

"It's getting even darker in here," she said.

Time to back off, Max decided reluctantly. "Go on, finish your point. You don't deserve my good opinion because...what? You lied about being a vegetarian?"

She sighed. "For starters."

"In fact, you concocted quite a few things on your résumé, didn't you?" he said.

Even in the dimness, he couldn't miss her startled expression. "You already know?"

He smiled. "Let's see, you won 4-H medals and grew up on a farm, but you don't know how to ride a horse, you were using cheat sheets from the Internet to plant the garden and— Need I go on?"

He could swear she was blushing. "Okay. The thing is, you only know half of it."

True confessions didn't interest him. "I know what matters," Max said. "You love the ranch. You're good with the kids. You've brought something special into our lives."

"I have? But I don't deserve…"

"You belong here," he said. "Let's not argue about it."

A man could wait only so long. Words weren't Max's strong point, not with his beautiful, sweet lady standing right in front of him, her heart shining in her eyes.

One short step and he gathered her into his arms. No more of that tentative exploratory stuff they'd tried before. No more getting to know each other in the kitchen or smooching in the pecan grove. This time, he meant business.

She flowed into his arms as if she'd been longing for him all her life. In her kiss, Max found the permission he needed to drop all restraint.

He didn't know where to start, or how to stop, so he did everything at once. Hugged her tight. Kissed her madly. Lifted her pullover top and slipped it off, removing her bra in the process.

"You don't fool around, do you?" Nancy whispered, sounding awestruck.

"I like to think of myself as a man of action," he

said, and proceeded to demonstrate by devouring her wonderful, firm breasts.

"I guess this is the way people do things on a ranch," she said, and made short work of his belt. Not an easy chore, since it had an elaborate Mexican silver buckle, but Nancy seemed determined.

He couldn't wait to see what else she was determined to do.

IN HER PREVIOUS encounters with men, Nancy had never taken such liberties with their bodies. Despite being incredibly intimate, she'd felt shy.

Not with Max.

This opportunity had been a long time coming and she meant to make the most of it. To strip off his clothes and run her hands over his skin. To touch him in places that were normally forbidden.

He was so glorious. So long and lean and responsive. She loved the way he gasped when she stroked his stomach and thighs. She loved to see his eyelids droop and hear the ragged breathing that signaled he was on the verge of losing control.

They managed to make it to the double bed. They didn't get the spread off, or all their clothes, either. Although Nancy yearned to savor every level of lovemaking, she had an urgent need to savor it in one, heart-stopping moment—now!

Goodness, Max was as long and hard in that department as in the rest of him, she discovered as he slid himself inside her. They were sprawled in a most undignified position sideways on the bed, holding on to each other as if afraid they might spin apart by the sheer force of their exuberance.

Grabbing Max's hips, Nancy arched upwards and kissed him again. "Amazing," he whispered when their lips unlocked.

"Beyond amazing," she said.

He thrust into her, harder and harder. Nancy didn't want this wild ride to end, and yet she couldn't stop the sensations rocketing through her. Didn't want to stop this mad rush toward a sunburst of pure, exquisite joy.

The best part wasn't her climax. It was having Max between her legs, feeling his bucking ecstasy and hearing his cries of unbearable pleasure. It was giving this man something so perfect.

"Now that," she murmured as he sagged against her afterward, "is what I call a real Fourth of July."

His laughter rumbled through her.

They must have fallen asleep, because Nancy awoke in darkness. She heard Max fumbling and then a small light switched on.

His grin gleamed at her, magical in the semidarkness. "Having a good time?"

"The best." As she plumped up a pillow behind her, Nancy remembered that she hadn't finished telling Max about her deception. He'd already known about some of her fabrications and hadn't been upset. Still, he didn't know the full extent.

I don't want to ruin this. I don't want to risk losing him when we're barely getting started.

Yet there would never be a better time to talk than tonight, while the children were away. Nancy cringed inside as she said, "Remember what we were discussing before?"

"Frankly, no." Sitting up, he drew her to his side. "I know what we should have discussed."

"What's that?" She relished the way he smelled, of shampoo and sex.

"Contraception," he said.

"Oh." She wondered if he was worried about possible dangers. "I haven't been involved with anyone for a long time. I'm perfectly healthy."

"Same here. That isn't what I meant." Max fluffed out a few of her blond strands. "Your hair's so soft, I've got this weird desire to keep a lock of it in— What do people keep locks of hair in?"

"Baggies?" Nancy suggested.

"Lockets, I think," he said. "Anyway, getting back to my point, you might be pregnant."

She hadn't been concerned about that, for good reason. "You don't have to worry."

"I'm not worried," he said. "I'd be happy to have a baby with you."

"You've already got two." She'd assumed that was enough.

"I always wanted a big family," Max said.

Nancy's heart sank. She hadn't foreseen this problem. "You're sure?"

"You bet," he said.

So which major disappointment was she going to lay on him first? she wondered. Her infertility or her Ph.D. in psychology?

To her dismay, Nancy realized she couldn't tell him either one tonight, because it was just too heavy a load. She wanted to bask a little longer in sheer, unadulterated happiness.

It was wicked and selfish, she conceded, and snuggled tighter against him.

THE NEXT WEEK flew by, with preparations for the Skunk Days Festival occupying every spare minute of Max's time. Or, at least, every spare minute that wasn't devoted to mentally replaying that delicious night with Nancy.

After returning to the ranch house, they'd made love again. Twice. She hadn't insisted on protection either time, so he figured she liked the idea of having kids.

They couldn't make love after the children returned, since Max considered it important to set a good example. Or, he admitted with a touch of embarrassment, to appear to.

In any case, he meant to rectify this frustrating circumstance as soon as possible. The night of the festival, he was going to propose.

The situation got more complicated on the eve of the festival, when Bill and Beth drove up to the ranch house. In the excitement, he'd forgotten they were coming.

They were good sports about being assigned to the den, thank goodness. Since they arrived near dinnertime, Beth tried to help Nancy cook, but proved so distractable that she was quickly shooed out of the kitchen.

Kirstin spent the first few hours hanging around her parents, showing them her kitten. She chattered on about the sleepover at the Witherspoon ranch and the adventure with Melissa, taking pride in how she herself had helped save the day.

At last she noticed that they were only half-listening. Her enthusiasm waning, she retreated to her room.

Max knew his brother and sister-in-law were absorbed in their own tensions from the strained formality with which the two spoke to each other. He wished they would try harder to pay attention to their daughter, though.

Finally the big day arrived. Max went into town early to help set up booths.

Luis, JoAnne, Rudy and Randolph volunteered as well. The twins had taken a particular interest in the festival after they learned that two attractive sisters, new in town, would be staffing booths.

"I'm a little embarrassed," Idabelle said as she greeted them all. "Last night, my skunk finally showed up to eat the cat food."

"How do you know it's the right one?" asked JoAnne.

"I'll show you." The woman produced a plastic animal carrier. From inside, she lifted the strangest-looking skunk Max had ever seen. Its proportions were wrong and the tail, although feathery, was too narrow.

"It's a cat," Luis said. "Isn't it?"

Max studied the black-and-white coloring, the fluffy tail and the pointy noise. "Maybe it's a hybrid."

"I don't think they interbreed," JoAnne said.

Idabelle hoisted the creature in her arms. "It's purring. Skunks don't purr."

"You mean you've had a cat stalking you?" Randolph asked. "That's durn funny."

"No, it isn't. It's durn stupid," said a mocking voice from behind Max. He turned to see Dale Dwyer, gussied up in silver spurs and white chaps over black slacks and a turtleneck. Talk about stupid; the man was ready to die of heatstroke to make a fashion statement.

"I beg your pardon?" said Idabelle.

Dale waved over half a dozen friends. The women were scantily clad and the men wore expressions of condescending amusement. "What kind of person can't tell a cat from a skunk? Look at this!" He pointed to the cat.

"Don't call her 'this.' As of right now, her name is Up Yours," said Idabelle.

"The woman's got a sharp tongue," remarked one of Dale's friends.

Annoyance flushed the nouveau rancher's face. "Let's see what kind of animal this really is." Without warning, he grabbed the cat.

With a frightened hiss, the creature raked its claws across Dale's arm and leaped away. The man issued a string of cuss words before pressing his injured wrist to his mouth. He didn't bother to apologize to the ladies for his foul language.

JoAnne started after the escaping animal, too late. It scampered out of sight beneath a building.

"She'll come back at feeding time," Idabelle said.

"You plan to keep her?" Max asked, ignoring Dale. He figured a creep like that wasn't worth tussling with, even if the man did need to be taught a lesson in manners.

"I don't figure I've got much choice," the café owner said. "She chose me, remember?"

Dale and his fancy friends wandered off. Max assumed they planned to amuse themselves by sneering at the entire festival, a pointless endeavor since the event was tongue in cheek.

As he finished assembling a shooting gallery, he saw a bus rumble down Main Street. The regular parking slots had been roped off for festival activities, so the driver veered onto a side street.

On the front of the bus, the destination sign read: Skunk Charter.

Max wiped the sweat off his forehead as a large RV rumbled in the bus's wake. It looked large enough to house half the population of Skunk Crossing.

Luis exchanged glances with him. "Guess we're gonna get a crowd," the foreman said.

"The activities don't start for an hour."

"They can nurse a black-and-white cappuccino at the cafe," he said.

More vehicles followed. Max decided he'd better drive back to the ranch for his family or the town might get so overcrowded they'd have to walk the entire five miles.

As he headed out, he patted the shirt pocket where he'd tucked the engagement ring. He'd bought it this week at the general store after swearing the shopkeeper to silence.

Tonight when they got home, he was going to ask Nancy to be his wife. Max could hardly wait.

TRYING TO GET the family ready for Max's return was like herding cats. No sooner did Nancy get Melissa's hair fixed than Griffin fell in a mud puddle in the yard and had to be scrubbed.

Kirstin's spirits swung wildly, depending on her parents' tone of voice when they spoke to her or each other. As for Bill and Beth, being around them was like square dancing with porcupines.

Nancy was getting pricked enough by her own sense of guilt. She'd kept Max in the dark all week. As a psychologist, she knew she was practicing avoidance, big time.

Double-checking her makeup in the mirror, she glanced down at the letter she'd received yesterday from *Femme Fatale* magazine. The editor wrote that she'd be delighted to see the article as soon as possible.

"Be sure to make it sexy!" she'd written. "Our readers love sexy! And, oh, they love those cowboys!" They must love exclamation points, too, Nancy surmised.

She should have been thrilled. Instead, she couldn't believe she was exposing Max, even incognito, to the lustful daydreams of other women.

He belonged to her. Well, no, he didn't. That didn't mean she was willing to share him with anyone else.

Outside, she heard a truck pull up. Through the shutters, Nancy watched Max's tall, well-built figure stride toward the house.

Was it her imagination, or did the man glow in the sunlight? Amber coloring and tanned skin didn't begin to explain it. He looked happy, just pure happy, and the thought made Nancy's heart beat faster.

She'd spent all summer helping plan this event. She wanted to hog every golden moment of it, not share it or Max with the horny readers of *Femme Fatale*.

Maybe the article wasn't such a good idea after all. Maybe...

Max was coming down the hall, calling her name. Nancy hurried out.

As on the Fourth of July, Max had hired Luis's nephew Manuel to keep watch over the ranch. That meant he could stay out late and put his full attention on his family.

Bill and Beth followed Max's truck to town in their car, with Kirstin sitting in back. In the rearview mirror, he could see his brother and sister-in-law mouthing angry words at each other, and then Kirstin leaned forward. They both fell silent.

His twelve-year-old niece must be chewing them out, because they didn't say another word. By the time they arrived in town, both parents looked embarrassed.

When they got out, Bill took Max aside. "Kirstin said that if we don't change our ways, she's going to stay at the ranch and go to school here this winter," he said. "She says she doesn't want to live in a battle zone."

"She'd be more than welcome." Lightly, Max added, "She makes great brownies."

"I don't know how you did it, but she's grown up a lot this summer," Bill said. "She told us in no uncertain terms that we need to get counseling. She even cited facts and figures about how devastating divorce is to kids. It kind of shook us."

"I wonder where she learned that?" He hadn't seen Kirstin read anything but historical novels all summer.

"Apparently this nanny of yours is a superbrain. Kirstin says she can ask her almost anything and get lots of information."

"Really?" Max hadn't noticed. Of course, he wasn't in the habit of asking Nancy a lot of questions. "Maybe she looks it up on the Internet."

"Kirstin got more than I expected from the ranch experience," his brother said. "Beth and I promised to work on our marriage so she'll come back with us."

"Can I give you a bit of advice from my own experience?" Max asked.

"Sure."

"Choose a woman counselor."

His brother clapped him on the back. "I'll do that."

Melissa and Griffin came over and urged Max to hurry toward the carnival music. "I want to go on the pony ride!" his daughter said.

"I want to see the baby skunks," said Griffin.

"Let's go, then," Max said, shepherding them and Nancy along. His brother's family set off on their own, not exactly bouncing with joy, but at least not snarling at each other.

Main Street was so jammed Max barely recognized it. People lined up outside the café, children ran around waving black-and-white pinwheels, and he could practically hear the *ka-ching* of cash registers rescuing the town from its skunk-induced doldrums.

They passed City Hall Park, where carnival rides whirled. He bought both kids Skunk Days T-shirts at a booth staffed by Rudy and a giggly young lady who seemed smitten with him.

They passed up some home-baked goodies labeled Polecat Cheesecake and Licorice-Scented Skunk Muffins. Max was glad to see Randolph hard at work alongside a beaming young woman, both serving pastries in between feeding bites to eat other.

At the elementary school, they enjoyed the black-and-white pet show. Idabelle had recognized in advance that the local judges could never pick one pet over another, so all the cages bore blue or purple ribbons. Every entrant had won either first prize or best in show.

Melissa skipped ahead as, in the schoolyard, they neared the Drag Racing Stinkers. "I'm cheering for that guy!" she said, pointing to one of the racing skunks. "Hey, look, there's free clothespins for your nose. Anybody want one?"

After the skunks—which were actually trained and descented—waddled along the course and received their cheers, the next stop was the adopt-a-skunk booth. The children knelt by a cage, faces shining as they cooed over a couple of baby skunks.

Nancy, Max noticed, was beaming, too, except that her focus wasn't the skunks but the children. She sure did love them, he thought, and they loved her, too.

Nancy was a natural mother. And wife, he thought. His wife. As soon as they got a moment alone.

"Do they bite?" a man asked the woman in charge.

"Like any animal, they'll bite if they're frightened," she said. "They need affection and gentle training. And patience."

"How can you tell if a skunk is patient?"

"It isn't the skunk that needs the patience," the woman said. "It's you."

After Max and Nancy pried the pair free, they headed for the bed-and-breakfast. In the refrigerator, they found the sandwiches Idabelle had promised to leave in case the café got too full. He was, she'd pointed out, part owner of both enterprises and shouldn't have to wait in line.

They ate outside on benches. Nancy insisted they find seats in the shade. "I put sunscreen on the kids, but forgot myself. Do you think I'm turning pink?"

Max made a show of inspecting her face. The first thing he was going to do tonight, after she said yes to his proposal, was to kiss her nose, then her cheeks, then...

Griffin spoke up with a mouthful of sandwich. "There's Mommy," he mumbled.

"You're dreaming," said his sister.

"No, honest. She's over there," he said. "At the Indian jewelry booth."

Max's pastrami sandwich on white bread with black potato chips on the side turned to sawdust in his mouth. If he hadn't been so absorbed in Nancy, he'd have spotted Lilia earlier, on the other side of the street trying on a pair of earrings. With that red-gold hair, she stood out like a flame.

Since making love to Nancy, Max had almost forgotten about the phone call on the Fourth of July. Lilia must have heard about the festival and made it an excuse to come to town.

He wished she would go away. She'd spotted him, though, and didn't look at all displeased about it.

"Max?" Nancy prompted. "Is it her?"

"Yes." He figured he'd better explain. "She called last month. Things didn't work out with her new husband.'' He knew better than to say any more in front of the children. Nancy was smart enough to read between the lines.

''She's coming toward us,'' Melissa said.

As Lilia smiled and sashayed in their direction, neither of the kids made any move to greet her. That didn't surprise Max. His ex-wife wasn't exactly Mother of the Year.

He stood up. Better to waylay the woman and keep the conversation private.

''I'll go talk to her,'' he said, and trudged across the street.

12

"YOU AREN'T GOING AWAY now that our mother's come back, are you, Nancy?" Melissa asked.

"What?" She turned her attention to the child. "No. I sure don't want to."

In fact, now that she'd seen that child-dumping, husband-hurting redhead, Nancy wondered how she could possibly go back to Clair De Lune and hurt them all over again. *Oh, Hayley, what hast thou wrought?*

It was no use blaming Hayley. Nancy was the one who'd come here under false pretenses. Why hadn't she guessed, right from the start, that she ought to turn around and go home because otherwise she was going to fall in love with Max?

Nancy went rigid. In love. Her? Impossible.

No, not impossible. It had happened and suddenly, in a flash of insight, she knew that she might as well hang up her heart forever, because it belonged to Max. And to these kids.

She wished that stunning Lilia wasn't standing over there flirting so vivaciously. If she tried hard enough, the woman could take Nancy's whole life away. She went cold at the thought.

Griffin snuggled close and offered her the remaining bite of his sandwich. The grilled cheese had gone cold and gummy on the black bread. She ate it anyway to please him.

"Why are you staring into space?" Melissa asked.

"I'm having an epiphany," Nancy said.

"Does it hurt?" asked Griffin.

"A little."

How could she, a Ph.D. on a fast track toward tenure, give it all up to live on a ranch? It was crazy. Unthinkable.

But she was thinking it.

MAX STEERED Lilia around the corner. He didn't want Nancy and the kids to witness this discussion, in case it got heated.

Her red-gold hair fluttering in the breeze, his ex-wife fixed him with wide, green eyes. "Max! I'm so glad to run into you."

"I doubt it's a coincidence," he said. "Why didn't you let me know you were coming?"

"You weren't exactly Mr. Welcome Wagon the last time we talked." Lilia twisted her hands together. "Look, I want to apologize."

It was too little, too late. Max held his anger in check with difficulty. "You do?"

"I found out my husband was cheating on me with one of his patients," she said. "It feels awful to have your trust betrayed."

In spite of himself, he felt a twinge of sympathy. "Yes, it does."

"I was wrong to give you such a hard time about investing your money in the town, too," Lilia continued. "You must be doing terribly well."

"Well enough," he said.

"I miss the children." Her eyes misted over. It was a trick she'd used in divorce court, to great effect.

"Lilia, I won't interfere with your parental rights." Max figured she'd forget all about the kids as soon as she latched on to another man, anyway. "As for you and me, that's over."

"Are you involved with someone?" she asked.

From Lilia's tactics in divorce court, Max knew she could be vindictive when crossed. Since he wasn't yet engaged, he said, "Nothing that concerns you."

"Good." She gave him a sideways smile, green eyes aglimmer, that would have set his heart racing years ago.

Now it only made him itchy.

In Max's pocket, the cell phone rang. Rotten timing, just like on the Fourth of July. At least this time he knew it wasn't Lilia, because she was standing in front of him.

"Your gelding's been hurt," Manuel Ortega said when Max answered. "Something must have spooked him. He jumped a fence and took a fall. He's on his feet, but he's limping."

"How badly?"

"I can't rightly say. I'm no expert on horses."

Max depended on Copper, and he owed the horse his personal attention. "I'll come make sure there's no internal bleeding. Much obliged for the call."

"What's up?" Lilia asked after he clicked off.

"I have to go to the ranch," he said.

"I'll come with you."

"That isn't necessary," Max said. "See you around." He walked briskly away.

When he reached Nancy, Max explained about

Copper. "I'm leaving you in charge of the children," he said. "Kids, if your mother wants to join you, she has a right, but don't go anywhere without Nancy."

"I won't," Melissa said.

"Me neither," said Griffin.

He met Nancy's eye. "I'm sorry about this." He hoped she understood that he meant Lilia as much as the horse.

"We'll be fine." She spoke with quiet authority.

Max wanted to hug her, but Lilia was watching. "I'll see you in a couple of hours," he said, and left.

IT DIDN'T TAKE a psychologist to figure out the body language while Max was talking to his ex-wife, during the glimpse Nancy caught before they disappeared around a corner. Lilia was pushing and he was fighting the urge to flee.

It was a huge relief to see that he didn't welcome the woman's return. There was no denying Lilia's beauty. Male passersby kept turning to watch her, and one of Dale Dwyer's city friends was so smitten he walked into a fire hydrant.

As soon as Max disappeared, his ex-wife popped up. "Hi, kids." She didn't even greet them by name. To Nancy, she said, "You must be the new housekeeper."

"That's me." She introduced herself and they shook hands.

Lilia tagged along for a while. She soon got bored with rooting for the children as they played games, however. When they decided to attend the Pepe Le Pew Cartoonfest, she took off.

Other people stopped to say hello, mostly townspeople and ranchers that Nancy had met at church. When some out-of-town visitors discovered that she was the Skunk Days Web master, she got showered with compliments and suggestions for next year.

The children ran about laughing with a group of friends. She heard them discussing which teachers they might get at school.

Nancy had believed she was part of a community in Clair De Lune, but it hadn't been like this. In California, she was a tumbleweed blowing through town. In Skunk Crossing, she'd begun putting down roots, whether she'd meant to or not.

If only Max would return. This was supposed to be a day of happy celebration, and he was missing it.

Tonight, she hoped they could steal an hour together in her room. Or his room. Or both.

Then she was going to tell him the rest of the truth. Since his brother and sister-in-law were within earshot, maybe he wouldn't scream too loudly.

ALTHOUGH COPPER had bruised himself, there was no sign of a break or of internal injuries. As a precaution, Max spent over an hour reassuring the horse and walking him gently.

While he attended to the gelding, Max's thoughts skimmed back to Lilia. He remembered how awestruck he'd been the first time he saw her at the Houston hotel where he'd been attending a conference. He'd wondered if she was a visiting movie star until he realized she worked at the concierge desk.

He'd been elated by his good fortune when she'd agreed to a date. And, a month later, when she promised to marry him.

Max had never met anyone so charming. Lonely from the isolation of the ranch, he'd considered himself the luckiest man on earth.

Only gradually had he discovered how self-centered she was. He'd learned from her parents that, a week before they met, she'd broken up with a live-in boyfriend who got tired of paying her bills.

Perhaps she'd married Max to prove something to herself. Or she'd liked the fact that he owned a good-size ranch. Then she got pregnant right away, and they'd both tried to make things work. At least, he had, and he supposed Lilia would consider sticking around for seven years a major effort on her part.

Max put Copper into a stall and fed him. Nuzzling him, the horse nickered softly.

"Good fellow." Max stroked his nose. "I'm glad you're all right."

"Mr. Richter," called Manuel when Max emerged from the barn. The young man, a thinner version of Luis, wore an earnest expression. "I smell gas coming from the house."

"What?" Max burst into a lope. Right outside the kitchen door, he smelled it, too.

Very carefully, he opened the kitchen door. Inside, a frying pan holding two raw eggs sat on the stove, obviously forgotten. On the counter lay a novel he'd seen his sister-in-law reading earlier. The gas jet had been left on unlit.

He didn't know whether Beth hadn't realized there was no pilot light or whether she'd been distracted, perhaps arguing with her husband. The reason didn't matter now.

Easing into the room, he turned off the jet. Then he opened the windows and walked through the house, raising windows in other rooms as a precaution.

While he was waiting for the place to air out, Max remembered that Nancy needed her sunscreen. It wasn't in the hall bathroom or the utility room, so he ventured into her bedroom.

The last time he'd come in here, before her arrival, it had been an ordinary, rather bare room. Now it sparkled with Nancy's light fragrance.

Signs of her were everywhere. A silky nightgown hanging on a hook behind the door. Her brush set carelessly on a chair. The laptop computer, surrounded by papers on the desk.

There! He spotted the bottle of sunscreen on the edge of the desk and reached for it.

An envelope caught Max's eye. Printed with the name of a women's magazine, it was addressed to Dr. Nancy Verano.

He hesitated, puzzled. Was this some kind of gag?

Max didn't want to pry. On the other hand, he had an unpleasant feeling in his gut.

What was it that Bill had said earlier? Something about Nancy being a superbrain.

Slowly, he picked up the letter and read it.

NANCY'S EXCITEMENT at Max's return faded when she saw the fury in his face. Something terrible must have happened.

He held out her sunscreen. ''Oh, good,'' she said. ''Where did you find it?''

"Right next to the letter from *Femme Fatale* magazine," he said.

Her heart got stuck in her throat. "Uh-oh."

In a daze, she walked with him to JoAnne's booth. One look at Max's face, and the foreman's wife volunteered to watch the kids as long as he needed.

He steered Nancy to a quiet corner of the town's central park. "Max, I was going to tell you tonight," she said.

The ice in his gaze chilled her. "That's interesting," he said. "I was going to ask you to marry me tonight. That would have made a great climax for your article, wouldn't it?"

He'd meant to propose! She was stunned. "I came up with the idea before I knew you," she said. "I wouldn't have written about anything so personal."

"You're a university psychologist." Max folded his arms sternly. "You never intended to stay here."

"My sister Hayley applied for the job and then begged me to fill in for her," Nancy said. "At first, well, I didn't know what I'd let myself in for. Max…"

"I'm not some experiment for you to play with." Anger rippled through his voice. "Neither are my children."

"I love them. I love you."

"You're just like Lilia," he said. "No, worse. She may have manipulated me, but she didn't calculate it. She didn't plan it all out and sell it to a magazine."

Nancy wished she could go back through the past few months and hit the delete key a lot of times. Now she couldn't let him go without a fight. "I'd have said yes," she told him.

"To what?"

"Marrying you."

"That's great," he growled. "Just what I need, another wife I can't trust."

"Max, I'm not kidding. I've fallen in love with you," Nancy said.

"I fell in love with a woman I met this summer." He'd never looked so rigid or so far away, she thought. "Turns out she doesn't exist. She's somebody named Dr. Nancy Verano. Is that Ph.D. doctor or a medical doctor?"

"Ph.D.," she said miserably.

"Well, as soon as we can book you a flight, you can take your Ph.D. back to California," Max said.

Frantically, Nancy searched for the words to change his mind. She had to convince him that she wasn't the same woman who'd blithely set out to promote her career by observing cowboys.

Then she realized that she'd already told him, and he didn't believe her. "Please don't send me away yet," she said. "I know you're furious. We both need time to…"

He shook his head. "You don't even understand what you've done. What it means to be betrayed by someone you trusted so much that—never mind. I don't know the fancy psychological term for what I feel. That's your department."

He caught Nancy's arm and led her firmly back toward the booth. Among other people, she couldn't continue the argument, and he knew it.

Besides, she didn't know what to say. Maybe there were no right words.

AFTER LILIA'S treachery, Max had considered himself forewarned and forearmed. What a fool he was. A complete dupe.

Nancy had sneaked right under the radar. Did he have "Kick Me" tattooed on his forehead?

He was almost grateful when Lilia dropped by, bringing treats for the children and attaching herself to Max's arm. It gave him a good excuse for his dour expression.

After dinner came the day's culmination: a concert of parody songs in the park, performed by a local quartet with guitar accompaniment from the Reverend Audacious Powdermilk. The singers were JoAnne, the Witherspoons and Max.

He'd never felt less like singing. Still, his spirits rose as he gazed from the stage over the throng of people spilling across the park and neighboring streets.

The Skunk Days Festival was a hit. By the end of its three-day run, the town would be flush with income. Next year, with enough advance notice to get listed in more magazines and guidebooks, they should do even better.

The appreciative audience began laughing as soon as the singers launched into a parody called, "I Left My Skunk in San Francisco." By the climactic number, "There Is Nothing Like a Skunk," they were howling.

Applause exploded afterwards, followed by calls of "Encore!" JoAnne and Max exchanged startled looks. It hadn't occurred to them to prepare anything extra.

They were saved the trouble as an unmistakable,

sharp odor drifted across the park. Amid cries of disgust mingled with wisecracks, people dispersed.

Local veterans like Max and JoAnne weren't so easily driven off. They'd been catching whiffs of skunk odor for months, and this was no worse than usual.

Max's cell phone rang. It was Idabelle. "Did you smell that?" she asked.

"How could I miss it? By the way, where are you?" He hadn't seen his business partner at the concert, and had assumed she was still working at the café.

"I got worried about my new cat," she said. "I was driving around looking for her when I saw Dale Dwyer crouched down, poking a stick at this black-and-white striped animal. He said, 'Here, kitty, kitty, kitty,' and then it turned around and started to beat its forepaws. I rolled up my window fast."

"I guess we know who really can't tell a skunk from a cat," Max said. "I'll spread the word. With any luck, he'll be too embarrassed to show his face in town for a while."

"Luck has nothing to do with it," Idabelle said. "The way he smells, people will run screaming away."

Lilia had decamped, Max noticed when he rejoined his family. The hard part, for him, was ignoring Nancy's distraught gaze. If he weren't careful, he might fall for her tricks all over again.

"Can we come back tomorrow?" Melissa asked.

"I'll have to be here for the finale," Max admitted. "Otherwise, one day was enough."

"It was great," his daughter said. "I liked the racing best. What about you, Griffin?"

The little boy yawned before speaking. "I liked the part at the end where the skunk went off."

Max would have liked the part where he took Nancy aside and capped a wonderful day by asking her to marry him. Right now, in his pocket, the ring hung as heavy as a stone.

This should have been the happiest day of his life. What a fool he'd been!

13

THAT NIGHT, Nancy kept waking up and wondering how she was going to win Max's trust again. About 3:00 a.m., she rose and went to the computer.

A few minutes later, she was done. She'd have to present the results to him in the morning and hope for the best.

Breakfast was a noisy if sleepy-eyed affair. Immediately afterwards, Bill, Beth and Kirstin left for Dallas, with hugs all around. Then Melissa and Griffin headed for the barn to play with their kittens.

Nancy was washing the breakfast dishes when Max came in. "I booked you a flight out of San Angelo this afternoon," he said.

"Please let me speak." She held up a wet, soapy hand to stop his refusal. "Max, I come from a blue-collar family and helped raise my six younger siblings. All my life, I felt I had something to prove to myself."

"I guess you proved something, all right," he said.

She ignored the interruption. "All through school, and even after I earned my Ph.D., I felt like a pretender. Maybe that's why the role came so easily to me this summer. Well, I'm tired of trying to be something I'm not."

"You're not a psychologist?" he asked. "Or just not a very good one?"

"I'm good enough, I suppose, or De Lune University wouldn't have hired me," Nancy said. "But I'm far from brilliant. I just finished one grant project and I can't come up with a good proposal for another one. I must have been kidding myself to think I had something important to offer to my chosen field."

"How is this supposed to make up for what you did this summer?" Max asked.

She rinsed a pot and put it in the drainer. "It doesn't. I'm just, I don't know, giving you some background about me. There's something else I want to give you, too."

She patted her hands dry on her apron and, from her pocket, handed him a CD-ROM and a printout. "These are the only copies of my article," she said. "I wiped it off my hard drive. I guess you'll have to take my word for that. Read it and destroy it if you like."

He accepted the offering gingerly. "I suppose I have to be grateful I'm not going to be ridiculed coast to coast."

"I wasn't ridiculing you," Nancy said. "I would never do that. Please, Max. I don't want us to part this way."

If only he would make eye contact. If only he would extend the tiniest ray of hope.

"Now that we've put the skunk problem in perspective, I figure I can find a local nanny willing to live here," Max said. "Someone over fifty would suit me fine."

He walked out of the kitchen, still holding the article and the CD. And a grudge.

As THE TIME approached to leave for the airport, Nancy said goodbye to JoAnne in the vegetable garden. She was even going to miss the tomatoes and zucchini, she reflected.

"Like I expected, you're good for Max," said her new friend, picking tomatoes and putting them in a basket. Tall corn plants screened the late-morning sun. "He's an idiot."

"He has a right to be angry," Nancy said.

"Maybe if Lilia hadn't opened those old wounds, he'd have listened to reason." JoAnne shrugged. "Who can understand men?"

"Speaking of men, how are you and Luis getting along?"

Her friend grinned. "I guess you know he moved back in from the bunkhouse. It's a big relief, let me tell you."

"I'm so glad."

"We have you to thank," her friend said. "You know what? I'm even starting to like the durn trebuchet. One of these days, I might try lobbing a few bowling balls myself."

"E-mail me and tell me all about it," Nancy said.

A short time later, parting from the children proved much harder. They both cried and so did she. Max made himself scarce.

"Is it because of Mommy?" Griffin asked.

"No. Your daddy and I just think it's for the best," Nancy said.

"I'll bet you had a fight, like Uncle Bill and Aunt

Beth," said Melissa. "You could make up. You could see a counselor."

Nancy winced.

The prospect of a long truck ride with Max was too painful to endure. When Luis's nephew said he planned to drive into San Angelo to see his girlfriend and could drop Nancy at the airport, she accepted.

She said goodbye to Max outside, with her suitcases already in the car. Standing with his cowboy hat casting a deep shadow across his face, he looked immensely tall.

"I'm sorry." She could think of nothing to add.

"Have a safe flight." That was it. No hint of warmth.

Nancy's heart squeezed as she got into the car, and she peered out the passenger window as they drove away. She wanted to memorize every detail of the sprawling ranch house, the land stretching to the horizon, even the angle of the sunlight.

The children waved, and she waved back. Standing with his arms around Melissa and Griffin, Max didn't look up.

Nancy tried not to cry until they were all out of sight. *Goodbye, Max. I love you.*

HE DROVE THE KIDS to the Witherspoons' ranch, where they'd been invited to spend the day. Then Max went home to catch up on work he'd postponed because of the festival.

While he was cleaning some equipment, it occurred to him that he'd forgotten to tell Nancy how Beth had left the gas on. They ought to make sure to check the burners any time they left the house.

Of course, there was no point in telling her now, he reminded himself.

In the middle of training a yearling horse in the corral, Max decided that he and Nancy ought to make a ceremony out of restoring the dining room to its original state. Griffin and Melissa needed a treat to help them adjust to their cousin's departure.

He'd have to do it himself, he remembered.

Later, Max was eating a plain ham sandwich to which he'd forgotten to add tomato and lettuce when he finally admitted that he almost wished he hadn't gone into her room and stumbled across the letter.

Would she really have said yes? Would she really have stayed?

He checked his watch. By now, her plane had left Texas. She was long gone, his Nancy not-a-medical-doctor Verano.

Only she wasn't his. He might as well get used to that fact.

THE DAY AFTER she returned home, Nancy weeded her landlady's herb patch because she missed her garden. The effort fell short of success, however, because she dug up some tarragon that looked like a weed.

Also, she had dirt all over her face when Professor Hugh Bemling dropped by. He seemed startled to see her. "I was bringing some misdelivered mail to Dean Pipp," he said.

"How are you?" Nancy hoped he wasn't going to burst into song. On the other hand, her bruised spirits could use a little puppylike adoration right now.

"Fine, fine." He edged toward the mailbox, where

he stuck a letter that must have gone to her old office at the English department. "Blair's fine, too."

"Who's Blair?"

"A new teaching assistant in comparative literature," he said. "'With her long raven hair, a man dreams of Blair.'"

"Does she like your poetry?" Nancy asked.

"She'll love it when she hears it," Hugh said.

Everything, she mused as he sauntered away, was too small here. Hugh was too small. Her apartment was too small. The future was too small.

During the next three weeks, Hayley called several times, but was too busy on the set to drive out from L.A., to Nancy's relief. She hadn't told her sister the whole story and didn't intend to. Not until the pain subsided, anyway.

As the start of school approached, one of Nancy's colleagues asked her to critique a grant proposal, which she did. He was grateful for her insights. She, too, was grateful for an insight she gained.

Reading his document, she understood why she hadn't been able to come up with a new project. The dry terminology bored her, and so did the prospect of dealing with test subjects.

She was tired of being an observer. She yearned to go back to wading hip-deep through life's messy, unquantifiable bustle.

In short, she was ready for a new phase in her life. If only she'd realized that before she lied her way into Max's household, she might not have broken both their hearts.

The next morning, she awoke to the sound of knocking on her door. Her visitor must have been trying to get her attention for some time, which would explain why she'd been dreaming about a woodpecker.

"Nancy!" called an achingly familiar male voice. "I know it's early, but I've got to talk to you."

Her heart performed a rapid spin. She was so taken aback that, for a moment, she couldn't move.

By the time she got up and pulled on her robe, footsteps were retreating down the steps. As Nancy flew onto the landing, she heard Max say, "Pardon me, ma'am. Why are you taking my picture?"

Oh, no. Not Mrs. Zimpelman again!

Below, Nancy caught sight of him, politely but firmly confronting her neighbor. Mrs. Zimpelman was snapping his photo as if Elvis Presley had come to call. "You're so handsome!" said the elderly woman. "I think your young lady's caught a winner this time."

She wasn't exaggerating, Nancy thought, staring at the tall Texan. A breeze ruffled his shaggy hair and sunlight brought out the amber gleam in his eyes. She'd never seen a man dominate an entire street or indeed an entire town the way Max did, just by standing there.

He spotted her on the landing. "There she is. Wearing her favorite bathrobe, I see."

Heat rushed to Nancy's cheeks. She hadn't noticed she was putting on the robe with the bikini figure. "Sorry. Why don't you come inside? Mrs. Zimpelman, this is a private matter."

"Why doesn't a sexy young man like this ever come serenading me, that's what I'd like to know," said her neighbor.

"I only sing songs about skunks," Max said. "That's not very romantic."

"I've always believed the right man can make almost anything romantic," replied Mrs. Zimpelman. "Although I'm not so sure about skunks."

Light-headed from the implications of Max's arrival, Nancy led him inside. The apartment looked even more cramped than usual in contrast to his tall frame.

"Cozy," he remarked, gazing around.

"How are Melissa and Griffin?"

"Lonely." Max cleared his throat. "I read your article."

Nancy could hardly breathe. "Well?"

"Anybody would think you were in love with that cowboy you were writing about," he said.

"I am."

"I kind of figured that out."

So he'd come rushing west to see her. Well, not exactly rushing. It had taken him three weeks, but Nancy didn't care.

There was one more matter she had to come clean about, however. "Max, I—another thing—uh…"

"You mean there's more?" he asked. "A secret husband? You've taken a job in Alaska?"

"No." Nancy wrapped her arms around herself. "I can't have children."

He didn't reply. Apparently he was waiting for some explanation.

"When I was a teenager, I had to have surgery," Nancy explained. "It made me infertile. I know you want a big family…" She let the words trail off.

"I only said that because I thought you might get

pregnant,'' Max explained. ''Two kids is plenty for me. No, that isn't the real problem.''

Her hopes, which had begun swooping up, shot downward. ''There's a real problem? Is it Lilia?''

''She complicated my life for a while.'' He took a seat on the couch. ''She made noises about seeking custody. Finally she got the message that I wasn't going to take her back, so she hooked up with one of Dale's friends she'd met at the festival.''

Nancy remembered the man who'd walked into a fire hydrant. ''I hope they'll be happy.''

''Me, too,'' said Max. ''That way she won't come back.''

''How's Dale?'' she couldn't resist asking.

''Breaking hibernation at last,'' he said. ''Considerably subdued after his adventure, I'm pleased to say. You can still smell him if you stand downwind.''

''What about the boat?''

''The raffle winners were a couple from Austin, which has a terrific lake for sailing. They were very happy.''

In the ensuing silence, Nancy perched nervously on a chair. Why didn't he just come out and—

''I wanted to talk about your article,'' Max said.

''That's why you came?''

''Partly,'' he said. ''You told me you don't have much to contribute to your profession. I think you're wrong.''

''You're concerned about my career?'' she asked, puzzled.

''It's important,'' he said. ''You may not think so now, but it is.''

This conversation made no sense, Nancy thought.

Instead of coming to tell her he loved her, Max wanted to encourage her professional aspirations?

"You see to the heart of things, and you care about people." Judging by his calm tone, he was clueless about her agitated state of mind. "I was wrong to accuse you of treating us like lab rats."

She hoped he wasn't being sarcastic. "Thank you."

"I found something on the Internet that might interest you."

Nothing on the Internet could possibly interest me as much as you do. "Oh?"

"There's a new online university based in Phoenix," Max said. "It's accredited, and seeking full-time professors with top-notch credentials."

"I'm not sure I follow you."

"The professors need to be able to reach out to people from every walk of life. Nontraditional students," Max said. "I took the liberty of submitting your article as a sample of your work, along with your résumé. It was on the CD-ROM."

"You submitted my résumé?" Nancy wondered if she'd truly awakened a few minutes ago, or if everything beginning with the serenade had been part of a bizarrely realistic dream.

"I did a little pretending of my own," Max continued blithely. "I applied for a job, pretending to be you. They got right back to me and said you had the righ qualifications, no interview necessary. Congratulations." He handed over a printed e-mail, offering Nancy a teaching job.

The salary wasn't as high as she received at De Lune. There was no requirement for publishing or research, however, and she could teach the courses from her home computer.

"We can convert your bedroom into an office," Max went on.

"Where would I sleep?"

"With me, of course," he said. "Wouldn't you prefer it that way?"

"I think you left something out." Nancy had been listening closely. She was sure she hadn't missed a mention of marriage.

"I did?" His brow puckering, Max patted his shirt pocket. "What's that still doing in there?"

"Excuse me?"

From the pocket, he removed a gold ring sparkling with tiny diamonds. "I thought I gave this to you."

"I'm sure you didn't," Nancy said.

"I had this all planned out," Max answered. "Are you sure I didn't hand it to you right after I mentioned that I could tell from your article that you're in love with me?"

"The evidence is against you."

"So it is." His mouth quirked. "You must find this whole conversation very strange."

"But interesting," Nancy said.

Max leaned forward, elbows on knees, the ring glimmering between his thumb and forefinger. "When I gave this to you, I meant to explain that after years of mistrusting women, I was quick to read betrayal into your actions."

"Does that mean you forgive me?"

"Looking back, I can see that although your judgment was bad, you didn't betray me," he said, apparently sticking to his planned speech. "You know, all my life I've fought to save the ranch for my family. After you left, I discovered that the center of my family is you.''

"Are we getting to the ring part?" Nancy asked hopefully.

He took her left hand and slipped the gold circle on the third finger. "It's a little loose."

"Max!"

"What?" Understanding dawned. "Oh! Nancy, will you marry me?"

"Does that mean I get to live on the ranch?" she teased. After the way he'd dawdled in popping the question, he deserved to wait for his answer.

"I'm sorry that Internet U isn't all fancy like a real campus," he said. "It'll mean turning down the burner on your career, but at least the fire would stay lit. That reminds me, I meant to tell you that Beth left on a gas jet the day of the festival and nearly blew up the house."

"I don't think I've ever heard you string so many words together at one time," Nancy said.

"I'm a little nervous," Max admitted. "I'd like it if you said yes now."

"Yes."

"Is that, yes, you'll marry me?"

Tears pricked her eyes. "It is."

He pulled her onto his lap. "Did I mention that I love you?"

"If you did, you can say it again," she said. "Over and over."

Max kissed her for a long time. It felt wonderful. Almost as good was the fact that inhaling his scent transported her instantly back to Texas.

"I adore you," he said when they finally came up for air. "I'm miserable without you. I'd eat eggplant and bean sprout sandwiches for every meal if that was the only way to get you back again."

"You would?"

"I said if it was the *only* way."

Her future, which had narrowed as she looked ahead to years of pursuing tenure and grants, expanded joyously to include children and the garden and, above all, this amazing man. So what if Internet U didn't offer a fast track to professional recognition? Nancy was in no hurry, not when every day was going to be filled with happiness.

"I have to warn you," she said, "that I won't be the paid housekeeper anymore. I'll expect you to pitch in."

"I've already started taking cooking lessons from JoAnne," he said.

"You have?"

"She gave me no choice," Max said. "I tried to press her into service again and she said she'd teach me how to do it myself, or else I could starve."

"How's it going?"

"The kids help me nearly every night," he said. "Griffin's pretty good at spreading peanut butter on the celery, and my daughter learned how to make brownies. I think Kirstin taught her."

"Good for them." Nancy cuddled against him. "I can't wait to get home. It sounds like heaven."

"Oh, one other thing. The kids want a pet skunk so badly, I think we ought to get them one for Christmas."

"Almost heaven," she corrected herself, with a smile.

Shotgun
Nanny

Nancy
Warren

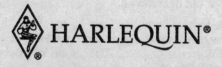

HARLEQUIN®

TORONTO • NEW YORK • LONDON
AMSTERDAM • PARIS • SYDNEY • HAMBURG
STOCKHOLM • ATHENS • TOKYO • MILAN • MADRID
PRAGUE • WARSAW • BUDAPEST • AUCKLAND

Dear Reader,

Don't you love those stories where opposites attract? I do. And when I set out to write *Shotgun Nanny*, I really went to town. I started with a free-spirited birthday party clown, hooked her up with an overprotective security expert (who's also an ex Royal Canadian Mountie), a young girl and a special dog, and the book just took off.

Kitsu, the failed police dog, is very loosely based on my own dog, Penny. Penny is a keeshond, not a German shepherd, but she sure loves her cookies and junk food. And she has one other trait in common with Kitsu, which I'm sure you'll figure out when you read the book.

One of the real joys of writing romance is being able to make everything work out right in the end. In the world of romance, women rule and, though they may struggle, they always get their heart's desire. I think this is true in our real lives, too. I believe in dreams and the ability of each of us to achieve our personal dreams.

My dream for a long time was to be a novelist. I love writing for Harlequin, and I've been privileged to work in three of my favorite lines: Temptation, Duets and Blaze!

I always try to mix sex and humor in my books— to me that's a winning combination. If you enjoy *Shotgun Nanny,* please watch for my next Blaze novel, *Whisper,* out next month.

I'd love to hear from you. Drop by my Web site at www.nancywarren.net or drop me a line at Nancy Warren, P.O. Box 37035, North Vancouver, B.C. V7N 4M0, Canada.

Happy reading,

Nancy Warren

This book is dedicated to the real Uncle Mark—
my brother Mark Weatherley,
and to my sister Sally, my very first fan.
With love and thanks.

1

HELP, Annie Mathers scrawled in big black letters. Then she outlined the word in ballpoint until she'd almost carved through to the picture side of the postcard.

She paused, took a sip of cappuccino, then tapped the pen on the blank space on the postcard. Underneath *Help* she wrote *Matter of life and death! Follow me.* She underlined *Follow me* with a dramatic slash of black ink. And, just like that, started to feel better. Action and movement always made her feel better, and as soon as her best friend, Bobbie, received the card, they'd be on their way.

She flipped the card over and discovered the aerial view of Vancouver harbor was marred by the thick ridges her pen had carved. With a sigh, she tossed the card onto the table—Bobbie would think she'd completely lost it. Which might be true.

She picked up a second postcard and made a more conventional start.

Dear Bobbie. Follow me to Vancouver. I need a vacation! Fly up TODAY. Matter of life and death—Gertrude's.

And if that doesn't get you, nothing will, she thought smugly. Bobbie loved Gertrude—she'd fly up from LA to save her, or at least save her alter ego's sanity. Of course she would. Gertrude had paid the rent several times when Annie and Bobbie had been financially strapped roomies.

Annie glanced up from the table and let the sun settle on her face. Sailboats bobbed beside the dock, rows of white hulls gleaming proudly in the early summer sun. She glimpsed a couple of kayaks scooting behind the brightly colored Aquabus. A soft breeze blowing across False Creek carried the briny ocean smells to mix with the restaurant scents—garlic, freshly cooked seafood, coffee.

The tables on the dock-cum-bistro were filling up with tired tourists and after-work yuppies. Much as she would have enjoyed swapping her empty coffee mug for a glass of wine and some of that mouthwatering seafood for dinner, she really needed to save her cash for the authentic sushi, Szechwan and Thai food she'd be eating once she and Bobbie got to Asia.

Annie signed the card with a flourish, addressed it, licked a stamp and pressed it to the corner of the postcard. She jumped up, obeying an overwhelming impulse to get Bobbie's postcard in the mail, as though she could conjure up her best friend just by popping the card in a bright red mailbox.

She reached down and deposited the backpacking guide to the Orient she'd been reading in her leather backpack, then dropped a tip on the table. Rising and turning in one motion, she collided with a brick wall. At least it felt like one. It was covered in a jean shirt and breathing but was still as hard and immovable as a brick wall.

She glanced into a pair of cool blue eyes set in a face of stone. He looked like a cop or private eye from one of the old movies she loved so much.

Maybe that was why this complete stranger struck her for an instant with an intense sense of familiarity. Even her body acted as if it knew him intimately. A sizzle of awareness zinged through her as she stared at the hard-planed cheeks, square jaw and a nose that would have been classical had it not sported the telltale crookedness of a break sometime in its owner's past. For an insane second, she wanted to lean into him as though he were a safe refuge.

Whoa! She'd definitely been working too hard. She must be nuts to go all gooey over a stranger. A big, handsome, tough-guy stranger who reminded her of her fantasy men—but she knew better. That kind of man only existed in black and white, on a movie screen.

Unpeeling herself from his warmth, she mumbled, "sorry," with a faint smile and made her way as quickly as she could away from the crowded patio.

MARK SAUNDERS'S eyes followed the woman, her spicy fragrance still in his nostrils. She was dressed in some kind of flowing thing in every color of the rainbow, and as she walked a shaft of sunlight shimmered through the fabric, outlining long slender legs and nicely rounded hips. Not even a superhero's X-ray vision could have caught a better view of the little triangle of fabric that seemed to be her entire contingent of underwear.

On her head was a floppy hat—maybe to keep off

the sun, but more likely she was one of those New Age types who always wore floppy hats.

Cute, though. And there'd been a nanosecond when she'd seemed more than cute, when he'd felt an electrifying sense of connection with her. He'd had to quash a bizarre impulse to invite her to join him in a drink.

But he was a sensible man. In his experience, spontaneous acts always led to trouble. Still, it didn't hurt to look. He smiled and turned to take the newly vacated table.

And froze.

Help, he read. *Matter of life and death. Follow me.*

The woman was sending him a desperate message, and he'd wasted valuable time watching her rear end.

Damn it to hell.

All his training slammed a lid on his emotions. Adrenaline pumped through his system, but he acted casual. Palming the card, he scanned the crowd to see who might be watching or following the girl. In the few seconds he'd wasted, she had disappeared, and so, it seemed, had anyone who was tracking her.

If only he'd acted on his impulse and invited her to sit down with him, he could have protected her. Damn it, maybe when she'd leaned into him and her green eyes had sparkled into his, she'd been trying to send him a silent message. Which he'd misinterpreted—totally.

Mark reached automatically for the radio at his side and groaned. No radio. He wasn't a cop anymore. When was he going to stop acting like one? He was on his own, no backup.

On the road he paused, eyes narrowed against the sun, allowing his gaze to scan the vicinity. Granville Island on a sunny day in June. What could be worse? Crowds of tourists ambled along enjoying the sunshine, browsing the shops, snapping pictures.

While one lone, sweet-looking woman was facing a life-and-death dilemma.

A hundred women looked like the one he'd bumped into, but his trained eye soon picked her out. It was as though a camera in his head had clicked a picture—he could have given her height, weight, eye and hair color and a reasonable description of her clothing to anyone who asked.

She strode forward with purpose, unlike most of the strolling crowd, and her head moved from side to side as though searching for someone.

Mark watched the people behind her. Many moved in the same direction. It was impossible to tell who might be following her. He pushed away from the protective wall and started walking, careful not to follow too closely or watch her too intently. Instead, he did his best to act like a guy enjoying the island, maybe on his way to buy fresh vegetables at the market.

He tried to formulate a plan as he walked. He had no sidearm, no weapon of any kind except his fists. No backup unless he passed a phone, and even then he didn't know if he'd dare stop—he might lose her in the crowd. If they passed anywhere near his vehicle, he had a whole arsenal of security stuff, but she was headed in the opposite direction. He'd even left his cell phone in the car. Whenever he met his buddy

Brodie he came unarmed, just to save himself the grief. In future, he'd take the teasing. But for now, he had to make do with what he had. Nothing.

His mind rapidly sorted possibilities. Drugs? Prostitution? Stalker? She looked pretty Haight-Ashbury, but his instincts told him it wasn't drugs—at least she didn't show any of the signs of a user or a pusher.

Prostitution? She appeared too fresh. He remembered the way she'd smiled at him, her green eyes frank and as assessing in their way as his were trained to be. In fact, her face was as clear in his mind as in that time-stalled moment they'd stood staring at each other.

Her lips, open in surprise, had been soft and pink without the aid of cosmetics. She had a pert little nose with a cinnamon sprinkle of freckles across the bridge and high cheekbones. Under the hat bits of reddish-brown hair stuck out helter-skelter, and there were three silver earrings piercing her left ear, four crawling up the right. But it was her eyes that had captured his fancy. Uptilted and sparkling with life, they'd made him feel momentarily reckless. And he was never reckless.

Had she made someone else feel reckless? A stalker? That was the most likely possibility. She was a good-looking woman, and he'd seen some pretty scary guys go after women who'd dumped them. But, if there was a stalker following the woman, he hadn't shown himself yet.

Abruptly she turned down a side street, speeding like a horse anxious to get to its stable. He picked up his pace, breaking into a run, knocking shoulders and dodging pedestrians as he raced to protect her. One more possibility occurred to him as he rushed forward—this could be a trap.

He halted, confused, as he rounded the corner and scanned the narrow street.

It was quiet, lined on both sides by little arty workshops and small businesses. But she didn't head for one of the doors. Her destination was the mailbox at the dead end of the alley.

She appeared to be alone.

Mark hated blind alleys. Sweat broke out on his brow as he glanced over his shoulder, then perused the surrounding area, focusing especially on the doors and windows. He detected no suspicious movement. It was just a quiet sun-filled alley.

As he watched the woman deposit something in the mailbox, his mind clicked through new possibilities. A ransom? With a deep breath, he plunged into the lane, senses super alert.

She turned from the mailbox and paused as Mark approached her, a half-smile on her face and a gleam of recognition sparkling in those eyes.

"Are you making a drop?" he whispered, putting as much of his body in front of her as possible in an instinctive protective gesture.

She moved closer, and once more that spicy fragrance teased his senses. In a heavy Bronx accent she whispered, "Let's hope Duey don't see us together!" She rolled emotion-filled eyes, her whole body expressing fear and dread.

He was keyed up for action, hating the vulnerability of this lane and not knowing who or where the enemy was. "Who's Duey?"

She laughed, a soft, rich sound that reverberated against his chest. He felt a bead of sweat trickle down his temple. If she went hysterical on him it could place both of them in greater danger.

"No, no," she said, chiding. "Your line is, 'Let's shake the heat, sister, and blow.'"

His line? What? "Ma'am, I can't help you if you don't tell me what this is about."

She took a step backward and glanced around, amusement changing to wariness. "You tell *me* what it's about!"

Mark also backed up a step, putting more distance between them and forcing a deep breath into his lungs. How had he missed the signs? The woman was a lunatic. He tried to recall if a full moon was expected tonight, but couldn't. He remembered how they'd all dreaded a full moon on the force. It was always a busy couple of days.

Keeping his voice calm, he spoke slowly. "Where do you live?"

Her brows rose, the green eyes dancing once more. "If that's your idea of a pickup routine, you were doing better before. Old movies may be corny, but they have the best lines."

She made to walk past him.

Old movies? Mark stepped in front of her, confusion turning to frustration. "Don't play games with me. I'm an RCMP officer—uh, ex-officer. I saw you drop something in that mailbox." Realizing he sounded accusing, he softened his tone. "I'm here to help."

She glanced at the mailbox, then at him, then raised her eyebrows. "Before you arrest me for mail fraud, Mr. Ex, I put a stamp on that postcard."

"A postcard like this?" He pulled the card out of his back pocket and held it in front of her nose.

She stared at the postcard, raised her gaze to his face, looked at the message she'd written, bit her lip. "You followed me because of that?" Her voice wavered.

Damn if he could make head or tail of this crazy woman. Was she in danger or wasn't she? "Yes!"

"Oh, I'm *so* sorry—" It was as far as she got. She gave a snort and burst into gales of laughter that seemed to go on forever, echoing off the buildings. "Ow, my stomach hurts," she gasped after an eon of one-sided hilarity. "Bobbie is just going to die!"

He was getting the feeling that this woman talked about death and dying in a different way than he did. "Is Bobbie the one in a life-and-death situation?"

"What? Oh. No. That's Gertrude. She isn't really dying. She's just tired from working too hard."

"So, you personally are not in any kind of danger at all?" He wanted to be absolutely clear on this point.

She touched the tip of her tongue to her upper lip and glanced at him from under her lashes. "Not unless you arrest me for writing postcards in bad taste. What would that charge be, anyway?"

She was so cute he couldn't stay mad at her, especially now he knew she wasn't in danger and his heart rate had slowed to normal. He rubbed his chin, thinking. "We could go with public mischief."

"Public mischief. Sounds serious. And the penalty would be…?"

He did his best to look stern. "They'd throw away the key."

Rich and earthy, her chuckle resonated in his chest. She started walking back the way they'd come, and he fell into step with her.

"I'm really sorry. I figured that postcard would get tossed. I never thought how it might look." Her voice wasn't the broad Bronx she'd first used. She must, he realized, have been mimicking some ancient movie he'd never seen. Her voice was softer, more West Coast. California, maybe.

"No harm done."

"You used to be a Mountie, huh?"

"Yes, ma'am."

"My grandmother just loved Nelson Eddy and Jeanette MacDonald. I grew up hearing them sing, 'When I'm calling you-oo-oo, will you answer too-oo-oo.'" She leaned into him and sang into his face, pursing her lips and puckering her eyebrows until she could have passed for an old-fashioned movie star.

She trilled the words in a high, clear soprano, and he was so caught up in the feel of her slight body leaning against him and the sweetness of her face that he forgot they'd rejoined the milling crowds. Until he heard a stranger's voice saying, "Yeah. You tell him, girl."

She broke away from Mark with a quick laugh. "Then there's the Musical Ride. I used to think the

Mounties was a singing group. Kind of like the Monkees only Canadian. And with horses.''

"That's us. Other cops get weapons training. We get voice lessons.''

"I learned the truth when I started watching a TV show about a Mountie. The guy was like a real cop, only in that awesome uniform. I just loved that red jacket and those killer jodhpur things. Ooh, and that hat was dead hip.''

"That is the RCMP dress uniform. No real officer would wear his dress uniform to work.''

Her face fell. She appeared so ludicrously disappointed he wished he hadn't told her. "But then they're just like any other cops.''

"Pretty much. Except for the singing.''

"Well. First you try and arrest me for mail fraud, now you destroy one of my cherished illusions about the Mounties. I'm just going to have to say goodbye.'' She smiled and extended her hand. "My car's over there.''

He gazed at her hand for a moment. Long, slender white fingers, a couple of silver rings, although nothing on the wedding ring finger, green nail polish. He grasped the hand in his, not at all eager to let it go, wishing he could prolong their acquaintance.

Briefly, he considered asking her out, then remembered what a total fool he'd made of himself. She'd probably laugh in his face if he asked her for a date. Besides, his life was complicated enough these days.

She shook his hand purposefully. Then turned and walked toward a parking lot jammed with cars, her skirt swaying and drifting.

He glanced at his watch and cursed silently. He'd forgotten all about Brodie. Reluctantly, he turned toward the restaurant.

"Hey!" the female voice stopped him, and eagerly he swung around.

A hand shielded her eyes against the sun as she called, "Thanks for trying to rescue me."

"I—" If it were this time last year he'd take a chance and ask her out, even if she did laugh in his face. But he had new responsibilities. Even if the lady was willing, he couldn't get involved with a woman right now. Not with Emily to worry about.

The woman was standing not twenty feet away, waiting for him to finish what he had to say, a slight breeze teasing him as it molded the flimsy dress fabric to her body then puffed it away again. So strong was the urge to close the distance between them that he felt like he was a magnet and she was true north.

"I, uh… Drive safely." He raised a hand in farewell then turned and walked the way he'd come. All the way to the restaurant where the bizarre situation had started.

And there was Brodie, sitting at a table, already halfway through a beer, his sunglasses reflecting the busy scene.

Beneath the reflective lenses, the mustache spread and tilted in a smile. "Did you get your man?" Brodie lifted the beer in Mark's direction.

Mark chuckled. His old buddies on the force liked to tease him that he was like the cartoon Mountie who always saved the damsel in distress and always got his man. He was zero for two today. He hadn't got his man, and he sure as hell hadn't helped the damsel in distress. Good thing he'd handed in his badge last year. "Not today."

"First time since I've known you, you're late."

Mark gestured to a waitress, who was unloading a tray at a nearby table, and sat across from his friend. He needed a beer.

"So," Brodie pressed, "What's up?"

Mark pulled the postcard out of his pocket and pushed it across the table.

Brodie leaned forward to read the card and then went absolutely still. He stared at the words for a few moments, then turned the postcard over and back again before glancing at Mark. "What's going on?" he asked.

Mark blew out his breath in a big huff. "I just made a complete jackass of myself." The waitress approached, and he ordered a beer.

"You ready for another one?" The perky redhead with the Australian accent gestured to Brodie's half-empty glass.

"Yeah," he replied, relaxing once more in his chair.

"Right." She smiled at Brodie, and Mark knew his old buddy hadn't wasted any time missing him. He'd been flirting with the waitress.

"Got her phone number yet?"

"I'm working on it." He pointed to the postcard. "You gonna tell me what's happening? Or do I read about it in tomorrow's paper?"

Mark told him, reliving the entire incident as he did so.

The sun was gleaming off Brodie's white teeth when Mark finished. He could see the physical effort it cost his old friend not to laugh aloud.

"Let it out, man," he said testily.

Brodie laughed, long and rich, stopping once to wipe streaming eyes. "Hey, I'm sorry, Mark. I know how you must feel, but God, that's the funniest thing I've heard all week."

"I just don't get it. Why would a woman write a postcard to a friend and put help and life and death and stuff on it? Whatever happened to weather great, wish you were here?"

"When you figure out what women mean, you let me know. They got no perspective. They break a fingernail and it's like the end of the world. Then they phone you and say, all casual, 'Hi, honey, can you fix my car this weekend?' You ask her what's wrong with it and she says, 'Oh, honey, I don't know. I think the engine fell out.'"

Mark grunted agreement.

"I'll never figure women." Brodie sighed. "But it's fun trying."

"I'll drink to that." Mark picked up the frosty mug that had been delivered and drank deeply.

"What did she look like?" Brodie asked.

Mark closed his eyes for a moment, then opened them. "Caucasian, five-seven, about one-thirty, eyes green, hair brown, age..." He wrinkled his brow. This was always the toughest one. "I'd say twenty-five to thirty."

"Looker?"

"Oh, yeah." He snorted; he was beginning to see

the funny side himself. "She must think I'm one terrific guy...."

"You acted just like you were trained to. If she'd been in trouble you might have saved her life."

"You're not helping."

"Maybe this'll help. Two tickets to the Grizzlies game Saturday." He pulled tickets from his shirt pocket and waved them in front of Mark's nose. "Basketball's not like women. There are rules in basketball. The same ones for both teams. And there's no talking about it."

Mark grinned. "You're still steamed at Shelley, huh?"

"Don't get me started. She wanted me to see a relationship counselor. Says I'm shallow and can't commit to one woman. This from a gal who makes her living taking her clothes off in front of hundreds of men."

Saturday afternoon at a basketball game. He didn't even let himself think about how much he wanted to go. He shook his head. "I can't. Emily."

"Can't your black-belt-in-judo nanny watch her?"

"It's her birthday party. The first one since..."

"Sure." Brodie stuck the tickets in his pocket. "Did you call that clown friend of Shelley's?"

"She's an ex-stripper. That's how Shelley knew her."

Brodie's eyes widened. "No. How'd you find out?"

"Standard background check."

His friend choked on his beer. "You did a security check on a birthday-party clown?"

"Good thing, too. Another family recommended a clown who checked out. I got her instead."

"Her? Is she good-looking?"

Mark rolled his eyes. "Did you ever see a good-looking clown?"

"No. But then I didn't catch the stripping clown. That could be interesting. Do you still have her number?"

"I don't know where you find the energy."

Brodie shrugged. "My motto is never pass on a pretty woman. You don't know when the next one's coming along."

Immediately, an image of the woman with the postcard rose in Mark's mind. Damn. He hadn't even asked her name. "I wish you'd told me that an hour ago."

"What? The life-and-death babe?"

"Yeah."

His buddy shook his head. "Uh-uh. You made a total ass of yourself in front of that one. My other motto is, if you fall flat on your face in front of a pretty woman, stay facedown until she's long gone. The good news about Ms. Life and Death is, you'll never see her again!"

2

ANNIE TUCKED a stray purple and yellow curl behind her ear, but it promptly boinged out to poke into her ear canal where it would tickle every time she moved. She grimaced with annoyance in the rearview mirror, making her huge red smile look like a burst sausage.

The hottest day of the year, and she was stuck in the tiniest car ever invented—you couldn't fit air-conditioning in it even if you could afford it—and the biggest wig. "Gertrude, honey," she told her clown reflection, "we need a vacation."

The little car crawled up the hill to an address high on the slopes of North Vancouver, just as she'd been told. Told over the phone, which was standard procedure when she took a clown booking for a birthday party, then told again in a follow-up letter containing detailed instructions on how to get to the house where the party was to be held and how to gain entry.

Gain entry? Annie read that part again. More than a simple knock on the door was required. First there was a key code she would have to punch into a security gate to get past the fence. This changed daily, the letter informed her. So they thought she might be a part-time clown, part-time jewel thief?

Okay, ahead of her the gate appeared. She drew

her little Smurf-blue putt-mobile up to an alcove that looked like a banking machine. She pushed in her number, waited a moment, and the gates swung open reluctantly.

After all the rigmarole, Annie expected a castle with a moat, at least, but the house was a family-size, modern-looking stone-and-cedar affair. Hardly looked like the Pentagon.

As the gates closed behind her, she started to get a claustrophobic feeling. For a second, she wished she'd turned back when she'd had the chance. The curse of an active imagination and a love of old movies was that she found herself picturing ridiculous scenarios. She was Philip Marlowe approaching the mansion where the two-timing dame was holed up, cynically wondering if he'd get out with his life.

The truth was even more ridiculous. She was a grown woman in a clown costume, wearing polka dots the size of asteroids.

She parked at the end of the drive and exited her vehicle as instructed. She swapped her trainers for Gertrude's huge floppy clown shoes and shuffled to the door, the plastic rose in her lapel bobbing to hit her in the nose with each step. She dragged her battered suitcase past perfectly manicured lawns, sterile-looking flower beds containing mostly small evergreen bushes, and up three swept steps. By the time Annie got to the intercom buzzer at the front door she was feeling wilted—not only by the heat. She noticed a small camera in the corner above the door and poked her tongue out as far as she could.

The door opened.

And so did her mouth, tongue only partly retracted.

Cool blue eyes, stubborn jaw, brick-wall chest. The guy from Granville Island. *Of all the joints in all Vancouver, I have to walk into to this one....* She nearly giggled hysterically. Brick wall was looking her up and down, noting the suitcase in her hand. He glanced behind her warily and only then opened the door fully.

"Mark Saunders." He extended his hand.

He doesn't recognize me. Relief shot through Annie. She went into her clown routine in high gear, suddenly thankful for the hot wig, hot suit, hot shoes, heavy greasepaint.

Behind the human wall, a gaggle of young girls gathered, gawking at Annie.

"Gertrude Smell-So-Good," she shrieked in her Gertrude voice. If that voice was a little more manic than usual, she was the only one who'd know. "Here's my card!" She reached into her pocket and pulled out a big plastic rectangle with her name emblazoned on it. As Mark Saunders reached for it, she squeezed the side, and a jet of water shot into his face. The girls shrieked with laughter—they always did. Nothing made them laugh harder than watching their parents get made fools of.

"Ha, ha." He wiped his face with his hand, still standing in front of Annie, preventing her from entering. "That's not the name I was given," he whispered fiercely.

"It's my stage name," Annie whispered back. "Anne Parker is my real name."

He looked a little foolish and backed away. *Here*

we go again, Annie thought as she waddled past him and gave her attention to the girls.

"I hear there's a birthday going on," she shrieked. "Now don't tell me, let me use my magic divining wand to guess who the party girl is." She fumbled in her oversize pockets, watching while the girls snickered and kept glancing toward one slight, dark-haired girl who hung back, blushing. *Bingo.*

Annie pulled out a long plastic rod and made a performance of running it in the air around each of the girls before approaching the shy one. She squeezed the bottom of the rod when she waved her wand over the blushing girl's head, and it lit up and played "Happy Birthday."

Gertrude jumped in the air. "The birthday girl, and don't tell me your name, let me guess…." She waved the wand around, hitting it on her head to make the music stop, then pretended to listen to it. "Ethel!" she cried.

The girls shouted with laughter.

"Oh, dear, that's not it. Wait a minute." She banged the wand against her head again and listened. "Amelia!" she yelled.

Another storm of laughter.

Again she hit her head with the wand and listened. "Ah, Emily."

The girl blushed more rosily and nodded in a totally adorable way. All the girls were talking at once. Annie turned to ask Emily's father to lead her to where he wanted the performance.

She surprised him watching the shy girl with a smile on his face. It lit him up, that smile.

"Where do you want the show?" she whispered.

When he saw she was staring at him, the smile disappeared. "Right this way," he said, and led the way down the hall, through a space-age kitchen and into a family room complete with bookshelves, TV, fireplace and masses of balloons and streamers. The maple furniture had been pushed to the edges of the room to leave Annie space for her performance, which was a magic show where she pretended to botch most of the tricks.

She had a great audience. The girls loved it, and there was lots of loud participation. When she said she was going to pull a red scarf out of her hat and instead came up with an egg, she knew, when she turned around looking puzzled, most of the girls would yell at once that the red scarf was hanging down the back of her pants.

Annie was surprised that Emily's father stayed in the room to watch the show. She wondered briefly where the mother was. She'd assumed the guy on Granville Island was single, maybe because of the brief tingle of excitement she'd felt when she bumped into him. It was strange and oddly disappointing to think of him with a family.

From in front of the group, she watched both father and daughter. Emily smiled a lot, giggled occasionally but never laughed outright. The father watched his daughter more than the clown. Annie sensed both pride and something almost like sadness when he gazed at his child.

"Now, girls, for my grand finale, I'll need help from everyone." She was handing out balloons as she spoke. "I want each of you to blow up your balloon, nice and big, and tie on a piece of ribbon. Emily and I will be back in a moment with a big surprise."

Annie held out her hand to a stunned Emily, who glanced nervously at her father before accepting Annie's hand. In the other hand, Annie carried her suitcase. "We need to go somewhere where no one will see us change. A bedroom or bathroom?"

"We can go to my room."

"Great, lead on." Annie still held the girl's hand in her own. It was a small hand, fine-boned and fragile.

Emily's room was predictably pink and white. Neat as a pin, with a violin case in the corner. Annie hefted her suitcase onto the frilly bedspread and snapped it open. She pulled out a child's wig and one-size-fits-all child's clown suit. "Put these on as quick as you can," she called over her shoulder, tossing the things behind her. She grabbed false glasses and nose, then two silver and gold capes.

"What's the matter?"

Emily stood stalk still, holding the wig in trembling hands. "I can't!" she whispered.

"Can't what?" Annie asked.

"I'm scared. At school, when the teacher made me stand up and introduce myself…I threw up," she admitted with the air of one making a grievous confession.

Annie smiled. "Emily may fall apart in front of people," she said heartily, "but Guinevere Get-Out-of-Here isn't afraid of anything or anybody. You put that costume on and you will be a different person."

Annie took the orange-and-green wig out of the child's hands, pulled it over her ponytail and eased it over her ears while she talked. "See, each clown has her own personality. Once you're all dressed up, you look in the mirror, and it's not you anymore. It's Guinevere. And you become Guinevere. That's what's so great about being a clown."

The girl's big eyes were fixed on Annie's while she pulled on the clown suit and fastened the cape. Annie didn't usually bother with makeup for the birthday child, but she sensed Emily needed all the help she could get. She dug in the suitcase for her makeup kit and painted a huge red smile and a few thick black lashes around the child's eyes. "Now the fake nose and glasses," she said, holding them out.

The girl stood motionless for a moment, biting her lip, but finally reached out and put them on. Annie turned her to the mirror, and Emily gasped, then giggled.

"See, everybody laughs at a clown. When your friends see you they'll laugh so hard their sides will hurt. You and I, we'll take advantage of that. We'll make them do something real silly, then they'll laugh some more. Trust me, you won't be shy, you'll be Guinevere. Here." She handed Emily a pair of huge polka-dot gloves.

"AND NOW, my assistant, Guinevere Get-Out-of-Here." With a flourish, Annie ushered the shrinking Guinevere into the family room. Out of the corner of her eye she watched Mark Saunders lean forward and surreptitiously grab a wastepaper basket from the corner. He, too, must have heard the throwing-up story.

Guinevere waddled into the room and was greeted by an explosion of mirth. Under the cover of all that noise Annie whispered, "You see, you *are* Guinevere."

Emily was one of the quietest assistants she'd ever had, but she didn't throw up, so Annie figured this was probably good for her. She let her off the hook, and everybody clapped loudly as she took her seat on the floor with the others.

"Okay, girls, you've been a great audience. Happy birthday, Emily." Annie went into her standard exit routine where she pretended to trip so she could fall on the floor and somersault out the door.

She took a huge, theatrical step forward, brought her left foot to tangle with her right, launched herself into the air.

But she didn't hit the floor.

In a blur of motion and thudding impact, she found herself in the arms of Mark Saunders. Those solid arms she remembered so well were rescuing her again. "It's part of the act, you idiot," she whispered. "Now we'll both have to pretend to trip and somersault."

"But…" Inches from her face, his eyes looked perplexed.

"Now!" she ordered. She pushed out of his arms and tried to roll, but he got knocked off balance and fell half on top of her.

The pair of them rolled and struggled helplessly on the floor, a flailing mass of polka dots, jeans, purple hair and plaid shirt. The girls thought it was a great exit and laughed harder than ever.

"Welcome to show business," Annie panted, blinking her huge spiky eyelashes into the face inches above her own. He was so embarrassed his craggy face looked like somebody had carved a modern Rushmore out of red clay.

"I don't know how to do a somersault."

"Figures," she gasped. "If you could move off me I might one day be able to breathe again."

He scrambled to his feet and helped Annie rise. "Oh, well," she said brightly—he was a paying customer after all, "no harm done. Do you want to pay me now?"

He shot a quick glance toward the bedlam in the family room, and Annie almost laughed. He looked like a hunted animal with nowhere to hide. "Do you have to leave right away?" he asked.

"Well, the show is an hour—I'm already over my time."

"Please, I'll double your fee, triple it, if you'll stay and help me with the rest of the party."

She did feel a little sorry for him. Experience told her the hilarity was approaching the peeing-the-pants stage. As though he sensed her weakening, he added, "My housekeeper was supposed to help, but she had to go home sick yesterday."

Somehow, he was so serious and so desperate standing there, all muscles and he-man tough, totally outclassed by a few eight-year-olds, that she felt kind of sorry for him. "You did say triple?"

He smiled his relief. It was a great smile. That

smile did things to her that usually only happened with men like Humphrey Bogart and Gary Cooper. "I'll make the check out now. Pizza's in the oven." Then he disappeared down the hall so fast she thought she'd imagined him.

Oh, well. The triple check would help fund her vacation.

Which was postponed for three weeks. Bobbie had left a message on her service that she'd landed a couple of weeks of work on a TV series. Which was great for Bobbie's career, not so good for the clown with itchy feet. In her usual impulsive way, she'd already turned down every clown booking for the next two months. She might just have to go on ahead to Asia and let Bobbie catch up.

"Okay, girls!" She clapped her huge clown hands to get their attention. "Everybody visit the bathroom and wash your hands. Pizza's up."

Annie pulled off her huge gloves but left the rest of her costume on. Better not let Mark Saunders in on the secret of who she was or he might take back that triple check.

She took the pizza out of the oven. Pale green plates were neatly stacked on the counter—it looked like the family's best china. She was delighted he wasn't wasting precious trees by using fancy paper plates, but something about using the best china for his kid's birthday party brought a quiver of sadness.

He was trying so hard.

She liked to see a divorced dad pulling his weight. She just wished he'd lighten up a little.

They pranced into the dining room—a noisy, colorful glob of girlhood. Guinevere Get-Out-of-Here had changed into Emily and quietly trailed the noisy mob like a moth following the butterflies.

Annie had the girls seated around the table and loaded with pizza and pop before Mark returned. She pulled up a chair and joined the party, which soon became a joke competition. Knock-knock jokes and what-do-you-get-when-you-cross jokes. Her sides were hurting long before the pizza trays were empty.

MARK HEARD the boisterous mob hit the dining table and managed to botch yet another check so he could extend this refuge in his office. They seemed to be doing fine without him.

When guilt overcame him, he reluctantly crept toward the noise. He couldn't see the clown in the kitchen and felt a flicker of irritation. Shouldn't she be getting the cake ready?

He peeked into the dining room and felt his eyes bug out. There, at the end of the table, his very expensive clown was acting like one of the guests. In fact, she fit right in with a bunch of kids. She was doing an impression of Jim Carrey in *The Mask*. At least, he thought that's what those strange contortions were about. Her audience loved whatever it was, if the howls of glee were any indication.

He'd never seen an adult have so much fun—not that he was sure she qualified as an adult. Unable to help himself, he smiled. As he concentrated on her face, the expressive eyes flashing, it occurred to him that there was something familiar about her. It bothered him, the feeling that he knew her, it hovered in the air like a familiar fragrance he couldn't identify.

His gaze swung around the table and stopped at Emily, who was laughing as hard as anyone. He stood there watching her, feeling the painful love build in his throat. His shy little niece was acting as demented as the rest of the kids. Christy would have been so proud of her.

"I have a joke," Emily said in her quiet way.

The rest of the kids were being so noisy they probably hadn't heard her. He wanted to shut them all up and make them listen to Emily. But as she started to pinken and retreat into her shell, Annie laughingly called, "Quiet, quiet, Guinevere-Get-Out-of-Here has a joke." The smile she sent down the table to Emily suggested a shared secret. He watched the girl's spine straighten.

"Why didn't the boy take the school bus home?" she asked, reddening even more as everyone stared at her.

"I don't know. Why didn't the boy take the school bus home?" the clown repeated in the kind of theatrical buildup that would make the lamest punch line sound like a side splitter. She might be a complete nutter, but he appreciated the kindness behind the gesture.

"Because he knew his parents would make him give it back!" cried Emily.

Groans and laughter greeted her joke, and even after the attention switched away from Emily, the quiet glow in her face remained.

Mark backed into the kitchen and pulled the cake

out of the fridge. It was a clown cake to match the theme of the party. He'd even found a clown candle in the shape of an eight. This birthday party was just one in a line of hurdles he'd had to leap since Emily came to live with him. The whole thing was so baffling. What was in, what was out, what was too juvenile, what was too old. He wasn't even sure about the clown cake anymore—maybe he should have gone with the princess.

As he was getting cake plates out, the phone rang.

"I just wanted to wish Emily a happy birthday," Bea croaked. Her normally dour voice sounded like that of a witch. Then a coughing fit rattled down the line.

"How are you feeling, Bea?" he asked, hoping his nanny-housekeeper would have a miracle recovery by Monday. He was swamped with work. He needed someone to take care of the house and watch over Emily.

"It's pneumonia. The doctor says I have to stay in bed two or three weeks. I'm sorry, Mr. Saunders."

Damn. He didn't have time to do a security check on a temporary housekeeper. Not by Monday.

"You just rest, Bea. Don't worry about a thing," he said with false joviality. "I'll get Emily."

What the hell was he going to do? The timing couldn't have been worse. His company had been selected to handle security for a big Pacific Rim trading conference just two weeks away. He'd be working harder than ever.

He was barely into his first day of home life without Bea and he was only coping because he'd convinced the clown woman to stay. Not that she was much use in the kitchen, but she kept the girls occupied, and Emily clearly adored her.

The cake server clattered onto the stacked plates as inspiration hit him. Of course, the clown had already passed his rigorous security screening—and Emily adored her. He peeked around the doorway into the dining room. The clown's huge smile was smudging. She'd left her pizza crusts on her plate—she was as bad as the girls. Still, it was only temporary.

She wasn't the woman he would have chosen, but the woman in the purple and yellow wig was about to become Emily's new companion.

3

―――――

"BUT I'M NOT a nanny. I'm a professional entertainer," Annie protested.

She shook her head so violently her wig slipped, which reminded her how itchy her scalp felt. She wanted nothing more than to get home and take all the scratchy clothes and mucky paint off her face and body, then step into a nice, long shower. The last thing she needed was some big jerk treating her like a baby-sitter.

"So, entertain Emily," Mark Saunders argued. "You'll never have a better audience. She thinks you're fantastic."

Annie softened for a second. "She's one great kid," she admitted.

"It's only for a couple of weeks, and I'll pay you the equivalent of two parties a day."

Annie's plastic eyelashes scratched her forehead as she widened her eyes in surprise. "That's pretty expensive baby-sitting."

They were in the front hallway. She'd been about to leave when he halted her with his request.

Most of the girls had gone home after cake and presents, but a couple had stayed to watch a video with Emily. After the noise of the party, the house seemed amazingly quiet with just the mumble of the TV coming from the direction of the family room.

He ran a hand across his chin. "Look, it's not just that I'm desperate. I…I liked what you did for Emily today. Your first priority is her safety of course, but—"

"Safety? Is Emily in some kind of danger?" She remembered the elaborate precautions to get into the party and felt a prickle of unease and a protective fear for that sweet little girl.

"No more than anyone else," he said shortly. "I just know it's a dangerous world."

"That's right. You used to be a Mountie."

It was his turn to look surprised. He straightened and got all uptight again. "How do you know that?"

Annie smiled mischievously. "We've met before. In fact, I'd better come clean so you can withdraw the job offer."

"I thought I knew you." He peered closely at her face, obviously trying to work out who she was beneath the costume and paint. His nearness sent a weird kind of slurpy feeling through her belly. Which was odd, because big, uptight guys just weren't her type outside a film canister. She always went for the artsy, lyrical ones whose promises were poetry, even if they never came through.

If Mark Saunders ever made a promise he'd stick to it or die trying, which made her feel trapped. Just like he did. No, it couldn't be attraction making her feel this way. She must have drunk too much soda pop.

Resisting the urge to step out of range of all that

macho sexiness, she said, "Not really, we sort of, ah, bumped into each other at Granville Island."

"Granville Island…" His puzzled gaze scanned her up and down then narrowed in concentration. She knew the moment he figured it out—an expression of pure horror crossed his face. "You're not the girl with the life-and-death postcard?"

"Yep!"

He groaned. He actually groaned.

"I had a great time. Thanks for having me today." She held her hand over the pocket where she'd tucked that huge check, wanting to leave before he demanded it back. She put her hand on the doorknob and turned it, but the door wouldn't open.

He was standing there looking as if somebody had just told him his parents were really aliens from Mars.

"The door seems to be stuck," she said.

He shook his head like a dog shaking off water. He opened a panel in the wall—Annie wouldn't have known it was there—and punched a series of numbers onto a keypad. This time when she turned the knob the door opened.

"So, will you let me know tomorrow?"

"Let you know what?"

"If you'll take the job."

"You still want me?"

He paused for a moment as if doubting his sanity. She could understand his need to check. Then he shrugged. "I'm desperate."

She bit her lower lip to keep from laughing and got a mouthful of stale greasepaint.

Did she want to wait for Bobbie or didn't she?

She'd already sublet her apartment—the guy was due to move in in a week. She had a few bookings that she hadn't had the heart to cancel. If she took the nanny job she could wait for Bobbie and still do a few clown gigs. Truth was, she could use the extra money for her trip.

She leaned against the door, thinking. He said he was desperate, but was she really his only option? "I know this isn't my business, but couldn't Emily's mother help out?"

A spasm of pain crossed his face. "Emily's mother is dead."

"Oh. I'm sorry." No wonder he gazed at the little girl in pain. She must remind him of his dead wife. "You must have loved her very much."

He nodded. "Emily's all I have left of Christy. She and her husband were both killed a year ago."

"Your wife was a bigamist?" *Wow.*

"No. An archaeologist. And Christy was my little sister, not my wife. She and her husband were on a dig together in Africa. They caught some kind of jungle fever."

"So Emily's your—"

"Niece. That's why I have to take extra good care of her. Her mother entrusted me with her most precious possession. I can't let her down."

Annie's mind was made up in that instant. Mark Saunders might not be able to do a somersault, but he'd taken on a child when he could so easily have sloughed off the responsibility. "I'll need weekends and evenings off for my clown work."

"I don't have a problem with that."

"What exactly would I have to do?"

"You have to get Emily ready in the morning and drive her to school. Pick her up at the end of school, drive her to her music and dance lessons, prepare dinner. Keep the house neat. School ends in a couple of weeks. If Bea's still sick, it would be a full-day thing."

She could see a couple of flaws in the plan already. Cooking and cleaning weren't high on her list of things she did well. And the word "morning" snagged her attention in an unpleasant sort of way. "When you say morning, what did you have in mind?"

"You arrive at seven. You'll prepare her breakfast, make sure she has everything she needs and drive her to school by nine."

She thought it over. She could make it work. Earn some extra cash and wait for Bobbie. "I'll have to sleep over."

"Uh—"

Yep. She could definitely make it work. "You have a deal," she said.

"Do you know any self-defense?"

Her chin jutted up, making the wig itch. "I can take care of myself."

"And while we're on the subject, that postcard mentioned life and death."

"I already told you that was just a joke. I'm planning a backpacking trip to Asia. I was trying to hurry my friend up."

A gleam of amusement entered his eyes. "I can see that would be a life-or-death situation." He leaned back on his heels, hands in his pockets, and her attention was caught once more by that brick-wall chest of his. A little springy hair peeked out from the vee of his shirt. *Mmm*. It looked good.

"Come tomorrow afternoon, and I'll go over some basic self-defense moves." His words dragged her gaze to his face.

"You're kidding!"

"I never kid about Emily's safety."

She sighed. Short-term pain... "Okay. I'll see you tomorrow."

"I CAN'T BREATHE!" Annie complained, trying to hoist the muscular bulk of Mark Saunders off her solar plexus. It was getting to be a bad habit.

He rolled smoothly to his feet. "That was better. You put up more of a struggle. Let's try it again. The trick is to go for my vulnerable areas and get me unbalanced."

"You don't have any vulnerable areas. And I'm the one who must be unbalanced! Besides, you're three times my size." She grabbed his outstretched hand and hauled herself to her feet with a groan. "This is hopeless."

"I'll give you a hint. The bad guys don't usually go for people bigger and tougher than they are. They go for the smaller and weaker."

"Hey, I'm not weak!" she said, stung. "I take yoga and I run." *Sometimes.* He was starting to tick her off with his cocksure attitude, tossing her around his basement gym like a rag doll. Just once, she was determined to land *him* on *his* back.

"That's what this little exercise is all about." He talked to her as if she were completely dense, which ticked her off even more. "Sure, I'm bigger. But you're quicker and more agile. You can use those things to your advantage."

"And I can do a somersault," she replied cheekily.

He rolled his eyes. "That should come in real handy if you're being attacked."

She felt hot and sticky. She yanked off her sweatshirt. Under the cropped tank top, her sports bra was maiming what it was meant to support. She slipped her hands under her shirt and tried to rearrange things. A dark vee of sweat marked the front of her top, and she was breathing heavily.

Mark Saunders's gray T-shirt hadn't even come untucked from his sweatpants.

With a prickle of awareness, she noticed that he'd stopped talking and stilled. She glanced up to find his gaze aimed at where she was rearranging her underwear. Which upped her irritation level another notch.

"See something you like?" she asked with saccharine sweetness.

His gaze dropped lower, from embarrassment, she was certain. Then his eyes widened. "What is that?"

"My birthstone. A diamond for April." She fiddled with the gem nestling in her pierced navel. "Actually, it's a zircon. Can't afford a real diamond. Like it?"

He seemed transfixed. "You let Emily get one of those things and you're a dead woman." His voice was ferocious, but he couldn't drag his gaze from her glinting belly.

She might know squat about judo, but she knew

when a man was getting turned on by her. A testosterone haze shimmered around him like an aura.

She swayed her hips with gusto, hoping the jewel in her navel would catch the light and blind him while she moved toward him as seductively as she knew how.

Letting her mind drift to Rita Hayworth, Ava Gardner, Hedy Lamarr, she imitated exotic and smoldering.

It appeared to work. He seemed completely mesmerized. In that moment, control of the situation began to shift her way.

"Did anyone ever tell you you should relax a little?" she murmured in a throaty purr.

"Frequently." His voice was unsteady, and for the first time since the self-defense lesson started, his breathing was fast.

She glided to a stop in front of him, gazed into eyes that were sending her a whole host of steamy messages. Her breath caught as responsive shivers raced over her skin. Damn. Hedy, Ava and Rita had taken over her mind. Big, tough he-man Mark was their kind of guy. Not hers. She had a point to make, she reminded herself. But still, she was kind of getting into this.

Those cool blue eyes could turn amazingly hot, scorching everywhere they gazed. He might be a bit of a stuffed shirt on the outside, but those eyes hinted at something wild hiding inside. Something that could be altogether exciting, and maybe just a bit scary.

She smiled her sexiest smile and leaned into him. For just a moment she let herself enjoy the way he made her feel—safe, feminine, wanted. It was a totally sexy combination, and if she didn't do something soon, she'd forget to make her point.

That mesmerizing gaze held hers, and he lowered his head slowly. Her lips parted all by themselves, tingling with the anticipation of his kiss.

Hanging on fiercely to her self-control, she hooked her leg around the back of his calf, pushed against his chest and toppled him like a three-hundred-year-old redwood.

"Timber!" she called softly as he crashed to the floor.

4

"NOW, CONCENTRATE." Mark had his security expert voice on again, and it probably fit him better than his birthday suit. She'd been concentrating so long her brain felt like it was going to implode. "When you leave the house, enter the security code to open the door."

"Yeah, I remember from yesterday."

"Good. Here's the code." Slowly, he reeled off a list of numbers.

"Wait a sec." She dug into her bag and rummaged for something to write on. She came up with a program from a play she'd seen at the Arts Club Theater and a purple felt pen. "Okay, tell me the numbers again."

"You can't write them down." Mark leaned against the wall and crossed his arms, a pained expression on his face. "That's why we have secret codes. So they'll be secret."

"Look. I already memorized the code to get in here. Why can't I use the same one to get out?"

He opened his mouth to argue, looking so frustrated she thought he might burst. A staccato beeping came from somewhere. Annie glanced at the wall panel, feeling hot and panicky. This was way too much for a girl who never bothered to lock her car door.

"Yeah," Mark said, and she realized the beeping had come from a cell phone he'd had hidden somewhere on his person. Maybe his shoe? Never had she believed she'd end up living in the middle of a sitcom, but that's what this baby-sitting gig was starting to feel like.

She watched him talking on his phone, a frown gathering, and wondered if she'd imagined the almost-kiss earlier in his downstairs gym. It was as though falling to the ground had knocked out the sexy, passionate man who'd been about to embrace her. When he'd stood, the polite, impersonal brick wall had been in place.

"It's not—" He stopped talking and listened intently. Then let his breath out in a huff. "All right. I'll be there as quick as I can." He flipped the phone into a square so tiny it wouldn't have a hope of being recovered if it ever found its way into her bag. She watched, disappointed when he didn't stick it into the heel of his shoe.

"You even have the same initials," she said with a giggle.

"What?"

"You and Maxwell Smart."

He was getting that expression on his face again, like she was some airhead dimwit. "Who?"

"You and Maxwell Smart. From 'Get Smart.' I bet Mark is your code name." She dropped her voice and struck a sultry pose. "And you can call me Ninety-nine. It's my secret code name. I'd tell you my real name, but then it wouldn't be a secret anymore."

A pause ensued. She had a strong feeling he was counting silently to ten. "I don't have time for this. I have to go. I'll change the outgoing code to match the incoming one, but only temporarily. I'll expect you to memorize a new one in two days. Now, if somebody gets to the door and you don't like the look of them, push this button."

"The green one."

"Yes."

She depressed the button, noting as she did so that her nail polish needed a touch-up. Judo wasn't the best activity for a manicure. Then she jumped out of her skin. From somewhere, a ferocious dog was barking its head off. She glanced around quickly. It sounded as if it was under their noses. "What the—"

"Realistic, isn't it?" Mark managed a teensy, tiny smirk.

"You have a fake dog?" She could not believe this guy.

"It helps deter prowlers. You can also activate it from this remote." He handed her a key chain with several buttons, including a green one.

"And the blue button?" She motioned to the one beside the green button.

"That activates the security system from a remote location. Just in case you forget to activate it when you leave the house. Which I'm sure you won't." His expression warned her she'd better not.

"I'm scared to even ask what the red button does."

"That's the panic button. You'll find them all over

the house, as well as on the key chain as a remote personal alarm. Push that button, and help will be on its way immediately.''

"How will you know where I am?'' She shook the key chain. "Does this thing have a phone in it?'' That would be cool. A Barbie-size cell phone.

"It contains a personal tracking device.''

Only the fiercest act of will prevented her from rolling her eyes. "Naturally.''

"Here's a cell phone for you to use. That button there gets you directly to me.'' Another small square of black plastic appeared in his hand. Where did he hide those things?

"Cool.''

He glanced at his watch. "Any questions?''

"Yes.'' She gestured to the wall panel. "What's the deal?''

His lips thinned. "There's a break-in somewhere in America approximately every twelve seconds.''

"Not in this neighborhood.''

"I don't care if you think I'm paranoid. I—I can't let anything happen to Emily. I promised her mother.'' He shook his head as though to clear it. "I look after what's mine. And Emily's the most precious thing I've got. Think whatever you like about me, but you'll do this my way. Do we understand each other?''

"Yes.'' She squelched the *sir* just in time. He was never going to help Emily by keeping her a sheltered princess in an impregnable castle. Still, he was right about one thing. He was the boss, and Annie had agreed to take on this assignment. She'd have to do it his way.

"Right. Um…" He looked embarrassed.

"Don't tell me. I can't shower without an armed guard?"

She wished she'd bitten her tongue. His gaze jerked to lock with hers, and she had a sudden vision of them both in a steamy hot shower. She could imagine his strong but gentle hands soaping her naked body while hot water streamed over them. She could as easily imagine taking the bar of soap from him and rubbing it all over that chest and down…

She knew darned well he was picturing the same thing. His eyes had that intense sexy expression he'd worn in the gym when he caught sight of her belly ring.

She was amazed, and a little scared, at how attractive he could be when he let his sex appeal surface. She had to remember he was a guy who liked his women locked in a fortress. Too bad, because the eyes told her there was a completely different man hiding behind the tough-guy exterior. That shower might be pretty entertaining.

He shook his head and glanced past her. "It's about today. There's a problem at work. I know you don't start work until tomorrow, but—"

"You want me to start today." She pretended to think about it, just to make him squirm a bit. "Luckily for you, I don't happen to have a clown booking today. I'll do it, but don't make a habit of this."

He smiled his relief and gripped her shoulder in what was probably supposed to be a warm, friendly manner. She wondered if he'd leave a bruise. Or a scorch mark. So much pent-up sexiness—if that guy ever let go of his iron control he'd flame like a blow-torch. "Thanks. I owe you."

"Don't mention it." Besides, it would give her a few more hours to cram for her new assignment as Special Agent Annie. She hoped Emily could help her sort out all these gadgets before her uncle figured out there was a darned good reason Annie had picked clowning over national security as a career.

It had to do with electronics. Anything to do with gadgets and gizmos made her nervous. She was more a simple-living kind of gal.

Mark trotted happily down the hall to his bat cave while she contemplated the electronic junk in her arms. Which button made the dog bark?

As he was leaving a few minutes later, Mark stopped at the front door and fiddled with the control panel for a while. "I've changed the code, so incoming and outgoing match. Just for two days."

"Yes, sure." Damn. She couldn't remember the first code. No way she was letting on, though. She'd figure something out.

"The fridge is stocked with food. Just make dinner for Em and yourself, I'll grab something out."

She flashed him a big phony-reassuring smile and hoped to goodness there wasn't some kind of kryp-tonite lock on the fridge. Also that Emily believed, as Annie did, that food closest to its natural state was healthiest. That was about all she knew how to cook.

"WHAT IF I hatched a frog from a chicken's egg?" Annie mused as she tore spinach for a salad.

"Are you a witch?" Emily's eyes widened, not with fear but fascination, as she glanced up from the 3-D castle puzzle she'd received as a birthday present.

Annie chuckled. "A few of the guys I've dated might say so. But I was thinking about adding some new tricks to my clown routine. What do you think if I took an egg like this one—" she lifted an egg out of the carton, squinting at the white sphere while she pondered "—and cracked it, and out jumped a frog?"

"Would it be a real frog?"

"No. Probably a plastic one." She pictured it in her mind, but it didn't seem right. "Oh, I know. How about one of those rubbery ones. I could make it look like it was leaping out of the egg."

Emily's face creased into a puzzled frown. "But frogs hatch out of slimy ponds, not chickens' eggs."

"I know. That's the point of the trick. It's supposed to be funny."

Emily gazed at Annie in a way that made *her* feel as if she'd hatched out of a slimy pond.

"Okay. It's not funny. What if I juggled eggs and—"

"Frogs."

"—broke one."

"Juggled them."

Annie paused, her eyes widening. "Did you say frogs? You mean juggle frogs?" She started to chuckle. "That's different. But if I drop one nothing happens. Where's the magic in that?"

"It could go ribbett."

"Wait. I know." Annie started getting that quivery feeling she got when she was onto something. "I could start with eggs, and every time I drop one it hatches into a frog.'' What would the logistics be? She started working it out in her head, ripping spinach leaves while her mind drifted.

After a while, Emily's voice interrupted visions of cracking eggs, hopping rubber frogs, ribbeting chickens, clucking amphibians…and came back to earth. ''What?''

''What are you making?''

''Spinach salad. What's the face for? It's very nutritious.'' She glanced at the bowl and saw a mass of tiny green bits that looked like used green tea leaves. She'd been so busy fantasizing about her new trick she'd turned the spinach into dark green mush.

A glance proved she'd missed not a leaf. Trying to hide her dismay, she opened her eyes in an assumption of innocence. ''It's like coleslaw,'' she assured Emily. ''Only with spinach instead of cabbage. You'll love it.''

''Could I have a hot dog?''

Oh, Lord. Day number one, and she was a complete disaster as a nanny. ''Hot dogs are junk food.''

''I'd eat it all up.''

She nibbled her lip. Mark Saunders had given her thousands of instructions on how to protect Emily with her life but no information at all on what he expected in the way of meals.

As though reading her mind, Emily said, ''Uncle Mark and me eat hot dogs all the time when Bea's not here.''

Oh, ho. So Mr. Brick Wall indulged in junk food, did he? It wasn't much of a weakness, but it was something and certainly made him more human. "Tell you what. If you promise to eat the spinach slaw, I'll give you a hot dog with it. Fair?"

"I guess." Her charge eyed the bowl of green stuff doubtfully. Annie had to admit she'd prefer a hot dog herself. But she raided the cupboards and started throwing things in—raisins, pine nuts, chopped oranges and some kind of bottled gourmet salad dressing she found in the fridge. When she'd finished, her spinach slaw was really quite delicious.

Her confidence rose when Emily sampled it and declared it "kinda good."

"Look how pretty it is on your uncle's green plates," Annie said as she dished up. The dark green spinach appeared designer coordinated against the pale green pottery plates she'd noticed at the party. She'd assumed it was the good china, but there didn't seem to be anything else in the kitchen. It struck her as odd that a bachelor would bother with nice china, but she was beyond being surprised by Mark Saunders.

"It's not Uncle Mark's china. It's my mom's." Emily corrected her in a matter-of-fact tone.

"I'm sorry, Emily. I didn't know. Would you like me to use something else?"

"Uh-uh. I like this. It helps me keep remembering Mom and Dad. Mom and me went shopping and I helped pick the china. Green is my favorite color." She fetched knives and forks and set the table as though it were a chore she performed every day, while Annie felt tears prick her lids at the thought of this poor little girl who'd lost both parents so suddenly.

But Emily seemed to be coping well. Apart from the shyness, she was able to talk about her parents, and obviously that would help her deal with her grief. Good for her. And good for Mark Saunders for understanding that she needed to use her china now, when it gave her comfort, not store it in a box for when she was older.

Automatically, Emily set the table for three.

"I don't think your uncle's coming home for dinner. He said he'd grab something out."

"He always says that. Bea makes dinner for him anyway. And he always eats it."

"Hope he likes omelettes and spinach slaw," she mumbled, cracking more eggs into a bowl.

"He pretty much eats anything," Emily assured her.

"He hasn't tasted my cooking."

Minutes later, Annie choked on her spinach slaw. "Oh, my God!" She gasped as a light began flashing rhythmically from a wall panel just above one of the ubiquitous red panic buttons.

She dove across the room for her backpack and frantically started tossing things to the ground searching for the multi-buttoned emergency key chain thingy she'd scoffed at earlier.

Here it was, her first day on the job and already they were having a break-in. Just her luck.

From the corner of her eye she saw the flashing stop. Great, the intruder had disarmed the system already. Must be a professional. She recalled all those scary thrillers where the bad guy cut the telephone wires just before...

"Emily. I want you to go upstairs to your room and lock the door."

"Did I do something wrong?" The small face creased with worry.

Annie mustered a brave smile, but it felt kind of wobbly. She turned her bag upside down, then shook it until a cascade of stuff came tumbling out. Where was that key chain? "No. I'll explain later."

"But Uncle Mark's home. Can't I say hi to him first?"

A feeling of immense relief washed over Annie at the news.

Mark was here.

He'd be more than a match for any scary burglar or phone-line cutter. Then, an instant later, relief turned to embarrassment as she realised there was no break-in. That flashing light must have signaled Mark's return to the house.

"Looking for something?" Amusement tinged the deep voice coming from the kitchen doorway.

"Just my sanity," she mumbled as she stuffed things into her bag. Her passport, traveling toothbrush—she'd been wondering where that was—wallet, half-used pack of tissues, an open roll of mints with a grubby gray mint peeking out the top.

She felt him behind her. He dropped to his knees and started handing her things. The sound of a chair dragging on the ceramic tile floor caused her to turn her head until she caught the enticing rear view of Mark Saunders and nothing but.

His head and arms were under the table as he gathered more of her stuff. Toned and muscled, his back end was rivetting.

He emerged backward from under the table, a bottle in his hand. He glanced at it and raised his eyebrows. "Water purification tablets?"

She shrugged. "I travel a lot. I like to be prepared for anything."

"So I see," he drawled, discreetly handing her the object in his other hand. An open box of condoms.

She would not blush. She was a modern woman of the twenty-first century. A third-millennium crusader for women's rights. A woman in charge of her own life and her own body.

She blushed hotter than a vestal virgin at an orgy.

Rising in one clean motion, Mark turned to his niece. Even with his back to her, Annie was certain he was grinning. "How was your afternoon, Em?"

"Good. We were thinking up new tricks for Annie. Do you think frogs hatching out of chicken eggs would be funny?"

"Sidesplitting."

Officially, she hadn't even started the nanny job yet, and already she wanted to quit. Having fastened the bag, she rose and fetched his plate with the slaw already on it and pulled the omelette out of the warm oven. "Here's your dinner."

He glanced at the plate. "You shouldn't have bothered." And the way he said it she knew he meant it. Maybe he suspected he was about to lose his desperation nanny, for he suddenly smiled that killer smile that reached right into her heart and gave it a hug. "But thanks. It looks great. I'll just go wash up."

By the time he got back, Annie's color was back to normal, her heart rate was back in the training range, out of the imminent cardiac arrest zone, and she was able to face him across a small table with a semblance of calm.

"Did you get things sorted out at the office?" she asked, sounding just like one of those sitcom moms from the fifties. She noted the horrified fascination on Mark's face as he examined the green stuff.

Manfully he shoved a forkful of mush into his mouth, and she had to hold back a smirk when his face flooded with relief. "This is delicious," he said in obvious surprise.

"It's an old family recipe."

"Today went fine. My company's handling the security for the Pacific Rim trading conference in two weeks. Things are pretty hectic."

"Wow. I'm impressed."

"I will be, too, if we get by without a disaster."

There was a small pause. "Does that red light go on every time somebody comes in the house?" she asked, not wanting to be caught making a fool of herself a second time.

"Yes. I had it wired so you always know when somebody comes in or goes out."

"And if it's a burglar?"

"Major alarms go off. Here, at the police station and at Saunders Security."

"Just so I know and don't go making a fool of myself again."

"Sorry." He compressed twitching lips. "I guess I didn't get a chance to finish showing you around the security system."

"Uncle Mark, where's Annie going to sleep?" Emily asked.

Those innocent words sent an invisible sizzle crackling through the atmosphere between the two adults. Mark glanced Annie's way, his eyes smoky with desire. The effect was amazing. Her heart rate kicked up again, and her breathing rate increased.

She was getting a whole cardiovascular workout just having dinner with these people.

She willed herself to stop the blush from rising to her cheeks. Oh, God. Maybe he thought she'd brought condoms for his benefit, when the truth was she hadn't even remembered they were in her bag until they'd turned up under the kitchen table with a few other escapees from the backpack.

"Well, uh..." Mark began.

Cutting him off at the pass, just in case he had any suggestions she'd rather Emily didn't hear, Annie said, "I would have put my stuff in one of the spare bedrooms, but I wasn't sure which one."

There were two bedrooms apart from Emily's, which she'd seen, and Mark's, at the other end of the hall, which she hadn't. Emily had pointed out the closed door, and even though she was curious, she hadn't wanted to pry.

There was a second bedroom next to Emily's that was a sort of playroom for the child, with toys, a desk, bookshelves stacked with an entire library of books—mostly educational and the classics. She'd bet her purple and yellow wig he'd bought the works from a specialty kids' store.

The other bedroom was set up with bedroom furniture and boasted its own bathroom. Obviously it was the guest room, but it was way too close to Mark's room for her peace of mind.

"Why don't you take the guest room?" he asked.

Because we'd be sharing a wall, and I'd never get any sleep. "I thought you might be expecting guests." She shrugged. "I could put a cot or something in the room beside Emily's, then I'd be there if she needed anything in the night." As opposed to being available to him if he needed anything in the night.

"I don't think we have a cot." Amusement dawned in his eyes as if he'd figured out what was causing her hesitation. The glance he flicked her way was pure challenge. As if he were daring her to take the room next to his.

Annie had never turned down a challenge in her life. She forced a carefree smile. "Oh, well. I'll take the guest room then."

When they'd finished their dessert of sliced apples and oranges, Emily asked if she could be excused to do her homework.

"Sure thing," her uncle replied, giving her ponytail a playful tug as she walked past on her way out of the kitchen.

Annie rose to collect the dishes and almost collided with Mark, who was bent on the same task. "I'll do the dishes," she protested.

He shook his head. "Ground rules. Once dinner's over, you're off duty. I do dinner dishes."

She watched him collect Emily's pale green dishes with exquisite care. "Am I allowed to help?" she asked softly.

"Optional. Your call."

She helped him stack the dishes on the polished granite counter then dried while he washed. He'd explained he didn't put the green dishes in the dishwasher, to help preserve them. Always the protector, she thought, enjoying the sight of his square, masculine hands covered in suds washing Emily's dishes with such care.

It gave her the same kind of sensation in the pit of her stomach that she got seeing a big hunky man with a baby. The occupation didn't make him less rugged or tough—it emphasized his masculinity.

She enjoyed watching soap bubbles gather around his knuckles, the way the water pasted dark hair to his forearms, the way the muscles worked together in such harmony as he methodically washed and rinsed each dish. He washed everything by hand, even the things that could easily have gone in the dishwasher. Annie had no idea whether he did this every night or whether he was enjoying working side by side as much as she was.

"You live in a family home in the suburbs, you own your own business, you even do dishes. How come there's no woman in your life?" Maybe it was insensitive and prying of her to ask, but the question had been bothering her since the birthday party.

He glanced up from the dishes. "I didn't always

live like this. A year ago I had a condo in Kitsilano." He mentioned the trendy part of town near the university almost with regret. "I was an RCMP officer and a single guy living in a city famous for beautiful women."

"Really? Vancouver's famous for beautiful women?" Darn. She should have checked that out before she moved here.

"I bet more men's magazine centerfolds come from Vancouver than any other city," he informed her with obvious pride. "Not that I personally know any," he hastened to add.

"Naturally."

"My friend Brodie dated a centerfold once. She was a nice girl." He shrugged, scraping a glob of egg stuck to the frying pan. "Then Emily came to live with me. Things changed."

Now that was an understatement. He'd given up his lifestyle and changed to a safer job for the sake of his niece. *Wow.* A memory of her dad, who'd left his family when the responsibility became too much, flashed across her mind, and she felt a frown develop.

But that was silly. Her dad was a great guy, as fun and adventurous as she was. He hadn't been cut out for permanence any more than she was. Emily was pretty darned lucky that Mark was cut from a different cloth. "It's been quite a year for you."

"Yes. And obviously, I can't get involved with a woman while Emily is still settling in."

"She seems pretty settled to me," Annie said, and then, panicking that he might think she wanted him to get involved with *her,* she quickly added, "I mean, she's able to talk about her parents quite naturally and seems like a normal eight-year-old. She's a little shy, but lots of kids that age are.''

"I'm glad you think so. I don't know much of anything about kids. I pretty much bought out the bookstore on parenting books and stuff about the grieving process. And there's some good information on the Internet.''

She stifled a grin. She might have known he'd search out an instruction manual on how to raise a child.

Once all the dishes were put away and the kitchen was spotless, its high-tech patina gleaming, an awkward pause ensued.

Annie had no idea what to do next. She had the sense that whatever she did now would begin the laying down of a routine, and she wanted it to be the right one. Something that put lots of space between her and Mark Saunders. A man like him could trap a woman like her into the kind of life she never, ever wanted.

"Well,'' he said. "I usually read to Emily at night and then it's lights out at eight-thirty. I'm getting behind on my paperwork, so I'll probably spend some time in my office.'' He gestured down the hall in case she'd forgotten where it was.

She nodded. "Maybe I'll just go up and say goodnight to Emily first, then.''

"Sure. You know where the family room is if you want to watch TV or some old movies or something.'' He grinned, and she knew he was remembering their insane conversation at Granville Island that first day.

"And help yourself to the gym downstairs if you want to work out."

Yeah, that'd top her fun-things-to-do list. "Thanks. I'll probably unpack and get to bed early." She gave a theatrical groan. "I've got an early start in the morning."

"The early clown catches the frog."

"Was that a joke?" Her eyes bugged wide open. She had a feeling her mouth had done the same.

"A pretty lame one," he said sheepishly.

"It's a good start. Shows you have a sense of humor. You'll need it if you're going to be living with me," she assured him. Then, seeing the startled expression in his eyes—which could go from arctic to meltdown in about three seconds—she hastily revised her statement. "I mean staying in the same house. Temporarily."

5

_____

"WHAT'S THE DIFFERENCE between a clown and a wizard?" Emily asked when Annie entered her room.

The child was in bed with a book about a child wizard propped on her chest. Annie had read the series, and as she recalled, the boy was an orphan, too.

Cuddled in Emily's left arm was a very ratty, clearly much-loved stuffed lion with an advanced case of mange.

"Well, a wizard has magical powers. A clown's job is to make you laugh."

The child stroked the lion's patchy tail while she considered this. "But you do magic, too. Do you have a racing broom? Magic potions and spells that turn people into animals?"

"No. My magic is just pretend. When I make things disappear, I really hide them when the audience isn't looking. I'll show you sometime if you're interested."

"Really? Would you show me how to do a magic trick?"

"Sure. Maybe we can work on some tricks you could show your friends." She glanced surreptitiously at her watch and discovered it was eight-fifteen.

After a hasty good-night and a peck on the cheek,

she made her way to the safety of the guest room, where she spent seven or eight minutes unpacking her backpack into the empty drawers of the pine dresser.

It took another good minute to unpack her toiletry bag in the bathroom. That done, she glanced at her watch.

Eight twenty-five.

What on earth was she going to do with herself? Normally she didn't go to bed until well after midnight and rarely woke before eight in the morning.

Luckily, the guest room came equipped with a clock that looked like it required an advanced degree from MIT to operate. Fiddling with that until she thought she had the alarm set for six forty-five a.m. helped use up another few minutes. Then she heard Mark's low voice saying good-night and Emily's soft reply. His tread descended to the main floor.

By eight thirty-five she had all the bed's pillows piled behind her back and her feet up while she tried to read her guidebook to Asia.

Usually butterflies of excitement flitted in her stomach when she read about all the exotic and exciting places she'd be visiting soon. But somehow, tonight, it couldn't grab her attention.

Her mind kept drifting to one brave little girl and one very sexy ex-Mountie. The little girl brought a rush of feeling that was both unfamiliar and unmistakably maternal. The ex-Mountie brought on feelings that were definitely not maternal.

With a sigh she put down the book. She felt restless and keyed up. Maybe she should go out. But she no sooner had the idea than she abandoned it. She'd have to remember too many codes.

With a sigh, she hauled herself off the bed and went to stare out the window. She saw what any prisoner must see—a fence and a gate. Heavily secured. She felt what many prisoners must feel—a sense of claustrophobia and an almost irresistible urge to escape.

"What have I done?" she asked the moon that taunted her from its position of utter freedom outside the gates.

She was going to go bananas if she stayed cooped up in this room all night. He'd mentioned old movies. Maybe she could go out and rent one, or better still, maybe he had a movie station or satellite dish.

If she was very quiet and kept the sound down, he need never know she was there. With that in mind, she crept down the stairs. As she made her way to the family room, she passed the kitchen and caught Mark in the act of building himself a very large sandwich.

Mayonnaise and mustard jars, a package of what looked like luncheon meat, a block of cheese, a pickle jar and a decimated loaf of bread were lined up neatly in front of him. As she watched, he cut the triple-decker sandwich with the precision of a surgeon and chomped into it.

She let him chew unobserved for a moment, frankly enjoying the sight of his enjoyment. A little daub of mayonnaise spotted his upper lip, and she watched, mesmerized, as it rode up and down with his rhythmic chewing.

Did she move? She didn't think so, but suddenly the chewing stopped and he turned his gaze her way.

She had to laugh. His expression was exactly that of a little boy caught red-handed in some mischief. "My cooking's not enough for you?"

"No. I mean..." He replied thickly, then swallowed and wiped his mouth with a paper napkin. Without the mayonnaise on his lip he appeared all grown up again. "I, uh, get hungry sometimes in the evenings." Sheepishly, he gestured to the sandwich fixings. "Want one? I do a terrific club sandwich."

Affecting an air of virtue, she shook her head. "I never snack."

"Most important meal of the day." He stood there, too polite to take another bite, and she stood there, watching him.

A moment passed.

"Did you want to make some tea or something?"

She started. "No. I, uh, just came down to watch a movie. If you have anything good."

"I've got the best DVD collection in town. Schwarzenegger or Van Damme, take your pick."

She smiled politely. "Do you have anything else?"

"I've probably got some Stallone somewhere."

If she hadn't witnessed him make a joke earlier, she might have fallen for it. But his expression was too innocent.

"I'll just look under that pile of *Sports Illustrated* and *Muscle Car* magazines and see what I find," she replied.

He chuckled. "The movies are in the bookcase. If you need help give me a shout."

"Thanks."

When she got to the family room she discovered he hadn't lied. He did have a good representation of the three actors he'd cited. But he also had a wide range of titles from sappy romantic comedies to intellectual European cinematic statements.

Gleefully, she pored through the romantic comedies, pulling out several of her favorites. She loved everything about old movies, especially those with cover pictures of the stars. Clark Gable, William Holden, Cary Grant all grinned at her, vying for her attention. What bliss.

"Find anything you like?" a much more contemporary but equally sexy man asked from the doorway.

"So many men, so little time," she replied dreamily.

"Well, you've got all night."

Was there a hidden message? Was he suggesting she could move on from celluloid men to the real flesh-and-blood thing if she wanted? Was the ex-Mountie coming on to her?

Hard to say. When she turned to see, he was gone.

She curled up on the couch and prepared to escape. While the black-and-white images flitted across the screen, she was in the best of all possible worlds, where women always looked elegant, always thought of something appropriate to say, and in less than two hours had the impeccably dressed hunky hero eating out of their hands.

Sure it was corny. And she enjoyed every single minute of it. When the music reached a crescendo and the couple kissed, she sighed aloud with pleasure.

Then heard a very unromantic snort from behind her.

Startled, she turned to find Mark staring at the screen with an expression of disgust on his face. "Real men don't kiss like that," he informed her.

"Too bad they don't."

"He's so scared he'll muss her hair he's hardly even touching her. What kind of kiss is that?"

She leaped to her feet. How dare he make fun of her favorite movies? "Tough talk, mister. I'd like to see you do any better."

"Oh, yeah?" He was teasing her, but there was a disturbing glint in his eye.

Her heart took to hammering away at her ribs as she tried to think up the kind of comeback Jean Harlow or Katharine Hepburn would have lobbed his way. But, naturally, her mind was blank.

Before she could think up a suitably annihilating retort, it was too late. He was in front of her, his hand cupping the back of her head while she gaped at him.

"First you muss the hair," he told her in a voice that sent shivers racing through her as his fingers slid through her curls.

"Then you get in real close." He fit his body against hers, and she forgot about the urge to tell him off. Ooh, he was warm. And rock solid. Everywhere their bodies touched, she tingled.

"Then you smudge her lipstick." His tone dropped to a sexy growl. She opened her lips to tell him she wasn't wearing lipstick, but before she could form a single word, it was too late.

He was kissing her.

His other arm came around her back, pulling her closer.

It had started as sort of a joke, but the minute their lips touched the joking was over. This was serious, high-voltage necking. And he was right, she admitted dimly, a designer dress and thick lipstick would definitely get mussed. In fact, everything from her hair to her heart rate was getting seriously mussed.

His tongue teased her, just tracing the edges of her lips before plunging deeper with gentle control.

Her arms went around his broad back and clung, pulling her body further into his embrace. Desire roared to life until she ached with it, wanting him here and now, right on the floor in front of the flickering TV screen.

Their tongues teased and played while the pressure built until she couldn't stand still. Her pelvis started wiggling against his, where she could feel his own pressure building. She hadn't felt this excited in a very long time. Somewhere in her foggy brain, she reminded herself that this was a bad idea, but she was having too much fun to care. She'd worry about that in the morning.

Just as she thought about using her one effective judo move to get him on his back on the floor, he began to pull away.

A little panting moan left her lips as he stepped back.

Even as she put her hands around his neck and tugged, trying to get back to that warm and infinitely exciting clinch, he was gently loosening them and putting them at her sides.

''That's my idea of a real kiss.'' He tried to sound casual, as if he'd just been demonstrating what he meant. She wasn't fooled for a second. She heard the sexual need in his tone as clearly as she felt its echo inside herself.

''Keep working at it. You might have something there.'' She affected the same casual air, but her voice was a dead giveaway.

He kept walking backward until he'd left the room. As she heard him return to his office, she flopped to the couch on rubber legs. Yep, she'd been right. Kissing Mark Saunders had been a very bad idea.

OF COURSE she couldn't sleep. She'd known she wouldn't. When she wasn't worrying that she'd sleep through the alarm, she was thinking about Mark. Recalling the strength of his arms around her, the amazing passion of his kissing. He'd stuffed that shirt with a whole lot of raw sexual energy.

Intellectually, she understood why he'd broken off the kiss just when things were getting exciting. It was very controlled of him. Very sensible. Naturally, it would be awkward for them to start an affair while she was his employee and Emily was asleep upstairs.

If he hadn't called a halt, she would have. Another minute and she absolutely would have pulled away.

About as easily as she could eat just one truffle and put the box away. Munch a single potato chip. Watch only half a good movie. She stuck the pillow over her head and groaned softly. Truth was, she'd been his for the taking. And they both knew it.

Who knew why? He wasn't her type. But, in flash-back images, she saw him when they'd been throwing each other to the ground in the self-defense class, remembered the sight of his soapy forearms, slick and wet and muscular. But mostly it was the expression in his eyes that fascinated her. They could be colder than steel, and harder, or they could be so hot they got her blood simmering.

A quick fling with him could be fabulous. But she didn't need a degree in psychology to see he wasn't casual. About anything. It was a very good thing he'd pulled back after no more than a little necking. Let a man like that in her life, and it would be nothing but trouble.

He was a hunk of major proportions. But he was resistible, as long as he didn't do anything stupid like put on his RCMP dress uniform.

6

"WHAT?" Annie dreamed she was in the middle of a war. Sirens screeched, guns boomed, voices commanded. She wanted to run and hide, but she couldn't get away. She dove for cover in some kind of cave, and it was better for a while.

"Annie!" She was shaken by the shoulder.

"No! Don't shoot!" she mumbled, opening her eyes to blackness, her heart pounding.

Where was she?

"Annie, wake up." It was a command. Mark. She'd recognize that deep, sexy voice anywhere.

Batting him away dislodged the pillow that had somehow got on top of her head, and she discovered daylight streaming in her window. She was in bed, and Mark was switching off the screeching alarm.

Never at her best in the morning, she struggled to her elbow to try to figure out what was going on. Then remembered belatedly that she'd been asleep in bed. Sleeping as she always slept—naked.

Trying to work up a good glare was tough on so little sleep. She settled for a peevish tone as she yanked the covers to her neck. "What are you doing in here?"

"I just about banged the door down trying to wake you. I have to leave, it's seven-thirty."

"Seven-thirty?" She rubbed her eyes. "But I put the alarm on for six forty-five."

"I know. It's been ringing for forty-five minutes." Pointedly he faced away from her.

"I'm not a morning person," she admitted on a yawn. Like he hadn't noticed.

"Directions to Emily's school are on the kitchen counter," he told the open doorway. "Make sure you check in with me by three-thirty. I'll want to be certain Emily's home from school."

"Yes, sir," she said to his back, sorry he couldn't see her salute.

"HEY, EM!" Annie called, waving madly to the slight figure ambling up the school path alone.

The serious little face broke into a smile when Emily saw Annie, and her slow steps quickened to a run. "Hi."

"It's such a great day, I thought we'd head to the beach. I've packed us some snacks and a Frisbee. You could invite some friends if you want."

The smile widened. "The beach? But aren't you going to make me practice my violin?"

"Sure. When the sun goes down. This city gets enough rain, you have to get out when the sun shines."

Small white teeth worried a small pink lip. "But I have some reading to do, and I didn't finish all my math in school."

"We'll get your homework finished first, then we'll play. Come on, we'll have fun."

"Okay."

"Do you want to invite some friends?"

The little girl glanced at clusters of noisy kids streaming out of the school, then shook her head. "No. Could it be just us?"

"Sure."

In minutes they were off. Being a responsible nanny, Annie slathered sunscreen all over her charge and stuck a baseball cap on her head. The afternoon passed swiftly while they read, practiced times tables, played some Frisbee, even braved the cool Pacific waves all the way up to their ankles. When they got hungry they munched apples and cheese and drank the bottled lemonade Annie had brought.

By the time they returned home, sandy and giggling, it was almost six o'clock. "Do you like tofu?" Annie asked as she approached the gate.

Her companion glanced doubtfully at her. "I don't think so."

Annie was still trying to convince her young charge of the benefits of soybean products when she realized she didn't have a clue what the code was to get into Fort Knox.

"I don't suppose you know the code?" she asked.

"No. I'm not allowed to come home alone."

She was about to start guessing when the gates opened. Slowly, like the jaws of death. And there, standing in the drive like the angel of vengeance, was Mark Saunders.

If Emily hadn't been sitting in the car, Annie might

have bolted, so angry did he look. His feet were planted wide, his arms crossed in a way that reminded her he'd been a cop. Waves of fury emanated from him.

She zipped through the gate and parked next to his vehicle, wondering how he'd known she'd forgotten the code.

"Hi, Uncle Mark," Emily said. "We had the best time. Annie took me to the beach."

His eyes had been boring into Annie's with retribution. He turned to his niece, his expression immediately softening. "That's great, Emily. I need to talk to Annie now. Can you go inside?"

The child looked uncertain. "Sure."

"It's okay, Em," Annie reassured her. "You'll get that tofu before you know it."

Mark waited until the child was inside then turned to Annie, his face blazing with anger. "How could you do this?"

"I'm no good with numbers."

His teeth ground audibly. "You didn't need a number to report in. You push a button. It's *almost* idiot-proof."

Her hand stole to her mouth. She'd forgotten to phone him at three-thirty. That's why he was so bent out of shape. "I'm sorry. I forgot."

"I might be able to forgive you if you'd answered the cell phone."

"It never rang." Really, who did he think he was? "Maybe instead of piling insults on me, you should check your equipment."

He pulled the phone from somewhere and waved it in front of her face. "It rang."

"Okay. So I forgot to take the phone." She was starting to get irate. "Emily had a wonderful time today, and she's perfectly safe. Don't you think you might be taking this security thing a little too seriously? The term is guardian. Not guard."

Beneath the anger, there was real worry in his eyes, and she wished she knew how to help him. "I couldn't get any work done. I couldn't concentrate, not knowing if she was all right...if you were both all right." He'd been worried about *her,* too? A flicker of warmth kindled inside her. It had been a very long time since anybody had worried about her.

"I'm sorry. Really."

"What about her homework? Her dinner?"

"We did her homework at the beach. Dinner's not going to take long. Trust me."

His eyes bored into hers, revealing anger and confusion. "I want to, but you make it tough."

Before she could retort, he'd turned on his heel and stalked into the house.

THE GERMAN SHEPHERD stared hard at Mark through bright, intelligent eyes, never moving from his seated position even though he quivered with alertness.

"He's a beauty," Mark said to the trainer, resisting the urge to run his hand over the silky fur. This was a trained police dog, never meant to be a pet. Only amazing good fortune and Brodie had made him aware that a couple of this season's dogs hadn't made the final cut for the K-9 squad.

Usually there was some slight flaw that made the dog ineligible for the crack dog squad. Mark was here to find out just where this one had failed. And if the animal would be any help in keeping his wayward nanny on a leash.

"What's his name?"

The uniformed officer who'd brought the dog out consulted a clipboard. "Kitsu."

At his name, the dog perked his ears even higher, but he never moved. Mark liked his discipline. Already he was getting a good feeling about this dog. Still, it wouldn't do to be too hasty. "Why didn't he make the cut?"

The officer flicked through several pages on the chart. "You could call the regular trainer. He's on shift again Tuesday. Kitsu got top marks for just about everything. But there's a note at the bottom in handwriting. 'Dog distracted on occasion.' And a word I can't read. Looks like 'squiggle.'"

With a shrug, the officer handed the clipboard to Mark, who flipped through it. The dog was clearly intelligent and had taken well to basic training. He was noted as being outstanding in scent training. He could be a first-class tracker, or maybe a bomb or a drug sniffer. Obstacle course, apprehension, all good. His lowest mark was in obedience training, although he still scored pretty high.

Mark had no idea what "squiggle" meant. But he wasn't looking for a dog who could sniff out drugs, only one who could guard two wayward females. His ferocious-looking presence would be a deterrent to potential troublemakers.

"Mind if I put him through a few paces?"

"Be my guest."

Mark approached slowly, letting Kitsu get used to him. He clipped a leash to the collar and stood to the right of the dog. "Heel," he commanded, and began walking. The dog followed, sticking close to his left heel, keeping perfect pace with Mark.

On and off the leash, the dog was perfectly obedient. Stop, sit, stay, come—Kitsu followed each command immediately and thoroughly.

At the end of the session, the dog gazed at Mark expectantly, tail wagging and sharp brown eyes never leaving his face.

"He looks like he's trying to tell me something."

"He wants his treat. Here." The trainer tossed a dog cookie Mark's way, and Kitsu's tail wagged harder. Still, he waited until Mark offered him the bone-shaped biscuit before delicately taking it with those sharp teeth and then crunching it.

The session over, Mark allowed himself a few minutes to pat the dog. "Good boy."

Already he could feel some of the tension leaving his shoulders as he thought about this dog watching over Annie and Emily. Annie was clearly too much of a flake to take the protection part of her duties seriously. He'd spent a big part of a sleepless night thinking about getting someone else. But every time he reached the decision to hire another nanny, he remembered the way she was with Emily.

In the fun-and-games department she couldn't be beat. Emily was acting more carefree than she had in a year. And, he had to admit, he enjoyed having a clown around the house. He never knew what she'd say or do next. She was fun, funny and sweet. This morning, she'd not only managed to get out of bed on time, she'd made pancakes for Emily and then decorated them to look like cartoon characters.

She'd cooked him one in the shape of a Mountie.

And she'd done it all while wearing some kind of tight skimpy top that definitely didn't have a bra underneath and a pair of shorts that showed off her slender long legs and her belly ring.

He'd almost choked on that Mountie.

Oh, he liked having Annie around, all right. And he knew she was good for his niece in many ways. If he could just assign a deputy to ensure their safety, he could quit worrying. Maybe Kitsu was the perfect answer.

"Think you can look after my girls?" Mark asked his new guard dog.

The intelligent eyes gazed at him, and Kitsu uttered a short, sharp sound, something between a yap and a yowl.

"I'll take that as a yes."

Giving the dog one last rub on the head, he turned to the stand-in trainer. "I'll take him."

"ANNIE, LOOK." Emily's voice was full of excitement.

Annie had never heard her so animated. She ran to the front of the house where the door was wide open for once and halted at the sight of Emily and Mark, both staring at a dog.

She leaned against the doorway, watching as Emily

slowly approached the animal. Mark spoke softly in the voice he used exclusively for his niece.

The child glanced to where Annie stood, and her smile was brighter than the sun. "I always wanted a dog."

Annie felt her smile grow as she watched the trio on the lawn.

Dog? Her goofy smile started to stiffen. Was that rigid canine shape really a dog or was it a garden statue? It sure didn't act like any dog she'd ever seen. Where was the barking? Jumping? Licking? The running around wildly that she always associated with puppies? Because if the German shepherd wasn't a puppy, he sure wasn't far from it. "How old is he?"

"Ten months," Mark replied.

"He's kind of quiet."

"He's just shy. Aren't you, boy?" Emily spoke with confidence as she approached the animal. His eyes were alive, and his ears perked up, but if he wasn't carved from stone, he was doing a darn good imitation of it.

Mark's voice continued, and Annie was almost certain he was giving some kind of instructions. Like how to plug the thing in or activate it in case of burglary.

Emily reached out and stroked the dog's head, and a quiver ran from its nose down its back. But still it remained sitting, watching Mark. Impulsively, Emily threw her arms around the dog and hugged its neck.

"No Em. You shouldn't do that." Mark's voice sharpened.

"Why not?" The smile faded in an instant. "Isn't

he ours to keep? Oh, please say we can keep him, Uncle Mark. I always, always wanted a dog, but Mom said no because we traveled so much. I promise I'll feed him and walk him every day and—''

''Yes. We can keep him.'' Mark dropped to his haunches, and Annie walked over to join the group on the lawn. ''But he's a very special kind of dog. He's a trained guard dog.''

A groan escaped her lips before she could suppress it. Emily wanted a pet, and he bought an attack dog. ''Great, just great.''

Mark glared at her, then turned his attention to his niece. ''His name's Kitsu.''

Emily laughed. ''He knows his name. Did you see the way his ears moved?''

''That's one rambunctious puppy you've got there,'' Annie said softly so only Mark would hear.

The jingle of keys got Mark's attention. ''What are you doing?''

She widened her eyes. ''I'm pushing the green button to make him bark.''

Mark snatched the key chain away. ''He's a real dog. Quit ruining Emily's fun.''

''You wouldn't know fun if it bit you in the—''

''Annie! I admit I got him to protect Emily. And you. The way you go through life worries me. So he can be a pet and a guard dog. What's the big deal?''

''You just don't get it.'' Emily wanted a dog she could play catch with, run around the yard with, whisper her secrets to and sneak up to her room to sprawl on her bed, muddy paws and all. She didn't want a dog that was like Mark only with pointy ears and a tail.

She gave the dog a reluctant pat on the head and announced she was going in to finish preparing lunch. As she entered the house she overheard Mark telling Emily how smart Kitsu was. "He can walk, sit, heel, lie down and stay."

"Sounds like a barrel of laughs," she muttered as she stomped to the kitchen.

"CAN WE TAKE Kitsu with us to the park after lunch?" Emily asked Annie.

That dog, if that's what it really was, was giving her the willies, sitting on the kitchen floor and staring at them while they ate. "I don't think—"

"It's a great idea," Mark interrupted. He caught her gaze and shot her one of those I'll-talk-to-you-about-this-later looks.

"He won't fit in my car," she complained.

"You can use my vehicle." His tone told her he didn't want to hear any more excuses, so she pursed her lips and forked her salad.

"Can you come, too, Uncle Mark?"

"Sorry, Em. I have to work."

"But it's Saturday."

"I know it is. But I've got a lot to do getting ready for the big conference. You have fun without me."

Ha. Annie grumbled the entire time she packed a dinner picnic and changed her clothes. She couldn't believe she'd been manipulated into taking a police dog to a picnic. And that was after she'd been conned into working on a Saturday when she was supposed to have weekends off. Not that she had anything better to do, as it turned out. And he was paying her time and a half. But still, it was the principle of the thing.

"Well, we're off for an afternoon of human and canine frolicking," she announced to Mark in a syrupy voice as they were leaving the house.

He took the picnic basket out of her arms and hefted it toward his truck while he shot her a sideways look. "That's what you're wearing for a day at the park?"

She glanced down. Her paisley-printed Capri pants were zipped. Her purple crop top was clean. Her purple sandals with the big plastic daisies were on the correct feet. "What's wrong with it?"

"There's so much skin showing." He dropped his voice. "And I can see you're not wearing a, um..." His gaze fastened on her chest.

"A bra, Mark. It's called a bra. I hardly ever wear them. Too restricting."

"It's a good thing I got that dog to protect you," he grumbled, forcing his gaze straight ahead.

"From who? You? You're the one who can't keep his eyes to himself."

The picnic basket landed in the back of his SUV with a thump, and she knew the flush on his face wasn't from exertion. At a single sharp gesture from him, the statue dog came to life and launched itself into the vehicle.

She lifted her sun hat and slipped on dark glasses while he closed and locked the rear door.

He held the keys out almost reluctantly and, as they

dropped into her hand, she stuck her chest out as far as a 32B with attitude would go. "Any more orders?"

He took a single step forward. It brought his chest to within almost touching distance of hers. Just a whisper away from contact, she felt the heat coming off him. Smelled the clean laundry and all-male scent of him. How could he infuriate and excite her at the same time? It just wasn't fair.

"Just one. Don't forget your poop and scoop bags."

7

_____

HOW ON EARTH had she gone from being a professional children's entertainer to being a professional poop scooper?

If she had any sense at all, she'd be in Asia. Maybe she'd practice her Japanese on Kitsu and totally confuse him.

Once they reached the park, Annie's annoyance began to lift. It was a beautiful sunny day, and children, lovers and families with real dogs played Frisbee, lounged on blankets and were having fun. The smell of barbecuing meat wafted in the air, and the sound of laughter drifted to her ears.

Annie found a spot near the middle of the huge field and laid out her red and white striped picnic blanket. Emily stood, holding the leash, and Kitsu halted obediently beside her.

"Help me unpack, then we can play some ball."

"Can I let go of the leash?" Emily asked in a doubtful tone.

Annie glanced at the motionless dog. "Yeah. I doubt if dynamite would move that dog without a command. Sit, Kitsu," she said in what she hoped was a commanding tone. The dog seemed to consider her for a few minutes, head cocked, before reluctantly complying and sitting rigidly, eyes on the alert, nose sniffing the air.

"Kitsu's so smart," Emily gushed. "He knows Uncle Mark's his master."

Annie had a suspicion the child was right. Just to be certain he'd obey, she took the leash and draped it over her wrist while she dug into her pack for the ball.

Emily meanwhile had opened the picnic basket. "Yum. Fried chicken." The rustling of cellophane informed Annie that her charge had already found the after-dinner treat. "And jujubes!"

"Those are for after dinner, Em."

"Can I have just one now? Please?"

"Well. Okay. Just one. I know that ball's in here somewhere," she grumbled. A shrill yap made her jump. Her bag tumbled to the blanket.

She was just in time to see the well-trained statue dog undergo the most amazing transformation into some kind of uber-beast. Instinctively she gripped the leash tighter as she watched those powerful legs crouch and prepare to launch the dog into motion.

"Kitsu, no!" she shouted even as the dog catapulted into action.

She felt her arm tugged practically out of its socket as she was yanked forward by an animal who was all muscle and speed.

"Stop, Kitsu! Heel!" Emily yelled from behind her while Annie brought her other hand around and tried to haul on the leash.

"'Scuse me," she panted as she found herself

dragged across a neighboring blanket and stumbling over a couple in a romantic clinch.

Dimly she wondered if the dog had sniffed out drugs or illegal weapons or whatever it was he'd been trained to sniff out.

"Heel!" She leaped over a ghetto blaster like an Olympic hurdler.

"Stay!" She ducked to avoid a Frisbee to the head.

"Sit! Roll over! Play dead!" Nothing slowed the galloping stride of the most powerful dog she'd ever seen in deadly pursuit of what or whom she couldn't see.

Did the police dog have to pick now to go on duty? Didn't he know he'd flunked out of police dog school? Whatever he was racing toward, she didn't want her young charge involved. "Em," she called breathlessly over her shoulder, "stay back."

If she hadn't glanced at Emily, following as fast as her much shorter legs would go, she might have seen the hedge.

"Look out!" Em screamed.

Too late. Laurel leaves and branches whacked her shins. With no breath left to yell at the infernal dog, she hung on grimly to that leash, grimacing in pain as he hauled her through the hedge. One of the perky plastic daisies in her sandal caught, and with a painful wrench she felt the shoe yanked off her foot.

"I'm going to kill you," she panted, so winded her threat came noiselessly from a parched throat. Another field, complete with a crowded children's playground, met her gaze, and desperately she tightened her sweaty hold on the leash.

What was the dog after?

There were no drug dealers or desperate criminal-looking types in her range of vision. In fact, all she could see was one wildly scampering squirrel.

The poor little thing looked like it was running for its life.

It couldn't be.

But it was. Even as the furry little creature veered wildly to the left, the crazed dog followed, closing in on that flapping bushy gray tail.

She wasn't sure which was worse, to be dragged into a drug ring or to witness the slaughter of an innocent woodland creature. The innocent woodland creature had a certain amount of native cunning, however, and headed straight for the crowded playground.

Limping and hopping from bare foot to flapping sandal, Annie screamed a warning. And suddenly, she was dodging swinging swings, dragged under a climbing apparatus and yanked through the sandbox. She had to give the dog some credit—he'd managed to carve a path between all the children. But still, as she sailed out of the playground, a glob of gum sticking to her foot, the sounds of screaming kids and yelling parents pursued her.

Beyond the dog's heaving flanks, the squirrel dashed madly for a stand of trees. Kitsu lowered his muzzle, and she saw that only inches separated those bared teeth from his quarry.

With the last of her strength she tried to put on the brakes, digging one naked heel and the back of one flimsy sandal into the patchy grass.

For her trouble, she was toppled onto her knees and

dragged forward. But she had managed to give the squirrel enough time to scamper up the trunk of a huge Douglas fir.

She may have thought the chase was over, but Kitsu had other ideas. Around and around the tree trunk he dragged her, a dog possessed. Barking and jumping, teeth snapping toward where, high in the branches, the squirrel began a high-pitched chattering.

Annie glanced up and was hit on the forehead with a well-aimed acorn. The squirrel seemed to have an arsenal of various missiles. Down rained acorns, peanuts, walnuts, a popcorn kernel.

That was the last straw. She'd saved that squirrel's life, and it was bopping her on the head with nuts.

She let go of the leash. "Knock yourself out," she told Kitsu. "I am out of here."

Turning, she massaged her sore shoulder and prepared to limp back the way she'd come. Somewhere in the bag she'd abandoned on the picnic blanket—if it was still there—was the magic key ring with the panic button. Let Mark come and collect his wretched beast.

She hadn't gone three painful steps when she saw Emily, hair flying behind her, hot on their trail.

Even in her fury, she managed a small smile. That girl was a trouper.

Emily was breathing hard when she caught up. Unable to speak, she collapsed in Annie's arms and watched Kitsu's insane behavior. He'd managed to wrap the leash so tight around the tree trunk that he almost strangled himself every time he leaped up, barking, while nuts rained down on him.

"What are we going to do?" the child asked in a worried tone.

"Do they make dog meat out of dogs? Or is that just horses?"

"Annie! You wouldn't?"

"With my bare hands."

"Kitsu!"

The dog spared her a glance, tongue hanging out, tail wagging, before resuming its pursuit of the treed squirrel.

"Come on," Annie said. "We'll go back and phone Mark."

"We can't leave Kitsu. Something might happen to him."

"We couldn't be that lucky."

"Please, Annie. Please. He'll get tired in a few minutes."

Privately, Annie thought it would take a rifle full of buckshot to get that dog away from the tree, but she kept her opinion to herself. "I guess I could use a few minutes to rest," she agreed and dropped to the ground, picking at the glob of gum welded to the bottom of her foot.

"Want a jujube?" Emily asked, gesturing with the package she was holding.

"Why not?"

The cellophane rustled, and Emily handed her a bright red candy.

"Look."

The dog's attention had been diverted. Instead of straining to get up the tree, he was straining toward the package in Emily's hands. "Do you think he wants a candy?"

"It's worth a shot."

The girl paused, open bag in hand, and a glimmer of worry crossed her pink cheeks. "Is it good for dogs to eat candy?"

"At this point I'd happily feed him arsenic."

"Kitsu, want a jujube?"

Amazingly, the dog did. He whined and pulled at the leash he'd managed to wrap snugly around the tree trunk until he was half choking himself trying to get to the shiny treat.

Emily approached him, holding out the sweet, which the dog snatched daintily from her fingers and greedily devoured, whining softly for another.

Annie was on her feet by this time, finding the end of the leash and walking in circles until it was free of the trunk.

Emily began dropping jujubes in a trail leading away from the squirrel, and the dog followed, gobbling each one.

They retraced their steps with the perfectly docile Kitsu, giving the playground a wide berth and silently praying they wouldn't meet any more squirrels.

When they returned to their blanket, miraculously everything was still there, but neither of them wanted to risk another squirrel incident, so they packed up everything and lugged it to the truck.

"Pass me a cranberry juice, Em," Annie said once they were all buckled in.

"Uncle Mark doesn't let me have food or drinks in his new truck," Emily warned her, as they drove off, her brake foot uncomfortably naked against the pedal.

"Really? I'll have a piece of chicken, as well. And have one yourself. I'll deal with Uncle Mark."

She didn't exactly *try* to get the steering wheel shiny with grease. But if Mark was stupid enough to stick them with the hound of the Baskervilles as a picnic companion, what could he expect?

THE BIG HOUSE seemed empty and quiet. Mark almost used the word lonely, but that was ridiculous. He'd just got used to Emily being there all the time. And since Annie had moved in, it was like living in the middle of a circus. No wonder it was quiet without them.

He should relax now that he had a police dog guarding the pair of them, but somehow it was impossible.

Annie had been in such a snit with him she hadn't left him any dinner, he noted when he opened the fridge hopefully. He could have cooked himself something, but it was just as easy to phone and get a pizza delivered.

He'd just sunk his teeth into a big gooey slice with all the toppings when he heard the door. He glanced at his watch and allowed himself a smug smile. They were earlier than they'd said they'd be. Kitsu was already making a difference.

As he was mentally congratulating himself on getting the animal, Emily and Annie walked in.

Walked was actually an inaccurate term. Annie limped—painfully, it seemed to him. Her hat and glam sunglasses were gone. As was one sandal. The other was muddy, and one half-plucked daisy hung by a thread. Those tight short pants she'd left the house in were grass-stained, and one knee was torn right out, showing a patch of grazed skin. Even the tight top he'd disapproved of mere hours ago wasn't perky anymore. It had a lot of threads pulled, and globs of dirt and some kind of vegetation stuck to it.

Emily looked better—but not much. Maybe they'd been playing baseball?

But one glance at Annie's face had him revising that idea.

She was wearing a scowl that warned him that whatever had happened, it wasn't a friendly game of baseball, and somehow it was all his fault.

"How'd it go?" he asked.

"Not well," Annie answered, slumping into a chair with a groan.

"It wasn't Kitsu's fault," Emily wailed.

Mark closed the pizza box. He was getting a bad feeling in the pit of his stomach. "What happened?"

Annie was pulling things out of the sole of her foot. Slivers maybe, the way she was wincing. He directed the question to his niece.

"He was really good, Uncle Mark. Until he saw a squirrel. Then he kind of went nuts and chased it."

"Kitsu chased a squirrel?"

"Yes."

"Didn't you call him to heel?"

"About a million times."

"And?"

"He, um, he ignored us."

"But he's a trained police dog. He'll always come to heel."

Annie glanced up at that, and he noticed her face was streaked with mud. "Not if he sees a squirrel, he won't," she assured him.

Suddenly, he remembered the police trainer's report. And that notation he couldn't read. It had looked like "squiggle." Maybe the word that trainer had written was "squirrel."

As though she'd read his thoughts, Annie said, "I think we now know why Kitsu flunked police dog school."

"You'd better tell me exactly what happened," he ordered with a sinking feeling in his gut.

By the time they'd finished their recital he knew he had no choice but to get rid of Kitsu. The guard dog was worse than useless. By dragging Annie all over the park, he'd effectively left Emily completely unprotected.

"But he came right to heel as soon as I gave him a jujube," his niece assured him, as though that would make Mark forgive the wayward canine.

He took a long pull of the beer he'd opened a few minutes ago, when the world had seemed normal. "I'm sorry," he said. He wasn't really sure who he was apologizing to—his niece or his shoeless nanny. All he knew was he'd made an uncharacteristic, but colossal, error in judgment. He'd been so eager to make everything work out, he hadn't researched the dog properly. He shuddered to think what disasters could have occurred because of his haste.

"Emily, honey, I need to speak to Annie alone for a minute."

"It wasn't Kitsu's fault, Uncle Mark. Really it wasn't. I'll go feed him his dinner now."

"All right," he said heavily.

He waited until she'd left the room. "I'll return him in the morning."

Annie glanced at him, her green eyes shining out of a grubby face. "I need a bath." That was all she said.

A few minutes later, Emily bounded into the room, the German shepherd at her heels.

His tongue lolled out, and his eyes gleamed with innocence, as though he hadn't terrorized a small furry animal, frightened a playground of little children and dragged Annie for miles, ignoring every command he'd been taught.

Tail wagging, he approached Mark with the tired whine of a dog who's spent a satisfying day. He lay at his master's feet, his head on his paws, and dropped to sleep.

Emily glanced from Annie to him, a worried look on her face. "You won't…you won't do anything, will you, Uncle Mark?"

"I'm sorry, Em, but Kitsu's going to have to go back."

To his horror, tears flooded Emily's eyes and spilled over onto her cheeks. "No! It's not fair." She'd been so brave all year, though he knew her little heart had broken when her parents died. He cursed himself for letting her get attached to the dog so quickly.

"Please, Em," he heard himself pleading. "Try to understand."

"You promised we could keep him. You promised." And with a heartrending sob, she threw herself into Annie's arms.

Over Emily's head, Annie shot him a look of reproach. But what was he supposed to do?

Frustrated beyond bearing, he took in the sobbing child, the glaring nanny and the snoring dog.

It was all too much.

While every sensible instinct told him he was doing the right thing in returning the beast, his softer emotions overruled him.

A tense minute passed for everyone except the happily snoring beast.

"Oh, all right," he snapped. "I'll give him one more chance. Just one."

Like magic, the sobbing stopped. Emily lifted her head from Annie's shoulder and turned a wet but smiling face his way. "Thanks, Uncle Mark. He'll be good from now on. I know he will." She jumped up and came over to give him a hug before dropping to her knees and giving the dog an even more loving embrace. Kitsu roused himself enough to stop snoring and lick her face with his huge tongue.

Determined to assert his authority in some small way, Mark ordered her to bed after her busy day, and without any argument or delay, she went. Followed by the useless watchdog.

He turned to his nanny with a feeling she wasn't going to be so easy to pacify. "You have a piece of peanut shell in your hair."

She grunted. "I probably have half of Stanley Park in my hair." Sitting slumped in one of the overstuffed chairs in the family room, she appeared much younger. And very, very cranky.

"Why don't you go and have that hot bath?"

With a tired sigh she nodded and rose.

"Do you want a glass of wine to take up with you?"

"I'll have it afterward. I hope you buy your wine by the gallon jug."

He half smiled as she limped out, so tired she didn't seem to notice she was wearing just one sandal. The plastic daisy bobbed hopelessly. He had a feeling he had as much hope of hanging on to his nanny as that shoe had of hanging on to that daisy.

A moment of panic speared him. What would he do without Annie? He was already down one guard dog. He had to find a way to stop Annie from quitting. He wracked his brain.

Could he flatter her into staying?

Beg her?

Change the outgoing code so she'd never get out of the house?

He'd start with flattery, he decided, and move on from there if he had to. He paused as he began assembling a tray of wine and glasses, remembering the sight of her grazed knee. Before he started on flattery, he'd better apply first aid.

It made an odd collection, once he had everything assembled in his rarely used sunken living room. A good bottle of wine, glasses, some slices of pizza on a plate, a first-aid kit. She was probably feeling the way he used to after a difficult arrest. Not only tired, but bruised. The way she'd been rubbing her shoulder, she could have strained the muscles. He went back and dug out the rubbing alcohol.

He put a jazz CD on, soft and soothing in the background. Then paused.

Would she think he was trying to seduce her?

He couldn't take any chances that she might misinterpret his intention. Irritably he jabbed the button, choking the sultry singer in mid croon.

He grabbed all the stuff and stomped to the familiar shabbiness of the family room.

And tried to think up something to say that would make her stay.

When she came into the room half an hour later, he still hadn't thought of anything. He glanced up, hoping inspiration would hit him, and noticed she was wearing the same multicoloured dress she'd worn the day he met her. Had she dressed up? For him? Damn. Maybe he should have stayed in the living room, after all.

She winced as she walked, lifting the hem of her dress impatiently until it was several inches above her knee, where the grazed skin was inflamed. "Ouch. I can't stand to have anything touch it."

"Don't you have a bathrobe?"

"Yep. It's somewhere in Spain. Madrid, maybe, or Barcelona. I never did figure out where I left it." She shrugged. "I never replaced it. It's just one less thing to lose."

What kind of woman didn't want a bathrobe? he asked himself. A woman who didn't want to be encumbered, that's who. A woman who would look at him and his life-style and see one big encumbrance.

She sat down, and he shifted an ottoman under her outstretched leg.

"First things first," he said, gesturing to the bottle on the table. "Red all right? Or I've got white in the fridge."

"Red's great."

He poured each of them a glass of Merlot and let her take a sip before clicking open his first-aid kit and dropping to his knees on the floor at her feet.

An amused smile flickered across her face as he cleaned, creamed and bandaged her knee. He did his level best not to notice how warm and soft her skin felt beneath his hand or to see the little patch of goose bumps that rose when he applied the antiseptic lotion.

Once he'd covered the grazed skin with a bandage, he couldn't smell the antiseptic anymore. Only Annie. And she smelled so good, warm and still damp from her bath. He caught the scent of tropical fruits and the nearer scent of woman.

He gently lifted the foot he'd seen her limping on and studied the sole. "What's this red patch?" he asked, concerned.

"Bubble gum," came the succinct reply. "I had to scrub with a nail brush to get it all off."

"Ouch. You've got a few slivers here, too." He shuffled through his first-aid kit.

"What are you planning on doing with that needle? And those tweezers?"

He grinned at her. "Drink some more wine. You won't feel a thing."

"That's what my first boyfriend said," she mumbled.

Deciding the safest response to that was none, he got to work, carefully digging splinters out of her foot. Apart from a little squirming and some mild whining, she let him get on with the job.

She had very nice feet. Not shapely like a dancer's, more broad and sensible, like a woman who does a lot of walking. Or running. The pads were firm and a little callused, the toes square and somehow sexy.

And he tried to forget all about the long, luscious legs they were attached to.

"That was a good thing you did. Letting Emily keep the dog."

He glanced up, a frown pulling his eyebrows together. "It was moronic."

Her gaze locked with his, and a sweet smile lit up her face. "No, it wasn't. Losing Kitsu would have broken her heart."

"That dog is a completely useless protector."

She tilted her head. "Oh, I don't know. I think it's safe to say we'll be protected from marauding squirrels with evil intentions."

He allowed himself a stiff grin and, putting her foot gently on the floor, flopped to the couch beside her. "It's not squirrels I'm worried about."

"You're worried about everything from unfriendly aliens to the bogeyman."

A spurt of righteous anger filled his gut. "I promised her mother—"

"Yeah, yeah. I've heard it. Do you think her

mother meant for you to wrap that child up in cotton wool and never let her experience life?''

Dull anger kept him silent.

''Do you?''

More silence.

''Life is risk, Mark. You're not helping Emily, keeping her trapped in this fortress. You've got to let her live.''

''Mighty fine talk from a woman who's so scared of commitment she doesn't even own a bathrobe.''

He had the dubious satisfaction of knowing he'd managed to make Annie as mad as she'd made him. Her cheeks flushed, and she glared. ''What does my bathrobe have to do with anything?''

''It's just so easy for you to waltz in here for a few weeks, load me up with advice and waltz out. I'll be seeing Emily into adulthood. I doubt you'll make it through the week.''

Her mouth opened and closed a few times. With shock, he noticed her eyes fill with tears. Her head drooped, and she said sadly, ''You're right. I guess things aren't working out that well.''

Belatedly he remembered he was supposed to be flattering her to make her stay, and here he was damned well taunting her to leave. What was Plan B again? Oh, yeah. Beg.

She drew a deep breath. ''Mark, I—''

He had to stop her before she quit. He had to. He grabbed her hand. ''Please. Don't let Emily down. She really needs you. It's just a few more weeks until Bea gets back.''

She shook her head sadly. ''I don't think—''

"I only let that useless dog stay because I knew I could count on you." *Liar.*

It worked, though. Her eyes opened wide. "You did?"

"Yes, ma'am." And in a way, he realized it was true. Annie would do her best to look after Emily. He just wasn't convinced her best was good enough.

"Well…"

He could tell he needed to give her something more than flattering words to prove how much he trusted her. He gulped. "I'll take the outgoing code off the door."

"You will?" Amazement shone in her eyes. He wasn't surprised. He was amazed himself. What was he doing?

"Sure. I'll have one of the guys come in and rewire it."

She smiled at him, a perky, provocative little smile that reminded him how cute she was and that her skirt was still pulled halfway up her thighs. "And I'll try harder to call in on time."

"Deal." He shook the much smaller hand he was still holding.

"And this is for letting Em keep Kitsu," she said, then leaned forward impulsively and kissed his cheek.

At the feel of those soft, sweet lips brushing his face, something happened. It was as though all the plucking splinters and dressing wounds had been an unusual, but very effective, form of foreplay.

For the moment her lips touched his cheek, he was lost. The soft brush of moist skin was as erotic as the most brazen caress. He'd been as restrained and as circumspect as any Canadian Mountie could be. But underneath, he was still a red-blooded male, and if the lady was going to start kissing him, well...

Her lips hovered for a moment, leaving his cheek but not pulling away. Not yet.

He tugged the hand he was still holding and she tumbled against his chest with a little coo of satisfaction. He turned his head, and she turned hers until their mouths met.

Hungrily.

8

ALL THE pent-up urges he'd been suppressing roared to life. He wanted to crush her body against him, but knowing she'd been battered by her little walk in the park with Kitsu, he held her gently, crushing only her lips beneath his.

She didn't seem to mind the crushed lips. In fact, she pushed her body closer to his until he couldn't restrain himself any longer and pulled her in tight. As her breasts flattened against his chest, he was glad for once that she wasn't wearing a bra. The natural feel of the flesh plastered to his chest and the two points tormenting him as she moved herself against him were wildly exciting.

All the sensible reasons they shouldn't be doing this were as easily crushed as her lips beneath his. She opened her mouth to him, and he didn't need a second invitation. Plunging his tongue inside, he found her hot and sweet. As intoxicating as the red wine he could taste on her tongue.

A low, rhythmic thumping came to his attention. It was too slow to be the beating of his heart. He pulled himself reluctantly away from Annie's mouth and glanced around to see Kitsu's tail thumping the floor in greeting. His muzzle pointed to the doorway where

Mark was just in time to see a flash of white that looked suspiciously like his niece's nightdress.

"Emily?" he called softly.

No answer.

Annie sat up, her eyes huge as she, too, stared toward the doorway. "Do you think she saw us?" she whispered.

"It's a distinct possibility," he admitted, and swore softly. He was always so careful. Not that his love life had seen much action since Emily moved in with him, but what there was had always been conducted elsewhere. His nanny had a way of making him lose his head so badly he felt like smacking it against the wall to try to scramble his brain into shape.

"I could go up and talk to her." Annie sounded full of doubt. Her hand crept to her ear, and she started fiddling with the array of silver earrings.

He tried to recall what he'd read in all those child-rearing books about how to handle situations like this, but he came up blank and decided to go with his gut instinct. "Let's just leave it for now. We don't know that she even saw anything. If she brings the subject up, I'll have a talk with her."

"You will?" Annie sounded shocked.

"Sure, why not? It won't be something I'll look forward to, but if she has questions, she deserves straight answers."

"My dad…" She stared at the dog, snoozing on the rug.

"Your dad what?" he asked, sinking back on the couch, knowing his niece had doused his plans for the evening. And a good thing, too. He must have been out of his mind to consider sleeping with Annie, a woman who abandoned men like bathrobes. Still, he was only human, and his body ached for her. If he couldn't make love to her, at least he could talk to her, and the serious tone of her voice told him she was thinking about something important.

"My dad never did any of the difficult jobs in our house. That was always my mom."

"When you say difficult, you're not talking about taking out the garbage, are you?"

She laughed softly. "No. My dad's the most fun person I know, but he can't take responsibility. My mom had to do everything from manage the family finances, which weren't pretty, to the discipline, to the dishes. And she got so resentful she started nagging my dad whenever he was home." She shrugged and shot him a bitter smile. "So he just stopped coming home."

"Nice guy."

"He is." She fired the words back. "He's just not cut out for the domestic scene. And I'm totally like him. I'm lucky I could learn from his mistakes. I'm not cut out for the family thing, either."

"Maybe you underestimate yourself," he said softly. Wondering who he was trying to convince.

"Uncle Mark?"

"Uh-huh?" He glanced up to find Emily hovering in his office doorway, fiddling with the ear of her stuffed lion. She'd carried that mangy thing around for weeks after her parents died. It gave him a start to see her with it again. Apart from sleeping with it every night, she'd pretty much detached herself from the flea-bitten creature. His gut felt queasy. She must be here to ask him what had been going on in the family room last night. He only wished he knew.

"I was wondering…"

"Yes, Em." He braced himself for what was coming. Please God, don't let the conversation lead to where babies came from or some mortifying aspect of femaledom he didn't feel qualified to answer. He marshaled his thoughts rapidly, trying to prepare a few answers. *Yes, I was kissing Annie, because I like her very much. Sometimes when grown-ups like each other…* The queasiness grew worse. This was going to be a lot tougher than he'd anticipated.

"Um, could I send Bea a get-well card?"

"What?" Could he possibly have heard right?

"Bea. I want to send her a card."

Relief made him able to breathe again. "Well, sure. But I think she's almost better now." Emily had probably just crept down to check on Kitsu and never noticed him and Annie tucked away on the couch. They had been pretty quiet. He slumped in his chair, vowing never to make out with Annie or anyone else again unless it was behind locked doors.

"I know. But I feel bad I never sent her one before."

"I sent her some flowers from both of us."

"But I really want to send her a card. Just from me." She glanced up, and he noticed a certain determination around the jaw that reminded him of her mother. He knew that expression well. Unless he wanted a knock-down, drag-out fight, that little face was going to get its way. And it was a perfectly nice idea.

He tweaked her hair. "Sure thing. We can go to the store and pick one out or we can make something on the computer."

She smiled right back at him. "Let's make one on the computer."

It didn't take them long to make the card. Then he helped her print the address on an envelope and stamp it.

"I can mail that for you tomorrow, Em. I bet Bea will be thrilled you thought of her."

Her face flushed. "No. I want to mail it. Please, Uncle Mark? Annie can help me tomorrow."

With Annie's help, Bea might get the card in time for Christmas, but if it made Em happy to do it all herself, he was proud of her just for seeing the project all the way through. Yep. Her mother's determination would take her far.

He watched her carry the card to her room and shook his head. He'd been ready to talk about grown-ups and sex and all she wanted to do was make a get-well card.

Kids.

"ANNIE?" Em's voice rose a little at the end in a way Annie was beginning to recognize as uncertainty.

"Mm?" They were adding toppings to pizza crust, each decorating her own. Annie added a couple more crescents of red pepper to the clown lips on her face. She had no idea what the finished product was going to taste like, but it sure looked cute. Red cabbage made awesomely curly purple hair.

She'd found some olives for eyes. Black would have been best, but as they didn't have any, she'd made do with stuffed green ones, kind of liking the red dot of pimiento for the pupil in the eye. Her clown pizza had red tomato cheeks, green pepper eyebrows and mozzarella cheese face paint.

Emily was attempting to render Kitsu in pizza. The result was interesting, to say the least, and since she'd promised to eat it, as well as the organic salad, Annie let her use chocolate-covered peanuts for eyes and cover some of the cheese with chocolate powder for his fur.

"We're having a take-your-mom-to-school project where we get to invite our moms to come and talk about what they do. If you don't have a mom, you're allowed to bring another grown-up lady who's special. And I wondered if I could bring you?"

"You want to take me to school with you?" Annie was surprised at the rush of warmth she felt at the compliment. Emily thought of her as a special woman in her life.

"Oh, yeah. Most of the moms do boring stuff like lawyer and dentist and stuff. Everyone would think it was so cool to have a clown."

Well, that brought her ego down a notch. So it wasn't that she was so special. It was because she was a clown that Em wanted her at school. "When is it?" She'd love to come, but she had to remember that she'd be on her way soon. They both had to remember it before there were any hurt feelings.

It was easy when it was a man she was leaving behind. But she'd never left a child before. She'd tried to stop herself from getting involved, and Emily from getting attached to her, but she wasn't sure she'd succeeded.

She was going to miss Emily, she suddenly realized.

And Mark? a little voice in her head whispered. What about him? Did she think she could just waltz out of his life with no regrets?

A red pepper strip snapped in her fingers.

It wasn't fair. She'd been very, very clear with both of them that she was on her way to Asia. This was a temporary thing. What was Emily doing asking her to be a stand-in mom? What was Mark doing kissing her breathless and then leaving her so full of sexual cravings she couldn't sleep?

Didn't they have any consideration for her feelings?

She was going to have to be firm. Make it clear that there was to be no emotional entangling happening in the next few weeks.

"Em, I..." She started forcefully enough. Then unfortunately made the mistake of glancing at the little face gazing at her.

"I, uh..." She had to refuse. It wasn't fair to raise any unrealistic expectations. But the pool of warmth kept growing. Emily saw her as a mother figure. "When is it?"

"In two weeks. Just before school ends."

"I'd love to come."

The grin of delight made her glad she'd accepted.

And it was pretty cool that Emily saw her as a mother figure. A sensible older woman she could confide in.

"Will you wear your costume?"

Annie giggled at her own absurdity. Em wanted Gertrude. She didn't see Annie as any kind of mother. Who would? "If you want me to."

The violent nod sent Emily's ponytail bobbing.

"Tell you what, why don't we both dress up and we'll do a couple of those tricks we've been practicing together?"

"That'd be sweet!"

She couldn't resist leaning down and giving Em a hug. But she had to make absolutely sure the child didn't get any wrong ideas. "You know I'm not here for much longer. Bea will probably be back soon."

A funny expression crossed Emily's face. The kid looked like some shifty character in the movies caught in a lie. But that was just her mind playing tricks on her. Probably she was projecting her own guilt. She knew she was a better nanny than Bea. Well, unless a cutthroat gang of ninja fighters decided to invade North Vancouver. Then Bea would have her beat hands down in the nanny department.

"But what if Bea didn't come back? Then you could stay."

"I can't Em. I...I'm not a real nanny. I do birthday parties."

"But you can do both, just like now."

"I'm also going on a trip. To Asia."

Em spooned mustard onto the pizza, drawing marks

on Kitsu's fur with her fingertip. "You could go any old time. Don't you like me?"

"Of course I like you."

"Don't you like Uncle Mark?"

In spite of herself, heat rushed to her face. Did she ever like Uncle Mark, and if she didn't get out of there soon, something more than necking on the couch was going to happen between them. "I like your uncle just fine."

"He likes you, too. I can tell."

"Let's get these pizzas finished, then we can take Kitsu for a walk."

"We're out of jujubes. We'll have to stop at the store first."

Annie had a funny feeling she'd forgotten something, then with a start glanced at the clock on the stove and saw it was already four o'clock. "Oops, better report in to our parole officer." She'd been a lot better about remembering to phone Mark at three-thirty—or thereabouts. Calling in half an hour late was practically on time.

"What?"

"Why don't you call your uncle and tell him how your day went?"

"Okay."

She heard Em's sprightly rendition of her day's events, then the voice turned accusing. "But you've worked late every night this week. Can't you get home early? Please? I want to show you how smart Kitsu is. We play catch with the rubber squirrel Annie bought him—"

The child turned from the kitchen phone to Annie

and rolled her eyes. "Yes. A rubber squirrel." She sighed. "Okay. See you later. Bye."

Annie felt her forehead crease. Every night since the one they'd spent kissing on the couch, he'd had to work late. She wished she knew whether it was the conference keeping him busy, or whether he was trying to avoid her.

This thing between them was driving her crazy. It didn't matter how late he worked, she heard him come in and move around his room late at night. Then she'd imagine him in his bed just a wall away from her. Did he sleep naked? Or was he a pajamas guy? She'd wonder, and then she'd start thinking about how much she wanted to be in the same bed with him.

As little as they'd been together in the past few days, she'd felt his presence every moment he was in the house. Glanced up to find his eyes on her, so deeply blue and smoldering she felt scorched.

And frustrated.

She wasn't like this. She was a normal, uncomplicated woman who liked sex. All this denial was definitely not healthy. He had a door that locked, and she had an escape hatch in the form of a trip to Asia.

A brief, uncomplicated affair was what they both needed. And tonight seemed like a good time to get started.

Once the decision was made, a delicious thrill of anticipation washed over her.

He was the one with the Mountie training, but she was the one about to get her man.

Just as Annie and Emily were leaving the house,

the phone rang. Emily answered it. "Hi, Brodie." She listened for a moment then turned to Annie. "Uncle Mark's's friend Brodie left his tennis racket here. He's going to play tennis and he wants to come pick it up."

"But we're just leaving."

Emily handed her the phone. "He wants to talk to you."

"Hello?"

"I hear you're beautiful," said the confident masculine voice on the other end.

She laughed. "Have you been talking to my mother?"

"No. To the most serious man in the world. If he says you're beautiful, you are. How 'bout I come round and see for myself?"

Mark had told his friend she was beautiful? She felt the compliment and was more flattered than she cared to admit. His friend was the kind of man she understood. Easy and casual. She knew instinctively he'd never try to tie her down. Quite the opposite, she suspected. Her kind of guy.

But not today. "Sorry, Emily and I are just on our way out."

He cursed softly. "I booked a game for this afternoon and forgot my racket was at Mark's place."

"Why don't I leave it outside the door?"

"It's a very expensive racket."

"I'll hide it behind the juniper bush out front, then," she said, improvising.

He sighed noisily. "I'd rather you gave it to me in person."

She glanced at Em, already waiting by the door, Kitsu on his leash. "Maybe another time."

"You got a date, babe."

"What are you laughing about?" Em wanted to know when Annie put down the receiver.

"Men, honey. Men."

After they found the racket and hid it behind the bush they got into Annie's little car and backed out. Only then did she remember the cursed security gate. Brodie was on his way, and she had no way of getting hold of him. She tapped the steering wheel in frustration, determined not to give up their afternoon outing because of Mark and his security paranoia.

Glancing around the car for inspiration, she noticed she'd left her white trainers in the back. Perfect. After backing the car out past the gate, she grabbed a shoe and hopped out, then wedged it into the gate so it couldn't close completely. The door of Fort Knox was still locked, so there was no way burglars could get in. With a clear conscience she drove to the beach, where they'd never yet seen a squirrel.

While they walked Kitsu, keeping pockets of jujubes handy and a weather eye out for furry-tailed creatures, Annie plotted Mountie seduction.

She didn't own a negligee and somehow disliked the idea of a contrived seduction scene. She finally decided she'd beard the lion in his den, as it were. She'd go knock on his door once he was in bed. She had a strong feeling that would get her man. Especially if she walked in on him in her usual night attire.

Nothing at all.

A brisk wind churned the choppy waves, and dark

clouds scudded across the sky, but Kitsu was well behaved, and Em had an idea for a new trick. She wanted to make pencils disappear when she brought Annie to school.

"That's pretty easy," Annie assured her. "We'll need a big handkerchief and a few hours' practice. We can also pluck an eraser from behind your teacher's ear if you want."

They giggled and planned until the first fat drops of rain plopped on their bare heads. "We should have brought an umbrella," Em wailed as the smattering of rain turned into a downpour.

"I don't own an umbrella."

"Uncle Mark does. He has lots."

"Why am I not surprised? Come on, let's run for the car."

"BAD NEWS, MARK. He's confirmed," said Amanda Kelly, his executive assistant, sighing and leaning into his office.

"The dictator?"

She nodded. Amanda looked as tired as he felt.

"Damn." He rubbed the back of his neck. Security planning for the conference had been going too smoothly. Now they'd have to add extra security for the unpopular dictator whose health had been failing and whom Mark had hoped would stay home. Mentally he began reviewing the extra precautions he'd need to take.

There'd be more political and law-enforcement liaisons to be added to the equation, tighter security all around. His job had just got a lot bigger. "Right. Set up a meeting with—"

He was interrupted by a redheaded, red-faced home security monitor, who brushed past Amanda. "Mark, your home gate's been breached."

He was on his feet and running. His team knew what to do without being told. What he needed to do was get home. An overwhelming fear began to build in his chest as he raced to protect his girls.

While he drove home as fast as he dared, he tried Annie's cell. No answer. His home phone. The service.

He decided to drive by his house and make a visual assessment of the situation, then he'd put a plan of action together based on what he could see.

He drove by the house, careful not to draw attention to himself by traveling too slowly, and squinted against the ominous gray clouds.

It didn't take long. A familiar running shoe propped the gate open. He slammed on the brakes and began cursing. And put an immediate plan together. Simple and expedient.

Fire the damn nanny.

9

"YIPPEE, Uncle Mark's home," squealed Emily as they drove through the gate.

A delicious quiver of anticipation danced in Annie's belly. He'd come home early today of all days. It was like a sign that they were meant to get up close and personal tonight. She had all evening to seduce him in subtle little ways. She could hardly wait to get started.

Even Kitsu was happy. He leaped from the tiny hatchback and jumped and danced toward the front door. He acted more like a puppy and less like a guard dog every day, she was pleased to note.

Checking to make sure her belly ring was in plain view and suddenly not minding so much that her shirt had got plastered to her body by the rain, she followed, wondering who belonged to the red sports car parked beside Mark's SUV and very much hoping the owner wasn't female.

Emily was in the door ahead of her, the dog bounding behind. "Hi, Uncle Mark. Hi, Brodie," she called in her singsong voice.

When she followed Em into the kitchen where two powerfully built men were drinking beer, Annie discovered two things. One, Brodie matched his voice.

He was slick, from his groomed mustache to the tennis whites he managed to wear with a rakish air. From his position, lounging against the counter, predatory hazel eyes scanned her openly and shouted, "Come to bed," loud and clear.

The second thing she noticed was that Mark was in a fine temper. His eyes were cold, hard, blue ice chips in a face of stone, the jaw so powerfully clamped she was surprised she couldn't hear his teeth cracking under the strain.

There were dents in the beer can he was gripping—dents just about the size of his fingers—and, far from lounging, he paced until he caught sight of her, then stood rigid as a totem pole and glared at her.

Seemed like her seduction wasn't going to be as easy as she'd planned.

"Hi," she said breezily.

"I see my friend here didn't lie. Hi, beautiful, I'm Brodie." He came forward with a cocky stride and an easy grin. Handshakes weren't usually sexy in her experience, but he managed to make his a come-on.

Mark reminded her forcibly of a volcano about to blow. "Don't you have a tennis date?" he asked his friend pointedly.

Brodie gestured with his beer can toward the nearest window, where drops of water splattered the pane. "Rained out. Besides, I wanted to meet Annie." He shot her a killer grin.

She returned it.

And heard a metallic ding as Mark added another dent to his beer can. "You'll have to postpone it. I need to talk to Annie."

"Look, buddy, it's my fault. I forgot about the gate. How was she supposed to know emergency alarms would go off at mission control?" Brodie asked in a tone that suggested he was repeating himself.

Alarms? Mission control? Oh, no. She'd done it again. With a sinking feeling in the pit of her stomach, she conceded that propping Mark's high-tech security gate open with a shoe probably hadn't been all that smart. She faced her stone-faced employer. "I'm really sorry. I never thought—"

"That's exactly the problem. You never do think. You just take off from one irresponsible, harebrained act to another." His words blasted her like a blowtorch.

"Uncle Mark, she didn't—"

"Go to your room, Emily. This doesn't concern you."

Both females stared at him in shock. He'd never used that tone with his niece before.

"Don't you yell at Emily!"

"She's my niece, not yours!" he shouted back.

"You better not do anything mean to Annie," Emily contributed. And with that she burst into tears and dashed out of the room.

Kitsu, not to be left out, rushed into the fray barking and growling at all of them indiscriminately. Then, catching sight of his rubber squirrel in the corner, he took his frustrations out on that, gripping it fiercely in his teeth and shaking it back and forth, growling ferociously the entire time. Having made his point, he glared at the three adults and trotted after

Emily, the mauled and sorry-looking rubber squirrel hanging from his mouth.

"The dog takes that round," Brodie commented.

Mark glared at him. "Would you take a hike?"

"Uh-uh. I wouldn't miss this for anything," Brodie said, lounging once more.

"I don't see what the big deal is," Annie said, starting to get seriously steamed. "The doors to the house were all locked."

Mark took a step toward her, and she fought an impulse to step back. She'd never seen him so mad. "The deal is, one—" he slapped one forefinger against the other "—when you breach the system you compromise everybody's safety. Two—" he banged his middle finger "—false alarms are expensive and time-consuming. Three—" his ring finger took the strike "—I've got a dictator coming to town—"

"To take lessons from you?" she interrupted.

A soft chuckle came from Brodie's direction. "I think Annie takes that game."

"Four," Annie shouted, so angry she felt like throwing things. One bullheaded ex-Mountie, for a start. "You are such a pigheaded, Neanderthal control freak, you can't stand to let anybody out of your sight."

"Set." Brodie mimed a tennis serve, but the two combatants were so intent on each other, neither paid attention.

"I don't dare—every time I turn my back you do something stupid."

"The only stupid thing I ever did was take this job

in the first place. Let me remove my harebrained, irresponsible, *stupid* self from your presence. I quit.''

She grabbed her leather bag and stormed blindly toward the door. She heard Brodie's voice like a sports announcer's. ''And match!''

''Where do you think you're going?'' She heard Mark stomping behind her and swung around. But before she could launch another verbal assault, Brodie was there taking her arm.

''She's coming for dinner with me.''

She opened her mouth to refuse, then heard Mark say, ''Oh, no she's not.''

She gave Brodie her most dazzling smile. ''Thanks, I'd love to.''

HE PACED the house like a caged beast. He was going to fire her.

How dare she quit on him?

And as for that Brodie… When he got his hands on his former friend the man was going to be sorry he was ever born. Only Emily being in the house stopped Mark from jumping in his vehicle to go after his former nanny and his former friend.

Instead he was stuck at home, cursing and waiting, knowing she'd probably end up in Brodie's arms for the night while Mark was the one who'd been aching for her ever since the moment he saw her. Maybe he was a Neanderthal, but if Brodie laid so much as one finger on her, he'd…well he'd think of something.

He made his peace with Emily, assuring her Annie would be back soon and hoping beyond hope he was right.

Then he went back to pacing. It was stupid to torture himself this way. He should start planning for the dictator's arrival at the conference. He should do some paperwork.

Work out.

Get some sleep.

Still, he paced. And wished he hadn't gone off the deep end. It was just that he'd been so damned worried. And scared that something had happened to them.

For the hundredth time he peered into the night. Her car was still there, so she'd have to come back sometime. He really didn't want it to be tomorrow morning, in Brodie's passenger seat.

She was right. He did worry too much. And she was responsible in her own way, he had to admit. He shouldn't have lost his cool. When she came back, he'd apologize.

Around midnight he gave up and had a long, hot shower, hoping to ease some of his tension. Then he shaved. He didn't stop to ask himself why. As he was drying off, he heard a car engine. A loud, in-your-face sports car engine. He knew that sound.

Bolting naked to the window, he was in time to see the passenger door of the red car open. The indoor light came on, spotlighting what happened next.

Brodie said something, and she turned to him. Even from this distance Mark recognized the sweet smile she turned on his old buddy. She shook her head, then leaned forward and brushed Brodie's lips with hers before getting out and shutting the car door behind her.

He had his bathrobe on in seconds and pounded down the stairs tying the belt.

By the time he got the door open she'd reached her car, and Brodie was long gone. The fact that her car was her destination, rather than his house, infuriated him all over again. He stomped up to her. "Going to Brodie's place?"

"None of your business."

"You didn't get enough? Mauling each other in his car like a couple of teenagers?" What he'd seen had been a chaste peck, nothing more, and he knew it. But damn if she was getting away before they'd finished the fight they had started.

At first, he thought she wasn't going to answer, then she turned to face him, and her green eyes caught the light of the moon, dazzling him. "Jealous?" she whispered in a voice that taunted even as it thrilled him. Her lips were soft and full, pursed in a sassy way.

"Damn right I'm jealous." He didn't even think, just grabbed her to him tight and kissed her like there was no tomorrow.

She gave a little whimpery sigh against his lips and then wrapped herself around him.

He thrust his tongue deeply, possessively into her mouth, and she licked up and down its length with her own, making him weak in the knees with the power of his desire.

"I'm sorry," he whispered when he came up for air.

"I'm sorry," she gasped in answer, and then they were kissing again.

Cool air currents eddied around them while the heat between them built. Then he felt cool air where it had no business being. She'd taken him in her hands beneath the parted robe.

He groaned helplessly as she touched and caressed him, knowing he had about three seconds of conscious thought left before instinct and desire took over completely.

They'd never make it upstairs, their need was too urgent, but neither would he risk even the remotest chance that Em might look out her window and see them. Annie was leaning against her little car, which wouldn't fit a pair of mating chipmunks, never mind two grown adults.

But his Jeep would.

He grabbed her hands and led her to his vehicle, found the spare key in its magnetized box and opened the back door.

He thought she might balk. Instead she swiftly stripped off her shorts, leaving her in nothing but a cropped, tight T-shirt and one of those thong things by way of underwear. He damn near lost it right there.

But the thing he needed most was upstairs in his bedside table. With a silent groan, he leaned his head on the door frame, which only gave him a better view of Annie, all eager for him in the back seat, the little jewel in her navel winking at him.

Then he remembered. "Your bag. Where's your bag?"

"I don't know. I dropped it, I think."

He found it in seconds on the ground beside her car. Rummaging through, he gave a silent crow of triumph. The open box of condoms was still there. He stuck them in his pocket.

He eased into the back seat, then shut the door with the quietest of clicks, plunging them into darkness. In his haste, he banged his elbow on a headrest, and his knee got tangled up in his bathrobe.

"I'm too old for this," he grumbled, groping around until he found her breasts. "Or not."

She chuckled softly. "Not too old, but definitely too big. You're squishing me."

With more grunting and shuffling and bumping of body parts, which only inflamed them more, they found a better position, sitting facing each other. Ignoring his cramped knees, he reached out and touched the soft flesh of her thighs.

With a little whimper, she opened her legs to him.

He made her wait just a little bit while he savored the soft tenderness of the inside of her thighs inch by soft, sweet inch, until at last he reached higher and cupped the crisp warmth of her nest of curls.

Even as she sighed against him, his hand stalled. "What happened to your underpants?"

"They melted," she whispered.

When he cupped the moist heat of her, he almost believed it. Beneath his middle finger he felt the slick wetness that told him she was as excited as he. Unable to stop himself, he slid that finger slowly deeper, letting her suck him in like hot quicksand.

Her head fell back, and her hips arched against him. She was so slick and so very hot. Crazy little sounds were coming from her lips, and deep within her he could feel a trembling begin. He plunged a second finger into her, and just like that she shattered.

He leaned toward her, wanting to taste her.

"Wait. Wait," Annie panted, pulling back.

He gazed at her dumbly, knowing he'd gone too far to stop now. She'd have to really, really want to call a halt before he'd give up on what they'd started, and one glance at her heated cheeks and drugged-looking eyes was enough to confirm that she didn't want to stop any more than he did.

What she wanted, he soon discovered, was to take control.

And he was happy to let her.

She straddled him, grunting when she hit her head on the roof, then dug into his pocket and efficiently sheathed him, turning it into a caress that left him burning for her.

She didn't make him wait long, but spread herself over him and slowly eased him into her. He felt the slight pull as she closed around him, so tight, so hot.

He wanted to plunge and thrust wildly, but he held himself rigidly still until she was ready.

"You are so big," she gasped once she held him completely inside her.

"I'm sorry," he said, contrite. "I should have warned you."

She giggled happily. "It's okay. Really."

Then she started moving, and he stopped thinking. And pretty soon he lost all control and plunged and thrust while she rode him until they both cried out and slumped against each other, spent and gasping.

He patted the leather seat beneath them. "Good thing this baby's got four-wheel drive. That was some wild ride."

10

___

Now THAT the first urgency was spent, they had time to go more slowly. But he'd had enough of the cramped back seat.

He dropped a kiss on her tousled hair. "Let's go to my room."

"But Emily might—"

"The door locks. Come on."

While she scrambled into her panties and shorts, he tied his bathrobe, returned the condoms to her bag and locked both their vehicles.

Then they crept into the house and up to his bedroom, pausing outside Em's room just long enough to confirm the regular, even breathing of a child's deep sleep.

Once inside his bedroom, he flicked on the bedside lamp, and she looked around her with obvious interest. "It's nice. Different than I expected. More..."

He watched her eyes scan the Scandinavian decor he'd liked so much he hadn't bothered changing it when he bought the house. Instead he'd purchased pale wood furniture of sleek Danish design to match. "More what?"

"Sexy, I guess."

"Haven't you seen it before?"

"No. I was curious. But I didn't want to pry."

He liked that. That she'd stayed out of his room. She had a lot of class, this crazy clown with the bra phobia. And speaking of bra phobia, he caught the outline of her breasts against the thin cotton of her little shirt, and his libido roared back even stronger than before as he studied the round swell of breast, the peak jutting teasingly forward. His fingers utterly ached to take that tiny peak, and its twin, well in hand.

He shut the door with a click, leaning behind him to lock it securely.

Her eyes widened when she saw what he was doing, and for a second he thought she'd flee. "I'm not used to locked doors." Then she seemed to pull herself together and smiled her tempting smile.

Leaning against the door, he watched her flit around the room, picking up his aftershave, uncapping and sniffing. Turning the security industry magazine he kept at his bedside toward her so she could read the headlines, then grimacing. He could tell her he'd been reading the dullest thing he could find trying to bore himself to sleep when only a wall separated them and he'd been driving himself crazy with images of her naked in that bed next door.

But he didn't. He let her take her time, her hands lighting on his things and passing on, almost like swift caresses. In some women it would be nervousness making them act this way, but it wasn't that with Annie. He felt she was using the opportunity to get to know him better, as though his things gave away secrets to his personality. Which, come to think of it, they probably did. He tried to see his room through her eyes and figured he'd seem as dull as she already thought he was.

Still, she was here with him. And she hadn't come to his room to show him her new juggling trick.

As soon as the tour of his room ended, he planned to prove to her that he had a few tricks of his own.

The way she touched his things was a kind of slow teasing. He was getting turned on seeing her run a finger over his hairbrush. And something tingling in the air between them told him she was getting turned on, too. They'd taken the edge off, but both knew what was going to happen between them—and she'd chosen to draw out the waiting.

"What's this?" she asked softly, reaching for a wooden frame half hidden behind a lamp on his dresser.

"Nothing," he said, grabbing for it.

She batted his hands away as a big grin split her face. Pressing the photograph to her chest, she raised her eyes skyward and cooed, "My hero."

He felt an unaccustomed heat mount his cheeks. He'd been so young in that photo, so proud of his new RCMP dress uniform. He should pack the infernal thing away in a box somewhere.

She gazed at the picture, then at him, then at the photo. "If you ever want to render me completely helpless, a love slave to your every desire, just put this thing on." He thought she was joking until he realized her breathing was getting jerky. Her finger traced his outline in the photograph. "Those jodhpurs. That hat. The sexy red jacket. Those boots.'' She practically moaned. ''Especially those boots.''

She began to sing softly, ''When I'm calling you-ooo-ooo...''

He'd had enough of the teasing. ''You watch too much TV,'' he informed her, advancing purposefully. He took the picture firmly from her hands and placed it on the bedside table, then reached for her shirt.

She shot him a perky, provocative glance.

He'd barely been able to see anything in the car. He wanted to see all of her. Taste her, touch her everywhere. Swiftly he pulled the shirt over her head.

As he'd already divined, she wasn't wearing a bra. Two of the most gloriously perfect breasts it had ever been his privilege to see taunted his gaze. Small but firm, they were as perky as her attitude, and as sexy. He leaned in for a kiss, saw her mouth purse to say something and changed direction, moving south to her breast.

She didn't talk, she sang. ''Will you answer too...ooh...''

Her voice petered out in a sigh, and he sucked a little harder at the perfect berry in his mouth. A faint scent of jasmine hovered between her breasts as he tongued his way from one peak to the other.

The beauty of a woman who wore so little clothing, he soon realized, was how quickly he could strip her naked. A little yank, and the shorts and thong came off in one motion.

He gazed at her slowly, taking in her beauty leisurely, allowing himself only to look, not to touch— not yet.

Apart from looking both delectable and aroused, she appeared...happy. He'd been with women who dived under the covers and only made love in pitch darkness and those who were coy and provocative when naked, but he never recalled seeing a woman just so darned happy to shed her clothes.

"What are you grinning about?" she challenged him.

"You. You seem to like being naked."

"Mmm, I do." She opened her arms wide and fell backward onto the bed where she shifted luxuriously, her skin pearly against the navy bedspread. "I feel so free and unrestricted when I'm naked. I should belong to a nudist colony."

"Might be kind of cold in a Canadian winter," he suggested, then grinned. "Course, I'd be happy to warm you up...anytime."

While he talked he dropped his robe and tried to be equally comfortable in his naked skin while she lay there, inspecting him with unabashed concentration.

HE WAS even more gorgeous out of his clothes than he was in them, Annie mused, letting her gaze travel from his broad shoulders and muscular, hair-sprinkled chest to the flat belly and finally lower.

"Mmm." She almost purred at the proudly upstanding erection. If she didn't know better, she'd swear he'd been lifting weights with that baby, it seemed so toned and muscular.

His thighs were a little thicker than average, bulging faintly with muscle. He could probably stop a speeding train with that body, she mused.

Her breasts felt tingly and amazingly sensitized from where he'd sucked at them. They were still faintly damp, and the air caressed them, reminding her of how exciting his touch had been. The sex in his car had been intense and mind-blowing. Now she wanted to take time getting to the main event. She was curiously lazy, prolonging each moment of waiting, loving being here with this very special man.

A flutter of unease crossed her belly. It felt almost like fear, but even as she named the emotion it was gone, and she knew it was ridiculous. She had nothing to fear from her gentle Mountie. It was normal that a healthy, unattached male and female living in the same house would start getting attracted to each other. This was the perfect way to let off a little steam.

He sank to the mattress beside her and ran his fingers over her face in a gesture full of tenderness. She wasn't looking for tenderness or anything that smacked of deeper feelings, the kind that might get hurt when she said goodbye.

That fluttery, scary feeling returned, even stronger, as a surge of answering tenderness filled her being. Determined to change the mood, she tilted her face, captured a finger in her mouth and bit softly, then started teasing it with her tongue.

He removed his hand and replaced it with his mouth. Just the feel of those strong but soft lips on hers had her melting into him. Warm and hair-rough, his skin rubbed against her while she wrapped herself around him like a vine.

The kiss built from light pressure to a hot, deep mating of tongues. Everywhere their flesh touched she burned, but most especially the soft place between her thighs where his erection naturally seemed to rub back and forth.

It was building up almost too fast. She felt frighteningly out of control and yet achingly empty. She nudged her hips forward, needing him inside her.

But he made her wait. "Not yet," he whispered, shifting away. Instead he moved his mouth downward. He took about a thousand years getting to her breasts, so long did he spend kissing and nuzzling her neck. Her breasts got another eon of attention, bathed by his teasing tongue while the tormenting heat built and tortured her.

He didn't seem clued in to how much she needed him right this second. Every time she tried to remind him in subtle little ways, like trying to roll on top of him, he pushed her right back where he wanted her and then, if anything, seemed to go even slower.

The man was completely maddening. She was so frustrated she wanted to scream. At last he finished with her breasts and moved down—all the way to her ribs.

She wriggled her hips around a little, in case he needed a hint, and she felt him smile against her burning skin. He was torturing her deliberately!

She gasped, "You are going to pay for this."

Another millennium passed while he kissed and licked every inch of her belly, taking extra time around the belly ring. "I can't believe how much this thing turns me on," he admitted.

He shifted away, and she heard the bedside drawer slide open and then the rustling that told her he was protecting her, as usual.

Yeah. Finally.

But not so. He parted her thighs wide and settled himself between them. Then he parted her most intimate place with his thumbs and gazed at her. He was so close she could feel his breath wafting across the burning, needy core of her.

She couldn't take much more of this. She grasped the bedcovers on either side. "Please," she begged.

Then his tongue was on her, and she thought she would die right then and there from the intensity of sensation. She was somewhere outside herself, able to hear her sobbing cries and the ragged panting that passed for breathing but helpless—her body belonged to him and he played her like a symphony.

When she was certain she could take no more, he raised himself above her and thrust home, hard and deep. Nobody had ever filled her so completely.

He didn't close his eyes. They stayed open, gazing right into hers. And because he didn't, she wouldn't. So they stared into each other's eyes while he entered her fully. The fear was back, along with a new emotion so warm she wanted to cry.

She reached up, planning to cup her hand around the back of his head and pull him down to kiss him, but he caught her hand in his and brought it to his lips. She watched the gesture, shocked to notice that her fingers were trembling.

Just as his body penetrated hers, so did he seem to be forcing some kind of penetration into her mind and heart as he was watching her. And she was staring right back, fascinated by the way the black pupils dilated into the blue, blue iris. Iris was exactly the right color, she mused dazedly. His eyes were the smoky blue of the Siberian irises her grandmother used to grow. Old-fashioned plants with great staying power.

A faint sheen of sweat on his forehead told her he wasn't as in control as he was pretending.

"Annie, I—"

She grabbed his head and planted her lips over his, arching her hips at the same time. A little growl rumbled against her mouth, and then he plunged into her again and again, letting go of all that control.

He was so hard, and filled her so completely, she felt her body clinging to him with each wet slide, arching even as he pounded down. The trembling had spread from her fingers to her entire body. Wordless sounds of pleasure and need filled the air, hers soft and high, his low and rumbling.

It was too much. Her heart was hammering so hard she felt as if she couldn't breathe fast enough to keep up. She was panting, reaching up, up, up... And then a swamping great wave came under her and lifted her high on its crest. Wave after wave rocked her very soul while she clung to Mark, who rode with her all the way.

The waves continued, ebbing until she was deposited lightly back to earth.

It wasn't just physical. An equally powerful wave of emotion filled her eyes as she lay with her head against his shoulder, watching the sweat-dampened hair rise and fall as his breathing slowly quieted.

She blinked back the tears, refusing to give a name to the emotion that flooded her.

11

ANNIE AWOKE with a start, heart pounding.

For a second she was completely disoriented. All she knew was she couldn't move, trapped by warm bonds that imprisoned her so she could barely breathe.

Shaking herself fully awake, she remembered.

A smile curved her lips. She was on her side, tucked into Mark's body, his arms wrapped around her possessively.

Much too possessively. With a jerk, she pulled herself away.

He grunted in his sleep, rolling forward until he was in the spot she'd vacated and she was teetering precariously on the edge of the mattress.

What had they done? What on earth had she been thinking? Mark wasn't a man a girl could have a few laughs with and move on. He was a protector, a possessor, a... There must be at least one more P word that would describe the sense of claustrophobia he induced. He was a—an imprisoner. That was close enough.

And Emily. What would Emily think if the nanny rolled out of her uncle's room in the morning?

A squint at the clock told her it wasn't even dawn

yet. Carefully, she eased out of the bed and gathered her clothes. She crept in the general direction of the door and after some silent detective work finally located it.

In less than a minute she was in her own room, in her own bed. Alone.

She found she was trembling.

It must be colder in her room.

"HI, GIRLS." The deep voice sent quivers of longing into the depth of Annie's very being. She checked the lentil casserole one more time, hoping the heat from the oven would explain the heat in her cheeks, then turned with what she hoped was her usual cheery employee-to-employer expression.

Unfortunately, he wasn't playing by the same rules. The expression he gave her was intimate and tantalizing. He came so close she thought he was going to kiss her.

She jerked her head Emily's way in warning. "Tell Uncle Mark about your day, Em," she said.

Later, his expression promised, setting off an urgent throbbing in her most sensitive areas.

Mark laughed when the child demonstrated the disappearing pencil trick she'd mastered, a carefree chuckle that brought a smile to Annie's face. When had he started to change from the stiff-rumped ex-cop? She wasn't sure, but she had a feeling last night was a part of it.

Strangely, last night had the opposite effect on her. Where she'd been carefree before, now she felt tense.

Like a trap was closing in, and she had to bolt before it was too late.

They'd miss her at first, but after she was gone, they'd continue, a healed and better family. She sighed at her usefulness to these two people she'd come to care for, feeling like an angel from TV who fixes a problem then flits away to a new situation next week.

Angel Annie. Had a nice ring to it.

They ate dinner, and nobody whined about lentils. Mark pretended he didn't know Kitsu was watching them like a hawk, not in case some crazed drug dealer crashed their family dinner, but in case a stray tidbit should fall from a plate.

It had become so much a routine that after dinner Emily would go upstairs to practice her violin and do her homework and Annie and Mark would do the dishes together that Annie didn't know how to get out of it without appearing to be avoiding him.

As soon as Em was out of the room, she jumped up and started gathering things off the table, anxious to avoid the intimacy of a tête-à-tête.

It was a useless plan.

"I thought about you all day," Mark growled against the back of her neck.

Darn it all, didn't he know that was probably the third most erogenous spot on her whole body? The whisper of his voice sent tingles all the way down her spine in some sort of biochemical ambush, igniting tiny flames in the top two erogenous zones. Carefully, she put the dishes on the counter before she dropped them.

By that time, he'd taken shameless advantage of the fact that her hands were too full to bat him away and he'd slipped his hand under her cotton sweater. "Do you think Emily's asleep yet?" he whispered in her ear.

"It's six forty-five. I doubt it," she whispered back, her voice husky.

His hands were caressing her breasts, and she could barely think clearly. She had a vague idea she should stop him, but she'd forgotten why.

"My office door locks," he suggested.

She wished he'd stop whispering in her ear like that. It sent more shivers through her body. They could have a lot of fun in his office with the door locked. She forbade herself to even think about how much fun. "We should do the dishes first."

"When did you get so concerned about housework?"

"When did you get so irresponsible?"

"You must be rubbing off on me."

Since his hands were currently rubbing her nipples, she groaned loudly at the horrible pun. She yanked his hands from under her top and thrust a dishcloth at him. "Here. Find something more useful to do."

He gave in good-naturedly, turning on the tap and squirting dish-washing liquid into the sink. Over the noise of running water he said, "I wanted to talk to you, anyway."

"You did?" She was always the one who used those ominous words, *We have to talk*. They always led into the goodbye speech. Surely he wasn't giving her the goodbye speech? After just one night?

"I always take Em on vacation during the summer holidays. It's getting late, and I've got to book something. I want...I mean, would you like to come with us?"

She felt a curious sensation, as if she were an overfilled balloon and the air was slowly leaking out of her. She fixed all her concentration on the green dish she was drying.

"But, ah, Bea will be back soon."

"I'm not asking you to come as Em's nanny, but as a, well, a friend."

"You mean like a girlfriend?" The words echoed strangely in her chest.

"You're going to rub the glaze right off that plate."

Realizing she was still polishing the same plate she'd started with, she carefully put it down. A glance showed his face wore that earnest, tender expression that scared the pants off her.

"Girlfriend...I guess so. I mean my girlfriend, not Emily's."

Girlfriend was one of those terms, like *retirement planning,* that gave her the willies. And yet, even as one part of her shied away in horror, another part was strangely attracted to the idea. A family vacation. She could pretend they were a real family. They'd play all day, and at night she and Mark...

"Where would I sleep?"

"With me."

"But what about—"

"Emily loves you, Annie. This is just a chance for

us to have some fun together. Nobody's asking you for forever.''

She flinched. There was another word she hated. *Forever.* As in, to have and to hold, forever… A couple of weeks would be just a little taste of forever. If it was only Mark, she might have said yes. But Emily was already getting attached. It wasn't fair to raise the child's expectations when Annie couldn't meet them.

Reluctantly, she shook her head, knowing she had to be strong enough to do the right thing for all of them. "I already have holiday plans. I'm going to Asia."

"Yes. I know. Couldn't you put it off for a couple more weeks?"

Of course she could. She could put it off permanently if she felt like it. They both knew that. But that trip was her escape hatch out of a situation that was starting to feel way too serious.

She sighed. It was the great sex that had got her into this horrible emotional tangle. Yesterday, Mark hadn't been asking her to go on vacation. He'd been accusing her of being a harebrained ninny incapable of looking after one eight-year-old girl. Today he used words like *girlfriend.* Why couldn't he get it through his thick head that she didn't want strings attached to this relationship?

All she wanted was the great sex.

And yet, it was that sense of connection that made the sex so great. *Not sex, making love,* a little voice whispered. And *love* was the scariest of all the scary words.

Her silence had stretched so long that Mark had gone back to washing the dishes. He was stacking them neatly in the space-age stainless-steel drainer. The dishes stood pale green and glistening with water while she stood there stupidly trying to decide what to do.

"I don't think so. I really need to get going to Asia."

"I understand." He glanced up with an expression of pain and resignation on his face, and she had a horrible feeling he did understand. A lot more than she wanted him to.

They continued the dishes in a kind of awkward, stilted way, their conversation sounding like bad dialogue. When they were done he didn't say another word, just headed down the hall to his office.

And he didn't invite her to join him.

It looked suspiciously as if she'd just had the shortest affair of her life.

MARK STRETCHED a cramped biceps and yawned as he approached the kitchen. He knew he was overdoing his workouts, but the basement gym was his refuge when he started thinking too much about Annie and how she was sleeping on the other side of the wall from his bedroom.

If she'd stay in her clown costume all the time it wouldn't be so bad. Like yesterday, when she and Emily had gone off hand-in-hand, big clown and little clown, to Em's school. Who got erotic fantasies about a woman in size nineteen polka-dot shoes and a baggy clown costume?

Well...he did.

It didn't seem to matter what she wore, or didn't wear. He wanted that clown and he wanted her bad.

If he hadn't botched it so badly the other night, he'd be having her, too. What in blazes had possessed him to invite her on holiday? You didn't need to be Freud to figure the lady had some kind of commitment phobia.

One night of heaven had been his. Just one glorious night. He knew he'd remember that night until the day he died. And it wasn't just him feeling as if he'd found the other piece of himself. He was almost certain of that. Annie had felt something, too.

And that scared her.

It wasn't as if he'd gone down on his knee with an engagement ring in his hand and asked her for a lifetime commitment. It was two weeks in a cabin somewhere, maybe on a lake, where they could hike or fish or go horseback riding.

But, apparently, even a couple of weeks was too much to ask. Those polka-dot shoes were ready to walk out on him and Em, and just keep on walking.

He hadn't asked for forever, but somehow, the fact that she couldn't even contemplate being with him a few weeks had soured him on the whole affair. To hell with it.

So, night after night, he punished his body, trying to exhaust himself so he could get some sleep. He couldn't take much more of this. Walking down the stairs, he stifled a groan. He'd really overdone it last night. No matter how many pounds he bench-pressed, he couldn't push away the image of Annie naked in his bed.

Even though she was the magician, not him, he felt as if he'd conjured her up when he entered the kitchen and saw her there. His bad mood vanished when he caught sight of her short shorts riding up her thighs. She was leaning over, trying to choose between three bags of coffee.

Plain old Colombian worked just fine for him, but she kept bringing home bags of exotic beans. He wasn't sure if she was drawn more to the colorful packaging or the name of the blend. Anything with a faraway country in the name seemed to appeal to her, he'd noted, as did anything with an extraordinary bird or plant in the name.

At the moment she appeared torn between three varieties. "Paraguay Parrot, Rain Forest Mocha, Kenyan Sunrise," she mused aloud, in an eenie, meeny, miny, moe voice, her back still to him.

Her small hand flitted from one to the other until he watched her shoulders shrug and she opened all three, pouring a liberal number of beans from each bag into the grinder. She pushed the button, and the mechanical whir filled the air along with the aroma that made getting out of bed worthwhile.

A few coffee beans had spilled on the counter. She picked them up, contemplated them, then started juggling them. He loved watching her. She was the only woman he knew who could make brewing coffee a game. She was completely absorbed in tossing and catching the beans in some complicated arrangement. Her pink tongue teased her upper lip as she concentrated, and he felt a rush of heat roar through his bloodstream.

Of course, she'd forgotten all about the coffee grinding itself into dust. In a couple of strides he'd crossed to the machine and pushed the button.

As quiet suddenly descended, she gave a startled, "Oh," and glanced his way.

Beans rained to the floor, rattling like hailstones in the sudden silence.

Their gazes locked.

He took a slow, deliberate step toward her, wanting to run his fingers through her sleep-tousled hair, kiss the soft lips. Under his gaze, her nipples came to attention beneath her shirt, resembling the size and shape of those foolish coffee beans she'd been juggling.

She swallowed. "I thought you'd be working today." She sounded as if she wished he were gone.

"It's Saturday," he reminded her. "We could both use a day off."

"But the conference—I thought—"

"The dictator had a heart attack yesterday. Not life-threatening, but enough to keep him at home. My job just got easier again."

"That's great news. I'll just, um…"

"Have your coffee first," he said and clomped down the hall to his office. She was so skittish all of a sudden and so obviously didn't want him around that he felt as sulky as a bear. And not just any bear. A big, mean grizzly. He would have liked to stomp through the woods roaring for a while, scaring small animals. That's the kind of mood Annie put him in.

He knew she was just scared of her feelings, but it didn't make her deliberate avoidance of him any easier to take.

With a sigh, he dumped himself in his chair and sorted through yesterday's mail.

What was Bea writing to him for? Mark wondered as he slit the envelope. He hoped she wasn't quitting on him. With Annie due to leave, he couldn't face finding yet another nanny for Em.

Puzzled, he found a short printed letter on plain white paper, the kind he used in his computer, with a yellow Post-it note attached. "You'd better read this," said the note, and Bea had scrawled her name.

He opened the letter fully and read.

Dear Bea,

How are you?

I am fine.

I hope you are feeling beter now.

We have a new nany. Her name is Annie and she and me are geting maried. Emily is being a bridesmade. She might ware a blue dress, or maybe green. But NOT pink.

Anyhow. We don't need you to be our nany anymoor.

Your frend,

Mark Saunders

Dropping his head into his hands, he groaned. That's what the get-well card was all about. Emily had found a way to get Bea's address and a stamp in an elaborate plot to get rid of the housekeeper, thereby making Annie stay. It would be a cute child-ish prank if it wasn't so damned sad.

In her innocent way, Emily wanted everything to work out like magic. Like one of Annie's crazy tricks where she could wave her magic wand and poof, they'd be a family. Poor Emily couldn't have picked a worse person on whom to pin a mother fixation. Annie couldn't commit to a two-week holiday. How the hell could she ever be a mother?

Or a wife?

A little spurt of excitement jabbed his gut at the thought of Annie as his wife. Annie being there every day with her clown pizzas, juggling coffee beans. Annie who made life a game. And yet, for all his reservations, she'd proven to be a reliable companion to Emily.

Okay, so she didn't phone in on time, if at all. He knew she'd do whatever she had to do to keep Emily safe. And she was giving the child something she hadn't had in a while. Fun.

Annie had given *him* fun, too. Not only the roll-in-the-hay kind, but the everyday fun of being alive. Of wondering what she'd say and do next. It might be outrageous, but it would never be mean-spirited or unkind. He glanced at the letter.

Em had a dream, and he'd do his damnedest to make it happen. Besides, he could think of worse things than being married to Annie.

She might pretend the other night meant nothing, but he knew better. He'd read the truth in her eyes, felt it in her body. He meant something to her. And so did Em. He wasn't sure how much they meant, but he intended to find out.

Still gripping the letter, he stood.

He found Annie in the family room with a steaming cup of coffee at her side and Walkman headphones stuffed in her ears, maniacally spewing out Japanese phrases in the most execrable accent he'd ever heard.

With a frown of fierce concentration, she barked at the towels she was folding. He translated as best he could, lounging in the doorway, watching. The monologue went, "How are you?" Pause while she listened to the tape, a frown of complete concentration on her face, eyes almost shut. "I am fine. Where are the violets?" That couldn't be right. He watched her do some complicated jaw exercise and rewind the tape. "Where are the toilets."

Aah.

"How much...? Too much."

She was really getting into it, he noted. Once more she reversed the tape. "How much?" she asked the blue towel.

Her lips pinched in horrified disapproval. She shook her finger at the red towel. "Too much! Can you please tell me where is the telephone?" The laundry basket didn't seem to know, so she moved to the next conversational gem. "My name is...Annie."

He crept across the room and slipped behind her. Based on what he'd heard so far, he could make an educated guess at what was coming next.

"What is your name?" she asked slowly, her accent improving marginally.

He pulled the earphones from her head.

She jumped, and her head swiveled to look at him.

"My name is Mark," he whispered in her ear.

She shivered.

If she hadn't shivered, he would have left it at that. But she had, in a full-body quiver that told him everything he wanted to know about how very aware of him she was. That shiver wasn't about being cold, it was about being hot. About sex. He nibbled her ear. Made a few suggestions in Japanese that had nothing to do with the price of sushi in Tokyo.

She tipped her head back, regarding him suspiciously. "I understood almost nothing. I think I caught the word 'bed' and something that sounded edible."

He grinned wickedly. "I have a big appetite."

Green eyes assessed him, as sexy upside down as they were every other way. Suspicion on the surface, with a sparkling interest deeper down. "Why do I think you're not inviting me out for dinner?"

"I am." He was surprised to hear the words come out of his mouth. *Duh.* What an idiot! He'd never even invited her out for a real date.

They'd gone from a working relationship to sex to him asking her on summer holidays. He'd completely screwed up the dating road map. Instead of traveling in some orderly sequence he'd taken them on a wild detour. He'd forgotten to ask her for a simple date. No wonder they were so far apart. "I'm asking you out for a date. Dinner and a movie."

"A date?" A tiny frown formed between her eyes. "Why?"

How the hell did he know why? The offer had

popped out of his mouth before he'd thought it through. Very uncharacteristic behavior. Mildly disturbing. Why? Lots of vague ideas swirled around in his head, but he couldn't grasp anything concrete. He went with something innocuous. "I want to spend some more time with you."

She lifted her head, picked up another towel from the basket and started folding it. Not very precisely. You could take an entire geometry lesson based on the shapes she'd managed to create in folded towels. "We eat dinner together every night."

He walked round her and grabbed another towel out of the basket. "Not in Japanese."

"Huh?"

"We'll go to a Japanese restaurant. You can order our meal."

"Really?"

"Sure." He gestured to the tape machine. "Then you can ask where the bathroom is, tell them your name and complain that it costs too much."

She shot him a tiny smile, then concentrated on the current parallelogram she was folding. "I just booked my ticket. For Asia."

He felt as if he'd been punched in the solar plexus. Too winded to speak, he nodded stupidly.

"I leave in two weeks. Your conference will be over by then, and Bea will be better." She wouldn't even glance at him. Her words came, low and quickly, while she fiddled with the towel. "I've just got one big commitment—a show at the Vancouver Beach Festival next week—then I'll be off."

It wasn't easy to assume a casual tone when he

wanted to throw her down on the towels and prove to her just how right they were together, how she should at least give this thing a chance instead of running away. But he managed it. "Then this can be a thank-you dinner, for all you've done for us. Next Saturday, after your show."

"What about Emily?" She glanced up then, and he had the impression she was disappointed he hadn't tried to argue her out of going.

"Bea can look after her." He was winging it, but it seemed like a good idea for Emily and Bea to spend some time together. Em had a few things she needed to clear up.

And speaking of Bea, he had her letter still in his hand. He handed the letter to Annie and watched her face crumple when she finished it.

She didn't say a word, just bolted off the couch and ran up the stairs.

"EMILY?"

Silence.

"Emily?" She knocked on the child's door, knowing full well she was being ignored. She counted to five then walked in to find Emily curled on her pink and white frilly bed, the ragged lion clutched in her hand. A book was stuck in front of her face, but given that it was upside down, Annie made an educated guess Emily hadn't been reading it.

"I'm quite busy." The little twerp could sound as formal and distancing as her uncle Mark when she wanted to. Annie wanted to sigh. Didn't they have a clue that this was hard for her, too? She caught a glimpse of the woebegone face behind the book, and her throat started to ache. She was no good for them. Why couldn't they see that? She was a clown, a wanderer, a free spirit. She wasn't cut out for the domestic scene.

She knew Mark had talked to Emily earlier in the day, and ever since Annie had suffered the silent treatment.

She wasn't walking out of Emily's life forever. She needed to make sure Em understood that. She sighed, a big noisy dramatic sigh that finally got the girl's attention.

Emily's eyes widened when she saw the object in Annie's hand.

"Emily, I want to ask you a big favor. I can't take Guinevere Get-Out-of-Here with me. She's feeling really sad right now." She nudged the wig so it drooped over the hanger and onto the chest piece of the child-size clown costume Emily had worn at her birthday party.

Emily stared at her.

She sat on the edge of the bed, and Emily immediately scuttled back against the headboard and pulled her knees to her chest. "You see, Guinevere hates it when I leave her. She thinks I'm never coming back. I thought maybe if I left her with you, maybe hanging in your closet, you could comfort her when she gets sad and remind her that I'm coming back in just a couple of months."

"But you won't be staying."

12

OF COURSE, it had to be the hottest day of the year.

But then it always seemed like the hottest day of the year when Annie donned her complete clown get-up. It might not have been so bad if she hadn't spent the past couple of weeks living in tank-tops and shorts, her feet either bare or in nothing heavier than strappy sandals.

Out in English Bay a boat tooted its horn in a long, loud wail. There were crowds of them out there, but nothing compared to the crowds of people squatting on grass patches, ambling the paved sea walk and lounging on blankets. The well-prepared had brought along picnic baskets and coolers. Those who hadn't brought food and drink were tempted by the sizzle of grilling hot dogs, the odor of popcorn and the tinkling music of the ice-cream vendors.

It was summer, it was a festival and it was crowded.

In spite of the carnival atmosphere and the enormous smile painted on her face, Annie's heart was leaden.

In two days she'd be on her way.

She should wow some of the many Asians in the crowd with her phrasebook knowledge of Japanese,

Cantonese and Mandarin. But she couldn't work up the enthusiasm. She'd be using it for real in a couple of days anyhow. What was the point?

She flipped back the orange and purple double frill of her cuff and glanced at her watch. Fifteen minutes till she was on.

Fifteen short minutes to turn one grumpy, depressed and sorry-for-herself clown into a laugh-a-minute magical trickster clown.

She wasn't sure she had that much magic in stock.

She schlepped through the crowd, her ginormous shoes slapping the ground and occasionally getting nailed to the pavement by somebody's foot as she made her sorry way to the big tent. The Celtic fiddling group was hitting the home stretch, and the toe-tapping music had drawn a huge hooting and yahooing crowd. A few flamboyant souls were doing what looked like their own private version of Riverdance.

Silently she cursed whoever put the schedule together. She couldn't possibly follow the fiddlers. She'd fall flat on her greasepainted face. Where was her edge? The combination of stage fright and in-your-face challenge that usually propelled her on stage no matter the odds?

Her heart was breaking. How could she be funny and magical when the very heart that pumped the blood to her vital organs—including wherever her magic was stored—was cracked?

If only she hadn't left Mark and Emily hurting. If only she could leave them laughing, not in tears and painful silences. If only...

Fiddles, flutes, guitars, drums built to a Gaelic

frenzy that lifted even Annie's depressed spirits. A few people had caught sight of her at the edge of the crowd and stared. Once in costume, she was supposed to be a clown, and clown she did. Beginning to stomp her feet to the rhythm, bobbing her head so the rose banged her nose, then rubbing her red proboscis and starting the whole thing over. It wasn't a bad segue, and when she was introduced, most of the crowd, having seen her antics and accepted her as part of the crowd, stayed on to watch.

She scrambled onto the stage lugging her suitcase with her.

Behind her, the musicians were packing up. Knowing that would happen, she'd decided to begin her routine with some stand-up comedy and move into her magic act when she had the stage to herself and room for volunteers.

She stared out at the sea of faces waiting to be entertained. Some of the faces sported zinc stripes over the nose, some had baseball caps, some had a lot of red, burned-looking skin on shoulders and cheekbones. All gazed at her expectantly.

She gave them a huge clown grin and moved to the microphone. In her Gertrude voice she shrieked, "Is it hot in here or is it me?"

A few titters while they waited for her to start making some jokes about the heat. And she had some. She had lots of them. She just couldn't, for the moment, remember a single damn one of them.

Her mind was as blank as the map of China. As empty as her future, stretching endlessly before her while she ran from what frightened her. And yet what she craved most.

Commitment. Love. Everything Mark and Emily represented.

The silence rang in her ears. She dropped her gaze and in a flash of desperation made a performance of lifting her foot and trying to fan herself with her big shoe. She dragged that out for a minute or so, hopping around the stage and trying to flex her foot back and forth rapidly.

A helpless gesture to the audience. She let them know that wasn't working, then tried nodding her head really, really fast. As an improv it wasn't bad, but it was definitely limited.

As the laughter started to peter out, she spoke again into the microphone. "It sure is hot today, it's so hot..."

Come on, come on. This had never happened before.

She was getting really and truly hot as embarrassment snuck up on her. She was going to humiliate herself if she didn't grab that elusive routine that was floating around in her head, that word just on the tip of her tongue.

In desperation, she started throwing a few insults at the audience. "How's the diaper rash, sir?" she called to a man who'd gone to town with the zinc on his nose.

The mike screeched, and she jumped in pretend alarm and did another panto routine pretending fear of the thing. Behind her a violin string caught on something and gave a faint whine.

She was close to tears.

Then, glancing up, she saw a very familiar trio hurrying across the grass to join the crowd watching her show. Her gaze caught Mark's, and her blood began to sing. Beside him, Emily gave her a thumbs-up, and even Kitsu had his ears tuned to her.

She could humiliate herself in front of a bunch of strangers, but no way she was going to let those three down. Yanking the mike off its stand, she dug deep into herself. If she had to do an entire improv routine, she'd do it. And have them rolling around on the ground in helpless mirth.

"Who wants to talk about the heat, anyway?"

Then, with an exaggerated wink in Em's direction, she shrilled, "Knock, knock..."

SHE WAS so full of life, Mark thought, watching Annie cavorting on stage. And talented, he decided, watching her get the crowd laughing with her body movement, her magic tricks and even her corny jokes. There'd been a moment, when he and Em had arrived, when he'd sworn an expression of panic had flashed in her eyes as she glanced their way. But maybe she was panicking because they'd shown up. Maybe she thought they'd try and beg her to stay... Again.

The smile her antics had painted on his face disappeared along with the carefree mood she'd put him in. There were probably fifty or sixty men, women and kids crowded around the tent, and she charmed every darned one of them. In front of him, a little kid clapped so hard, a wad of his cotton candy took flight and coasted to the ground where it was promptly stepped on.

Mark watched a couple of gulls fight over a half-eaten hot dog. There were streams of people in summer gear. Over the bay a Cessna flew a trailing banner advertising a fitness place. You could hardly fit a toothpick between all the people.

Next week it would be a lot quieter. The festival would be over, and life would return to some kind of semi-normal summertime routine.

And Annie would be gone.

He didn't want his life to return to normal. As he gazed at Annie he knew his life would never be the same. She had changed him in some subtle way he hadn't even noticed. Made him relax more. Made him believe in happy endings.

Then decided to take a perfectly good happy ending and turn it into a tragedy of unrequited love. Not even Romeo himself could have ached as much for his Juliet on her balcony as Mark did for the clown above him on stage. More clapping. She bowed, then reached for the mike.

"And now, I'll need a very special volunteer from the audience." Young hands, and even a few mature ones, shot up instantly.

She shook her head. "I'm sorry, children. The job I have in mind is very important. I'll need a big, strong man." A few hands remained raised. The clown put a hand above her eyes as though to shade them and scanned the crowd. Once her gaze skimmed him, twice.

Heads started to turn his way.

Oh, no.

Emily giggled, and before he knew what was happening, she'd clasped his hand in her small one and raised it as high as she could.

"Why, thank you. You, sir, in the back. The one in the blue T-shirt."

Giggling with delight, Emily yanked on Kitsu's leash. "Come on, Uncle Mark. You gotta go."

She was so eager and thrilled that he didn't have a choice.

He was going to kill Annie.

Feeling like the biggest idiot on two legs, he reluctantly made his way through the crowd and stalked up the stairs to the stage.

He trudged across it, deliberately taking one step more than necessary so he crowded her. Then he glared with all his might into her painted face.

Her eyes were laughing at him, full of good-natured teasing. When he'd crowded so close to her that he could smell the greasepaint, identify her lashes beneath the absurd huge plastic ones, her eyes stopped laughing, and his breath caught.

For an eternal instant, they gazed at each other, and in that moment he knew he loved Annie, with everything in him.

And it occurred to him, like a lightning bolt out of the clear blue sky, that she loved him, too.

He couldn't believe how stupid he'd been. Everything she'd told him about her past had broadcast a lively fear of commitment, and instead of easing her into a relationship, he'd tried to force her.

Maybe it wasn't too late to get her to change her

mind. Maybe he still had a chance, if he could just explain...

"Annie," he whispered, his voice husky.

Her lips parted, and he noticed a smear of red greasepaint on her front tooth. Her hands fluttered up, and he waited for her to touch him. Pink ribbons fluttered from her fingers, and as she caught sight of them, she jerked and glanced around as though she'd forgotten where she was.

He knew the feeling.

"Right," she squealed, and he took a step back as the amplified voice ripped into his ear. "I think you'll be a suitable volunteer." She began walking around him. "What's your name, sir?"

"Mark."

"Mark. Well, Mark, this job requires a lot of strength. Would you curl your biceps for me?"

"What?"

She shook her head at the audience, like he was a big, dumb galoot. "Like this." She demonstrated, bringing her two arms into a classic which-way-to-the-beach bodybuilder pose.

"I'm going to kill you, Annie," he muttered, giving her the most exaggerated pose he could manage, squeezing until his biceps bulged.

"Oh, my," she cooed, "Do you know the story of Samson and Delilah, sir?"

He nodded and went back to glaring at her. "Samson was a very strong man," she explained into the microphone while rapidly unpacking things from the trunk. He could see a big barbell that was obviously plastic. If he didn't love this woman she'd be in serious trouble.

"And he fell in love with the wrong woman."

Was it his imagination or did her voice wobble just a bit? "She found out all his strength was in his hair, and then she cut if off." She brandished the biggest pair of scissors he'd ever seen. "Now, in a moment, I'll ask for a volunteer Delilah, but first, we're going to give our Samson a little help, and make his hair longer and stronger."

And then, with a wicked grin, she started tying on hanks of fake hair with big, pink ribbons. Everybody thought that was pretty funny.

Everybody but him.

She was having a terrific time making a damned fool of him in public. And he was obsessed with having a terrific time with her in private. He had some big plans for dinner tonight. His future, and Em's, could be riding on it.

He had a reputation for always getting his man. This time he had to get his woman. He just had to. Not only for his sake, but for Emily's. The three of them were meant to be a family. He knew it just like he knew Annie loved him. And that, deep down, she wanted a family, too.

He was going to explain it all to her, sweet-talk her, ease her into things. He grimaced as she tied another pink ribbon into his hair. But first he was going to punish her for this. He was going to punish her thoroughly. He'd deprive her of sleep for at least a week. Make outrageous demands. He'd make her beg....

Something pulled his attention away from his fantasies. A sound that filled him with foreboding. It was the high-pitched yap of a dog. He glanced at where Emily had been standing at the back of the crowd and saw that she was already being dragged toward a crowded path. Any second he'd lose sight of her.

Bounding up, he shouted, "Emily, let go of the leash."

She turned a half-puzzled, half-panicked face his way, then like a bad vaudevillian performer being yanked off the stage, she jerked out of sight, swallowed by the meandering hordes.

"Em. Stop!" Annie shouted the words into the microphone so they boomed over the gaping spectators.

He didn't wait, but leaped from the stage and hit the ground running, pink ribbons streaming from his hair.

13
_____

"SORRY, FOLKS. Show's over. I've got a family emergency." He heard Annie's voice, tinny from amplification, while he shouldered through the crowd in the direction he'd last seen Em.

Even as he focused on tracking his niece, Annie's words hit him. A family emergency, she'd called it. He wondered if she was aware she'd automatically thought of them as a family.

Once this was over, he'd remind her of that. And a few other things. All he had to do was find Em. He wouldn't panic. Annie was right. He was overprotective of Em. She was an intelligent girl, and nobody would tangle with her so long as she and Kitsu were together.

"'Scuse me...pardon me." People bumped and blurred past him as he struggled through a sea of bodies, some smelling of sweat, some of suntan lotion, some of popcorn and hot dog.

Who'd have thought that damn useless dog could even spot a squirrel in all the melee? There was some kind of commotion up ahead. Maybe that was them. He sprinted forward, mumbling apologies.

IMPATIENTLY, Annie tissued off her face paint and struggled out of her costume. Underneath she wore

Shotgun Nanny

shorts and a tank top. She removed her wig, ran her fingers through her hair and peeled off the false eyelashes. The little trailer, set up for the performers to use between acts, was stifling.

She'd never changed so fast. Not because of the heat in the trailer, but because of the nagging sense of worry. Which was odd, because she never worried. It wasn't in her nature.

Leaving her case in the trailer, she walked the few steps to the tent where she'd performed. Since she'd cut her show short, there was a lag until the next act. She recognized a few of the audience members who'd been watching her perform, grateful she was unrecognizable without her costume.

Annie couldn't believe she'd cut her show short. She had performed through stomach flu, thunder and lightning storms, birthday kids throwing tantrums and having accidents on the floor, and she'd never stopped a show before. Never.

So a kid got dragged off by a dog to go see a squirrel run up a tree. Big deal. Why had she canceled the show?

As she glanced worriedly left and right, trying to stretch her vision, the answer came with a bump of recognition. She'd never felt that sick sense of fear before. Never.

She felt like a…a mother.

Minutes dragged by. She was hot, thirsty and scared. She bought a bottle of water from a passing cart and downed it while she stood, feeling like a small animal was gnawing at her lungs.

A squeal from the microphone caused her to jump

out of her skin. She'd been so focused on watching for her missing trio, she'd forgotten there was a stage behind her.

When the folksinging group started up, the crowd in front of the tent began to swell, and Annie found herself pushed farther from the stage. Darn it, she should have kept her purple wig on so Mark and Emily could find her easily. She was dying to get out and start looking, but she knew Em would come back to the tent when she got Kitsu under control, and Mark would head back as soon as he could. As much as she wanted to rush off and start looking, at least to be doing something, she knew she had to stay put.

A song about a wandering Gypsy gave way to a ballad about preserving the rain forest, and still there was no sign of them. Had they found each other and forgotten all about her? For once in her life, she wished she owned one of those hateful cell phones just so she could call Mark and find out where he was.

And then she saw him sprinting her way.

A glimpse of his expression told her he was alone.

Her face must have registered the same information to him, for he didn't even ask, just hauled his cell phone out of his back pocket.

He was breathing heavily, and sweat dripped from his hairline. His pink ribbons lay damp and tangled in his hair.

"Who are you calling?"

"The cops."

"But—"

He turned on her, his expression fierce. "No buts.

I've looked everywhere. I can't even raise a signal on her tracking device. Something's happened.''

In her heart, she felt he was right, so she didn't say a word, just watched his fingers jabbing at the phone.

Then she heard a very familiar whine and glanced down to see Kitsu at her side, heaving flanks and lolling tongue...and dragging leash with no Emily at the end of it.

"Mark, wait." She knelt in front of the dog and looked straight into his eyes. "Where's Emily?"

Again that whine, and she almost thought the timbre changed, increasing in urgency. The dog paced restlessly.

She glanced at Mark, who glared at the dog, cell phone still in hand.

"He's trying to tell us something. I think he wants to show us where she is," she insisted, picking up the dog's restlessness.

"You think that hellhound suddenly turned into Lassie?" Without waiting for an answer, he went back to the cell phone.

Ignoring him, she focused on the dog. "This is really important, Kitsu. You have to take me to Emily." At the child's name, the dog gave a shrill yap. "We all love Emily. We have to find her."

"I don't believe this. That dog's useless. You stay here and wait for the officers. I'm going searching again."

"No."

"Look. There's no time—"

"Give Kitsu a chance, Mark. Please."

"You're going to go chasing after goddamn squirrels while Em could be in trouble? I don't believe this!''

''You stay here and wait for the cops. I'm going.'' She grasped the leash firmly. ''Kitsu. Find Emily.'' And as though she'd pushed her foot to the accelerator, the dog raced off.

She heard muttering that she thought was a string of words Mark would never say aloud in mixed company, then everything was a blur.

She recalled an earlier trip with Kitsu a lot like this one, when she'd been dragged all over the park after a squirrel. For all their sakes, she hoped she wasn't on another wild squirrel chase.

The dog bounded ahead, slowing only when he needed to find a path around children. Every time there was a space, he'd put on another burst of speed.

Only fear and grim determination kept Annie hanging on to that leash. If anything, this race was worse than the last one. There were more people to bash into, more obstacles to be avoided, and even while her heart and lungs labored and her legs scrambled to keep up with the dog, the knot of fear—the possibility that this was all for nothing—cramped her belly.

''Find Emily, find Emily,'' she gasped over and over, hoping the dog would understand her and stay on task. Wherever they were going, the dog knew the way. He never hesitated. She'd see him sniffing the air and aiming his nose, and then his powerful body followed. Like a bouncing balloon on a string, Annie's much less powerful body jounced along behind.

"Please, let her be all right. Please," she prayed silently.

She stopped saying "excuse me," and the way ahead looked clear. With a sinking heart, she realized they'd left the most crowded part of the park. They were racing along a nearly deserted stretch of seawall, with the ocean on one side and lawn, trees and apartment buildings on the other. If they were chasing a squirrel, she was going to skin that dog with her bare hands.

Her breath pounded in her ears, and behind her she heard the pounding of footsteps. She didn't have the energy to turn her head, but she knew without looking that it was Mark. Against his better instincts and training, he was giving her intuition and Kitsu a shot at finding his niece.

They'd better not let him down.

She was so mindlessly accustomed to the pace, all her energies focused on following that blasted dog, she almost didn't notice when Kitsu stopped running. A few steps, and she bumped into his warm, hairy body. He was leaping back and forth, his nose pointing over the seawall, while he gave a loud version of his squirrel bark.

Praying silently, she peeped over the side.

And there was Emily, her small body sprawled on the rocky beach.

After the first ghastly stab of fear, Annie realized she was alive and conscious. She was sitting up, her head tipped backward to gaze at Kitsu with a tired smile. Her face was pale, but the relief shone from every feature.

Annie dropped the leash, and the dog leaped to the beach, pacing protectively between Em and the incoming tide. Annie put a leg over the wall and began to scramble down the four or five feet to the rocky beach below. Something dark hurtled by to her left, and Mark almost flew through the air, landing with a grunt.

By the time she'd reached them, Emily's bravery had deserted her, and tears poured down her face while she explained to her uncle.

"I hurt my leg. The tide started coming in. Ow. I can't move."

"Hold still, honey." All vestiges of panic were gone from Mark's face and voice. He sounded completely calm. Annie had to give him credit for hiding his feelings so well. "Did you hit your head at all?" He ran his hands down her arms, the sides of her torso and her back.

"Uh-uh. I just tripped and fell sideways on my foot."

"Which leg hurts?"

"This one." She pointed to the left.

He ran his hands down the right and then much more gently down the left. When he reached her ankle, she sucked in her breath.

Annie sank down beside her and wrapped her arms around Emily, who hugged her right back.

"I was so scared."

Annie squeezed harder. "So were we." Her hands were shaking, and she fought a strange desire to cry, just like Emily. She was so glad to have her back.

"Kitsu dragged me here after a squirrel so I finally

let go of the leash, but I was so hot and dirty, I thought I'd rinse my hands and face in the ocean. But I guess my shoe got untied. I don't know. Anyhow, I tripped. And then I couldn't get up. And then the water started coming in.''

"You did fine, Em. Just fine." Mark soothed her with his matter-of-fact tone. "I don't think it's broken, probably just sprained, but we'll get it looked at to make sure."

"Kitsu stayed right with me. He must have heard me scream. Then I told him to go find you. And he went." She sniffed. The dog, hearing his name, had come forward to put his wet nose to her cheek. She giggled and hugged the dog to her. "He's a great watchdog, isn't he, Uncle Mark?"

There was a pause. "The best. But, Em, where's your tracking device?"

"In my pocket. I think I fell on it."

Mark glanced up and caught Annie's gaze. She thought he was going to say something, maybe admit for once that she was right and he was wrong. But when he did speak, it was to issue orders.

"Annie, here's my key. You can bring the vehicle up that road there, and we'll meet you." Rapidly, he described where he'd parked. "Em, I'm going to carry you up to the grassy area. It might hurt a bit, but I'll try not to go too fast. Okay?"

"I'm ready."

Annie waited until he'd scooped up his niece in his powerful arms and started walking toward the closest set of cement steps that provided beach access. With utmost care, Mark picked his way over the rocks while Emily clung to his neck, her lips compressed. Kitsu stayed at Mark's side.

Annie scrambled up to the path and half-sprinted, half-jogged to where he'd left the car.

By the time she'd negotiated her way through the crowded streets, detouring around those that were blocked off for pedestrians only, she was thankful to find the trio of man, dog and injured child just where they'd said they'd be. Even her fear that Kitsu would embarrass himself in front of his master was apparently groundless. Two squirrels wandered the grass, tails twitching, noses to the ground, seemingly oblivious to the squirrel-annihilation machine at Mark's feet.

The dog's eyes were fixed on his quarry, and even as she approached, a small begging whine came from his direction. "Don't even think about it," Mark warned in a voice that brooked no disobedience.

Impressed in spite of herself at Mark's control over the uncontrollable beast, Annie took a good look at Emily. Her color was a lot better, and she was chatting away to Mark with all the semblance of a girl who wasn't in a lot of pain.

"Thanks, Annie," Mark said, "I'm going to drive Em to the hospital and get that ankle X-rayed, just to be safe." He mussed his niece's hair. "I don't think it's very serious, but you'll probably get to lay around for a couple of weeks with your feet up and ignore all your chores."

The girl grinned at him impishly.

He glanced at Annie. "Do you mind getting your own car? I'd like to take Em right to the hospital."

"Of course. I'll meet you there."

He shook his head. Anger boiled up in her chest. If he thought he was going to shut her out now, he could forget it. But it wasn't that. "I need you to take Kitsu home. I can't leave him in the hospital car park. Who knows how long we'll be?"

She really wanted to go with them, just to make certain Em was all right, but obviously Mark was right. Swallowing her disappointment, she nodded. "I'll make dinner." She glanced at Em with a teasing grin. "Something with extra tofu in it."

After the girl had finished with the yucks and gagging motions, she leaned down to kiss her soft cheek. "See you at home."

She helped Mark get Annie settled across the back seat then grabbed Kitsu's leash. She waved until they'd pulled away from the curb, then she glanced at the dog, knowing they were heading through squirrel territory. "Do I need to put a paper bag over your head?"

A soft whine greeted her. The panting jaws opened in a big doggy grin, and the tail started wagging.

"Trying to butter me up won't work," she warned the dog as they started walking. "I'm not the woman I was a few weeks ago. I could flatten you with a well-aimed karate chop." She paused to inspect the muscled flanks and powerful throat. "Well, maybe." They walked on companionably.

"I'll tell you one thing, for sure, without Emily here, I'm not chasing you to hell and back. You go tearing off, you're on your own. And I gotta tell you, squirrel as a steady diet gets old real fast."

She wasn't certain if her threats had sunk in or if they were just lucky enough not to pass any of the bushy-tailed creatures, or whether the dog had just tired himself out. But amazingly, she made it to her car with only one small incident.

She'd stopped to pick up her clown gear in the trailer, and as she wended her way to her vehicle a guy with a huge belly drooping over his jeans and one too many tattoos lurched across the parking lot in her direction. He gestured with the open beer in his hand. "Hey, babe" he leered. "Wanna come to a party?"

"It's a tempting offer, but no, thanks."

With a fatuous grin on his face, he kept coming until he was close enough to get a look at Kitsu, who could appear amazingly ferocious when he chose. Teeth bared, hackles up, a low growl took care of the drunken partyer in no time.

"You know, you're a good dog to have around."

She opened the rear car door, and he balked. "I know, it hasn't got the headroom you're used to. You'll have to slum it till we get home."

With a big, huffy pant, he scrambled into the back.

She walked to the driver's side and opened the door. "I don't believe it!" He was sitting in the passenger seat grinning at her.

"I guess you earned the privilege. You did good today." She leaned over and patted him, getting a big tongue slurp for her trouble.

"Okay, Kitsu. Let's go home."

But she made a couple of stops on the way.

"How do I stop her from leaving?" Mark wondered for the thousandth time.

"What are you mumbling about, Uncle Mark?" Em asked from the back seat. Her voice was a little slurred, probably from the painkillers the doctor had given her. As he'd hoped, it was just a sprain. Her ankle, swathed in an elastic bandage, looked huge. Tomorrow he'd have to get her some crutches.

He sighed. Aloud he said, "How do we stop Annie from leaving us?"

In the rearview mirror he caught her puzzled frown. "But you said we have to let her go."

"I changed my mind."

She was silent for a moment or two. "Maybe we could phone the plane and tell them Annie's a criminal and they should kick her off. I saw that on a movie me and Annie watched."

"Not bad, kid. Apart from the breaking-the-law aspect, it's a pretty good plan."

"We could steal her passport."

"You really are headed for a life of crime, aren't you?"

"Well, let's hear your ideas, Mr. Smarty!"

"We could set Kitsu to guard her. Which would be fine until a squirrel came along."

"I know, I know! We could give away all her clothes."

"Now you're talking."

By the time they pulled into his gate, they'd pretty much figured out a million ways to make Annie's life hell. Neither of them seemed to care, so long as they could keep her with them. As he turned off the engine, they both fell silent. It had been fun to fantasize that they could make Annie stay, but real life had once again intruded.

Or had it?

He hauled Em in his arms. Just as he got to the front door, it opened. He damn near dropped her. She gasped in his ear, then started to giggle.

Everywhere he looked were balloons.

Not just any balloons. His crazy clown had fashioned balloons into dogs and squirrels. Shiny red dogs, blue dogs, yellow dogs chasing bright balloon squirrels in orange, pink and purple that hung always just out of reach. They chased each other across the hallway floor, hung from the ceiling in a moving tableau.

And there was Annie, a huge smile on her face, holding a balloon doll with yards of toilet paper wrapped around its left ankle. And finally, Kitsu, a big helium balloon that said Get Well Soon attached to his collar.

"How are you feeling, Em?" she asked, handing her the balloon doll.

"Okay. Kind of tired. The doctor gave me some pills."

"Are you hungry?"

"Yeah."

Annie then turned her attention to Mark, and he noticed she'd put on some makeup and brushed her hair. Her clothes were different, too. She wore a tight-fitting long skirt in a kind of leaf pattern and a green top that lifted whenever she moved, just enough to give him a glimpse of the faux diamond glinting from her navel.

If he didn't get that thing between his teeth before the night was through, it wouldn't be for want of throwing everything he had at her.

He must have been staring. She tugged the top down, as if it would stay there, and said, "Thanks for phoning from the hospital. Dinner's almost ready."

"What's for dinner?" Em asked.

"A special surprise."

"If it's green, I'm not eating it."

"Emily, mind your manners," Mark chided.

Annie preceded them into the kitchen, and his eyes widened. The table was set with the usual green china and linen napkins, but in the middle were ketchup, mustard and relish, a big plate of pickles and a bowl of potato chips.

He glanced over to where Annie was busy slipping wieners in buns.

"Hot dogs?" Emily exclaimed in awe.

His eyes narrowed suspiciously. "This isn't some New Age bean-sprout wiener, is it?"

Her eyes danced. "No. It's a real old-fashioned hot dog."

"Wow," Emily said. "The bun isn't even whole wheat."

"Come on. I'm not that bad."

Mark shifted his gaze to Em, who was nodding. "Yes, you are," they chorused.

"I even got some soda for you, Em. Do you want some, Mark?"

"After the day I've had, I need a beer. How about you, do you want some wine or something?"

"A beer would be great. Thanks."

"Come on, Em, we'll go wash up, then I'll carry you to the table."

IT WAS LIKE so many meals they'd had, and yet so different. For one thing, Em didn't usually need a second chair with a pillow on it to prop up her leg. For another, Annie was in love. She had to admit it to herself. Not just with Mark, but with Em, as well. She even loved the overgrown squirrel terrorizer who gazed with rapt attention at the hot dogs, though he'd already wolfed down the two she'd slipped him for a reward, plus the jujubes Mark had slipped him when he thought no one was looking.

Maybe it was her new appreciation of her feelings, but the atmosphere around the table was subtly different. They still told stupid knock-knock jokes in between Emily and Mark telling her about the hospital visit. But she found herself superaware of the man across the table. She kept sneaking little glances his way simply for the pleasure of seeing the man she loved.

She hoped he'd like her surprise.

Emily made it halfway through her ice cream before her eyes started drifting shut. Annie and Mark shared the kind of conspiratorial smile she'd seen parents exchange countless times.

He stood and reached to lift Em into his arms while Annie picked up the pillow and supported the foot all the way up the stairs. Once in the child's room, Em's eyes half opened as her uncle lay her on the bed. "Don't forget to phone the plane," she mumbled to him.

He smiled and kissed her cheek. "Good night, Em."

"I'll get her into her nightclothes and then come down to help with the dishes. And, uh, we have to talk."

"The four most terrifying words in the English language." He shook his head with a grimace that made her grin. "See you downstairs."

"No. It's good—" She started to explain, but he was already gone. "At least, I hope it's good."

When she emerged downstairs, butterflies were doing the Watusi in her belly. What if he said no? She bit her lip, knowing she deserved his rejection and deciding she'd have to be forceful about what she wanted.

With his usual efficiency, he was wiping the counters when she got to the kitchen.

"Come on into the living room," he said.

"The living room?" She'd never seen a soul in there.

"It's a good place for serious discussions, don't you think? All that leather."

As long as she lived, she'd never understand men. What was serious about leather furniture? "You didn't think my leather skirt was serious?"

"Honey, nothing that small could ever be taken seriously." Then he grinned at her, and she started to feel woozy. He'd called her honey.

He flicked on a couple of lamps, and soft pools of

light appeared. Headed for some kind of mission control panel, he stopped and turned to her. "Is this discussion too serious for music?"

"Uh, no. Not at all."

"Good." Methodically, with the same care and precision he did just about everything, he chose a CD. Soon soft jazz filled the air. He pushed another button, and a gas fireplace added a pool of flickering light.

"How about a cool drink?"

For some reason, she was getting more nervous. It was becoming clear that he had a hidden agenda. Or a secret joke, probably at her expense. She cleared her throat. "A drink would be great. I think I have some beer left."

He returned in a few moments with a bottle that most definitely did not contain beer. Her eyes widened. "Champagne?"

"This is a celebration, isn't it?"

"Is it?" Her voice was squeaky all of a sudden. Maybe she was coming down with some kind of laryngitis. She cleared her throat again.

"We found Emily. And Kitsu finally did something useful." A slow, thumping noise came from behind the couch.

"Did that dog follow us in here?"

"I asked him to. He's a chaperon."

A soft pop, and the wonderful fizz of champagne pouring came to her ears. He handed her a glass that felt cool against her skin. Unable to help herself, she gazed into his eyes, and the butterfly Watusi turned into an acrobatics competition. He touched his glass to hers. "To us."

It was the opening she needed. Taking a quick, delicious sip of the pale gold wine, letting it crackle and fizz on her tongue, she swallowed. Then took a couple more deep sips, hoping to drown those darned butterflies.

He was still watching her, and there was definitely amusement in his eyes…mixed with something she didn't even want to think about. She forgot the speech she'd prepared and skipped to the chase. "I want my job back."

He refilled her glass. She couldn't believe it had been emptied so fast. He must use really small champagne flutes. "You can't have it."

She'd been prepared to have to argue her case, but somehow the bald refusal stunned her. She sipped more champagne while she dredged her mind for the reasons she'd prepared in case he was doubtful.

"I know you think Bea's better qualified in the self-defense department—and I grant you she is. But I really think I'm good for Em."

"You are. That's not the reason."

"Oh. Um, if it's my cooking—"

"Your cooking's fine. A little more fat, a few more grams of cholesterol once in a while might be nice…but overall, no complaints."

"You probably think a clown isn't a very good role model for an impressionable child. However, studies show—"

"I think you're terrific with Em. I already told you that."

"If it's about our personal relationship—"

"Now you're getting warmer," he said approvingly, adding more wine to her glass. He sank down beside her on the leather couch, addling her brains.

"It's just that—I was scared."

"I know." His voice rumbled deep and rich in her ear, sending little shivers chasing each other down her spine.

"My trip. I, well, I figured out a week ago I didn't even want to go. I mean, I'd love to see the Orient. Traveling is very educational and culturally enriching. And fun. But I was using my trip as an excuse to run away. To avoid responsibilities."

He seemed so calm and quiet beside her, totally relaxed, while she couldn't seem to stop babbling.

"I've loved the time I've spent with Emily. I'd really like to stay."

"How about me?"

"Huh?"

"How do you feel about the time you've spent with me?"

A warm flush stole its way up her body from her toes to her ears. "I, um, enjoyed that, too."

In the same reasonable, conversational tone that made her want to slap him, he continued. "How about making love with me. Did you enjoy that?"

A little whimper quivered through her lips. Unable to form an actual word, she nodded vigorously.

His lips tilted in the semidarkness, and she longed to lean over and kiss them. "I hope you can begin to see why you're completely unsuitable to be Emily's nanny."

That was just so unfair. "But you had sex with me, too. And you're her guardian."

"I'm planning to change that."

Her heart sank. Surely he wasn't even thinking—he couldn't be planning to send Em to someone else. She couldn't let that happen. It would break the little girl's heart.

"I want to adopt Emily legally."

"What are you—"

"I don't think she needs a nanny and a guardian. I think she needs a mother and father again."

"What are you saying?"

He picked up her hand and began toying with her fingers. "I'm saying I love you."

Ooh.

"And Emily loves you. She was trying to figure out ways to stop you from leaving. But there's only one thing that will stop you. And that's if you love us enough to settle down. Enough to make a commitment."

"Oh, Mark. I do love you. I do."

He half grinned. "I kind of thought you did when the travel agent phoned and left a message. Something about canceling your ticket."

"She phoned? But I was saving that for my surprise!"

"The thing is, I know you're terrified of commitments, and marriage probably terrifies you more than anything. If it was just me, I wouldn't care. But Emily needs someone who'll be there permanently."

"Are you asking me to marry you?"

"Yes."

She waited for the fear to grip her and choke the life out of her. But it didn't come. She played a game with herself, waiting for it to happen. She tried to put all her scary words out there at once. "So, I'd be your wife. You'd be my husband. We'd wear rings and have anniversaries and life insurance policies and, ah, retirement plans."

He nodded gravely.

She gulped. "Mutual funds, a dental plan, his and hers towels?"

"I might have to draw the line at the towels. But I do have full medical coverage."

"More children?"

"It's a definite possibility," he agreed.

"So I'd be, like, a mother?"

Little gleams of blue fire burned in his eyes. "You're the most likely candidate."

It was a miracle! She didn't feel even a twinge of fear, only a strange kind of elation. She could imagine it all. Children, grocery lists, dentist appointments. Golfing in her golden years with this man and actually having a pretty good time. Of course, she'd have to buy him outlandish golf shirts, just to keep things balanced.

"You won't mind being married to a clown?"

"Not if she's you."

She chuckled. "Life is going to be pretty interesting."

"And a whole lot of fun, my love. A whole lot of fun."

He leaned forward and kissed her, then reached into his pocket to withdraw a jeweler's box.

She eased open the box, and the unmistakable dazzle of diamond sparkled at her. "An engagement ring?"

He grinned and shook his head.

She took a closer look and started to laugh. "I thought you hated my navel ring."

"Are you kidding? I'm crazy about it. And I think it's time you had a real diamond in your navel."

"Sometimes you're not such a stuffed shirt, after all."

"By the way, that ticket's not canceled. It's postponed. For your honeymoon. Japan, Thailand, Europe—anywhere in the world, you just pick your favorite place."

"How about right here," she murmured, pulling him down on top of her.

C'mon back home to Crystal Creek with
a BRAND-NEW anthology from

bestselling authors
Vicki Lewis Thompson
Cathy Gillen Thacker
Bethany Campbell

Return to Crystal Creek

**Nothing much
has changed in
Crystal Creek...
till now!**

The mysterious Nick Belyle has shown up in town,
and what he's up to is anyone's guess. But one
thing is certain. Something big is going down in
Crystal Creek, and folks aren't going to rest till
they find out what the future holds.

*Look for this exciting anthology,
on-sale in July 2002.*

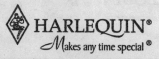

HARLEQUIN®
Makes any time special ®

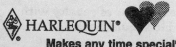

Princes...Princesses...
London Castles...New York Mansions...
To live the life of a royal!

**In 2002, Harlequin Books lets you escape to a
world of royalty with these royally themed titles:**

Temptation:
January 2002—*A Prince of a Guy* (#861)
February 2002—*A Noble Pursuit* (#865)

American Romance:
The Carradignes: American Royalty (Editorially linked series)
March 2002—*The Improperly Pregnant Princess* (#913)
April 2002—*The Unlawfully Wedded Princess* (#917)
May 2002—*The Simply Scandalous Princess* (#921)
November 2002—*The Inconveniently Engaged Prince* (#945)

Intrigue:
The Carradignes: A Royal Mystery (Editorially linked series)
June 2002—*The Duke's Covert Mission* (#666)

Chicago Confidential
September 2002—*Prince Under Cover* (#678)

The Crown Affair
October 2002—*Royal Target* (#682)
November 2002—*Royal Ransom* (#686)
December 2002—*Royal Pursuit* (#690)

Harlequin Romance:
June 2002—*His Majesty's Marriage* (#3703)
July 2002—*The Prince's Proposal* (#3709)

Harlequin Presents:
August 2002—*Society Weddings* (#2268)
September 2002—*The Prince's Pleasure* (#2274)

Duets:
September 2002—*Once Upon a Tiara/Henry Ever After* (#83)
October 2002—*Natalia's Story/Andrea's Story* (#85)

**Celebrate a year of royalty with
Harlequin Books!**

Available at your favorite retail outlet.

Visit us at www.eHarlequin.com

HSROY02